WHERE SHE

Belongs

WHERE SHE
Belongs

A NOVEL

JOHNNIE ALEXANDER

Revell

a division of Baker Publishing Group
Grand Rapids, Michigan

Published by Revell
a division of Baker Publishing Group
P.O. Box 6287, Grand Rapids, MI 49516-6287
www.revellbooks.com

Printed in the United States of America

Library of Congress Cataloging-in-Publication Data
Alexander, Johnnie.
  Where she belongs: a novel / Johnnie Alexander.
    pages ; cm.—(Misty willow ; #1)
  ISBN 978-0-8007-2640-9 (pbk.)
  1. Title
PS3601.L35383W48 2016
813'.6—dc23   2015018608

16 17 18 19 20 21 22   7 6 5 4 3 2 1

To Hebe

my sister, friend, and alpaca-wrangling buddy

Acknowledgments

My deepest appreciation to my clever critique partners and eagle-eyed early readers. Imagine That! Writers: Patricia Bradley, Rob McClain, Renee Osborne, and Chandra Smith. Kindred Heart Writers: Clella Camp, Karen Evans, Laura Groves, and Jean Wise. And treasured friends: Carol Anne Giaquinto, Joy Van Tassel, and Mandy Zema.

My warmest thanks also to Sara Jo Dusterhoft, a once-upon-a-time missionary kid and dear friend; Beth Scheckelhoff, Ohio State University Master Gardener, Julie Hilton Steele, Greg Buckley, Joyce Sidwell Piper, and Karen Preskar for their gardening advice; Lisa Harris, missionary in Mozambique; and Marion Ueckermann, a resourceful overseas pal and reader of books at traffic lights.

My love to the family who shares my childhood memories of The Brick (the inspiration for Misty Willow): my parents John and Audry and my siblings Tony, Adam, and Hebe. And also to the family God blessed me with: my children Bethany, Jillian, and Nate; sons-in-law Justin and Jacob; and the grands.

Thanks and a hug to my agent Tamela Hancock Murray, my editors Vicki Crumpton and Kristin Kornoelje, and the Revell team for their encouragement and support.

And here at the end, a smile and a wink to my niece Payton Alexander, because . . . well, you know.

My prayer is that God brings us all into spacious places.

> He brought me out into a spacious place;
>> he rescued me because he delighted in me.
>
> I will be glad and rejoice in your love . . .
> You have not given me into the hands of the enemy
>> but have set my feet in a spacious place.
>>>> Psalms 18:19; 31:7–8 NIV

- 1 -

*I*n an upstairs room as neglected as all the others, AJ Sullivan flicked the grime from a broad fireplace mantel, then rubbed his fingers on his jeans. Mahogany. Whoever built this place had used the best materials. But more than 150 years later, no one cared.

Except some woman who was about to free him from this millstone.

Pulling her letter from his pocket, he walked across the pitted wood floor to the bay windows. Sunlight filtered through tall, narrow shutters hanging askew on their hinges. He gingerly opened one, and a spider scooted across the marble sill. Through the unwashed glass, dust motes danced in the sun's beam.

He didn't need the light to read the letter. Shelby Kincaid's emotional plea to buy the house scraped an ache he'd thought was buried. When he'd shown the letter to his grandmother, her agitated response had plucked at his heart as desperately as her arthritic fingers had plucked at his shirt sleeve.

He scratched his arm, barely aware of the gesture as Gran's words echoed in his mind. *Find a way. Bring peace to the past.*

Tires crunched on gravel, and a motor accelerated a few seconds then idled. He peered through the angled bay window. A

9

slender woman stood by a beige sedan near the end of the drive. Though she was too far away to make out her features, there was something pensive about the way she stared at the house. Chestnut hair blew across her cheek, and she gracefully tucked it behind her ear.

She had to be Shelby Kincaid—the woman who so desperately wanted this forsaken place. He hadn't expected to meet her until their afternoon appointment to sign the papers at Richard Grayson's office.

After a moment, Shelby slid into the driver's seat and drove at a snail's pace toward the house. She steered the car around the lane's deep ruts and parked near the porch behind his Jeep Cherokee.

As she emerged from the car, sunshine reflected the golden highlights in her shoulder-length hair. A frown puckered her delicate features as she gazed at the house. When she looked upward, AJ's pulse quickened, and he stepped back from the window.

She'd be coming into the house any moment, and here he was feeling as awkward as one of his freshman students on a first date. Time to pretend to be Cary Grant, Gran's favorite movie star.

He tucked the letter into his pocket and bounded down the stairs. One of the thick exterior doors stood ajar, just as he'd left it when he entered the house. He stepped onto the decrepit porch. Shelby, wearing boot-cut jeans and a V-neck sweater, stood on the bottom step, fiddling with her watch.

"Hey, there," he said. "You must be Shelby Kincaid."

She jumped, her startled green eyes softening as she faced him and exhaled.

"Sorry. Didn't mean to scare you. I'm—"

"My hero." She flashed an excited smile and extended her hand. "I'm so glad you're here. The place is quite a mess, isn't it?"

"Not surprising." As he took her hand, a long-forgotten warmth charged through him. "It's been empty more than a decade."

She flushed and quickly withdrew her hand. "Ever since the Sullivans stole it."

"Stole it?" He took off his Ohio State ball cap and tapped it against his leg, unsure whether to be amused or insulted. "You're kidding, right?"

"This house was built by my great-great-great-great-great-grandfather." She grinned at the repetition and lightly caressed the wooden porch railing. The splintered white paint chipped beneath her fingers. "I just have a hard time understanding . . . I mean, what kind of person takes a family's home and leaves it empty year after year?"

AJ had never given a thought to how his grandfather acquired the Lassiter farm. After inheriting it, AJ had cared even less. Still, the old man must have had his reasons. "A shrewd businessman?" he asked.

"There's nothing shrewd about letting a perfectly good house go to ruin."

Good point. "A man with a grudge?"

"Against my grandfather?" Shelby seemed to drift into the past, her eyes tender in memory. "There was no finer man. I don't think he had any enemies."

"It's a mystery then." She didn't need to know that Granddad had enjoyed his grudges. Or that the old man collected enemies like trophies. AJ leaned against the porch railing and grinned. "Anyway, you're here now, taking the old homestead back from the evil Sullivans."

Shelby's eyes brightened with anticipation. "That's right. In just a few hours, the farm will be mine. Back in the family where it belongs."

"Do you plan to live here?"

"Absolutely. How long do you think it will be before we can move in?"

"I have no idea."

"I suppose all the wiring will have to be replaced. Have you checked it out?"

He pointed at his chest. "Me? Why would I do that?"

"That's why I hired you . . ." Her brow furrowed. "You're not the contractor?"

11

"High school history teacher. And assistant football coach. Varsity."

"AJ Sullivan." She practically spat his name as she wrapped her arms around her stomach.

"Guilty."

"Shouldn't you be in school?"

"Personal day."

"What are you doing here?"

"It's been awhile. Thought I should see what I'm signing away."

"This house doesn't mean anything to you, does it?"

Only a reminder of Granddad's unrelenting anger. A legacy he wished he could forget.

He spread his hands in a placating gesture. "What happened in the past doesn't matter. I don't want this place; you do. After we sign the papers, it's as good as yours."

"Why didn't you take care of it?" Her voice was a raw whisper.

Gazing into her eyes, dull with tension, he struggled to come up with an answer. The truth would pain her, but anything less seemed dishonorable.

AJ twisted to face the road as a dusty white pickup turned into the lane. Saved by the contractor.

"You hired Nate Jeffers. Good choice."

"You know him?"

"His son's my best running back." AJ jumped over the broken steps, then turned and offered Shelby his hand. After a moment's hesitation, she took it and stepped warily over the split boards.

The contractor greeted them, clipboard in hand, and smiled broadly as AJ made introductions.

"I'm pleased to meet you, Mr. Jeffers," Shelby said. "You come highly recommended."

"Glad to hear it. I talked to your uncle Richard just a few minutes ago. He said to tell you he couldn't get away from the bank right now, but he'll see you in his office this afternoon."

"Thanks for letting me know."

Nate scanned the exterior of the house, craning his neck upward to see the aged widow's walk above the porch roof. "The old Lassiter homestead. I can't tell you how honored I am to work on this place. I moseyed about the place yesterday. Shall we go inside?"

"Could you give me a moment first?" Shelby asked.

"Take your time. Coach and I can walk around the outside." He strolled to the corner of the porch and knelt by the foundation.

AJ faced Shelby. "Are you all right?"

"Fine."

"I saw a spider upstairs," he said lightly, but she averted her gaze. The Cary Grant charm didn't seem to be working.

"Please tell me." She stared at the ground, her voice so low he leaned closer to hear her. "Why didn't you take care of the house?"

"I kept the yard mowed." Only because he had to.

Her mouth twisted, and she briefly closed her eyes before pinning him with her gaze. "It's all a joke to you."

Apparently he wasn't getting out of this one. He jammed his hands into his pockets. "This place was my punishment."

"I don't understand."

"I do." But his transgressions and Granddad's vengeance belonged in the past too. Locked away and buried. He tapped her elbow and gave her a brief smile. "Be careful in there."

Before she could answer, he jogged to where Nate was disappearing around the corner of the house.

~

Finally alone.

And perplexed. How could anyone think of this magnificent place as a punishment?

Shelby took a few steps backward and squinted against April's pale sun. The abandoned brick house, elegantly situated beside massive oaks, would soon be hers. Just as she'd always dreamed.

At the end of the porch, tangled vines held a splintered trellis in

13

place. A weathered swing hung crookedly from a length of rusted chain. If the interior looked anything like this . . . She gazed back toward the road.

The pungent smell of freshly cut grass filled her nostrils. AJ Sullivan had kept the place mowed all right, including Nanna's prized irises. A grassy carpet covered the ground where the colorful blossoms once flourished.

Shelby closed her eyes for a moment, breathing deeply as she tried to imagine the fragrance of the obliterated flower garden. But the sweet fragrances of lilacs, honeysuckles, and peonies that once heralded spring had faded long ago.

Unlike her dreams.

Treasured childhood memories of playing tag on the long rectangular yard, of catching fireflies in mason jars, flitted through her mind, swift and intense.

Solitary snatches of ordinary moments frozen by loss.

Shelby gingerly stepped across the splintered stairs and onto the porch. To cross the threshold into the house was to cross the threshold into a new chapter of her life.

A chapter in a place where Gary had never been, where memories of their early years together didn't taunt her.

One of the thick double doors stood ajar, and she gave it a little push. With a soft creak it swung backward, and Shelby entered her grandparents' home for the first time in fourteen years.

The realization that she could divide her life almost exactly in half pierced through the tough scab shielding her heart. Those *before* days, her golden childhood and early teen years, warmed her spirit with their light; the *after* . . . She pushed the thought away. She had come back to create a new *after*. To give her daughters the legacy that once belonged to her.

Dirt spotted the pine floors of the long hallway, and she could see AJ's telltale footprints. She kicked at the closest one with her shoe before entering the room to her right.

The parlor, Nanna had called it, laughing at her own pretentiousness. Cobwebs formed lacy valances in the upper corners of the window alcove. More spiders. Ugh.

Ashes, a partially burnt newspaper, and trash littered the hearth. She knelt beside it, pushing at the debris with a stick. The fireplace was smaller than she remembered, and not nearly as grand. She pushed aside the niggling disappointment. It only needed a good cleaning. Along with everything else.

She went through an arched doorway to Grandpa's old study, then opened the door to the space under the stairs. The secret place. Smiling to herself, she gently jumped up and down. The solid hickory floor didn't give anything away. She doubted either AJ or Nate Jeffers knew about the room hiding beneath this closet and the study.

Returning to the hall, Shelby carefully climbed the broad stairs to the upper story and entered the room where she'd stayed during summer vacations and holidays. The pink floral wallpaper she and Nanna had selected hung in ragged strips. They'd had so much fun choosing the pattern and matching material for the curtains and bedding. The hours she had spent within these four walls, dreaming dreams derailed by circumstances she didn't understand.

Not then. Not now.

Pushing aside the brittle window shade, she gazed through the cracked glass at the abandoned shed and the neglected patch where the kitchen garden once thrived.

She did not look at the barn.

One end of the window shade and rod fell, and she startled as the hardware skittered across the bare floor. With a sheepish smile, she laid it on the sill, then wandered back to the landing. Running her hand along the wide banister, she smiled at the temptation to slide down it. Why not? Her parents weren't around to say no.

She lifted a leg to straddle the banister, then heard voices outside the front double doors. Walking sedately down the stairs, she joined the men on the porch.

Nate doffed his hat. "Good news, Miz Kincaid. The foundation is solid. This house may be old, but it was well built."

"Grandpa always said so." Shelby smiled with pride. "How long will it take to upgrade the wiring and plumbing?"

"How soon do you want to move in?"

"As soon as possible after school is out. In about six or seven weeks."

"Are you a teacher too?" AJ asked.

Shelby shook her head. "I have a first grader. And a three-year-old."

"You're married?"

As AJ's brown eyes flitted to her left hand, she self-consciously folded it into her waist. It'd been over a year since Gary's death, but she still wore her wedding band. More for her daughters' sakes than her own.

"I was." Ignoring the curiosity written all over AJ's face, she focused on Nate. "Will that give you enough time?"

"Not sure about that," Nate said. "First thing we need to figure is how to get rid of the critters in the attic."

"What critters?" Shelby's voice raised an octave.

"Pigeons, for sure. Probably bats."

"Mice have been in the kitchen," AJ said.

Shelby involuntarily shivered. She should have known spiders wouldn't be her only unwanted guests. "Any suggestions?"

"Let me do some thinkin' on it. Right now, I want to go over a few other things with you." Using the pickup's hood as a makeshift desk, Nate reviewed his notes with Shelby. "I'll need to take this back to the office to make some estimates. Usually, that would take a week or so, but given your time frame, I'll work on it this evening."

"That would be great. Thank you."

"If you'd like, I can come back in the morning and check out the attic. Nine o'clock too early?"

"I'll be here."

"All right then." Nate stuck his pen in his pocket and faced AJ. "Coach, you could have knocked me over with a feather when I heard you were selling this place. Bet your grandfather's just a-churnin' in his grave."

16

"No doubt." AJ paused, his eyes darkening to an even deeper shade. "But it's what Gran wanted me to do."

"Miss Joyanna's a fine lady. How's she doing?"

"She's been better."

"Tell her we're praying for her." Nate dug keys from his pocket and opened his truck door. "I'll be going now. See you in the morning, Miz Kincaid." He waved as he backed up, then drove down the lane, dust flying up from behind his tires.

"Your grandmother is ill?" Shelby studied AJ's profile as he avoided her gaze.

He nodded, his jaw as rigid as stone.

"I'm sorry."

He nodded again, then faced her and seemed to force a smile. "How about going into town for lunch? My treat."

"With you? No."

"This may surprise you," he said, a teasing lilt in his voice, "but I'm not my grandfather."

Shelby gazed at the broken swing. "Uncle Richard told me you've owned this house about five or six years."

"Six."

"What exactly did you do different than your grandfather?"

A wounded frown replaced AJ's amiable smile, and his eyes brimmed with pain. Regret gripped Shelby's heart. She'd meant the words to sting a little, but not to cut.

She opened her mouth to apologize, but he turned on his heel and headed toward his Jeep before she could say a word. Opening the driver's door, he glared at her over the roof.

"See you at the signing."

"I didn't mean—"

"I think you did." He disappeared into the Jeep and started the ignition.

As the vehicle bounced down the lane, Shelby's heart jolted. It was as if she were fourteen again, as lonely and abandoned as the house behind her.

– 2 –

*H*esitating outside the open door of the bank's conference room, Richard Grayson took a moment to compose himself. Never had he anticipated this turn of events. His sister Aubrey's granddaughter and his best friend Sully's grandson entering a business arrangement together.

No good could come of this.

Not that he hadn't tried to stop it. Despite his admonition that the house was beyond repair, Shelby would not be dissuaded. He'd almost had a heart attack when she called and told him about that ridiculous letter she'd written AJ.

But even worse had been Joyanna Sullivan's interference. Instead of leaving matters alone, she'd encouraged her grandson to find a loophole that would free him of the house. Given her blessing, AJ had quickly found one.

Feeling momentarily light-headed, Richard placed his palm on the wall to steady himself and pasted on a smile. Shelby would expect him to be delighted to see her after all these years. He started to enter the room, then paused again as he heard her voice.

"I truly am sorry." Her voice shook just a little. "About what I said."

"Forget about it." AJ sounded dismissive.

A spat? Richard's spirits lifted slightly. Perhaps it wasn't too late to end this transaction before it ever took place. Then maybe Shelby would stay in Chicago. Or find some other place to raise her girls. Anywhere but here, where the past lingered too close to the present.

With a confident stride, he entered the room and smiled broadly at his great-niece as she rose from her seat.

"Shelby," he said, enfolding her in an embrace. "How much you've grown."

"Hello, Uncle Richard." She kissed his cheek. "It's so good to see you."

He grasped her hands as she stepped away. "I'm only sorry it couldn't have been under happier circumstances."

She tilted her head, a bemused expression in her green eyes. "This is a very happy circumstance. A dream come true."

"I know how much the house means to you. But I can't help being sorry about"—he deliberately paused and willed concern to show in his eyes—"the loss of your husband. Are you sure he would have wanted you to uproot the children this way? After all Elizabeth and Tabby have gone through, is it wise to make this move?"

Her stunned expression told him he'd hit his mark, but he controlled his satisfaction. She looked away briefly then faced him again, her smile grim and cheerless. Before she could speak, he turned and shook hands with AJ.

"Good to see you, as always. How's your grandmother?"

"The doctor isn't holding out much hope."

Richard shook his head, genuinely sorry for Joyanna's decline. It seemed like only yesterday that they'd been young and energetic, full of life and dreams of their own. He and Joyanna often double-dated with Aubrey and Sully, the four of them big fish in Glade County's little pond. Then the Korean War had come along, throwing their lives into turmoil.

Ancient history now.

With the strange consequence that Aubrey's granddaughter and Sully's grandson faced each other across a table, oblivious to the heartaches, the betrayals, resonating from the past.

"Richard?" AJ's voice brought him back to the present. "Are you all right?"

"Fine, yes." He took his seat at the head of the table. "Considering your grandmother's health, I do wonder if this is the best time for you to be involved in legal matters."

"But, Uncle Richard—"

He placed his hand on Shelby's arm. "We must be sensitive to AJ's concern for his grandmother. She's very ill."

"Of course." Her eyes darted from him to AJ and back again, as if her confusion searched for guidance. "But if we don't do this today . . . my house in Chicago is already under contract. Where will we live?" She turned to AJ. "Please don't postpone this."

AJ seemed unable to take his eyes from hers. "I'm not postponing anything."

A sense of déjà vu reeled around Richard. Sully, before the war, gazing at Aubrey with that same steadfast intensity.

Perhaps it'd be best to get these proceedings over with. As quickly as possible.

He cleared his throat and opened the folders he'd carried in with him. "I know you both have reviewed the details of this contract with your respective attorneys. But before signing, let's cover the high points to ensure there are no misunderstandings."

"I think we both know—" AJ broke off at Richard's disapproving look. He leaned back in his chair, palms up in surrender.

"As we are all aware, the terms of Anderson John Sullivan II's estate plan forbade the sale of the Lassiter farm, legally named Misty Willow, for ten years after the date his grandson, Anderson John Sullivan IV, took possession of the property." Richard pointed the end of his pen at AJ. "That would be you."

"I know that." AJ's eyes flickered to Shelby, and the corners of her mouth turned up slightly.

Ignoring their amusement at his expense, Richard continued. "It will be four more years before the property can be sold outright. However, this contract leases thirty-two acres, including the homestead, to Ms. Shelby Lassiter Kincaid while the remaining acreage remains in the possession of Mr. Sullivan. As long as Ms. Kincaid makes the required payments, the leased property will become hers at the end of the four-year period. The negotiated payments are listed on page two."

As if on cue, Shelby and AJ flipped to the second page of their contract copies and skimmed the details.

"It's really mine?" Shelby's eyes lit up like a child's on Christmas morning.

Richard smiled indulgently. "For all practical purposes, yes."

"But AJ . . ." Shelby hesitated and corrected herself. "Mr. Sullivan technically owns the land?"

"It's not much different than a bank holding a mortgage."

Shelby's face drained of color. "Things haven't changed much, have they?"

Richard's pulse quickened at his poor choice of words, but long years of hiding his thoughts behind an impassive expression served him well. "It's your home now, Shelby. As soon as the papers are signed and filed."

"You'll take care of all that?"

"Of course." He directed the signing of the multiple copies, smoothly rotating the pages and pointing out signature lines.

When they finished the process, Shelby handed AJ an envelope. "Your first check."

"Thank you." He restlessly tapped the envelope on the table. "I hope you and your daughters will be happy there."

"We will be."

Richard stood and gathered the signed copies into a neat pile. "Our business is concluded then. Congratulations to you both."

Shelby squeezed his arm. "Thank you for everything, Uncle Richard. You've been so helpful."

"I apologize again for not being available for dinner tonight." He patted her hand. "I promise to make it up to you another time. You will forgive me?"

"Of course," she said, smiling up at him. "I'll be fine."

"When do you leave for Chicago?"

"My flight's at two-something tomorrow afternoon."

"Next time you're in town, I'll take you somewhere special. To celebrate."

"It's a date." She kissed his cheek. "Thanks again."

She practically floated from the room. After all she'd been through, she deserved some happiness. But Richard couldn't help wishing she'd found it in Chicago instead of here. At least he'd been able to avoid spending any more time with her. Now to get rid of AJ.

"I can take care of depositing your check for you. If you'd like."

"Sure." AJ removed it from the envelope and endorsed the back. "It looked like you hadn't seen Shelby in a while. Seems kind of strange since you're her uncle."

"Great-uncle, actually. But you're right. It has been a long time."

"How come?"

"Her parents are missionaries in Mozambique. She lived overseas for several years. When she returned to the States, she went to college in Chicago, married, and stayed there."

"Did you know her husband?"

"I never met him." Richard took the endorsed check and put it in his pocket. "They eloped."

"How did he die?"

"He was a police officer. Killed in the line of duty a year or so ago." Richard gestured toward the door. "Now if you'll excuse me, I have another appointment in a few minutes."

"I'm going to see Gran. She seemed anxious about the legalities." AJ glanced at his watch. "Thanks for taking care of all this."

"It's what I do." What Richard had always done for the Sullivans. Cleaning up messes. Straightening out entanglements. He had wearied of them long ago, but old habits died hard. "Tell Joyanna I asked about her."

"I will."

"And AJ?"

"Yes?"

"Don't concern yourself with Shelby."

– 3 –

*A*fter changing out of her suit into jeans and a sweater, Shelby grabbed her shoulder bag and headed out the front door of the bed-and-breakfast where she was staying. In an earlier era, the three-story B and B had been home to one of the town's founding families. According to information she'd found online when she made her reservation, the landmark had been transformed into a six-suite historic destination.

She stepped outside into a pleasant spring evening. Shade trees lined the sidewalk, their freshly sprouted leaves lightly dancing in the setting rays of the sun. The Dixie Diner's sign flashed on the corner, but earlier today she'd spotted an Italian café a couple of streets over. The perfect place to celebrate her perfect day.

Perfect except for running into AJ Sullivan at the house. To think she mistook the fiend for Nate Jeffers. And called him her hero.

As if.

The restaurant wasn't busy this early, and the hostess seated Shelby right away. Deciding on lasagna and a small salad, she handed the menu to the waitress, sipped her water, and looked around at the typical red-checked tablecloths and colorful murals painted on the walls.

A cute little place. She'd have to bring the girls here after they moved. If only there wasn't so much to do before then.

Pulling a notepad and pen from her bag, she jotted down a few notes. Priority one—rid the house of its four-legged and eight-legged inhabitants. Hopefully, Nate Jeffers had a plan for that project.

Suddenly realizing someone was standing near her, Shelby looked up with a polite smile.

AJ Sullivan.

The smile froze in place as she stared at him, too stunned to speak. He carried a royal blue gift bag and a different OSU ball cap than the one he'd worn that morning. No doubt he spent every spare moment glued to some sporting event. That seemed the American male obsession, one she'd marveled at when she returned to the States for college.

At least Gary hadn't been caught up in that craze. At least not too much.

He'd preferred video games.

"Do you mind if I sit down?" AJ's question jerked her back to the present.

"Of course not." Biting her lip, she fervently wished her mother hadn't drilled good manners into her quite so deep. Then she could just tell him to get lost.

"I was driving by and saw your car." He sat across from her and gestured at the notepad. "Making plans?"

"There's a lot to do."

"Anything I can do to help?"

"I think you've done enough." She closed the notepad. "Or, more accurately, *not* done enough."

"It's just a house."

"Not to me."

"Hey, AJ." The waitress appeared by his side. "What brings you to town on a Thursday night?" As her eyes flickered to Shelby, the generous smile she'd given AJ faded. What did the woman think, they were on a date?

It would never happen.

"Hi, Tiff," AJ said, then faced Shelby. "Let me treat you to dinner. Seeing as how I've just come into some money."

Before Shelby could reply, Tiff gushed. "What happened, AJ? Did you win the lottery?" Her laugh grated like fingernails on a chalkboard.

"I gave it to him," Shelby heard herself saying as AJ's brown eyes held her gaze. Her cheeks warmed as an unexpected charge tingled her spine. Unexpected and unwelcome.

"I've got other tables, you know." Tiff squeezed AJ's shoulder. "What are you going to have, handsome?"

Shelby glanced around the barely occupied room and ducked her head to hide her amusement. But AJ must have seen the gleam in her eyes. He bent his head to catch her gaze. "I can stay?" he asked softly.

"Yes." She tried but failed to sound exasperated.

AJ grinned as he looked up at Tiff. "Just bring me the usual."

"One 'usual' coming right up." Her hips swayed as she flounced away.

"Your girlfriend?" Shelby asked coyly, then sipped her water.

"Tiff?" AJ shook his head. "Um, no."

"Does she know that?"

"Tiff is"—he paused as if choosing his words carefully—"friendly."

"I see."

Surprisingly, color crept up his neck, and he plopped the gift bag in front of her. "This is for you. From my grandmother."

"Why would your grandmother give me a gift?"

"Open it and you'll see." Folding his arms on the table, he leaned forward.

Shelby pushed aside the blue and white tissue paper and lifted a large key from the bag. A weeping willow was engraved into the top of the key. Curved above the tree's crown was written "Est. 1842."

She gasped, covering her mouth with one hand as she cradled the key in the other.

"You recognize it?"

"It's the original key. The year is when the house was built."

"Gran thought you'd like to have it. Now that the place is yours."

"This is amazing." Shelby blinked away tears. The original doors had been replaced long ago, but the key had been a family heirloom, hanging decade after decade in the hallway near the double doors. She thought it had been lost, as so many other heirlooms had been lost when her grandparents died.

"Please tell your grandmother thank you for me."

He pulled his phone from his pocket. "Let me take a picture. You holding the key."

"Why?"

"For Gran. It'd mean a lot to her."

"I guess that would be okay." Shelby held up the key and smiled. She didn't like the idea of AJ having a photo of her, but neither did she want to appear ungrateful for his grandmother's gift. He snapped the photo, looked at the phone display, then held it out to her. In the photo, her eyes appeared too bright, her smile uncertain.

"Do another one. Please."

"Sure."

She took a deep breath then smiled, a genuine smile for the elderly woman who'd given her a precious keepsake from the past.

They examined the photo together. The lighting wasn't the greatest, but at least her expression was more relaxed.

"Much better," she said. "You will tell her how much this means to me?"

"I will." AJ pocketed his phone. "Does this mean you aren't mad at me anymore?"

"I was never mad at you."

"Could have fooled me."

"It's not that I'm mad." She hesitated, wanting to corral her emotions into the right words. But how could she explain the unrelenting anger she carried for the family who had caused her such grief? Until today, when she met AJ, a faceless family who had appeared in her nightmares as ogres with red eyes and grasping fingers that clawed at her heart.

Nothing at all like the man who sat across from her with his Cary Grant cleft, warm eyes, and easygoing demeanor.

"It's that . . . you're a Sullivan."

"You don't like me because I'm a Sullivan?"

"It's reason enough." She lifted her chin, trying to impose solidity where there was nothing but foolishness. She wasn't being fair. But life hadn't been fair to her.

Tiff arrived at the table with two steaming plates of lasagna. "Bon appétit," she said. "Let me know if you need anything." She leaned closer to AJ. "Anything at all."

"Thanks, Tiff." He barely smiled. "I think we're good."

Thankful for the distraction, Shelby placed her napkin on her lap and picked up her fork. "May I ask you a question?"

"Sure." AJ took a breadstick from the basket and tore it in half.

"What did you mean earlier about the house being a punishment?"

He bent his head, but not enough to hide the set of his jaw. She cut into the lasagna with the side of her fork and jabbed at it.

"You don't need to answer. It's just hard for me to understand. It's a beautiful house. At least it was. Once."

He lifted his eyes, drawing her into deep brown pools of light and warmth. Her breath caught as an unexpected thought beat rhythm with her pulse.

If only she had met AJ Sullivan under different circumstances.

~

"I'm sure it was. Once." AJ bit into the soft, hot bread. Shelby's green eyes mesmerized him, but her mercurial attitude confounded him. One minute, he felt like her enemy. The next, as if they could be best friends. Maybe even something more. "But the first time I saw it, the house had already been empty several years."

"You didn't want to fix it up? Live in it?"

"It's kind of large for one person, don't you think?" He ventured a grin. Thankfully, she nodded agreement.

"You could have rented it out. Made some money."

He searched for a noble reason why he hadn't done even that. But the simple truth was that he wanted nothing to do with the house or the memories it embodied. Shelby might be hurt by that truth, but perhaps his explanation would make up for whatever wrongs his family had done to hers.

"Granddad—everyone called him Sully—had several business interests," he said. "And three heirs. My two cousins and me. I got Misty Willow, and they got everything else."

"To punish you?"

"Yeah."

She didn't ask, but he read the question in her eyes. *What had you done?*

He gave a casual shrug, as if what he'd done wasn't that big of a deal. Except that it was. He didn't need to tell Shelby the whole story, though. Only the part that most people knew.

"I'm his namesake. His only son's only son. Naturally, I was supposed to be a lawyer so I could take care of his legal affairs. But I dropped out of law school and became a teacher instead."

"So he pretty much disinherited you?"

"Except for your farm, yes."

"Why the 'you can't sell this for ten years' clause?"

"According to Richard, who's the trustee, Sully thought I was too headstrong. That I didn't think before I acted. Forcing me to keep the property was meant to teach me patience." AJ leaned back in his chair and traced a pattern on the tablecloth. "For all his faults, he was a visionary. The farmland around here becomes more valuable every year. The commute to Columbus isn't that far. Seems people want to raise their kids in the country."

"I understand that."

"I guess you do. Anyway, what the commuters don't get, developers will."

"Not Misty Willow."

"Nor the rest of the acreage. I kind of like the land the way it is."

"I wish I could have afforded to lease all of it now."

"I wish you could have too." Apparently, the numbers hadn't worked out for her to lease more than the thirty-two acres. At least that's what Richard had said. AJ wasn't sure what difference it made in the long run, though. He gave her an encouraging smile. "But you have first options on the rest, and it's not going anywhere."

"I guess that means we'll be doing business again in the future."

AJ lifted his glass of tea. "To the future."

A slow smile brightened Shelby's features as she clinked her glass against his. "To the future."

With her perfect timing, Tiff sidled to the table with separate checks and routine questions about to-go boxes. AJ paid both bills then escorted Shelby to her car. The moon hung low on the horizon, and only a few stars gleamed in the night sky.

Shelby clicked the remote to unlock the car. "Thank you for supper."

"Thanks for letting me sit down." Stepping in front of her, he opened the door.

"Thank you for the key too. Tell your grandmother it means the world to me."

"She'll be glad."

Shelby started to get in, then halted, standing so close her delicate fragrance beckoned him even closer. "You're very close to her, aren't you?"

AJ's throat tightened. "Very."

"It's hard. Losing a grandmother." She stared past him. "The pain eases, but it never goes away."

"Would you want it to?"

She looked at him a moment, her eyes dark in the dim light of a nearby lamppost, then barely shook her head. "Good night."

"Night."

30

AJ stood on the sidewalk, staring at the taillights as she drove away. When she turned a corner, he jammed his hands in his pockets and strode to his Jeep. He envied her. That's why he couldn't stop thinking about her.

He envied her passion for a rundown house. He envied her happy childhood memories. He was even jealous that she had kids.

There had been a time when he thought he could change the dysfunctional Sullivan legacy. Become a respected husband and loving father.

But God couldn't trust him with a family of his own. Not after the way he'd messed things up.

As he slid into his Jeep, he vowed not to think of Shelby Kincaid's dazzling eyes or delicate features. Ever again.

– 4 –

Shelby opened the attic door, the hinges eerily squeaking, then stood aside so Nate Jeffers could climb the steep wooden stairs. As they neared the top, the overwhelming stench caused her to gag. She adjusted her nose mask. "This is awful."

"I take it you don't think much of your current tenants." Nate laughed as he entered the attic. The scurry of movement sounded along the far walls. Shelby stayed on the stairs and watched the beam of Nate's flashlight play across decaying pigeon carcasses. She gagged, swallowed her rising bile, gagged again, and barely kept herself from vomiting.

"You okay?" Nate turned the light to her. Lifting the mask, she wiped her mouth on her sleeve.

"I'll just leave this to you." She backed down the attic stairs and hurried into the second floor bathroom. Somehow the claw-footed bathtub and porcelain vanity had survived the years of neglect.

She tore off the mask and turned the ivory-handled faucets. Pipes groaned, but no water appeared. Plopping on the closed toilet, she buried her head in her arms to scrub away the mental image of the dead birds. But the grimy feathers, the mottled bones, wouldn't go away.

If only Gary were here. To teasingly make fun of her grandiose plans. He'd always laughed when she dreamed of buying the house, restoring it. "Someday," he'd say, his hazel eyes glinting with humor. But he hadn't meant it.

He could have attended the police academy in Columbus, but he wouldn't even apply. Chicago, not Misty Willow, was his dream place.

Shelby pulled her knees to her chest, guarding her heart as best she could. God knew, she wanted Gary back. The Gary she fell in love with when they were college students at the University of Illinois. Except if Gary were still alive, she wouldn't be here, in this house. Where she belonged. Where all was right with the world.

Her head ached with the impossibility of wanting two opposing things so much.

"Anybody home?" The voice echoed up the stairs, and Shelby's stomach lurched. Not again. Last night in the restaurant, she had let herself be lulled into a truce. But the return of her nightmares had reminded her of all the grief and heartache the Sullivans had caused. It might not be rational, but the less time she spent with AJ the better.

Reluctantly, she walked to the hallway and peered over the banister. AJ waved at her. "You coming down, or should I come up?"

"What are you doing here?"

"I was curious about the attic."

"Nate's up there now." She gestured for him to come up. It'd serve him right if he got sick at the sight of all those . . . Her stomach heaved, and she wrapped her arms around her belly.

"Are you all right?" AJ rounded the banister and rested his hand on her shoulder. She recoiled from his touch.

"I'm fine. It's just, all those dead things."

"You mind if I go up?" His brown eyes danced, a mischievous schoolboy bent on adventure.

Shelby exaggerated a heavy sigh. "Go."

"How do I get there?"

"You don't know?"

33

"How would I?"

She pressed her lips together, preparing herself for the anger she expected to feel at this blatant reminder of his misdeeds. But it didn't come. "Through there," she said, gesturing to the open room that housed the attic stairs.

"You sure you're okay? You look queasy."

"It's so awful up there."

"Sure you don't want to go back up?"

"I need to change before driving to the airport." She tucked her hair behind her ears. "Guess I'll do that now."

She stepped around him, rushing down the stairs and through the open double doors to get a change of clothes from her car. As she stepped onto the porch, a faded blue pickup pulled up and parked behind her rental. The driver wore jeans and a work shirt, sleeves rolled above the elbows. A cap bearing a feed store logo shielded his eyes and sun-darkened face. He headed for the porch, a younger version of himself following closely behind.

"Hello, miss." The farmer removed his cap, and the teen did the same.

"Hello." Shelby stepped forward and extended her hand.

"You may not remember me, but I'm Paul Norris. This is my boy Seth. We're your nearest neighbors."

"Paul Norris." She broadened her smile. About fifteen years older than she, he'd sometimes worked for her grandfather. "Of course I remember you. How are your parents?"

"Doing well. They moved to town a few years ago, a nice little house. My family's at the farm now."

"No better place to raise a family."

"Heard tell you're buying this place from AJ."

"That's right. I hope to move in as soon as the house is ready."

"I bet AJ's granddaddy is spitting nails." Paul gazed upward, seeming to appraise the house. "But I'm sure glad to have Lassiter kin back in the old place."

"Thank you, Mr. Norris. That means a great deal to me."

"AJ may have told you, I rent the pastures on both sides of the house."

"Of course." She remembered now, seeing his name on the contract. "I'm glad you do."

She turned at the sudden commotion behind her, loud footsteps on the stairs. A moment later, AJ and Nate spilled through the door, laughing uncontrollably.

"It's an animal graveyard up there," AJ said, gripping his side.

"There's a raccoon. Big one." Nate held his hands a couple of feet apart, like a fisherman measuring the one that got away.

"I thought it was dead," AJ sputtered.

"Now you know better." Nate took off his hat and wiped his forehead with his sleeve. "Never saw anyone move so fast in my life."

"It scared me. I'm not ashamed to admit it."

"What is all this?" asked Paul.

"My attic," Shelby said, almost wishing she had seen AJ's encounter with the raccoon. "It's a nightmare."

"I want to go up." Seth Norris spoke for the first time, and Shelby marveled at the appeal. She hoped never to step foot in that dark, infested place again.

While the men inspected the attic, she washed up the best she could with bottled water and changed into fresh clothes in the downstairs bathroom. Gazing at her reflection in the mottled mirror, she refreshed her makeup and brushed her hair into a neat ponytail. Now that the papers were signed, she was anxious to get home. To have supper with her girls and tell them all about the house and the farm. But not about the attic.

Shelby carried her overnight bag to the front doors and met the men coming down the stairs.

"I think Seth and I can help you out," said Paul.

"With the critters?"

"Yes'm. We can get started on it next week, if that'd suit you."

"That would be great." Shelby glanced at Nate, wondering if

he knew the going rate for removing animal carcasses. Though Gary's life insurance policy had been substantial, she had to keep a close eye on her budget. "What would you charge for the job?"

"I owe your dad a favor, and I've been waiting a long time to pay him back." Paul glanced around the hallway before looking straight at Shelby. "I figure this will do it."

"It must have been a very big favor." AJ lounged on one of the lower steps, his long legs casually stretched before him.

"Sure was," Paul said, then clapped Seth on the shoulder and moved to the door. "We best be getting along. Your mom will be wondering what happened to us."

"Mr. Norris, I can't let you clean up that mess without paying you something."

"Please, it's Paul. And it's already settled."

"Shelby," AJ said softly. She turned to him, and he barely shook his head as he stood.

He picked up her bag as they followed the Norrises and Nate out of the house.

"I'll be putting locks on all the doors this afternoon," Nate said to Paul. "Okay if I give you a key at church in the morning?"

"That'd be fine, if Shelby has no objection."

"None at all. Thank you." She smiled nervously, unsure how to accept such generosity. "Thank you so much."

"Once you get settled, we'll have you over for supper. If you'd like."

"Yes, I would. Thanks."

Standing on the porch, she waved at the Norrises and Nate as their trucks kicked up dirt down the long lane.

"That driveway needs new gravel," AJ said.

"I know." Shelby let out a deep sigh. "One more thing to add to the list."

"Let me take care of it."

"You? Why?"

"If I'd paid more attention to the place, your list wouldn't be so long."

"True. But I don't need your help now."

"Consider it a housewarming gift."

"Gravel for my drive?" Shelby tried but couldn't stop from smiling. "That has to be the strangest housewarming gift ever."

"You'll accept it, then?"

A flash of blue caught Shelby's attention, and her gaze followed the aerobatic jay as it swooped into the midst of a silver maple near the fence line. Her mind drifted to her younger self, sheltered by those outstretched branches, her back against its broad trunk.

Reading, thinking, dozing. Dreaming of the future. Imagining her Prince Charming.

But nothing had turned out as she expected.

"Is that a yes?"

Lost in the past, Shelby startled. "Thanks for offering, but it's too much."

"It's a lot less than what Paul and Seth volunteered to do."

"I would have paid them. Why did you tell me not to?"

"Pay him if you think you can. But I know Paul Norris. He'll just figure out a way to give it back to you."

"You know, anything to do with this house is no longer any of your business." Shelby punched the key remote to unlock the car. "It's mine."

"True." Frowning, he placed her bag into the trunk. "When will you be back?"

"Right after Mother's Day." She opened the car door and tossed her purse inside.

"I live over on the next road. I could drive by here. Keep an eye on the place if you want."

"Now you care about it?"

"Just tryin' to be neighborly. That's what we do around here."

"And one of the reasons I want to live here." She glanced at the widow's walk above the porch, a simple balcony outside the twin windows of the upstairs hall and what had been her grandparents' bedroom. The room she'd make her own. Living in the house would give her a chance to recapture the spirit of the girl she'd been.

But she couldn't build on the pleasant memories with AJ Sullivan hanging around, reminding her of the bad.

She faced him, praying her voice wouldn't shake. "We can be neighbors," she said softly. "But never more than that."

AJ pressed his lips together in a thin line, then shook his head as if in defeat. Pain hardened his eyes. "I didn't ask for more than that."

His words slammed into Shelby's stomach, their impact more hurtful than she would have thought possible.

"Of course not." She slid into the car, but AJ grabbed the door before she could close it.

"Shelby, wait."

"I have to get to the airport."

"Just . . ." As he leaned in, she breathed the woodsy notes of his aftershave. Drawn to the fragrance, she bent her head slightly toward him while avoiding his gaze. "Travel safe."

"I will." She turned the ignition, watching through the windshield as he climbed into his hunter green Jeep. A lump pressed against her throat, and as she drove to the airport, her thoughts were haunted by the ache she'd seen in his eyes.

She knew that ache. She saw it in her mirror every day.

- 5 -

AJ rode the elevator to the eleventh floor of the downtown office building, breathing a prayer of thanks this wasn't his daily routine. Some people might like the prestige of a prosperous business, the panoramic view of the Columbus skyline. But not him.

He preferred his high school students, even the uninspired ones, over contract negotiations, power lunches, and wearing a tie every day. His cousin was welcome to those so-called perks.

Pushing open the glass door to Somers, Inc., he shook his head at the irony. Sully had left the business he'd founded, Sullivan Investments, to his new favorite grandson, Brett Somers. Less than a month after the estate was settled, Brett had changed the company's name.

AJ greeted the latest receptionist, another mini-skirted blonde. "I had a summons from your boss," he said, only half joking. Brett had refused to tell him what he wanted over the phone.

"Your name, please." The blonde gave him the once-over beneath fluttering false lashes. Where did Brett find these girls?

"AJ Sullivan. Would you please tell Brett I'm here?"

She consulted a calendar program on her computer. "Oh, you

can go on in. Brett"—she giggled—"I mean, Mr. Somers is expecting you. Would you like me to show you the way?"

"I've been here before." Though not that often since Brett had taken over their grandfather's corner office. Sully's original plan was for Brett to run the company's day-to-day operations, and for AJ, with a law degree backing his name, to have control. Until the argument. Then everything had changed.

AJ rapped on the door of Brett's office and entered.

Wearing a blue shirt that almost perfectly matched his eyes, Brett commanded a large oak desk, his back to a wall of certificates, plaques, and VIP photographs. He smiled at AJ. "See, Amy. I told you he'd come."

AJ followed Brett's gaze to the brown leather sofa. His cousin Amy, impeccably dressed in a lilac linen suit, stood and pecked AJ on the cheek. "Where have you been hiding? I don't think we've seen you since Christmas."

"You're probably right." Christmas. Funny how they still celebrated the holiday together, though only Gran truly enjoyed the family togetherness. The traditional brunch eaten around her antique table. The exchanging of gifts. Her only grandchildren promising to get together again soon before they went their separate ways.

"Can I get you something? Coffee?" Brett asked, walking around his desk to the built-in bar.

"A soda, if you have one."

"Ice?" Brett pulled a Coke from the mini-fridge, and AJ reached for the can.

"This is fine." He popped the tab.

"Sis?" Brett turned to Amy.

"I'm good." She swirled the contents of her crystal glass at him. "Here, AJ, sit beside me."

AJ followed Amy to the couch while Brett settled in a nearby chair. Double-teaming. So that was their game. He took a long sip of the soda as his cousins exchanged furtive glances.

"Do you still enjoy teaching?" Amy asked.

"I do." AJ gazed at her. Same ash blonde hair and clear blue eyes as her brother. As in all things, AJ was the odd one out with his darker coloring. His cousins had inherited their father's Scandinavian features, their mother's social superiority.

"But you didn't drag me here to talk about my career choice, did you?"

Amy lowered her eyes as if embarrassed, though AJ knew better. She crossed one shapely leg over the other and pulled at her skirt. Another of her ploys. "Have you heard about the Glade Valley Refuge project?"

"Who hasn't? There are signs up everywhere, editorials. What about it?" The controversial Glade Valley watershed project was a proposed federal initiative designed to control runaway development in the large geographical area southwest of Columbus.

"There's a very good chance that project is going to be fast-tracked. When it gets approved, it's going to upset some people's plans."

"What does that have to do with me?"

"A private consortium has hired my consulting firm to assist them in getting the approvals for an exclusive retreat within that area," said Amy. "Upscale cottages, golf course and clubhouse, pool, very chic. But if the refuge goes through, the land they want will be federally protected. The consortium will have to find another site in the same general area."

AJ shrugged. "And . . . ?"

"And that's where," Brett said, pausing dramatically, "our Midas touch turns land into gold."

"What land?"

"Our land." Brett chuckled. "Okay, your land. But considering that Amy can broker the deal and I can negotiate for top dollar, it'd be to our advantage to form a partnership."

"The three of us?" AJ widened his eyes. He'd known to expect the unexpected when Brett asked him to come to the office. But he hadn't foreseen a proposal like this. "Let me make sure I have this right. We form a partnership so someone can build a retreat on my land."

"That's right," Brett replied. "Earlier than the old man stipulated in his will, but we'll get around that legal stumbling block. Amy already has a friend looking into it."

"Too bad you didn't finish law school," Amy said. "Then you could have done it yourself."

"If he'd finished law school," Brett said, "Sully would have stuck either you or me with that wasteland."

"It's not a wasteland," AJ protested. He hated admitting that he'd ever agreed with Brett on something. But that's what he'd thought of the farm until he realized how important it was to someone else. Somehow that made it important to him too.

More than a week had passed since Shelby had flown back to Chicago. He drove by the house every day, sometimes stopping in if either Nate Jeffers or Paul Norris was there. Both men were making great progress. And the gravel he had ordered would be delivered and spread out in the next couple of days. A surprise for Shelby. Though what she'd say about it . . .

"The land may prove to be valuable," Amy said, frowning at her brother. "But we need to have everything in place so that when the refuge goes through, we have something else to offer my client."

AJ shifted to face Amy. "Aren't you being paid to make sure the refuge doesn't go through?"

"I can't always get my clients what they want," she said, posing her lips into a pout. The girl never quit, not even with her own relatives. "Besides, this way I'll know their plans, and I can steer them to Brett."

AJ leaned back, folding his hands behind his head and staring at the ceiling. This could be fun. "How many acres will they need?"

"All of it. And more."

"Who's most likely to sell, do you think?" asked Brett. "Jason Owens or Paul Norris?"

The Owens family owned land to the west and across the road from Misty Willow; the Norris land lay to the east.

"Neither," AJ said.

"But which one might?" Brett insisted.

"Jason might."

"Great." Amy scooched forward. "Why don't you invite him to have dinner with us one day next week? Perhaps at the Buckeye Club. I'll make the reservations."

"I'm not sure Jason has as much acreage as your client needs."

"I think he does." Brett's smug tone irritated AJ. "I did a search. Owens's farm added to Misty Willow should be more than adequate."

"I wouldn't be so sure about that." AJ stood and walked around Brett's chair, hands sunk in his pockets. "Even if I agreed to add my acres to this project, Shelby Kincaid will never give up hers."

"Who is Shelby Kincaid?" asked Amy, bewilderment distorting her features.

"The new owner of the old Lassiter homestead. The house and thirty-two acres."

"What house?" Amy's strident voice echoed in the room.

"The new what?" Brett spoke at the same time as his sister.

"Do you still want me to talk to Jason?" AJ asked with pretend innocence.

"What I want is for you to explain why you sold the house." Brett rose from his chair and paced the room before facing AJ. "And how."

AJ bristled at Brett's threatening tone. He'd punched his cousin once before, and he wouldn't mind an excuse to do so again.

"I don't have to explain anything to you," AJ said. "And I'm not interested in selling my acres for a retreat. But thanks for including me in your plans."

"How could you sell?" Amy stood and crossed her arms like a petulant child. "Sully's will specifically said—"

"Gran told me to."

"I don't believe you," Brett said.

"It's done."

"Undo it."

"No."

"Boys!" Amy placed her manicured hand on AJ's arm. "Tell me again. Who bought the house?"

"Shelby Kincaid," AJ said. "Her grandparents owned Misty Willow before Sully did. She loves the place and wanted it back in the family."

"What sentimental . . ." muttered Brett. "When did this happen?"

"A little over a week ago."

"Does Richard know?"

"He was at the signing."

"It can't be legal."

"And yet it is." Fed up with his cousins, AJ strode to the office door. "Forget this development plan. Both of you. Shelby won't give up her land. And I won't sell mine."

- 6 -

$\mathcal{S}$helby savored a bite of the decadent chocolate mousse. "Delicious." After a month away, she'd flown into the Columbus airport only a few hours earlier, hoping for a restful evening. But Uncle Richard had insisted on driving back to the city for dinner.

"I'm glad you like it." His fond gaze blanketed her, piercing her with longing for Grandpa. If only he were sitting across from her instead. Except he wouldn't have brought her to this pretentious place. They'd have celebrated her return with grilled steaks and potatoes slowly baked amongst the hot ashes in the stone fire ring outside the house.

Another memory she needed to re-create for Elizabeth and Tabby.

"Richard, is that you?" A blond man with crystal blue eyes, wearing a tailored navy suit and crisp white shirt, approached the table. "What brings you to the 'big city'?"

"A rare evening out." Rising from his chair, Richard shook hands with the newcomer. "Allow me to introduce you. Shelby Kincaid, this is Brett Somers."

"She's a little young for you, isn't she, Richard?"

Unaccustomed butterflies flitted in Shelby's stomach as the gorgeous stranger held her gaze. "I'm pleased to meet you," she said, her voice betraying her sudden embarrassment. He took her hand, and his light touch electrified her fingers.

"Shelby is my great-niece. Her grandmother was my sister." Richard gestured toward a chair. "Join us, won't you?"

"I don't want to intrude."

"I imagine I've bored Shelby with enough of my stories for one evening," Richard said. "Have you eaten?"

"A business dinner." Brett took a seat and gazed at Shelby. "My guests left a few minutes ago."

"What type of business are you in?" Shelby asked.

"Investments. Property development." Deep dimples appeared on either side of Brett's engaging smile. "What about you?"

Shelby pressed her lips together and slightly shrugged. She'd graduated with a bachelor's degree in anthropology but was pregnant with Elizabeth before starting any kind of career. This handsome stranger wouldn't be interested in that. "I just bought my . . . a farm. The house was neglected for several years, so I'm restoring it."

Brett's eyebrows arched. "You're planning to farm?"

"The pastures are rented to a neighbor. I just want to live there. With my children."

"Children?"

The question he didn't ask hovered in the air. Before Shelby could explain, Richard covered her hand with his.

"Shelby's husband died about a year ago. She's moving here with her two daughters." Richard squeezed her fingers and smiled. "Would you both excuse me? I need to make a call. It'll only take a few moments."

Richard pulled out his cell phone as he walked toward the restaurant's lobby, his shoulders barely stooped with age. Funny that he hadn't mentioned a call before. If Shelby didn't know better, she'd think he had deliberately left her alone with Brett. Embarrassed by her sudden awkwardness, she focused her attention on the table's floral centerpiece.

"So moving here is a starting over for you?" Brett's blue eyes glistened with sympathy.

"More like coming home."

"You're doing a brave thing. But is it the best thing?"

"Why wouldn't it be?"

"My parents divorced when I was a kid. I know it's not quite the same thing, but if I'd had to change schools, leave my friends . . ." He shrugged, then folded his hands on the table in front of him. Nicely shaped hands.

She frowned, his words opening the Pandora's box of doubts she'd been carrying around with her since morning. They had whispered in her ear as she said good-bye to the girls, leaving them in the care of Gary's parents. Then the doubts accompanied her onto the plane, setting up camp in her heart. But this move had to be the right thing. Where else could she find peace?

"I'm sorry about your parents," she said. "And I know it'll be hard, especially for Elizabeth. But it's what I have to do." She forced a smile. "I just flew in this afternoon, and then Richard insisted on bringing me here. It was very nice of him, but—"

"But you're tired."

"Yes."

"Not of me, I hope." Brett flashed his dimples, startling Shelby with his handsome smile. Her cheeks warmed, and she played with the crystal stem of her water glass.

"I've embarrassed you."

"No, you didn't."

He laughed softly and stood. "I'll find Richard and tell him you're ready to leave."

"Thank you."

"I hope to see you again, Shelby Kincaid."

He strode from the room, his gait confident and sure. Flustered by his attention, she took one last bite of the mousse. No man of his caliber could possibly be interested in her. She'd probably never see him again.

~

Shelby skipped church the following morning, though guilt gnawed her stomach. But the thought of seeing people who remembered her, who had known her grandparents and parents, was too overwhelming. They'd be asking the same questions, and she'd be repeating the same answers.

Yes, my parents are still missionaries. I live in Chicago now. Two children, both girls. I'm widowed; yes, it is sad. Yes, we'll be moving to the old homestead as soon as it's ready.

Besides, her flight had arrived too late yesterday to go to the house. She was eager to see what progress had been made during her absence.

As soon as she turned into the drive, she braked, staring through the windshield at the long straight line of pristine gravel leading beyond the house and also encircling the broad grassy oval at its side. She stepped from the rental, then picked up a handful of pebbles and let them fall between her fingers.

How dare he! After she specifically told him not to.

She'd give AJ Sullivan a piece of her mind . . . if she only knew how to get hold of him.

As she brushed the pebble dust from her hands; she imagined the argument with AJ. While she raged at him, his brown eyes would dance with amusement. After all, what could she do? Insist he take it back? She'd just have to pay him for it.

She drove the rest of the way to the house, pleased despite herself that she didn't have to avoid any more ruts.

Parking in front of the newly built porch, she admired the renovation. The broken trellis and porch swing were gone, the brush cleared away. She climbed solid steps and pulled the key Nate had sent her from her pocket.

Once inside, she explored the downstairs rooms. Stripped of

paint and wallpaper, the walls appeared fresh and smooth. The floors hadn't been sanded yet, but debris no longer cluttered the corners and filled the hearths.

The last of the electrical and plumbing work still needed to be finished, but Richard had told her at dinner last night that the attic was "critter free." She trusted his word for it, not being courageous enough to check out the attic alone.

Things were going almost too perfectly. She waved away the superstitious thought. Things were going well because restoring this house was the right thing to do. And with Nate's recommendations, she had the right people helping her do it.

Wandering into the kitchen, she discovered the old cabinetry and appliances had been removed. Redesigning the layout and choosing new cabinets was a top priority this week. She opened her three-ring binder and flipped to the "kitchen" tab. Her favorite magazine photos and internet printouts filled several sheet protectors. Sitting on the floor, she imagined cream walls with yellow and blue accents. Gleaming appliances. Herb pots in the windowsill over the sink.

A delightfully sunny room where she and the girls would enjoy pancake breakfasts on lazy Saturday mornings and bake chocolate chip cookies in their new oven.

A knock sounded on the doorframe, and she jumped.

"Anyone home?"

Handsome as any teenage heartthrob, Brett leaned against the doorframe almost as if posing for a photo shoot.

Shelby quickly stood, brushing the dirt from her jeans. "What are you doing here?"

"You look beautiful."

Heat warmed her cheeks, and she pushed her hair from her forehead. "How did you know where to find me?"

"Amazing what you can find on the internet. And I just took a chance you'd be here." He gestured at her open notebook. "Planning your new kitchen?"

"Trying to."

"Have you had lunch?"

"Not yet."

"I was hoping you'd say that. Why don't we take a drive into town?"

"I'm sorry, I can't."

"Aren't you hungry?"

She hadn't been until he mentioned food, but that was beside the point. She nervously twisted her wedding ring.

Brett entered the kitchen and stood within arm's reach. Near enough for Shelby to catch a whiff of his sophisticated aftershave, far enough not to crowd her.

"It's only lunch." He grinned, showing off his cute dimples. "Nothing fancy."

She wavered, unsure how to respond. Her dating days ended long ago, and her experience even then hadn't been extensive. Besides, her dusty jeans and worn sneakers made her feel unkempt next to his pressed and polished appearance.

"Would it help if I got a little dirt on my pants?"

As if he'd read her mind.

"It might."

"Then why don't you show me around the place, and I'll see what I can do."

Eager to shed the momentary awkwardness, she quickly agreed. "I'd love that."

Leading him through the rooms, she shared her plans. He appeared genuinely interested as he admired the craftsmanship of the woodwork. When she told him about the attic, he insisted on climbing the steep stairs. She followed him, gazing in awe at what had to be the cleanest floor in the house. Even the odor was gone.

After returning to the kitchen, they went out a side door to a concrete patio that curved in the L formed by the house. At one end of the patio, a two-story brick structure with a wide door and window openings was attached to the side of the house.

"This used to be the smokehouse," Shelby said. "They hung the meat up there and built the fire down here. My grandparents turned it into a playhouse for me. I had a table and chairs, an old chest of drawers. But everything's gone now."

"I can see why you love this place." Brett surveyed the property, then focused on Shelby. His clear blue eyes were like magnets, drawing her into his world. "I just hope you're not making a mistake."

"Why would I be?"

"For what you're putting into this place, you could build something new. Think of it, Shelby. A brand-new place for your brand-new start. For you and your girls."

"This is where we belong." Shelby shrugged. "I don't know how else to explain it."

"No explanation necessary." He looked down at his pants. They weren't nearly as pristine as when he'd arrived. "Am I dirty enough for you now?"

His easy flirtation sent butterflies flitting through her stomach.

"Come on, Shelby," he said, adding a bit of a country drawl to his voice. "We both gotta eat."

How could she refuse?

"Nowhere fancy."

He smiled triumphantly. "I promise."

She locked the kitchen door, and they walked around the house to Brett's jet-black Lexus. He opened the passenger door for her, and the butterflies flitted again, in nerve-racking formation this time.

"I'll drive separately," she said. "I've got a few errands to do, and that way you won't have to bring me all the way back here."

"Whatever you say."

She locked the front door of the house, then climbed in her rental. He surprised her by turning left at the end of the drive instead of heading toward town. She didn't have much choice but to follow behind. After a few minutes, she got her bearings and realized they were headed for a little crossroads with a gas station and a cluster of houses. Too small to even be called a village. When they arrived, Brett turned into a dirt parking lot in front of a squat building. The sign out front screamed "Boyd's Bodacious BBQ" in big red letters.

Shelby parked beside the Lexus and closed her eyes. Suddenly she was a little girl again, riding beside Grandpa in his blue "pick-me-up" truck. Coming here for the best pulled pork this side of the Ohio River.

Brett knocked on her window, and she opened her door. "If you're disappointed, we can go somewhere else."

"This is perfect." She hugged the memory to her heart. "Absolutely perfect."

"I used to come here with my grandfather sometimes," Brett said, an almost wistful tone in his voice. "A long time ago."

"Me too." She laughed self-consciously. "I mean with mine."

Brett flashed his dimples and grabbed her hand. "Let's see if it's as good as we remember."

They were soon settled across from each other in a wooden booth with barely padded seats. After placing their orders, Brett leaned back. "What do your parents think about your restoration project?"

Shelby shifted uncomfortably in her seat. "I haven't told them."

"Why not?"

"They're in Mozambique." She'd have to tell them soon, though. At least, before she actually moved. "It's too much to explain in an email."

"Mozambique? What are they doing there?"

"They're missionaries."

"Did you live there too?"

Shelby nodded. "For a few years. Until I came back for college."

"I admire people who can give up so much to do something like that. I don't think I could."

"It isn't so hard when you love what you're doing. When you have a purpose."

"Did you love it?" The gentleness in his voice touched a tender spot in Shelby's heart. Perhaps he would understand, like she thought Gary had, how difficult her teen years had been. She'd never really fit in with the other kids overseas. Then when she came back to the States, she didn't fit in here, either.

"The whole time I was there, I looked forward to the day I could leave. But when that day came"—Shelby shrugged her shoulders—"I wanted to stay." She gave a small laugh. "I guess that doesn't make much sense."

"I don't think we ever appreciate what we have until it's gone. Especially when we're kids."

"Were you like that?"

"I didn't handle it well when my parents divorced. I doubt you want to hear about that."

"Of course I do. That is, if you want to tell me."

"I thought we were a happy family, that there was something special about us. But it turned out that Dad was sleeping around. Mom retaliated by doing the same." He said it lightheartedly, but sadness tinged his words. "They tried reconciling, but by then it was too late."

"Are you close to them?"

"There was an accident. They died."

"I'm sorry." She resisted the urge to reach for his hand, to offer any other condolences. Words could be so empty.

"So am I."

"Do you have any other family?"

"A younger sister." His lips parted in a teasing smile. "And I have Richard."

"You're related to Richard?"

"No, it just seems that way. He's my mentor. He helped me when I was restructuring my business. And with a few other projects."

The waitress appeared with their BBQ baskets. The somber mood lifted as they made small talk while enjoying their sandwiches and fries.

"I don't want you to take this the wrong way," Brett said, dipping his last fry in a pool of BBQ sauce. "Maybe I shouldn't say it."

"Now you have to."

"This is like a time warp." He gestured at the red plastic baskets and Mason jar glasses. "We could be high school kids on our first date."

"But this isn't supposed to be a date. Just a late lunch."

"It's not too late to call it our first date."

"I . . . I can't."

"You miss your husband."

"Yes."

"I doubt he'd want you to spend the rest of your life in mourning."

"You might be surprised." Immediately she wanted to take back the words. The expression in Brett's eyes flashed from surprise to curiosity to what appeared to be a conscious decision to politely ignore what she'd said. She silently thanked him.

"You're scared. I understand that. But you can't stay cooped up in that big old house forever. Give dating a chance. With me."

Averting her gaze, she focused on the salt granules dotting the wax paper nestled in the basket.

"I know it isn't easy." He gave an exaggerated sigh, snaring her attention as dejection clouded his fine features. "I can't tell you how many women I've dated trying to find the right one."

Catching the mirth in his eyes, Shelby tried to match his teasing mood. "What woman wouldn't want to marry a handsome, successful, well-to-do businessman?"

"Not a one, or I wouldn't still be single."

Shelby gasped at his good-natured conceit, and they both laughed.

"Will you be at the house tomorrow?" he asked.

"Plan to be."

"How about we have a no-date supper tomorrow? Though not here."

"Not a date?"

"Not a date."

She wanted to ask him why, but her mouth refused to form the word. Why would a sophisticated man like him be interested in someone like her? A missionary kid, a stay-at-home mom?

"Is that a yes?" Brett asked.

The question echoed in Shelby's mind, reviving a memory as Brett's blue eyes morphed to AJ's deep brown ones. *Is that a yes?* AJ had asked the same question, with the same tone, when she hesitated over his offer to gravel her driveway.

"Are you all right?"

"For a moment you reminded me of someone."

"Who?"

"Nobody important." She dismissed the strange resemblance. AJ Sullivan had none of Brett Somers's charm or magnetism. The men were polar opposites in every way.

"So . . . ?" Brett's brilliant blue eyes shone with the confidence of a man used to getting what he wanted.

"Yes." Goose bumps chilled Shelby's arms. "It's a yes."

- 7 -

*S*helby massaged her aching neck and surveyed the parlor. After several hours spent taping, edging, and rolling, fresh primer covered the walls. One room down, too many more left to do.

But she remained determined to do as much of the work herself as possible. Though she had earmarked a decent amount for the house's restoration, the remaining principal from Gary's life insurance needed to provide a sufficient income for several years. She didn't want to think about finding a job until the girls were older.

Picking up her cell phone, she frowned. Almost four thirty, and no word from Brett. They'd exchanged numbers before going their separate ways the day before. She tapped the screen till his name popped up, and her thumb hovered over the call button. Closing her eyes, she took a deep breath and willed the temptation to pass. She might be a modern woman, but calling him was not an option.

A photo of Elizabeth and Tabby appeared as she returned to the main screen. Her adorable little girls, dressed in their Easter finery and smiling at the camera, were the reason she was here. Not Brett Somers.

She shoved the phone onto the mantel.

Raising her arms one at a time, she stretched the kinks from her back. Even the soles of her feet ached from standing on the ladder rungs in her paint-spattered sports socks. Tomorrow she'd wear sneakers.

A knock sounded on the windowpane, and a man's smiling face appeared through the new glass. Red hair stuck out beneath a John Deere ball cap, and freckles sprinkled his complexion. He waved, and Shelby's momentary tension subsided as she hurried to the porch.

"Jason Owens."

"The one and only." He grabbed her in a bear hug and swung her around. Shelby squealed and laughed.

"I'm so glad to see you." She gripped his arms, steadying herself after the dizzying swing. "It's been too long."

"We were fourteen the last time we saw each other." His face reddened slightly, then he gleamed as a petite brunette appeared by his side. "This is my wife, Cassie." He gave the woman a sideways hug. "Cassie, Shelby Lassiter."

"It's Shelby Kincaid now." She extended a hand, and Cassie responded with a warm smile.

"Welcome home, Shelby. Jason has told me so much about you, I almost feel like we're old friends."

Jason laughed. "Only about a few of our adventures."

"More like misadventures. Your hubby and I had a knack for getting into trouble."

"It's great to have you back." Jason rested his hand on the new porch railing and rubbed the wood grain with his fingers. "To see the old house coming to life again somehow sets things right."

Cassie gave him a good-natured jab. "And you say I'm the fanciful one."

"I mean it. This place has been empty long enough."

"Too long." Shelby released a contented sigh. "But school ends in a couple of weeks, and we're moving the very next day."

"You and your daughters?" Cassie asked. "Are they here?"

"My in-laws are staying with them."

"One of them is in first grade, right?"

"Yes. Elizabeth is six, and Tabitha is three."

"We have a first grader too. A boy, Austin." Cassie's brown eyes sparkled with an almost childlike glee. "Do you mind if we take a look inside? Jason dropped by last week when Nate was here, but I've never been."

"Just wanted to give Nate a helping hand," Jason said. "I put up the drywall in the dining room."

"Did you really?" Shelby led the way into the house. "That was kind of you."

"Glad to do it."

Cassie glanced into the parlor. "You're doing the painting?"

"As much as I can."

"Would you like some help?"

Jolted by the offer, Shelby stammered. "I don't like asking."

"You didn't ask, I offered."

"I won't say no."

"Great." Cassie smiled engagingly. "We're just down the road, you know. And I'd like us to be friends."

Shelby glanced at Jason, and he gave an encouraging smile. Just like when they were kids, he'd understood her unspoken question. Back then, he'd been part of her dreams of the future. Dreams she'd taken for granted would come true.

And so had he. That's why he'd chiseled their initials into the engagement tree.

S. L. + J. O.

The carving broke Lassiter family tradition—only formally engaged couples were supposed to add their initials to the weeping willow back by Glade Creek. Maybe that's why everything went so wrong.

Shelby shook away the ridiculous thought. Things started going wrong before Jason flaunted the Lassiter rules. And he'd meant it as a promise, that someday her topsy-turvy world would be righted again.

But then Shelby had been dragged overseas, and she'd let his letters go unanswered. Eventually, he'd stopped writing.

Jason's smile told her all was forgiven. Their paths had separated and now were coming together again. In friendship.

"I'd like that too." Shelby returned Cassie's smile. "Very much."

They wandered through the other rooms, chatting about Shelby's plans and updating her on other local families she had known as a girl. After Jason and Cassie left, she sealed the brushes and rollers in plastic bags, then closed up the paint can. A hot shower would have to wait till she got back to the B and B, but she couldn't risk getting paint on the seat of the rental car. She washed up in the bathroom, thankful Nate had gotten the water running, and changed into jeans and a T-shirt. On her way out of the house, she retrieved her phone.

Still no call from Brett.

~

Brett swiveled in his desk chair and gazed through the glass wall at the Columbus skyline. He rotated his cell phone between his fingers, then tapped it on the chair arm.

Rotate, tap. Rotate, tap.

Almost five. Next on his agenda, a workout at the gym. Then meeting the guys at Gallagher's for wings and the best selection of beers in the region. As usual, they'd swap stories about their weekend exploits. He imagined telling them about his impromptu BBQ date with a widowed mom. They'd never believe him.

Truth was, though, he'd enjoyed the afternoon more than he expected. Shelby's transparency, her lack of sophistication, were a refreshing change from the dolled-up plastics he too often encountered.

Shelby may have been hesitant to accept his offer of dinner tonight, but she wanted to see him again. If he knew women—and he did—she'd spent the day with her phone nearby, ready to snatch it up at the first ring.

He glanced at the time: 4:58. Right now, no matter what else she was doing, Shelby Kincaid's thoughts were consumed with him. He'd bet money on it. Exactly as planned.

Guilt fluttered his conscience, but he swatted it away.

A knock sounded on his door, and he swiveled to face his receptionist. Tracie's long bare legs emerged from a tight teal skirt, and a matching jacket skimmed her curves. Earlier in the day, the top two buttons on her snowy white blouse had been open, providing Brett an enticing view whenever he towered over her desk.

Now the third was undone.

Brett allowed his eyes to linger on the deep V formed by her neckline.

Her manner of dress might not be the epitome of corporate professionalism, but it was for moments like this he had hired her. And all the gorgeous leggy blondes preceding her. The primary role of any receptionist at Somers, Inc., though none of them seemed to realize it, was to beguile his colleagues with their teasing necklines and heady perfume.

Brett's team of virtual assistants handled the firm's important business.

"I'm about to leave." Tracie posed in the doorway. "Is there anything else you need before I go?"

"Did you order those flowers?"

"I did."

"They'll be delivered today?"

"Any minute now. Just as you instructed." Her voice lacked its usual warmth.

"Is something wrong?"

"I was only thinking that it was a lot of money to spend on a bouquet. Your, um, friend, should be impressed."

"I'm sure she will be." After all, that was the point. Shelby needed to be kept off-balance, ignored then romanced, her thoughts directed to one object—him. It was only a matter of time before she'd be head over heels and eager to please. One quick signature, and he'd control the land. Then neither she nor AJ could stop his plans.

"You look absolutely wicked when you smile like that." Tracie's perfectly manicured fingers fiddled with her fourth button.

So his latest Gal Friday, threatened by an extravagant bouquet, was making her move. He leaned back and idly calculated how many buttons remained beneath the jacket. "I didn't realize I was smiling."

"It's your 'take no prisoners' smile."

"Does it frighten you?"

"Should it?" Her sultry voice softened the challenge.

He stood and walked around the desk. "How long have you been working here?"

"About ten weeks."

Longer than the average. Most of his receptionists didn't take that long to attempt trading in a paycheck for a credit card with his name on it. Usually he played along, though he had an unfair advantage. He knew, as the blondes did not, that the first kiss started a countdown clock. In two months, three at the most, she'd be without his credit card, without a paycheck. And while she cried with her girlfriends, he'd be laughing with the guys over another disappointed Mrs. Somers wannabe.

He considered waiting another day or two, curious to see her next ploy. But in the end, it didn't really matter.

Sliding his gaze appreciatively to the pointy tips of her black heels and up again to her beckoning eyes, he held out his hand. She sashayed toward him, and he pulled her into a tight embrace.

Unlucky Tracie.

The countdown had begun.

– 8 –

As Shelby entered the B and B, eager to get to her room, owner Martha D'Arcy appeared in the foyer carrying an enormous bouquet of yellow roses in a slender crystal vase. "These are for you, Mrs. Kincaid," she gushed. "Aren't they lovely?"

Breathtakingly so.

Shelby cradled the vase and inhaled the sweet fragrance. "Who sent them?"

"Can't say that I know, but there's a card tucked among the greenery."

"So there is. Thank you." Probably Richard had sent the bouquet. No one else would send her flowers.

Mrs. D'Arcy gave Shelby the once-over. "Looks like you've had a busy day. Painting, huh?"

"I got the primer coat on one room."

"I don't envy you the job. My husband and I did most of the work on this place. Never again. 'Course, we're not as young as we once were."

"Guess I better get cleaned up." Shelby fished her room key from her bag as she headed for the stairs. "Thanks again."

Inside her room, tastefully furnished in a blue and white Victorian motif, she set the vase on a bedside table and opened the card.

Hope this makes up for breaking our "not-a-date." My time hasn't been my own today, but I promise we'll get together before you leave. Brett

She smiled and read the note again. Her tired achiness seemed to disappear as she breathed in the aroma of the roses. It'd been a long time since anyone had given her flowers. Except at Gary's funeral, but that wasn't the same.

She popped into the shower, emerging twenty minutes later refreshed by the steamy water.

And hungry.

The Dixie Diner, the town's greasy spoon and only a short walk away, would have to do for tonight. She tucked her e-reader into her purse, slipped on flip-flops, and headed downstairs.

As she crossed the B and B's parking lot, a hunter-green Jeep Cherokee pulled up beside her. The driver, wearing an OSU ball cap, leaned out the window.

"May I give you a ride?"

Of all people.

"What are you doing here?"

AJ shrugged. "Thought you might want to treat me to supper."

"Why would I want to do that?"

"It's your turn."

She almost smiled. Almost. But his expression told her she hadn't hid her amusement soon enough.

"I'm mad at you." She meant to sound mad, but somehow the words came out pouty, almost flirtatious.

"What did I do now?" His tone made it clear he wasn't taking her supposed anger very seriously.

"The gravel."

"Oh." He drew out the syllable and tapped his fingers on the steering wheel.

"I told you not to."

His eyes, dark pools beneath the bill of his cap, looked mischievously into hers. "But I bet you're glad I did."

He had her there. Maneuvering around the ruts had *not* been fun. "Are you getting in?"

Gracious, the man was persistent. She pointed at the Dixie Diner's neon sign. "I'm only going over there."

"Have it your way." He eased onto the main street, then pulled into the restaurant's lot.

By the time Shelby had reached the diner, he had parked and was waiting for her at the front door.

"You've got a lot of nerve, you know that?"

"I'm just a hungry guy looking for a bite to eat." He opened the door and followed her inside.

The place hadn't changed much in the years Shelby had been away. A Formica counter and round stools stretched along one wall. Back-to-back booths, covered in red vinyl, lined the windows. A teenaged girl in khakis and a red shirt pulled two menus from a nearby stack.

"Hi, Coach." She looked with curiosity at Shelby. "Table for two?"

"What do you say?" AJ nudged Shelby with his elbow. "You aren't going to make me eat alone, are you?"

"I should. But you look so pitiful."

"You really do, Coach."

"Just take us to a table, Jillian."

The teen giggled. "This way."

"Are you ready for exams?" AJ asked as he settled on the bench seat. After removing his cap, he ran his fingers through his short hair.

"I hope so."

"You'll do fine." He turned to Shelby. "Jillian earned a full-ride scholarship to Dartmouth."

"That's impressive." She smiled at the teen. "Have you selected a major?"

"I've been accepted into the honors history program."

"Wow! Congratulations."

"I owe it all to Mr. Sullivan. He wrote the most amazing recommendation letter."

AJ spread his hands. "I only told the truth. You're the one who did all the hard work."

Jillian beamed, then left to welcome a family entering the diner.

"She seems like a sweet girl."

"She is. Hardworking too." He opened the menu. "Any idea what you're getting?"

"The only thing one should ever get at the Dixie Diner."

Their eyes met as they simultaneously recited, "The Dixie Deluxe."

Shelby laughed. "Are they still the best burgers in town?"

"Even better."

AJ ordered the signature cheeseburger with fries and chocolate milkshakes for both of them. The place was surprisingly busy for a Monday evening, and AJ seemed to know practically everybody who walked in the door.

"One of the perks of teaching," he said with a characteristic shrug.

Shelby gave up on keeping names straight with faces as AJ introduced her to the other diners who stopped by their booth. Not surprisingly, a few of the older folks knew her grandparents and were interested in Shelby's restoration of the old homestead.

She could splurge for granite counters in the kitchen if she had a dollar for every time one of them said something about how AJ's grandfather must be spinning in his grave. AJ seemed bothered by the comments too. Though he responded with good humor, the light in his eyes dimmed a little each time.

Funny, Nate Jeffers had said something similar that first day at the house. Come to think of it, so had Paul Norris.

When she was a teen, Anderson "Sully" Sullivan had been the scapegoat for all her rage. As the years passed, that rage simmered into bitter enmity for the faceless monster who had driven her beloved grandparents to their deaths.

That same monster had punished AJ from beyond the grave by leaving his grandson a property he considered worthless. Simply because AJ chose to teach high school students—apparently very well—instead of practicing law. How cruel.

When the waitress brought the check, AJ picked it up, but she quickly pulled it from his fingers.

"My turn, remember?"

"Come on, I was teasing about that."

"I insist." She dug out her credit card. "I also insist on paying you for the gravel."

"There's no need."

"You won't win this one, so don't even try."

"It was a gift."

"One I can't accept. How much was it?"

"You're not going to change your mind, are you?"

"Nope."

He leaned forward, arms crossed on the table. "How about I ask you to do something else instead?"

"Like what?"

He lowered his voice. "Figure out a way to give it to Jillian."

"The hostess?"

"She's a great student, but things have been hard for her family the past couple of years. The scholarship is a big help, but you know how it is. There are other expenses that won't be covered."

Shelby leaned forward too, leveling her voice to his. "You could have just given her the money in the first place rather than using it to buy gravel for my drive. I wish you had."

"I bought the gravel as a kind of, I don't know, peace offering." His mouth twitched, deepening the adorable Cary Grant cleft in his chin. "Her parents won't take charity. Besides, it's hard for me to do something for one student if I can't do it for all of them."

"I'm glad to help, but I don't know why they'd take money from me if they won't take it from you. I'm a total stranger."

"You're probably right. I'd just like to find a way to make things easier for her."

Throughout the conversation, their whispers had drawn them close enough for her to see the dark ring around his brown irises. His aftershave teased her nostrils, and without realizing it, she leaned closer.

His eyes widened, and she sat back as heat warmed her cheeks. Whatever had just happened shouldn't have. But she wasn't sure what had.

Mindlessly stirring her milkshake with her straw, she took a deep breath. "I'll try to think of something."

"Thank you, Shelby." He drummed a fast rhythm on the table. "This has been a fun evening."

"For me too." Surprisingly, she meant it.

~

Outside the diner, the evening's first stars glimmered in the darkening sky. AJ settled his cap on his head. "How about I walk you home?"

"You mean over to the B and B?" Shelby pointed to the looming house. Electric lanterns shone white ambient light along the eaves of the wraparound veranda. "That's really not necessary."

He patted his stomach. "It'll give me a chance to walk off that cheeseburger."

"Oh yeah, a one-minute walk is quite the workout," she teased.

"Two minutes. I'll have to come back for my Jeep."

She shook her head and headed for the sidewalk. He hesitated half a second then caught up with her. After all, she hadn't said no. A nearby street lamp came on, casting a soft glow on the golden highlights in Shelby's hair as they passed under it.

When they climbed the steps, Mrs. D'Arcy greeted them. Rocking in a white wicker chair, she held up a glass of iced tea as if to make a toast. "So you were the one," she said to AJ.

"The one what?" Placing his palm on his chest, he glanced from Mrs. D'Arcy to Shelby and back again. "What did I do?"

Mrs. D'Arcy gave him a knowing look. "Sent that enormous bouquet of yellow roses to our Ms. Kincaid, of course. I wish you could have seen her face. She was impressed."

"Oh no, the flowers weren't from him." Pink spotted Shelby's cheeks. "AJ and I are just . . ."

Friends. With a sinking heart, he waited for her to say the inevitable, but she appeared to choke.

Taking a breath, she shrugged. "We're just acquaintances."

Even worse.

AJ's heart plummeted. He didn't know what he had expected. Until this moment, he hadn't realized he expected—or wanted—anything. True, thoughts of Shelby seemed to pop into his head too often, but that was only because of the work being done on the house.

"I should go," he said. "Thanks again for dinner, Shelby. I had a nice time."

"So did I."

"You don't need to sound so surprised." The words came out more gruffly than he intended. He jutted his chin as Shelby's eyes widened, then grew cold. The easygoing atmosphere between them now seemed charged with uncertainty. An enjoyable evening sabotaged by a bunch of roses.

He needed to get out of there.

"Good night, ladies." He bounded down the broad steps and jaywalked across the street. After getting in his Jeep, he drove slowly past the B and B. Shelby stood on the porch, staring at him. He waved. She slowly raised her hand, but she didn't smile.

It was just as well. Especially since she apparently had a boyfriend. Somebody in Chicago, probably, though it seemed strange she never mentioned being involved with anyone. Stranger still that she was so gung ho to make this major move if she was in a relationship.

Though how serious could she be about someone when a wedding band still adorned her finger?

His cell phone rang, and he glanced at the display before pressing the answer button.

"Hi, Gran."

"It's Candace." His grandmother's live-in nurse had called from the landline. "I think you better come."

~

AJ leaned against the highboy dresser near Gran's bed and tracked the uneven rise and fall of her chest beneath the multicolored quilt. He had stood vigil through two grueling nights and into this afternoon, only eating when Candace insisted.

Gran's rasping breaths came in shallow gasps that raked his heart. Her waning strength pulled at him, but he clenched his stomach muscles into an iron fist that controlled his grief. He would not fall apart. Not here.

His cousin Amy perched on the edge of a chair, her crystal blue eyes narrowed by worry. Her features, usually so composed, were pale and drawn. She rested her hand gently on Gran's arm, as if her touch could keep their grandmother's life from flying away.

The bedroom door slowly opened, and Brett slipped in. "Any change?"

AJ shook his head.

"Sorry I'm late. I had a business matter to take care of."

"What's her name?" AJ regretted the question as soon as it left his mouth, but it was like some kind of strange Pavlovian response. An automatic retort to his cousin's excuse. "I'm sorry," he said hurriedly. "I shouldn't have said that."

Brett scowled. "For your information, my expertise was needed on a multimillion-dollar deal. Believe me, if I could have postponed it, I would have."

"I said I was sorry."

"What you are is jealous."

"Jealous?" AJ shook his head. "Of you? I don't think so."

"Admit it. You can't stand my success. With business and with women."

"Stop it!" Amy's harsh whisper cut through the animosity. She choked back a sob. "Just please stop it."

Gran's gnarled fingers pulled at the quilt, and her mouth opened and closed.

AJ and Brett hurried to opposite sides of the bed, each clasping one of Gran's arthritic hands.

"It's all right, Gran." AJ swallowed against the stone pressing against his throat. "Everything's going to be all right."

"She should be in a hospital." Brett's voice shook, and Amy gripped his arm.

"That's not what she wanted," AJ said.

"AJ's right." Amy gently caressed Gran's fragile arm. "This is where she wants to be. With us."

"Yesss." The word was barely a breath. Gran inhaled, and her three grandchildren leaned closer. "Love. You." Her eyes blinked open, and a slight smile parted her lips. She seemed to garner all her strength before speaking again. "Be good. To each other."

Her eyes closed, her head relaxed against the pillow, and the hand clasped in AJ's went limp. He squeezed her fingers, willing life to return as his chest tightened. He gulped air, shutting his eyes and clenching his jaw.

Amy's heartrending sobs broke through the muffling fog. He opened his eyes and, through a mist of tears, endured another squeezing pang. Brett, fighting back tears of his own, embraced his sister. Amy clung to her brother as grief wracked her thin body.

They had each other to hold on to through this storm. Just as they had when all their parents died. When Sully died.

While AJ stood alone.

Without Gran, he was all alone.

As if she read his thoughts, Amy raised her eyes to his and stretched her hand across the bed. AJ hesitated the briefest of seconds before clasping one hand in hers while still holding on to Gran with his other.

The goodwill born of shared sorrow probably wouldn't last beyond the funeral, but for now he accepted Amy's comforting gesture. For a few minutes, Joyanna Sullivan's beloved grandchildren stood beside her, united in their reluctance to let her go.

After Brett and Amy left the room, AJ tenderly kissed Gran's cheek. Her skin crinkled like thin paper beneath his dry lips.

"What am I going to do without you?" he whispered. "No one loved me like you."

Except for Me. The words breathed into his heart. *My steadfast love is with you always.*

– 9 –

*S*helby dragged the red wagon to the sweeping branches of the treasured willow that overhung Glade Creek, then lifted Tabby over the wagon's wooden railing.

"Everybody out. We're here."

"Is this the 'gagement tree?" Elizabeth's eyes, more green than blue today, shone with wonder. Her long dark hair, so like Gary's, was pulled back in a single braid and tied with purple ribbon. Standing in the wagon bed, she grasped a long slender branch of the weeping willow and pressed it against her cheek.

"It sure is. Come see." Shelby took both girls by the hand and swung their arms as she counted. "One. Two. Three." She ducked beneath the branches, and the girls giggled as they slipped between the feathery fronds.

"Look here." Shelby picked up Tabby and balanced her on her hip, then pointed to a set of initials surrounded by a heart. "C. Z. and A. L. That stands for Adam Lassiter and Catherine Zema. Your grandma and grandpa."

"Your mommy and daddy," Elizabeth said. "In Africa."

"That's right." She moved around the tree and pointed to another heart. "This one belongs to *my* grandma and grandpa."

Tabitha slowly recited the letters as she traced them. "A. G. What's this?" She touched the plus sign.

"That means 'and.' What are these letters?"

"T. L." Tabby gleamed.

"That's right."

Elizabeth touched the heart. "What are their names, Mommy?"

"Aubrey Grayson and Thad Lassiter." She let Tabby slide to the ground. "My grandma Aubrey is Uncle Richard's sister." Richard had been at Misty Willow when Shelby and the girls drove in from Chicago. He had welcomed them to their new home with American Girl dolls and accessories. Too extravagant of a gift, but kindly meant.

That was almost a week ago. After a few days unpacking, Shelby couldn't wait any longer to explore the land that belonged to her again.

"Who belongs to these letters?" Elizabeth pointed to a heart, lower than all the others, on the other side of the tree. "S. L. and J. O."

The initials that shouldn't be.

"The S. L. means me. S for Shelby and L for Lassiter."

Elizabeth narrowed her eyes in puzzlement. "Your name is different?"

"My name was Lassiter. When I was a little girl like you. Then when I married Daddy, I changed my name to Kincaid."

"Daddy's initials are J. O.?"

Shelby stifled her laughter at Elizabeth's skeptical expression. She could almost see her daughter's mind working, trying to puzzle out this mystery.

"No, Daddy's initials are G. K. For Gary Kincaid."

"Then why does it say J. O.?"

Elizabeth had met Jason and Cassie a few days ago when they brought over lasagna and salad. How to explain to a six-year-old why Jason's initials were paired with hers on the 'gagement tree?

"I think that's enough family history. Who's hungry?"

Both girls responded with shouts and jumps as Shelby retrieved the insulated tote from the wagon and spread a blanket in the shade near the bend in the creek.

"We came a long way, didn't we, Mommy?" Elizabeth plopped on the blanket.

"We sure did." Not that far really as the crow flies. But because of the wagon, she had to skirt the woods and follow a fencerow through a pasture. The house was hidden by distance. "But worth it, don't you think? Isn't it nice out here?"

Elizabeth gazed at the sun-dappled water of the broad creek as if in deep thought. "I like it."

"I like it too." Tabby dropped next to Shelby and folded her hands. "I pray."

Shelby and Elizabeth echoed Tabby's amen. After they ate their sandwiches and sliced apples, Shelby washed their juice-stained lips and sticky fingers.

"Time for wading." She helped Tabby take off the top and shorts she wore over her bathing suit while Elizabeth undressed herself. "Leave your tennis shoes on," she instructed. "No walking barefoot in the creek."

As they splashed in the cold water, their laughter and squeals warmed Shelby's heart. She sighed as a contentment she hadn't felt in years soothed her spirit. This was why she had pleaded with AJ to sell her the land, why she had uprooted her children from the only home they had known.

To create memories in this place where their ancestors had created memories. To add their laughter to the merriment of those who had been here before them.

Perhaps even to find romance. Brett had sent a huge basket of fruit, snacks, and candy as a housewarming gift. Though she hadn't seen him since their arrival, he called or texted almost every day. Nothing would probably come of it—and she definitely wasn't in a rush to marry anyone—but the flirtatious attentions from such a handsome and successful man made her pleasantly light-hearted. Flattered by his interest in her opinions, she appreciated their grown-up conversations. Even when they disagreed, he didn't make her feel naive or uninformed.

A turtle about the size of Shelby's fist crawled onto a rock jutting from the creek bed. Tabby clapped her hands in delight as it waggled its head, apparently curious about its visitors.

"Don't get too close," Shelby warned. "We don't want to frighten him."

"Can we take him home?" Elizabeth asked.

"This is his home, honey. He wouldn't be happy anywhere else."

Hearing a soft whistle behind her, Shelby twisted around. AJ Sullivan, a fishing pole slung across his shoulder, approached the bend. Tan cargo shorts and a high school T-shirt revealed muscular arms and legs. He had tanned since she last saw him that evening at the Dixie Diner. Such a fun evening it had been with their juicy cheeseburgers and thick milkshakes.

At least she had thought so. But without meaning to, she'd upset him. It bothered her more than she cared to admit.

Ever since she and the girls moved in, she had expected him to pop in. But there'd been no sign of him. Maybe she shouldn't have been surprised. After all, he was still a Sullivan. Probably more like his grandfather than she knew.

The less contact with him the better.

He halted when he saw them, as if uncertain what to do. She gave a hesitant wave and self-consciously pushed loose strands from her face as Elizabeth stepped behind her. Slender damp arms encircled her neck.

"Nice day for wading," AJ said, coming toward them. "Looks like you're having fun."

"We found a turtle," Tabby spoke up before Shelby could answer.

"That so?" He waded to the rock and bent down by Tabby. "I know this turtle. He always comes out here on a good hot day to get a suntan. And then when the moon comes up, he slides back into the water and swims home to his family, and he tells them about the people he met."

"What's his name?" Tabby's baby blue eyes sparkled.

"His name is"—AJ paused, grimacing at Shelby over Tabby's head—"his name is Tommy. Tommy Turtle."

"Very original," Shelby said in a stage whisper.

He shrugged sheepishly.

"Can I touch him?" Tabby asked.

Shelby nodded permission. As AJ reached for the turtle, it receded into its shell. Tabby stretched out one small finger, barely touched the shell, and pulled her hand back with a shriek.

"It's hard," she said, reaching out to touch it again.

"Can I touch it too?" Elizabeth asked, peering out from behind Shelby.

"Of course, honey."

Elizabeth tapped the turtle's hard shell and smiled at Shelby.

"Turtles are pretty lucky, I think," said AJ. "They carry their houses with them on their back. When they get tired, they just go right into their doors and windows."

"We have a big house," said Elizabeth. "It's too big to carry around."

"I could carry it," Tabby boasted.

"I bet you could." AJ placed the turtle back on the rock, but it stayed inside its shell. "I guess this means you're all moved in."

"Moved in, yes," Shelby said. "Completely unpacked, no."

He grinned at the girls, squatting to their level. "Will you tell me your names? Or should I guess?"

"I'm Tabby." She poked her chest with her thumb.

"So glad to make your acquaintance, Miss Tabby. And who's this lovely lady?"

"Elizabeth." She smiled shyly.

"My grandmother's middle name was Elizabeth. It's one of my favorite names."

Was. Shelby stared at AJ. His jaw clenched, but he talked to the girls as if he didn't have a care in the world.

"Is Tabby one of your fav'rite names too?"

AJ poked her tummy, and she giggled. "It sure is."

"You haven't told us your name," Elizabeth said.

"My name is, are you ready for this? Anderson John Sullivan the Fourth."

Elizabeth's eyes grew round. Even Shelby had to admit it sounded impressive when he said it like that.

"What's this for?" Tabby grabbed the fishing pole.

"Fishing." AJ casually extricated her grip.

"You won't catch anything with us splashing around," Shelby said. "It's time we headed home anyway."

"I can fish another day. I don't want to spoil your fun."

"Will you wade with us, Mr. Fourth?"

Shelby and AJ glanced at Elizabeth, then at each other, and stifled their laughter.

"His name isn't Mr. Fourth, sweetheart." Shelby squeezed Elizabeth's shoulder. "That just means he's the fourth person in his family with the same name."

Elizabeth's mouth formed a small O, and she hung her head. Shelby stroked her hair, brushing stray wisps from her pale cheeks.

"You can call me AJ, if you want. All my friends do." He glanced at Shelby. "If that's okay with your mom."

Elizabeth gazed up at Shelby, her green-flecked eyes pleading. "Is it okay, Mommy?"

Shelby wavered. Normally she didn't let the girls call adults by their first names, but Elizabeth had been mortified by her mistake. She didn't suppose they'd see much of AJ anyway, so it didn't really matter.

"How about you call him Mr. AJ?"

Elizabeth's thankful smile told her she'd made the right decision. Tabby tugged at the hem of AJ's shorts. "Fish now."

"Tabitha Jean," Shelby said in her you-don't-talk-like-that-to-grown-ups voice.

"I wanna know how."

"You don't know how to fish? That's terrible." AJ's brown eyes were wide with exaggerated horror. "If you're going to be a farm girl, you gotta know how to fish."

"I wanna be a farm girl." Tabby jumped up and down. "Farm girl. Farm girl."

"You started this." Shelby pretended to glare at AJ as she crossed her arms. "What are you going to do now?"

"Teach her to fish. Unless you'd like to."

"You go ahead. I need to clean things up a bit." She knelt on the blanket, then placed the picnic leftovers back in the insulated tote.

AJ gathered his fishing equipment and led the girls a few feet up the creek to a deeper bend. Bored after about five minutes, Tabby wandered back to Shelby and was soon asleep in her lap.

Elizabeth and AJ were too far away for Shelby to hear their conversation, but once in a while, her little girl's laughter or AJ's chuckle floated on the light summer breeze. The sound warmed Shelby's spirit. AJ's quiet patience obviously filled a hole in Elizabeth's grieving heart. Shelby couldn't dislike him for that.

Her eyelids grew heavy in the summer heat, but she startled, immediately alert, when Elizabeth squealed. Wind bent the long grasses near the bank, and the creek reflected graying clouds.

"I got one!" Elizabeth shouted. "I got one!"

Shelby gingerly moved Tabby from her lap and walked to the bend. With AJ's help, Elizabeth reeled in the line. A silvery fish, no more than five or six inches long, struggled on the hook.

AJ held it up. "I told you we'd get one. Just takes patience."

"I caught it, Mommy." Elizabeth grabbed Shelby's hand, her eyes gleaming with excitement. "All by myself."

"You did great, honey."

"She sure did. Just like a pro." AJ knelt in front of Elizabeth. "What do you say we throw him back in the creek? Give him a chance to get a little bigger."

Elizabeth stared at the little fish wiggling in AJ's palms. "Can I do it?"

AJ carefully unhooked the fish and slipped it into her upturned palms, cupping them with his own. Together they knelt at the edge of the creek and placed their hands in the water. The fish quickly swam away.

A stronger gust stirred up ripples in the creek, and the sky darkened. Black clouds melded together, racing toward them.

"Storm's coming," AJ said.

"I need to get the girls home."

"You'll never make it. My place is closer."

"I couldn't—"

"I suppose you've found something else to be mad about." He glanced at Elizabeth still kneeling at the creek bank, and lowered his voice to a bare whisper. "What is it this time?"

"You're the one who's mad," Shelby whispered back.

"What are you talking about?"

A lightning bolt flashed in the sky, and Elizabeth rushed to Shelby's side. Embracing her daughter, Shelby gazed at the gathering clouds. AJ was right. She'd never make it home before the storm hit. "Where do you live?"

"That way." He gestured southwest. Gusts of wind swept across the pasture, bending the long grasses and stirring up dust eddies. The willow's branches danced wildly.

AJ closed his tackle box and picked up his pole. "Are you coming with me?"

Staring toward her unseen house, Shelby considered her options. It'd taken them almost an hour to get here. The storm wouldn't wait for them to reach home.

"We're going with you."

- 10 -

AJ packed the wagon and parked it beneath the willow while Shelby helped the girls pull shorts and tops over their swimsuits.

"Ready?" he asked.

Nodding, she finished tying Tabby's sneaker.

"I'll take her." AJ picked up Tabby, still drowsy from her nap, and led the way alongside the lazy curve of the bank until the creek veered sharply north beside a cornfield. As they walked single file through a corn row, the green stalks rubbed his bare legs. At the edge of the field, they crossed a wooden bridge over a narrow branch of the creek.

"My place is just over that rise," he said when they reached the other side. "Not much farther."

"Are we going to beat the storm?" As if to answer Shelby's question, thunder cracked overhead, and another bolt of lightning split the sky. She flinched and grasped Elizabeth's hand. Giant raindrops pelted their heads, gaining momentum with each passing second.

"Come on." AJ tucked Tabby's head beneath his chin and raced awkwardly up the hill on the well-worn footpath. Halfway up, he glanced back at Shelby. Her head was bent against the downpour, and her arm was around Elizabeth's shoulder. Together they stumbled up the path several feet behind him.

When he neared the top of the hill, he paused and waited for Shelby to catch up.

"The grass will be slippery going down," he said. "Can you make it?" He followed Shelby's gaze to where his cottage nestled into the hillside. The rectangular house, painted pale beige with deep brown trim, seemed practically a part of the hill itself. A secluded place, hidden by the rise on one side and surrounded by tall hedges and taller trees on the others. When Gran lived in Columbus, the cottage had been her refuge. Now it was his.

"We'll manage."

"Let's go." He half-ran, half-slid down the slope, praying he wouldn't fall. Or die of asphyxiation from Tabby's arms gripping his neck. Who knew a three-year-old could be so strong?

Reaching the back door, he fumbled in his pocket for his key and unlocked the door. Once inside the tiny kitchen, Shelby and her girls stood in a huddle, water pooling around their soaked feet.

"Doggy!" Tabby exclaimed.

His dog, a creamy Labrador retriever, plodded into the kitchen and sniffed Tabby's outstretched hands. White bandages encased one foreleg.

"This is Lila. She had a wrangle with a mean old groundhog a few days ago."

"Poor Lila," Elizabeth murmured, patting the dog's head and whispering in her ear. "Does it hurt much?"

AJ gazed at Shelby, wishing he could read her thoughts as she looked around the small room. His cottage, not much wider than a double-wide trailer, couldn't compare to Misty Willow with its many rooms.

At least he'd washed the dishes.

"The bathroom's through here." He opened the door and stepped inside. "Plenty of towels. Use whatever you need. I'll try to scrounge up some dry clothes."

Grabbing a towel for himself, he slid open the pocket door on the other side and entered his bedroom. He closed the door behind him, quickly dried off, and changed into jeans and a sweatshirt. After rummaging through his drawers, he came up with sweatshirts, a pair of navy sweatpants for Shelby, and three pairs of thick white socks. He grinned at how big they'd be on the girls, but at least their little legs would be warm.

He knocked on the pocket door. "Are you decent? I've got clothes."

"Decent enough." Shelby slid the door halfway open, and he handed her the stack. "Thanks," she murmured before disappearing behind the closed door.

"Come on, Lila." The retriever sprawled across his bed. "I bet those girls would like some of my famous hot chocolate."

Unable to take the shortcut through the bathroom to the kitchen, he went the long way. Lila followed him into the study next to his bedroom and down a step into the long room that ran the front length of the house. Built-in cabinets and shelves lined the lower half of the long wall, a row of windows above them. Outside, the rain came down in thick gray sheets, obscuring his view of the trees and hedges surrounding the place. Thunder rolled overhead.

He stepped up into the kitchen, Lila close behind him. She caught the treat he tossed to her, then curled into a tight ball under the table.

As AJ stirred milk into his melted chocolate and sugar mixture, he heard Shelby's soft voice. His chest tightened, a pang for what he didn't have.

A wife. Children.

Carrying Tabby through the rain, being mindful of Shelby and Elizabeth behind him . . . He shook his head against the aching truth. For a short time, their need had fulfilled his instinct to protect. But now they were safe, and his heart beat with yearning.

The bathroom door opened, and Shelby's girls spilled out in

oversized sweatshirts that hung below their knees. The rolled-up sleeves still reached to their wrists.

"Do you have a bag I can put these in?" Shelby held a folded stack of wet clothes.

"You can put them in the dryer. Right there." He pointed his wooden spoon at a bifold door in the corner. She opened it, revealing a stacked washer/dryer unit, and fiddled with the dryer settings.

"Hot cocoa coming up." AJ pulled a bag from the pantry and shook it at Elizabeth and Tabby. "Who likes marshmallows?"

The girls raised their hands, chanting, "I do, I do."

The hum of the dryer lessened when Shelby shut the door. "How can I help?"

"Do you mind if they have cookies?"

"Not at all."

"Cookie jar's beside the fridge."

Shelby picked up the ceramic jar, a calico kitten peeking out from a wicker basket, with both hands. "Aww. This is so adorable."

He shrugged sheepishly. "It was my mom's when she was a little girl."

"An heirloom."

"I guess so." More like a reminder of happier days, a time when he was too young to realize the depth of turmoil swirling around the adults in his life. But his parents couldn't hide their dislike for each other from him forever. No matter how hard they tried.

Removing the pan from the burner, he ladled the steaming hot chocolate into mugs and sprinkled tiny marshmallows on top. "Cocoa's ready."

Once the girls were settled at the table with their snacks and napkins, Lila sat between them. Her wagging tail beat a rhythm on the linoleum floor.

"This is a cozy place." Shelby leaned against the counter, twisting a cookie in two. And looking too cute in his too-big clothes.

"It suits me." He handed her a mug, the steam rising through a creamy blanket of melting marshmallows.

"I'm sure I was on this road hundreds of times when I was a kid. I never knew this place was here."

"Most people don't. The hedge along the road hides it. Would you like the tour?"

They stepped down from the kitchen, and Shelby gasped. "So many windows. It's more like a vacation house than a home."

Heavy raindrops pinged the glass in a melodic harmony punctuated with thunder. Irregular lightning revealed flashes of the lush property.

"It was my grandmother's retreat. When I got my teaching job at the local high school, she insisted I move here. I installed central heating and A/C, but otherwise it's pretty much as it's always been."

"Even the pool table?" Shelby brushed her fingers along the polished wood.

"That's also my addition," AJ said with a chuckle. "Do you play?"

"Not well."

"You want to shoot a few?"

"Thanks, but no." She turned from him, wandering past a square pub table toward the seating area and television at the other end of the room.

"We might as well sit down. This rain is going to last awhile."

As they settled in midnight-blue club chairs, Shelby tucked her feet beneath her. "May I ask you something?"

"Of course."

"I'm afraid it's going to sound ungrateful. But I'm only curious."

"Now I'm curious. What is it?"

"Who was trespassing today? You or me?"

"Good question. I sure didn't mean to give up my favorite fishing hole."

"Do you really catch fish there? I mean anything bigger than what Elizabeth caught today?"

"Are you questioning my angling abilities?"

"Just asking."

"Like most fishing holes, it's best for thinking." And praying. "Lila likes it there too."

"So that piece of the farm still belongs to you?"

"I honestly don't know. Does it matter?"

"I very much meant to buy the willow."

"Very much meant?" he teased.

"You know what I mean."

"Why the willow?"

"There's an old family story." She stared in her mug, seemingly fascinated by the melting marshmallows. Her cheeks flushed.

"Tell me."

She peered at him under long dark lashes. "Are you sure you're interested?"

"I teach history. Of course I'm interested."

"According to Lassiter legend, a Rebel soldier escaped from a prisoner-of-war camp near Lake Erie. My great-great-great-great-grandmother found him, near death, beneath that tree. She hid him in an old hunting cabin near the woods east of there."

"What hunting cabin?"

"It's long gone. Though if you know where to look, you can still see the outline of it. At least, you could fourteen years ago."

"Did the rebel ever make it home?"

"Only once. For a brief visit." An engaging smile curved her delicate lips. "He's my great-great-great-great-grandfather."

"The family accepted him?"

"Not at first. It took time for him to gain their trust. My ancesters were part of the Underground Railroad."

"You know a lot about your family history."

"Because of the willow. Jeb Lassiter was the first to carve initials on the engagement tree. His and Eliza's. My 'four-greats' grandparents."

"The engagement tree?"

"You've never noticed all the initials carved on the weeping willow?"

"Can't say that I have. But I'll look next time I'm out there."

Coloring slightly at the thought of him noticing her initials, she set her mug on the pine table beside her chair and picked up a framed photograph. Her eyes narrowed as her casual curiosity turned into something more intense. "Who is this?"

"My grandmother." He leaned forward, hands clasped and his elbows resting on his knees. "Joyanna Stewart Sullivan."

Shelby's knuckles whitened as she gripped the frame, and her lips quivered. "Your grandmother?" she asked, her voice quaking. The color seemed to drain from her face.

AJ moved near her and carefully pried the frame from her icy fingers. He clasped her hands in his, trying to warm them. "What is it? What's wrong?"

"I saw her. By the willow." She swallowed hard, blinking back tears. "I thought she was an angel."

- 11 -

"Mommy, Tabby's climbing."

"No, I'm not."

A crash and a yelp sounded from the kitchen. Her heart in her throat, Shelby sprinted to her girls.

Tabby lay beside an overturned chair amid pieces of broken ceramic, her eyes scrunched up. Elizabeth knelt beside her, smoothing her little sister's hair from her face.

"Oh, Tabby, what did you do?" Shelby moved the chair and gathered the sobbing girl in her arms. "Are you all right? Where does it hurt?"

"Here," Tabby whispered, pointing at her chin and hiccupping as she tried to stop crying. An ugly bruise formed around her scraped skin.

"She wanted another cookie," Elizabeth said. "I told her not to, but she didn't listen."

"Should we take her to the hospital?" AJ asked as he squatted beside Elizabeth. She leaned into him, and her green-flecked eyes, red-rimmed and watery, sought reassurance. He gave her a smile, and her pixie face relaxed.

"Just ice, if you have any," Shelby said.

AJ immediately retrieved an ice pack from his freezer. "Try this."

"Thanks." She placed the pack on Tabby's chin, rocking slightly back and forth.

"I broke the kitty." Fresh tears dampened Tabby's cheeks as she stared at AJ. "I sorry."

"It's okay, Tabby. These things happen." He brushed a tear from her cheek then busied himself picking up the pieces. Elizabeth bent to retrieve a broken shard from beneath the table, and AJ clasped her hand. "I'll get it."

"But I want to help."

"Tell you what." AJ gently swung her hand back and forth. "Take Lila in the other room, okay? We don't want her cutting her paws, do we?"

Elizabeth shook her head, then took Lila by the collar. "Come on, girl. Come on."

Shelby kissed the top of Tabby's head as Elizabeth led Lila from the kitchen. "I'm so sorry, AJ. She should have known better."

"She's just a little girl." He placed the larger pieces in the trash, then grabbed the broom.

"But it was your mom's." She blinked back the tears that burned her eyes. AJ didn't have a lot of knickknacks cluttering up the cottage. He must not have many keepsakes from his parents. And now something he treasured was gone. She should never have left the girls alone in the kitchen.

The broken pieces pierced her heart, tangible reminders of the heirlooms she'd lost when her grandparents died. She buried her face in Tabby's damp hair. All she'd wanted was to take her girls to the creek. To let them play where she had played as a child. To give them a memory. How had she ended up in this predicament?

"I'm so sorry," she murmured again.

AJ swept the last of the debris into the dustpan and knelt beside her. His deep brown eyes were solemn, and his voice low. "At the end of the day, it's a thing. And things are never as important as people." His gaze shifted to Tabby. "God has been good to you, Shelby."

Her arms tightened around her daughter as his words floated into her heart. She gave thanks for her daughters every day, and yet the gratitude was mostly from habit. For too many years, God had taken more than he gave, forcing her to regain as much as she could on her own.

Some *things* were too important to ever give up. Things like Misty Willow.

She kissed Tabby's temple, then tilted her head, listening to the drops splattering the kitchen window. "The rain's letting up."

AJ picked up the overturned chair. "Looks that way."

"I think we should go home now."

"The Jeep's out front."

"We have a slight problem."

"What's that?"

"I don't suppose you have a car seat."

"You suppose right."

"I know it's only a few miles, but I can't take a chance . . ."

"Of course not." He poured the remaining cocoa into a pitcher and set it in the fridge. "I've got an idea, but I'm not sure you'll like it."

"I'm listening."

"You stay here with the girls, and I'll go get your car."

A memory pricked Shelby's heart. Gary had spent the day helping a buddy fence his yard. The job took longer than expected, so he called Shelby to have her join them for supper. That's when she realized he'd driven off with two-year-old Elizabeth's car seat. It had just been one of those things, but he pouted the rest of the evening as if it were her fault.

"You sure you don't mind?" Her stomach knotted waiting for his reply.

"Unless you're going to walk," he said, grinning, "it's the only thing to do."

He was right, but he didn't have to be so good-natured about it.

"Of course, you'll have to take me home with you so I can get my Jeep."

"If I must, I must," she teased as she pulled a leather cord over her head. "Here's a key to the house. The car key is on a hook inside the kitchen door."

"I'll find it." He turned on a television show for the girls to watch, then selected a ball cap from a rack by the front door.

Shelby walked outside with him, arms wrapped tightly around her chest against the chill. "Be careful."

"I'll be back soon." He settled the cap on his head and jogged to the Jeep parked several yards away on a cement slab. Gravel formed a curving drive from the slab to a gate, barely visible in the tall hedge.

Shelby shivered in the rain-drenched air, then returned to the house. Lila climbed on the couch between Elizabeth and Tabby while Shelby washed the mugs and folded their dried clothes. In the last couple of minutes, the storm had strengthened again. It was too chilly to put the girls back into their shorts and tank tops. She hoped AJ didn't mind if they wore his clothes home.

After returning to the main room, she settled in the club chair and studied the photograph of AJ's grandmother. Silver hair framed vibrant eyes and a porcelain complexion. Her engaging smile exuded warmth and confidence.

The same dear face Shelby used to see in her dreams. The same smile that bestowed affection and comfort when she had needed it most.

AJ's grandmother. Joyanna Sullivan. Apparently staying at the cottage. Wandering to the creek. Finding fourteen-year-old Shelby, distraught, practically hysterical, beneath the weeping willow.

Tires crunched on the gravel outside. Shelby peered out the window as AJ parked the Jeep and jogged to the porch. She hurriedly opened the door for him.

"I thought you were bringing my car."

"The road's flooded on the other side of the bridge. I wasn't sure your car would make it through." He took off his ball cap and ruffled his hair. "But I got the car seat."

The girls balked at leaving Lila behind so AJ put her in the Jeep too. He drove cautiously, expertly maneuvering through the flooded section of the road. When he turned into the drive at Misty Willow, he glanced at Shelby. Her features were drawn and tired.

"Bet you're glad of this gravel on a day like today."

As he hoped, fire lit her eyes and enlivened her face. Then she unexpectedly laughed.

"Not just today. Every time I pull in this lane, I'm thankful."

And who said gravel couldn't be romantic? He smiled before squelching the flame her laughter had ignited. To her, he was still a Sullivan. She'd never let him into her heart. Even if she wasn't already seeing somebody else.

He parked in the oval drive near the kitchen patio. Shelby ushered the girls and Lila into the house while he wrestled with the car seat. Despite the pelting rain, he fastened it into Shelby's Camry then sprinted up the back steps and into the kitchen.

"I put Tabby's seat in your car," he said, hanging Shelby's key on its hook.

"You didn't have to do that." She handed him a towel, and he dried off as best he could.

"Didn't want you to have to. Might be nice if you had a garage, though."

"I'll add it to my list. One garage." She directed a stony glare his way. "And I better not come home someday and find one from you."

"I wouldn't dare." He surveyed the kitchen with its gleaming appliances and cherry cabinets. A square table, covered in a blue cloth, sat in the middle on a new wooden floor. "Sure looks different than the last time I saw it."

"There's still a lot of work to be done upstairs." Shelby spread a layer of frozen fries on a baking sheet and stuck it in the oven. Delightful squeals and a splash of water came from the nearby bathroom. "So we're only living downstairs for now."

"What about the attic?"

"Completely clean, thanks to the Norris menfolk."

"Did Paul ever tell you what your dad did for him?"

"No, he didn't." She disappeared behind the open refrigerator door, then peered at him over the top. Uncertainty filled her eyes. "Hot dogs and fries for supper. Would you like to stay?"

AJ twisted his head, exaggeratedly looking behind him, then faced Shelby with a grin. "You talkin' to me?"

She gave an exasperated sigh. "It's nothing fancy, but . . . well, I'm sure you didn't expect to spend the day entertaining wet children. Thanks for taking us in."

"Does this mean you don't hate me anymore?"

"I never hated you." She closed the refrigerator door, holding a package of hot dogs. "It was just the house. That you didn't do anything to fix it."

"Maybe I wasn't meant to." He gazed into her eyes, so vulnerable and lovely. "Maybe God meant that task for you."

"Maybe. I hadn't thought of that." She held up the hot dogs. "Yes or no?"

"Yes." Despite the lingering chill from the rain and his futile attempt to guard his heart, warmth exuded from his chest clear to his fingers and toes.

The girls squealed again.

"I'll be right back. They'll turn to prunes if I don't get them out of the tub."

"We wouldn't want that." He took the package of hot dogs from her. "I'll fix these."

"You will?"

"Sure. Just tell me what to do."

"We like them grilled." Rummaging through a cabinet, she pulled out a grill pan and set it across two burners.

"How many?"

"Three for us plus however many you want."

The hot dogs were ready when Elizabeth and Tabby scampered

into the kitchen wearing nightgowns and slippers. Lila padded behind them, her tail swinging happily.

Elizabeth got ketchup and mustard out of the fridge, and Tabby found buns in the bread basket in the large pantry. By the time Shelby returned to the kitchen, the table was set, milk had been poured into glasses, and the fries were just coming out of the oven.

While Elizabeth said grace, AJ glanced at Shelby sitting across from him. Her head was slightly bowed, her eyes closed, and her expression serene.

"Bless Mommy and Tabby and Mr. AJ," Elizabeth said solemnly. "And thank you, God, for Mr. AJ showing me how to fish. Amen." She opened her eyes and gazed at him, her pixie face radiant. "I had so much fun."

"So did I." AJ grinned at her. "Maybe we can do it again sometime."

"Me too," said Tabby. "I wanna fish."

"You too." He tapped her nose, and she giggled.

Throughout the meal, Elizabeth and Tabby peppered him with questions about fishing, Lila and the mean groundhog, and teaching. Elizabeth talked about her teacher in Chicago, and Tabby bragged that she could write her name.

When the girls finished eating, Shelby shooed them out of the kitchen, Lila at their heels, and stacked the dirty dishes.

"They're fun kids," AJ said, returning condiments to the refrigerator. "Though the next time we go fishing, we should figure out a way to drive there. Tabby's heavier than she looks."

Shelby carried the dishes to the sink, her back to him. "There can't be a next time, AJ."

"Why not?" He tried to sound nonchalant, though he already knew the answer. Maybe he'd find out a little more about this mystery boyfriend.

Busy rinsing the plates, she didn't look at him. Her shoulders appeared tense. "I just think it's best they don't get too fond of you."

The refrigerator door closed with a soft click. He went to her side, stifling the desire to put his arms around her. "Don't you think it's a little late for that?"

"Not if they don't see you again." She scrubbed an already spotless plate.

"I see." His stomach turned to stone. "Guess I should get on home then."

"Wait a minute." She turned off the faucet and dried her hands. "I meant what I said earlier. If you hadn't been there . . ."

"You would have managed."

She scrutinized his face as if she didn't believe he meant what he said. Apparently satisfied he wasn't being sarcastic, her mouth thinned into a tight smile.

"Before I go," he said, "I need to ask you something. What you said about my grandmother. When did you see her?"

Shelby's eyes shifted, becoming glassy as she seemed to retreat to a place of incredible sorrow. She clutched the sink, focusing on something outside the window. "It was a long time ago. Years and years."

"You talked to her."

A wan smile barely lifted the corners of her mouth. "Mostly she talked to me."

"What did she say?"

A long pause bound them together, the only sound the quiet hum of the fridge and the distant noise of a television. Shelby bit her lip, reminding him of Gran the day he'd read Shelby's letter to her. Biting her lip, gripping his hand. "Find a way," she had urged. "The house belongs to Shelby."

Shelby finally spoke. "She said what I needed to hear."

He shook his head, puzzled, desperate to know. "What?"

"It's my memory. I've never told anyone."

"She wanted you to have this house. It was all that mattered to her at the end." He blinked as the remembrance of Gran's final moments stung his eyes. "It eased her last days to know you were fixing it up. Making things right again."

Shelby faced him, the moment wrapping itself around them as if time had no meaning. He held her gaze, willing her to share this hidden fragment of Gran's life with him.

"When did she die?"

"About three weeks ago." He swallowed past the lump pressing against his throat. "I got a call after we left the Dixie Diner. It was a couple days later."

"But I was here then." She sounded confused.

"Yes."

"Uncle Richard didn't tell me. If I'd known . . ." She reached for his hands, her gentle touch unsettling him even more. "I'm very sorry. I know how much it hurts."

The lump thickened in AJ's throat, making it impossible for him to speak. His eyes ached with the dam of unshed tears pushing against them. He stared at their hands, his and Shelby's, clasped warmly together.

He didn't want her to ever let him go.

- 12 -

Holding hands with AJ wasn't right, but Shelby didn't want to move. Sympathizing with his grief, she had impulsively reached out to him. But when her hands touched his, something clicked within her heart, and an unexpected thought burst into her mind.

This is where I belong.

No. That couldn't be true. AJ was a nice guy, but he was still the grandson of the ruthless monster who'd stolen her grandparents' farm.

Still, she was unwilling to end the moment. Despite the thunder and the raindrops pelting the kitchen windows, an intimate silence lingered around them till she believed she could hear the beating of her own heart.

"Shelby." He breathed her name, his voice husky and soft.

She lifted her eyes. His were rimmed in the red of sorrow but narrowed with longing. He stepped closer and bent his head, his gaze flickering to her lips. His hands moved to her waist, and, scarcely aware of her movements, she rested hers on his muscular biceps.

He moved closer, and panic seized her stomach as her conscience demanded to be heard. *What would Gary think?* And then, as if that might not be enough reason to push AJ away, her conscience flung up another thought.

What about Brett?

As if on cue, the ring of her phone shattered the fragile moment. She jumped back with a nervous giggle as if she'd just been caught doing something wrong. Grabbing the phone from the counter, she checked the display.

Brett.

Perfect timing.

She tapped the ignore button and sent the automated text message saying she'd call back in a few minutes.

"A friend." She stuck the phone in her pocket and absentmindedly picked up the dish towel. "I'll need to call him back soon."

"Him?"

She nodded, biting her lip.

"Friend, huh?"

"Yeah."

"I see." He seemed to wait, probably wanting some clarification. But she had none to give him. She liked Brett, and she didn't like AJ. What had almost happened between them was no more than two hearts who had both known sorrow wrapped up in the romance of a thunderous rainstorm.

Because everyone knew there was nothing more romantic than eating grilled hot dogs with two children and a wet dog. She flung the dish towel on the counter.

"Guess I should go so you can return that call." AJ picked up his ball cap from the table. "Where do you suppose I can find my dog?"

"This way."

Shelby led the way through the hallway past a couple of rooms and the stairs to Nanna's parlor. Except she had transformed it to their family room. The girls cuddled with Lila on a kid-friendly leather sofa as they watched television. The Labrador raised her head when AJ entered but didn't budge.

"Sorry about her being on the furniture," AJ said. "I guess I've let her get away with bad habits."

"It's okay. I imagine the girls encouraged her."

"Time to go, Lila." AJ patted his leg. "Come on."

Lila didn't move.

"She likes us," Elizabeth said, hugging the dog.

"I'm sure she does, but we need to get home. C'mon, Lila. That's a good girl."

Lila stretched and slowly stepped from the couch. Elizabeth and Tabby got up too, bestowing hugs on Lila and AJ both before Shelby could stop them.

"Thanks for helping me fish." Elizabeth swung his hand. "It was fun."

"Thanks for the cookies. And the cocoa. And riding in your Jeep. And the . . ." Tabby tilted her head, trying to come up with more to say.

"That's enough," Shelby said, gesturing to the door that opened to one end of the curving patio. "You can go out this way."

Bending down, he adjusted the plastic wrap he'd used to protect Lila's bandages from the rain. "I guess we're all set. Thanks for supper."

"It was the least we could do after you saved us from the storm."

"Rescuing lovely damsels in distress is what I do best." His mouth smiled, but not his eyes. "Night."

Head bent against the downpour, he and Lila disappeared into the dusk.

Shelby pulled the screen door closed and locked the latch. Rain slanted through the mesh, dampening her hair and face. But she didn't move away or shut the wooden door until the Jeep's taillights disappeared.

What happened in the kitchen couldn't happen again. It mustn't.

She plopped down on the couch, one arm around each of her girls. Holding them tight, she kissed one dark head and then the other.

"Mr. AJ's nice, isn't he, Mommy?"

"Yes, he is, Bitsy." Too nice.

"I like him." Tabby emphasized the *like*.

"He likes us too, doesn't he, Mommy?"

"I think he does." Too much.

The girls watched the rest of their show in silence, then put up the usual fuss about going to bed. When Shelby finally had them settled, she retrieved her phone and returned to the family room. Now she could enjoy a conversation with Brett without interruption.

A little thrill tingled her spine in anticipation of hearing his voice. He'd say "It's you" in that special tone he always used when she returned his calls, as if nothing was more important than talking with her. That greeting would wipe away her heart's traitorous preoccupation with Anderson John Sullivan the Fourth.

Curling up in a wingback chair by the empty fireplace, she looked down at her phone and groaned.

She was still wearing AJ's clothes.

Which reminded her. One more thing to do before calling Brett.

It took some searching, but finally she found what she was looking for on a Vermont antique store's website. A ceramic calico-cat-in-a-basket cookie jar. She dug her credit card from her wallet and placed the order, spending the extra for express delivery. It couldn't replace the one Tabby broke, but this was the best she could do. AJ had hidden his feelings well beneath his concern for Tabby's injury, but seeing the pieces of his mom's cookie jar scattered across his kitchen floor had to be hard for him. Especially since he seemed to have so few heirlooms. His biggest collection appeared to be OSU ball caps. At least a dozen dangled from the wall rack.

Must be a guy thing.

Her phone rang, and she stared at the screen with dismay.

Brett.

How could she have forgotten to return his call?

- 13 -

As AJ and Lila got out of the Jeep, Elizabeth came running out of the kitchen door. Her pixie face beamed as she raced down the stairs toward them.

"You're here." Throwing her arms around Lila, she giggled as the dog got in a kiss or two.

"Were you expecting us?"

"I hoped. But Mommy said you wouldn't."

"Did she?" Dropping by uninvited was a calculated risk, but one he'd decided to take. Something had happened between Shelby and him yesterday. She might choose to ignore it, but she couldn't deny it.

The screen door thwacked, and Shelby walked to the edge of the patio. "Hey, there. What's going on?"

"They came." Elizabeth dashed across the yard while Lila limped behind.

"I see that." Shelby joined AJ at the Jeep. He opened the rear hatch and lifted out the wagon. The insulated tote and blanket were inside.

"I would have called, but I don't have your number. Thought you might want these."

"You went out to the willow?"

100

"Yep." He closed the hatch and casually leaned against the bumper. "I wanted to see the 'gagement tree."

"I suppose you looked at the initials." With a sheepish smile, she sat on the bumper beside him.

"I did." Glancing at her profile, he caught the whiff of a delicate floral scent. "My favorite was S. L. and J. O."

She buried her face in her hands. "I should never have told you about that tree."

"Let's see. S. L. probably stands for Shelby Lassiter." He nudged her arm. "That's you, isn't it?"

She nudged him back.

"And if I were a betting man, I'd bet J. O. is, drum roll, please . . . Jason Owens."

"You think you're so smart."

"So you and Jason planned to marry?" he teased.

"We were kids. Best friends."

"What happened?"

"I left the country." Her somber tone shifted the mood away from playful banter. "He wrote to me, but I never wrote back. Eventually his letters stopped coming."

"Why didn't you write him?"

"Too angry, I suppose." She dug the toe of her shoe into the gravel. "I couldn't have explained it then, but now I think it was because his letters reminded me of what I was missing. Not just this place, but all the things I had taken for granted. Going to football games on a Friday night. Sleepovers with my friends." She smiled. "Pizza."

"Sounds like you had a tough time."

"I did. And I didn't handle it well." She hesitated, as if needing time to form her thoughts into words. "My parents had always dreamed of serving God as missionaries. Misty Willow, the family legacy, hindered that dream. They came to see losing the farm as a blessing. But I couldn't accept that. I still have a hard time accepting that."

AJ didn't respond. Instead he let her words settle around them. She'd given him a gift by sharing her heartache. He didn't want to ruin the moment by saying the wrong thing.

The peacefulness of the summer day was broken only by Elizabeth's laughter and Lila's occasional bark as the two played a game only they understood.

He ached for moments like this one. A tiny taste of what it would be like to belong to this family, this house. To be a father. A husband.

"I'm glad you didn't marry Jason."

Shelby's eyebrows furrowed. "Why?"

"Because then you'd be living down the road instead of here. You belong here."

"I think Jason's happy with the way things turned out. He and Cassie are perfect for each other."

"But are you? Happy with how things turned out, I mean."

"There are things I wish had been different. But I try to trust that God has a plan for me." She stood suddenly and faced him. "How about you?"

"What about me?"

She bent her head as if giving him the once-over. "You're a decent-looking guy. Thoughtful. Caring." A teasing smile brightened her face. "Why isn't there a Mrs. Fourth?"

He chuckled and shook his head. "I guess I don't want to make the same mistakes my parents did."

"What mistakes?"

"Mistakes." He shrugged. "Forgetting they once loved each other."

Her smile faded, but her eyes studied him. "I don't think you would."

"I haven't been willing to take that chance." Until now. But he couldn't tell her that. Time to change the subject. "Where's Tabby? I'm surprised she hasn't come outside."

"She's napping. We had a busy morning clearing up branches from last night's storm."

"Did a bit of that myself. So what's with the stakes out front?" He'd noticed the sticks when he drove in.

"Eventually it will be a flower garden. My grandmother had a variety of lovely irises planted in that area."

"Before long this place is going to look just like it used to."

"Not exactly. I plan to add a few special touches of my own."

"Like what?"

"Perhaps a trellis or a sundial. Or maybe a small gazebo. I haven't decided yet, but I'm gathering ideas and photos for inspiration."

"Sounds like quite a project."

"But a fun one."

"Gran grew irises at her house. 'Course, when she moved there, she wasn't able to do much of the planting herself, so that privilege was mine."

Shelby grabbed his hand and examined his thumb.

"What are you doing?"

"Just checking to see how green it is."

"Not very. But I'm real good at following Gran's directions." His stomach tightened, and he stared across the amber wheat field to avoid Shelby's sympathetic gaze. "Least I was."

~

Shelby released AJ's hand as she considered how to respond. And to figure out what in the world she was doing. When she said there couldn't be a "next time," she'd meant it. But her pulse had unexpectedly quickened when she saw his Jeep parked in her drive. Instead of saying thanks for the wagon and sending him on his way, she had actually flirted with him.

And enjoyed it when he flirted back.

Now the rawness of his grief scraped her heart. When her grandparents died, too many people avoided talking about them in her presence. Even as a young teen, she had been hurt by their misplaced compassion. Ignoring her grandparents' existence didn't lessen the pain of her loss.

103

"Tell me about her."

"What do you want to know?"

"Something special. When you weren't planting irises, what did you do together?"

"That's easy." A casual grin spread across AJ's face. "I think we've seen every movie Cary Grant ever made a dozen times."

She widened her eyes. "Me too. Nanna adored Cary Grant."

"'Everybody wants to be Cary Grant. Even I want to be Cary Grant.'"

"I love that line."

"How about this one. 'Insanity runs in my family. It practically gallops.'"

"*Arsenic and Old Lace.*"

"That's one point for you."

"My turn. 'Not that I mind a slight case of abduction now and then, but I have tickets for the theater this evening.'"

"Too easy." AJ smirked. "*North by Northwest.*"

"We're tied. One point each."

"So it's a competition now?"

"For biggest Cary Grant fan."

"Okay. Try this one. 'There must be something between us, even if it's only an ocean.'"

"Every woman in the world knows that one."

"Then what is it?"

"*An Affair to Remember.*" Shelby sighed dreamily. "And you can't watch that one without watching *Sleepless in Seattle.*"

"Another of Gran's favorites."

"Did you really watch all those movies with her?"

"Sure did. About once a month or so on a Sunday afternoon, we'd have a movie marathon." His eyes softened as he revisited the past, then he grinned. "Sometimes I drifted off to sleep. So did she, but we both pretended we didn't."

"Sounds like a pleasant way to spend a Sunday."

"It was." His grin widened. "Two to one. Your turn."

Shelby thought a moment, her mind sifting through Nanna's favorite movies. Only one quote came to mind, but she hesitated to share it.

"Can't think of any others?" AJ teased. "I'll do another."

"Not so quick." With unaccustomed boldness, she touched the cleft in his chin. "'How do you shave in there?'"

Surprise brightened the gold flecks in his brown eyes, and her head spun as he held her gaze. Her hand slipped from his chin to his chest, and he covered it with his own. A palpable charge electrified the space between them. Stepping back, she withdrew her hand and broke the connection.

"Shelby, I . . ."

"Give up?" The question spilled out too quick. To cover her embarrassment, she pasted on a broad smile.

Thankfully, he allowed his mood to follow hers.

"Never." He stressed the final syllable in a teasing growl. "But that's not a Cary Grant line."

"Still a Cary Grant movie."

"Audrey Hepburn. *Charade*."

"One of my favorites."

"Mine too." He checked his watch. "Guess we'll leave it two to two. Lila has an appointment at the vet to get her bandages removed."

"Is she all better now?"

"I hope so."

"Me too. And thanks for getting the wagon. I was trying to figure out the best way to bring it home."

"Just being neighborly."

"That reminds me. I washed and dried your clothes. I'll be right back." She hurried into the house, grabbed the bag of folded sweats and socks, and rushed out again.

Elizabeth stood beside the Jeep while AJ coaxed a reluctant Lila to get inside. Finally he picked her up and placed her on the seat.

"Will you come again tomorrow so we can play?"

"Afraid not, sunshine." AJ bent over, hands on knees, and chucked her chin. "I'm going on a weeklong camping trip with a couple of buddies in the morning."

"Is Lila going too?"

"She sure is. Though she won't be able to do as much hiking as she usually does."

"I want to go camping."

Shelby put her hand on Elizabeth's shoulder. "Someday we will, Bitsy." She handed AJ the bag. "Enjoy your trip. And thanks again for everything."

"Anytime." He climbed into the Jeep, waving as he drove away.

A week. She should be glad he wouldn't be dropping in unannounced—at least not for the next seven days. Instead, an emptiness settled around her.

"I like Mr. AJ." Elizabeth snuggled close to Shelby. "He listens with his eyes."

Puzzled, Shelby looked down at her daughter, then at the disappearing Jeep. "What do you mean?"

"He looks right at me when we talk."

"He does, doesn't he?"

"You like him too, don't you, Mommy?"

"Yes, I do." Maybe too much.

- 14 -

Brett hummed along with the classic country western station he'd found on his XM car radio. It wasn't his typical music, but he was familiar with the oldies. Listening to Willy Nelson croon about the woman who was always on his mind eased the drive into last-century farm culture.

He'd told Amy she owed him big time for the sacrifice he was making—taking a day away from the office to romance a woman he would have ignored under any other circumstances. Not that Shelby wasn't attractive. Only that she had committed the unpardonable transgression of having children.

The stakes were high enough, though, that he planned to romance the kids too. Right under Shelby's cute little nose.

Amy considered his scheme to be a colossal waste of time. To her vindictive little mind, an attorney should have been bought, the lawsuit filed, and the judge distracted by her sleek legs. But Brett didn't want to give up on his plan yet. He wasn't going to admit it to his sister, but he enjoyed his phone conversations with Shelby. He'd quickly learned that shallow chitchat bored her, and she could discuss a wide range of topics with warmth and intelligence. And unlike the tiresome Tracie, who wasn't nearly as irresistible as he let her believe, Shelby had no hidden agenda, played no games.

That was another reason he was anxious to see her. When he finally reached her late Thursday evening, the night of that big storm, he detected something different in her voice. She said it had been a long day and that she was just tired. He could understand that. He'd be nuts spending a whole day shut in a house with two rambunctious rug rats.

When they talked yesterday, she sounded more like herself. But if she had something on her mind, he wanted to know about it.

He had considered driving down over the weekend, but he couldn't take a chance that AJ would drive by and see his car parked at Shelby's house. But yesterday he'd found out that AJ had taken off on one of his frequent summertime camping trips.

Good riddance.

As he pulled into Shelby's drive, his pulse quickened like it did before investment strategy sessions. Today's venture promised its own special appeal.

He parked at the side of the house in the graveled loop behind Shelby's Camry. Such a huge place. At least ten rooms, not counting the bathrooms. Maybe she was exhausted from all the work she'd been doing.

And he hadn't done anything to help. Why would he? After all, his plan was for her to vacate the property. The sooner, the better.

Yet it might not hurt for him to do something. He surveyed the graveled drive. Unaware of their relationship, she'd told Brett about AJ's unwelcome gesture. Only his idiotic cousin would try to win a woman's heart with gravel. But then AJ didn't have the benefit of Brett's calculated expertise. Otherwise, AJ would never have let that college co-ed ruin his relationship with Sully. Brett sure hadn't.

Wonder whatever happened to her.

Shrugging away the thought, he gathered the flowers from the passenger seat. A bouquet of pink tulips for Shelby and two bud vases, each holding three pink-tipped carnations, for her girls. He paused by the steps leading up to the patio to consider if he should go around to the front door.

Before he could decide, the kitchen screen door opened, and Shelby greeted him with a warm hello. Surprise and delight mingled in her eyes. She looked adorable in cutoff shorts and a paint-splattered T-shirt.

Cute wasn't his usual style, but maybe it should be.

"Look at you," he said as he climbed the patio steps. "You look lovely."

"I look a mess."

"Not to me." He held out the bouquet. "For you."

She blushed slightly as she accepted the flowers and inhaled their fragrance. "Why didn't you tell me you were coming?"

"I wanted to surprise you."

"That you did."

The screen door opened again. The younger girl practically tumbled out of the house while the older one never took her eyes off him as she walked to Shelby's side.

"Hello, ladies," he said, flashing his most charming smile and holding out the vases. "I brought you flowers."

"Just like Mommy?" Tabby oohed and aahed as she gripped the vase in both hands. "Wow!"

He grinned at her delight. "You're Tabby, right?"

"Uh-huh. I this many." She clutched the vase to her chest with one hand and held up three fingers on the other.

"I never would have guessed." He turned to the older girl and knelt to her level. "You must be Elizabeth. This one's for you."

"Thank you." She took the vase, smiling slightly, then buried her nose in the carnations.

"Girls, this is Mr. Brett. He's the nice man who sent us the basket of goodies when we first moved in. Remember?"

"We liked the basket," said Tabby. "I ate all the pwetzels."

"I'm glad." He stood and smiled at Shelby. "Looks like you're busy painting."

"Yes and no. We were working on a little craft project, that's all."

"Good, because I have another surprise for you." He pulled four movie tickets from his pocket. "The new Pixar movie is showing in town. I thought we could go."

Even Elizabeth's eyes lit up as he dangled the tickets in front of them. Shelby opened her mouth in protest, but he pretended he didn't notice.

"Who wants to see the movie?" he asked energetically.

The girls' eager cheers made him laugh.

"Brett." Shelby pulled at his sleeve. "You should have talked to me about this first."

He immediately looked contrite. "Did I do something wrong?"

"No, of course not. It's just that . . ." She looked at her daughters' uplifted faces, their expressions wavering between hope and disappointment. "Are you sure you want to do this?"

"I cleared my calendar to do this."

"What if we hadn't been home?"

"I took a chance." He ran his finger lightly down her arm. "It's just a movie. Not a date."

She smiled at that, just as he knew she would.

"Come on, it'll be fun. Right, ladies?" He appealed to the girls, confident Shelby couldn't resist their pleas. He was right.

She glanced at her clothes then at the girls in their shorts and tees. "We need to change."

"You've got time."

"Do you want to come in? Get something to drink while you wait?"

"I'll just stay out here. Count the cars that go by."

"We won't be long." She herded the girls inside, oblivious to what a pair of gorgeous legs clad in cutoff shorts could do to a man.

When the kitchen door shut behind her, he sauntered to his car. So far everything had gone as planned. A movie was the perfect outing. He'd be spending time with the girls without needing to interact much with them. And even at a kids' movie, sharing a bucket of popcorn with Shelby could be fun.

If all went well today, she'd say yes the next time he asked her out. Too bad Friday night's charity event was too soon. Could be fun showing her off to the guys. But for now he needed to keep her off-balance.

He grinned, pleased with himself and with the world. He almost didn't care if Amy turned out to be right. Shelby might not fall hard enough for him to give up her land. But he planned to enjoy every minute of the chase. Should he win, the victory would be that much sweeter.

Meanwhile, Tracie still had four or five more weeks before he let her go. If he could stand her pouty lips and cloying voice that long. As predictable as her predecessors, she now arrived to the office late, left early, and took long lunch hours. It seemed more of her clothes appeared in his closet with each passing day as she obviously planned to become a permanent resident. He'd let her believe that for now. It was part of the game. No wonder he was already bored with her.

In a couple of weeks, he'd place an ad for a new receptionist. Same merry-go-round, different painted filly.

Dismissing Tracie with a shake of his head, he propped himself against the bumper of his car and scrolled through the email on his phone. A few minutes later, Shelby and her girls came out of the house clothed in pastel sundresses and sandals. Both children wore their dark hair in a single braid tied with matching ribbons. Shelby's chestnut hair was swept off her neck and held in place with a silver clasp.

Brett wolf-whistled, and Shelby's blushed cheeks reddened even more.

She dangled a set of keys. "Do you mind if I drive? Tabby still uses a car seat, and it's already strapped in."

He glanced at his Lexus, disconcerted by the unexpected request. He didn't like the idea of riding shotgun. But a car seat? In his car? Not happening.

"I suppose we could follow you." She shooed the girls toward her Camry.

"No, that's all right. I'll come with you." He jogged to her side. "I'm just not used to not driving."

She admonished him with a steely look, softened by a delicate smile. "I didn't know you were so old-fashioned."

"I'm not old-fashioned."

"Then get in." She pointed to the passenger side. "Over there."

His head screamed *no*, but his feet listened to Shelby. He climbed in, muttering, "I can't believe I'm doing this."

"What did you say?" She fastened her seat belt and drove toward the road.

"You're the old-fashioned one, not me."

"Why do you say that?"

"Stay-at-home mom. Craft projects. This is the twenty-first century, you know. Women in the real world have careers, goals."

"The *real* world?" she said, her voice quiet but firm. "Believe me, Brett, if my life is some kind of fantasy, I would be imagining something different."

Her soft rebuke stung like a slap. Heat rose up his neck, and he stared out the window. The rhythmic click of the turn signal filled the silence between them. The road was clear, but Shelby didn't turn out of her driveway.

"Maybe this wasn't such a good idea." She still spoke quietly, almost as if apologizing.

He twisted to take a quick glance at the girls, but they didn't seem to be paying attention to what was going on in the front seat. Elizabeth turned the pages of a book, and Tabby clutched a worn pale pink blanket. "They'll be disappointed."

"I'll still take them to the movie."

But without him.

The unspoken words hung in the air.

When had he lost control? The answer smacked him upside the head, it was so obvious. He took a deep breath and slowly exhaled.

"I'm . . . sorry. That was an insensitive thing to say."

"Apology accepted." She didn't pull onto the road.

He mentally ran through his usual lines, but nothing fit. How could he have been so stupid? He studied her profile, surprisingly intrigued by the delicate curve of her ear and the fine line of her jaw. Dark sunglasses, resting on the curve of her cheek, hid her eyes.

Something stirred deep within him, tender heart-stirring feelings he'd buried long ago beneath unspeakable pain.

Resisting the overwhelming urge to reach for her hand, he cleared his throat. "May I accompany you to the movie?"

"Why?" She pushed the sunglasses into her hair, glanced into the backseat at the girls, then faced him. "Why do you, of all people, want to go to a children's movie?"

"Because I want to spend time with you." He met her gaze, unafraid of the truth she'd see in his eyes. "I wanted to meet them." He tilted his head toward the girls.

She seemed to weigh his words before she responded, her voice still low. "Every choice I make, everything I do, I do for *them*."

"Of course you do." He gave an exaggerated sigh then an apologetic smile. "And I can ride in the passenger seat without acting like a brat."

The smile worked. She smiled too, then adjusted her sunglasses, checked the road, and made her turn. He sat back, relaxing as best he could when he wasn't in the driver's seat, and replayed the strange conversation. He hated to admit it, even to himself, but he'd learned a couple of things.

First, Shelby had a backbone. And for his plan to work, he'd better not forget it.

Second, he'd meant what he said about wanting to spend time with her. He just hadn't realized it until a few minutes ago.

~

After the movie, they returned to the house, and Shelby gave Brett a quick tour of the downstairs renovations.

"What about up there?" he asked, propping his arm on the banister post.

"I'm saving that for autumn. It's too hot to work up there now, and the second air-conditioning unit still needs to be installed."

"Sounds expensive."

"I suppose."

"It's a big house for three people."

"I know. But it's my house, and I love it."

He was right, though. There were four rooms downstairs, plus a bathroom and the kitchen. Beyond the kitchen was the back room, used for laundry and storage. A tiny room at the rear of it had once stored coal. A rickety set of enclosed stairs led to two small rooms that hadn't been used for decades.

For now, Elizabeth and Tabby shared the room across the hall from the family room while she'd claimed the small room that had been Grandpa's study as her temporary bedroom. Arched double doors separated it from the family room, and its windows looked out onto the curved concrete patio.

She opened the front doors, and sunlight spilled into the hallway followed by a welcome breeze scented with the freshness of outdoors. She'd often thought that if scents had a color, this one would be green.

"I hope you still love it this winter when you get your heating bill."

"I'll manage."

Brett glanced at his watch. "I need to get going."

"You could stay for supper if you want. I'm baking a chicken."

"Sounds delicious, but I already have plans."

Of course he did. Probably with some statuesque bimbo . . . She reined in her thoughts before they could go any further. What Brett did was none of her business, and she had no right to be jealous.

"A few guys and I get together on Monday evenings. A networking kind of thing."

She smiled with relief while inwardly admonishing herself for being glad he wasn't seeing another woman. *We're only friends. That's all. Only friends.*

"Did you have a good time today?" she asked as they walked outside to his car.

"I did."

"Honestly?"

He chuckled. "Honestly. How about you?"

"Absolutely. I love it when my daughter spills her drink on someone's clothes."

"They'll wash. Besides, it was really my fault."

"You keep saying that, but I don't believe you." Shelby hadn't seen the mishap, but Tabby could be stubborn about doing things by herself. When she had trouble getting her straw into the drink's lid, Brett tried to help. Somehow the lid popped off, and his pants leg got soaked.

"Accidents happen."

"Thanks for being so nice about it." She gazed into his clear blue eyes. It still seemed incredible that he had taken a day from work to spend time with her and the girls. But she was glad he did. The movie was laugh-out-loud funny, and he'd spoiled them with popcorn and treats. Much more than she should have allowed. "Thanks for everything. I had a really good time."

"I'm glad. When we talked the other night, you sounded a little upset."

She glanced away and frowned, remembering how close she'd come to kissing AJ. How much she had wanted him to kiss her. He'd been her hero that day, that's all it was. Naturally she'd been grateful. But it wouldn't happen again.

"Do you want to talk about it?"

The concern in Brett's voice washed over her, reminding her how much she missed having someone to confide in. But her close call with AJ wasn't something Brett needed to know.

"Talk about what?"

"Whatever that was I just saw in your eyes."

"It was nothing."

"It must have been something," Brett persisted. "I'm a good listener."

"We got caught in the rain," she said, fumbling for an explanation. "The guy who owned this place had to bring us home."

"The same guy who gave you the gravel?"

"The very same." A slight breeze blew a strand of hair across her cheek, and she tucked it behind her ear. "The girls really like him, but they're still grieving for their dad. Especially Elizabeth. I hated to hurt his feelings when he'd been so kind to us, but I asked him to stay away."

"He has to understand you're only looking out for your children. That's what good moms do." Brett reached for her hand and intertwined her fingers with his. "Besides, I hope I'm the only guy in your life."

She smiled slightly, then sighed. What was true of AJ was also true of Brett. She needed to have a similar conversation with him. Now.

"The girls and I had a great time today, Brett." She withdrew her hand from his and rubbed her arms. "But I can't let them get too fond of you, either. Not yet."

He stared at her, as if gauging whether she meant it, then exhaled. "I see."

"Do you?"

"No more surprise trips to the movies, right?"

"You must think me so ungrateful. I'm sorry."

"Don't be." Taking her by the shoulders, he drew her into a gentle embrace. "Can I still call?"

"If you want to."

"I want to." He brushed his lips against her hair, so lightly she wondered if she'd imagined it, then drew back and looked into her eyes. He hesitated, as if making up his mind about something. "There's a charity event I need to go to Friday night. For wounded military. Come with me."

Her pulse quickened, whether from excitement or nerves she wasn't sure. "I don't know."

"I'd really like you to." His hopeful smile tugged at her heart.

But her mind swirled with indecision. The thought of going out on an actual date made her stomach queasy. And yet, she liked Brett. He obviously liked her. Take away all the silly excuses, and only one thing might prevent her from going out with him. "I'll have to find a babysitter."

His smile broadened, and he jumped into his car as if rushing to get away before she could change her mind. "I'll call you with the details."

She waved good-bye, and the Lexus kicked up gravel as it headed down the lane. After it disappeared around the curve, she wandered across the yard to the mailbox on the other side of the road. A date with Brett. To a charity event. What should she wear? Nothing in her wardrobe was suitable. That meant a shopping trip. Tomorrow.

She reached the mailbox and pulled out the day's delivery. Typical junk stuff and one official-looking envelope from Trainum and Trainum, Attorneys at Law. She opened it as she walked back toward the house.

The letter asked her to come to the law office Thursday afternoon to discuss a small bequest left to her by the recently deceased Joyanna Sullivan.

She read the letter again, her heart pounding. Why would AJ's grandmother leave her anything?

- 15 -

As irrational as it was, AJ felt like a vulture. He'd left his buddies fishing near the Appalachian Trail in Virginia to come home for this meeting. Leaving fresh mountain air to be in the same suffocating room as his cousins was especially galling.

Now here he was, a little before noon on a Thursday morning, preparing to discuss Gran's will as if her personal assets could ease the aching hole in his heart caused by her absence.

Yep, he felt like a vulture.

Six years ago, after Sully died, Gran had sold their Columbus mansion, bought a few acres less than a mile from AJ's cottage, and built her bungalow. Wanting a new attorney, someone who had never been involved with Sully's personal or business enterprises, someone whom Sully hadn't bullied into making unethical compromises, she'd found Trainum and Trainum.

A massive desk commanded attention in the center of the office. From a gilded frame, Patricia's father, the firm's original Trainum, glared at the room's occupants. The wall's dark paneling absorbed the rare bit of sunlight that managed to penetrate through the heavy drapes.

AJ resisted the urge to pull down the curtains only by imagining he was trapped in a Dickensian novel. Perhaps *Bleak House*.

118

That story was all about the law and inheritances and never-ending court cases.

His only consolation was that Amy and Brett, sitting in chairs next to him, appeared just as uncomfortable.

Patricia cleared her throat and straightened the papers stacked on her desk. "Your grandmother requested I bring the three of you together after her passing. When she updated her estate plan, she talked to me for quite some time about how much she wanted you to get along with each other. To mend—"

"She updated her plan? When?" Brett glared at AJ.

"Don't look at me," AJ said. "I don't know anything about it."

"How could you not know? She tells you everything."

Patricia removed her bifocals and stared at Brett. "Your grandmother asked me to come over about a month before she died. But only to add an extra proviso. As I was saying, she wanted the three of you, her only grandchildren and the heirs of the bulk of her estate, to be together when her final wishes were made known. May I continue?"

Brett flipped his hand, as if giving royal permission.

"As all of you probably know, Joyanna's estate consists of two trusts. The first is the estate she inherited from her husband. Your grandfather. This trust is to be divided equally among the three of you."

"The three of us?" Brett shifted in his chair and glanced at Amy. "Are you sure that's right? Sully practically disinherited AJ."

AJ turned his head toward the window, wishing he could see beyond the burgundy and blue drapes to the sky. He slightly loosened the tie that he'd worn out of respect for the solemnity of the occasion. Leave it to Brett to turn it into a farce by bringing up ancient history.

"Be that as it may, after Mr. Sullivan's death, your grandmother controlled the trust and could do with it whatever she wanted."

Brett started to speak, but Amy placed her hand on his arm.

"Forgive our interruptions, Patricia," she said with practiced diplomacy. "What about the second trust?"

"The second trust is made up of a small legacy left to your grandmother by her parents and then additional investments added over the years. Except for a few charitable donations and other small bequests, this part of the trust will also be divided equally."

AJ pulled again at his tie. Most people might be thrilled to be handed this kind of monetary legacy. But it almost made him sick. He'd grown up in a life of privilege—private schools, expensive vacations, a fire engine red Camaro when he turned sixteen.

But all that luxury hadn't made anyone happy. Not his grandfather, whose greed could never be satisfied. Not his parents nor his aunt and uncle, who made their marriages into a blood sport before the four of them died in a fiery airplane crash.

Not even his grandmother, who grieved over the rifts in her family.

Even without the boon that Brett and Amy had received from Sully when he died, AJ had a comfortable nest egg from his parents. But he lived on his teacher's salary, much preferring the uncomplicated life he'd chosen after Sully disowned him.

"We might as well get her house on the market right away," Brett said. "Can you recommend a realtor?"

"That's not your decision to make, Mr. Somers."

"Why not?"

"Your grandmother's real estate, strange as it may sound, isn't part of the trust. The cottage property where AJ currently resides and—"

"And she left it to AJ." Brett smirked. "No surprise there. Though why anyone would want to live in that drafty old place out in the middle of nowhere . . ."

AJ pushed himself out of his chair and strode to the window. Amy stood too, and wrapped her arm through his.

"Be quiet, Brett," she admonished. "AJ's cottage is charming and secluded."

"Thanks, Amy, but I don't need you to take up for me." AJ yanked off his tie and stuffed it in his pocket. "Is there anything else?"

Patricia had half risen when AJ stood but returned to her seat and picked up a piece of paper. "Your grandmother asked me to specifically say, 'I am leaving my real estate, both the cottage and my current home, to AJ because of the ill-treatment he received from his grandfather. Brett and Amy, I ask that you understand and respect my wishes.' There's more, but you can read it at your leisure."

She pushed three envelopes across the desk. "She wrote each of you a separate letter."

"Of course we respect Gran's wishes." Amy retrieved the envelopes and passed them out. "Don't we, Brett?"

"Absolutely," he said flatly, folding the envelope and tucking it into his inner jacket pocket.

"The contents of your grandmother's home are also yours, Mr. Sullivan, to do with whatever you'd like." Patricia pulled out another sheet of paper and held it out to AJ. "Except for these few items. Your grandmother specifically requested that they be given to a Ms. Shelby Kincaid."

"To Shelby?" AJ scanned the list. It showed a photo and detailed description of each item Gran meant Shelby to have.

"Your grandmother was quite anxious about making the change. She said those particular items belong to Ms. Kincaid. It was the reason for our last meeting."

"I see." The list included a three-drawer lowboy, an antique washstand, and a few decorative items. It didn't take a genius to guess that the pieces once belonged to Shelby's grandparents.

"As the executor, you can arrange the delivery of the items. However, if you'd like, I can make the arrangements."

"No, that won't be necessary." AJ folded the list and placed it in his pocket. Suddenly the room didn't seem as claustrophobic. Now he had an excuse to call on Shelby. "I'll do it."

"Is there anything else Gran wished us to know?" Amy graced Patricia with a disarming smile.

"No." She came around from behind her desk. "The transfer of assets will occur over the next few weeks. If you have any questions or concerns, please feel free to give me a call." She handed each of them a business card, then escorted them out the door.

In the lobby, Amy grabbed both Brett and AJ by an arm. "You two could have behaved better in there. What would Gran say?"

"I didn't know she planned to leave me both properties." AJ's mood brightened, probably because of the sunlight pouring through the lobby windows. Strangely, Brett's mood seemed to have darkened.

"I'm not surprised she did." Amy smiled up at him. "What will you do?"

"I'm not in a hurry to sell Gran's house," AJ said, feeling generous and suddenly wanting to smooth things over, "but how about we get it appraised? Then I'll buy out what would have been your shares."

"There's no need." Amy shook her head. "The house is all yours. Brett and I have no claim on it."

"It's only money. More than I need."

Brett made a strange sound and shook his head. "Did Sully teach you nothing?"

Before AJ could reply, Amy intervened. "Now, boys. No more of this nonsense. Let's go to lunch."

"Lunch?" Brett stared at her.

"It's past noon, and I'm starving. Besides, it's not often I get to have lunch with my two favorite men."

"Only if AJ's buying."

"Why not?" AJ shrugged. "Where do you want to go?"

"How about that little Italian place across the street?" Amy suggested.

"Sounds great." AJ grinned. "They have a waitress there who'll cheer up Brett."

Brett glared, and AJ grinned even more. "Only kidding, cuz."

"Now that you mention it," Brett said, his glare softening into a teasing smile, "I'm thinking of hiring a new receptionist."

~

Shelby walked out of the law office, still in a daze after the brief meeting. It had only taken a few minutes for Patricia Trainum to explain Joyanna Sullivan's bequest, hand Shelby a copy of the list, and inform her that AJ Sullivan would be in touch to work out the details.

"Were we good, Mommy?" Tabby's yank on Shelby's hand brought her back to the present. "Can we have 'lato?"

"May we," Shelby automatically corrected. While parking the car, she had noticed the Italian café and promised gelato in exchange for good manners.

"You were both wonderful." She squeezed their hands. "Time for our special treat."

The light changed, and they crossed the street. Inside the café, the hostess welcomed them. As she escorted them toward a table, Tabby squealed and slipped her hand from Shelby's.

"Mr. AJ, it's me." Tabby ran to him, and he pushed his chair back to lift her onto his lap. Elizabeth hurried after her sister and leaned into him.

"Girls," Shelby called after them, only to be ignored. She smiled lamely at the hostess and followed her children. Two other people were at the same table, an attractive woman and . . . Brett?

AJ grinned at Shelby. "I'd get up," he said, "but I don't want to drop your children."

Before Shelby could answer, Tabby pointed at Brett. "I spilled my drink on him. It was an askident." She giggled. "He likes Mommy."

Brett stood and gave her an awkward smile. "Hello, Shelby. I'd like you to meet my sister Amy."

"It's nice to meet you," Shelby said.

"You too." Amy started to say something else, then seemed to think better of it. She took a sip of her tea and glanced at AJ.

Shelby followed her gaze. He held tightly to the girls, his body tense and his expression dark as he stared at her. "You know Brett?"

"Yes," she said haltingly. "Yes, I do." Somewhere in the back of her mind, she realized that only Brett and Amy weren't surprised at who knew whom.

"Mr. Brett gave all of us flowers," Elizabeth stage-whispered. "And we went to the movies."

"What's this all about, Brett?" AJ's low voice simmered with anger, and he pulled the girls a little closer.

"Nothing that's your concern." Brett's voice was equally hard, but his eyes softened when he turned to Shelby. "I can explain this."

"Explain what?" Shelby looked from one to the other as she tried to fit the pieces in their proper places. One man treated her like royalty, charming her with his wit and fine manners. The other, the one she couldn't quite forgive, had his arms protectively around her children. The puzzle didn't make sense. "Why didn't you tell me you knew AJ?"

"That wasn't part of the plan."

"What plan?"

Instead of answering, he took his jacket from the back of the chair and slung it over his shoulder. "Time to go, Amy."

"This isn't about your development scheme, is it?" AJ asked.

"You should never have signed away your land, AJ." Amy placed her napkin beside her plate and stood.

The words slammed Shelby's stomach. "You mean Misty Willow? It's mine."

Amy smiled, but her eyes were cold. "Not for long. Good-bye, AJ. Thanks for lunch." She took a few steps, then turned back. "Coming, Brett?"

Brett traced Shelby's jawline with his finger. "It wasn't supposed to work out this way. But we need that land." Stunned, she didn't move when he brushed his lips against hers. "And we're going to get it."

Staring at his back as he strode away, she longed for him to turn around, but he left the café without even a backward glance.

She looked helplessly at AJ. He smiled at something Elizabeth said, but his tense jaw and narrowed eyes betrayed his simmering anger. Her knees wobbled, and she sank into the seat Brett had vacated, her eyes downcast.

"How do you know him?" Her voice was a bare murmur.

"He's my cousin."

She closed her eyes as the revelation ricocheted against her temples.

"Mommy?" Elizabeth touched Shelby's shoulder. "Are you sick?"

"No, honey." How could she have been so naive to think anyone like Brett cared for her? But never could she have imagined such an ulterior motive. It didn't even make sense.

She pulled her daughter close, comforted by the little girl's touch.

"Are you girls hungry?" AJ asked, the cheer in his voice sounding forced.

"We were good at the lawyer's place, so we get gelato." Elizabeth took Amy's empty seat. "Mommy said it's like ice cream."

"The lawyer's place? Did you see Patricia Trainum?"

"Yes," Shelby said, her voice shaking, "She gave me a list."

"We went to the library first," Elizabeth said. "I got a book about dogs. Like Lila."

"You did? That sounds like a good book."

"I wanna see Lila," said Tabby.

"I'm sure she wants to see you too."

A waitress stopped by with menus. As if they were in a distant tunnel, AJ asked about the gelato flavors and the waitress recited the options. Elizabeth chose strawberry, and Tabby asked for chocolate.

"Do you want anything?"

Cousins? It couldn't be.

"Shelby?"

She roused herself from her stupor.

"Would you like something to eat?" AJ's gentle voice slipped through the thrumming in her ears. "Coffee?"

Barely shaking her head, she avoided looking at him. The last thing she wanted was his pity.

As AJ entertained the girls, she slowly emerged from the miserable fog surrounding her. When the last bite of gelato had disappeared, she wiped Tabby's mouth with a napkin. "We need to get home. Tabby's already missed her nap."

AJ walked with them to her Camry and waited while she made sure both girls were safely secured in the backseat. Before she could open the driver's door, he touched her elbow.

"Are you okay to drive?"

"I'm fine."

"We need to talk."

"About your family tree?"

"About you and Brett." He crushed his jacket in a death grip. "I can't believe you let him kiss you. Right there in front of Elizabeth and Tabby."

"I didn't *let* him." Her face burned as she barely resisted the impulse to slap him. But he wasn't the one who needed a good slap. That honor belonged to Brett.

"Where did you meet him, anyway?"

Shelby leaned against the car, arms wrapped around her chest, thinking back to that night in the restaurant when she first saw Brett. "Uncle Richard introduced us."

AJ stared at her. "Richard Grayson?"

"He didn't tell me." She gulped, repulsed by the sudden revelation of Richard's betrayal. "He never said."

"We have to talk about this."

"Just leave me alone." Unwelcome tears pooled in her eyes,

and she swiped them away. "Please just leave me and my children alone." After slipping into the car, she closed the door before he could stop her.

She drove home on autopilot, barely registering the traffic lights and turns. Her emotions whipsawed between shame for believing Brett cared for her and irrational anger at AJ. Then there was Richard.

Her great-uncle. Nanna's brother. A trusted family friend.

Why hadn't he told her that Brett was Anderson Sullivan's grandson? He knew how she despised all the Sullivans.

Now the entire dinner seemed like a setup. And she had been the victim.

The eager, willing victim.

- 16 -

*A*J pounded his steering wheel with his palm as he waited for the light to change. Shelby couldn't be in love with Brett. She just couldn't. But when Brett had walked out of the restaurant, she had looked as if her heart would break. The light turned green, and AJ floored it through the intersection.

His tires squealed as he swerved into the bank's parking lot and braked behind Richard's late-model Cadillac. Inside the bank, he headed for Richard's office. Chandra Coleman, the administrative assistant, stood as he passed her desk. "Mr. Grayson is with someone right now. If you could just take a seat . . ."

AJ ignored her and opened the door. Richard rose from his desk, and his eyes flicked to Brett standing near the window.

"You're not welcome here, AJ." Brett straightened, his body rigid.

AJ focused on Richard. "What are you doing to Shelby? She trusted you."

"Brett and I are having a private conversation," Richard intoned as he came out from behind the desk and grasped AJ's elbow. "It doesn't concern you."

AJ jerked his arm away from Richard's grip. "Anything involving Misty Willow concerns me." He faced Brett. "You're not getting that land, no matter how much you plot and scheme. So leave Shelby alone."

"Don't worry, AJ." Brett's voice dripped with spite. "I'd have given her back when I was done with her. I always do."

AJ clenched his fist and connected it with Brett's cheekbone. Flailing backward into a bookshelf, Brett struggled to maintain his balance. A framed photograph and a glass plaque fell to the floor.

"No more." Richard, his face stricken with horror, stepped between AJ and Brett. "You will not behave this way in my office."

AJ stepped back and shook his aching fist while keeping a wary eye on Brett. Blood glistened along his cousin's jawline.

Though his age made it difficult for him to bend down, Richard retrieved the photograph and plaque from the floor and placed them on his desk. "What would Joyanna say about this spectacle?" His hoarse voice rose in anger. "What if she'd seen the two of you behaving this way?"

"What would she say if she knew what you were up to?" AJ retorted.

"What am I 'up to,' AJ?"

"You introduced Brett to Shelby."

"So I did. And somehow that gives you the right to barge in my office? To assault your cousin?"

"You're lucky I'm not filing charges." Brett pressed his handkerchief against his jaw, then examined the bloody stain. "We'll talk tomorrow, Richard. I'm out of here." He slammed the door behind him.

AJ rubbed his bruised knuckles and closed his eyes against the memory Brett had unleashed. But it was too late. Overpowering regret and Meghan's distraught expression taunted him.

If only he could go back in time.

"I've been friends with your family for most of my life." Richard perched on the edge of his desk. "It pains me to see you and Brett fight the way you do."

"But you're *related* to Shelby."

"True."

Still nursing his injured hand, AJ plopped into a nearby chair. "How did we end up with Misty Willow?"

Richard returned to his seat and tapped a pen against his desk blotter. "What has Shelby told you?"

"She doesn't seem to know."

"Thad Lassiter borrowed money on the farm. Sully bought the loan. When Thad couldn't make payments, Sully foreclosed."

"Since when was Sully a mortgage company?"

"He had many business interests."

AJ sat in silence, his thoughts beating against his brain. "So he foreclosed on the farm, then ignored it?" Even the pastures and fields had been neglected until AJ inherited the property and rented them to Paul Norris.

A shadow flitted across the old banker's face, and he cleared his throat. "I'm sure Anderson had his reasons."

"What aren't you telling me, Richard?"

"Leave the past alone, AJ. For Shelby's sake, if not your own."

AJ rubbed his palms against the arms of the chair, then stood and leaned over Richard's desk. "After Shelby and I signed the lease agreement, you told me not to get involved with her. But then you introduced her to Brett. Why?"

Richard leaned back in his chair and rested his folded hands on his chest. "Shelby may have been infatuated with Brett. But she's a sensible girl with strong values. Even without today's misunderstanding, she'd have eventually broken things off with him."

AJ held Richard's gaze as he straightened. "Are you saying . . ."

"All I'm saying is that she would never fall in love with Brett." He turned from AJ's scrutiny, and his eyes seemed to dim. When he spoke, his voice was low, almost as if he were speaking to himself. "Brett's too much like Sully. And Shelby's too much like Aubrey." He sighed heavily.

"Where does that leave me?"

Richard startled and looked up in surprise, as if he'd forgotten AJ's presence in the room. "I won't let you break her heart."

"I never would."

"You already did." His eyes watered, and he pounded the desk. "You already did, Sully. And now she's dead. Aubrey's dead."

AJ froze, unsure how to respond. Aubrey, Shelby's grandmother, had died a long time ago. Perhaps Richard's grief over Joyanna had him confused.

"Are you all right? Richard?"

Tears flowed along the lines in Richard's cheeks. He wiped his face with a large white handkerchief, but the tears didn't stop. "It shouldn't have happened. None of it should have happened."

AJ rounded the desk and bent beside him. "What shouldn't have happened?"

"Aubrey and Thad." The words spewed out, seemingly propelled by anger. Then his tone abruptly changed to a gentle tenderness. "Sully loved her. But he broke her heart."

"I didn't know."

"Nobody knew. Except me." Richard swiped the handkerchief across his nose. He looked at AJ, and his vision seemed to clear as the past faded into memory. "AJ? Why are you here?"

"We were talking about Shelby."

"Ah yes. Lovely girl, my niece. So much like her grandmother."

"Richard, are you feeling all right? Would you like me to call someone?"

"I'm fine, fine. Just a little tired." He folded the handkerchief, dabbed at his face, then stuck the handkerchief in a pocket. "Is there anything I can do for you?"

"No." AJ shook his head and stood. "No, I was just leaving."

"Always good to see you. Please tell your grandmother I asked about her."

AJ hesitated, then inwardly sighed. "I'll do that."

When he reached the office door, he paused. Richard was already engrossed in a stack of papers, the fight between Brett and AJ apparently forgotten, the strange trip down memory lane as much a part of the past as the events he'd relived.

Chandra Coleman frowned when AJ stopped by her desk.

"I think you should keep an eye on Richard," AJ said. "He doesn't seem to be well."

"No wonder after the way you and Mr. Somers acted." Her voice wavered. Loyalty to her boss had overcome any reticence she may have had about chastising one of the bank's best customers. "You both should be ashamed of yourselves."

"I know. And I am." He examined his skinned knuckles, then met her gaze. Anger and disappointment hardened her eyes. "Richard seemed disoriented. He called me Sully."

Mrs. Coleman's expression softened. "He didn't."

"He thinks my grandmother is still alive."

"The poor, poor man." She shook her head and glanced at Richard's office door.

"You'll look in on him? Maybe you should call his daughter."

"I'll do that, Mr. Sullivan. Thank you for letting me know."

"I really am sorry about what happened in there."

"I believe you." She smiled slightly and spoke in a stage whisper. "And I daresay Mr. Somers deserved it. But you didn't hear that from me."

He grinned because she expected it. But as he walked out of the staid bank and into the bright sunshine of a simmering June day, his spirit sunk into gloom. He had awakened this morning concerned only with the pompous formality of hearing his grandmother's last wishes. That appointment, dreadful as it was, turned out to be the highlight of the day.

Except for spending time with Elizabeth and Tabby. He'd enjoyed their little girl chatter.

Too bad it had been overshadowed by the discovery that the other man in Shelby's life was none other than Brett.

Though nothing could beat the joy that coursed through his veins when the girls ran to him, so eager and happy.

To him. Not to Brett.

If only Shelby felt the same.

- 17 -

*B*rett kicked off his shoes and stretched out on Amy's couch. He'd prefer the peace and quiet of his own home after a day like today. But Tracie, the tiresome tart, had claimed that privilege for herself. She expected him for dinner, but facing her meant explaining the scrape on his jaw. Though it wasn't against his moral code to make up an interesting story, he didn't have the energy to endure her crocodile tears and hypocritical pampering.

On a day like today, the complex game he and his buddies had developed over the years was nothing but a tiresome complication.

"Take these." Amy handed him a couple of painkillers and a glass of water.

"Thanks." He downed them, then laid his head on a silk cushion.

"Hungry?"

"Not really."

"I could fix you an omelet."

He opened his eyes only wide enough to see her face. She sat in a chair across from him, her legs tucked beneath her. Her ash blonde hair flowed past her shoulders and halfway down her back. They'd inherited their coloring from dear old Dad. But Amy's oval face and spare chin reminded him of a photograph of their mother as a young woman. Dad had carried a print in his wallet, though it hadn't stopped him from romancing the ladies.

The airplane crash that killed their parents also destroyed the photograph. Now it was only a memory.

"Why are you staring at me?"

"I was just thinking about how much you resemble Mom."

"Mom was a brunette."

"You still look like her."

"You didn't answer me about the omelet."

"Maybe later."

Brett closed his eyes and tried to relax his tense muscles. His breathing settled into a steady rhythm, and for several minutes only the quiet hum of the air-conditioning made any sound.

"I told you it wouldn't work." Amy broke the silence. "Weeks have passed, and we're no closer to getting control of that land."

"It doesn't matter," he said wearily. "Someone somewhere will be eager to sell."

"I don't want 'someone somewhere.' I want Misty Willow and the acreage around it."

"Given the terms of Sully's will, you probably couldn't get it anyway. I'm surprised AJ figured out a loophole." Turning on his side, he studied the stubborn set of her features and prepared for an argument.

"And I can find another. My clients expect results."

"Give it up, Amy."

"I can't."

"Of course you can. It's not like you need the money."

"Do you think that's the reason? Money?"

"Isn't it?"

She played with the ends of her hair, unconsciously running her fingers through the silky strands. "How could you, of all people, be so naive? Money is only the means to an end."

"What end?"

"Power."

"I know my head's a little woozy thanks to our idiot cousin, but how does Misty Willow give you power?"

"My clients don't want the Glade Valley Refuge project to pass. They're paying me to make sure it doesn't."

"That part I know."

"What you don't know is that I have my eye on a state senator who has his eye on a congressional seat. And the surest way for him to get what he wants is for the Glade Valley project to become a reality." She leaned forward, her eyes gleaming with excitement. "It's unusual to find an issue supported by both the tree-huggers and the seed-planters. But both groups want this project."

"Seed-planters?"

"Farmers." Her dismissive tone revealed her disdain for the people who could give her what she wanted.

"That still doesn't explain your obsession with Misty Willow. Even if the Refuge passes and you're forced to find another property to appease your clients, it doesn't have to be Shelby's farm."

"It's not her farm. Not really."

"She has legal documents that say it is."

Amy straightened, and her blue eyes darkened. "You like her. Don't you?"

"She's . . . not what I expected."

"AJ has a thing for her too, you know."

"I don't care about AJ. And neither does Shelby."

"Are you sure?"

"She's told me."

"Her kids seem to like him. More than they like you."

"Yeah, well, they're kids." He shifted onto his back again and stared at the ceiling, reliving the moment in the café when Elizabeth and Tabby ran to AJ, overjoyed to see him. He wished he knew why.

"We can sue AJ." Amy's tone was meant to be nonchalant, but Brett detected her resolve. This state senator must be important to her. Strange she hadn't mentioned him before. He shifted again, trying to get comfortable. Maybe he should have gone home and faced Tracie instead of hiding out at Amy's. His sister's ambitious plans were worsening his headache.

"You want to sue your own cousin?" Brett exhaled in exasperation. "This isn't what Gran would want."

"Sully would understand."

"Sully died a bitter old man with more enemies than friends. Are you sure you want to follow in his footsteps?"

"I want to see how hard Shelby Kincaid will fight for her beloved farm. And how hard AJ will fight for her. Play your cards right, and she might come back to you for help."

Brett didn't bother to respond. After seeing the stricken look on Shelby's face and accepting he was the reason for it, he didn't expect her to ever speak to him again. Guilt nibbled at the edge of his conscience as he faced the truth.

Though they hadn't yet been on an official date, Shelby had shown him in a few short weeks what it had cost him to play his stupid games with women like Tracie. What once seemed entertaining now felt empty.

His cell buzzed, signaling a text from Tracie asking when he'd be home. Instead of answering, he flipped through the phone's photo album till he found a picture of Shelby taken outside the movie theater. Tracing her smile with his finger, he regretted what he'd never had.

∼

Standing by his bathroom sink, AJ winced as he dabbed an antiseptic ointment on his skinned knuckles. Glancing at his reflection, he frowned. Good-looking enough, judging by the giggles of his female students. But he didn't have his cousin's strong Nordic features.

Brett's gloating words mocked him.

I'd have given her back when I was done with her. I always do.

Jealousy, thin and strong as filament, wound itself around AJ's heart. Whose honor had he defended with that punch?

Shelby's? Meghan's?

Or his own?

He threw the ointment-stained washcloth in the hamper and retrieved a box from his bedroom closet. Lila jumped up on the bed, her hind legs stretched out at crooked angles, and he plopped beside her.

With time, his guilt and pain over Meghan had eased, yet she was always there, lingering on the edge of his mind. Preventing him from giving his heart to another. Not because he had loved her—though he had—but because he had failed her when she needed him most.

Lila nudged his hand, and he patted her shoulder before taking a deep breath and removing the box's lid. Rummaging beneath old letters and greeting cards, he found a small photo album with a brown suede cover.

The only tangible reminders of their autumn romance.

Memories washed over him as he studied each photo. Meghan at the park the day they met, khaki shorts revealing her gorgeous legs. The two of them at that little Mexican restaurant near her campus. A candid taken with his cell when she least expected it. Another, taken moments later. Her gray eyes sparkled as she smiled shyly for the camera. Smiled at him.

He flopped back on the bed with a groan, covering his eyes with his forearm. If only he could go back in time. If only he could have a second chance to make things right.

But it was too late. For him, and for Meghan. And from the look on Shelby's face this afternoon, he wouldn't get a second chance with her either. That realization hurt even more.

Lila rested her head on his chest, and he scratched behind her ears. "At least I've got you." She whimpered, and he clasped her paw. "You love me, don't you?"

A couple hours later, AJ awoke from a fitful nap disturbed by images of Tabby and Elizabeth. A third child played with Shelby's girls, but AJ couldn't make out the youngster's face. While he lay there, all the mistakes he'd made, all the hurts he'd caused, paraded in front of him.

Tired of guilt, tired of being afraid to love someone, he curled into a tight ball and whispered his prayer.

"O Lord. I know Shelby will never love me. My family has hurt her too much. But please show me how I can be her friend."

He took a couple of deep breaths, then wandered into the kitchen. As he poured a glass of sweet tea, an idea came to him. With Lila padding after him, he pulled Shelby's letter from the top drawer of his desk. The paper was wrinkled from his handling. Though he knew it from memory, he read it again, as if for the first time.

> *Dear Mr. Sullivan,*
>
> *Richard Grayson tells me you aren't interested in my offer to buy Misty Willow. I hope to change your mind. The house has been in my family since it was built by a long ago ancestor. I spent much of my childhood there, on weekends and in the summers. I'd like my children to know the heritage I still treasure and that was lost to us by means I don't understand.*
>
> *I remember one summer, when I was about ten years old. I was sitting with my grandfather on a stack of hay bales. Nanna's chickens were scratching in the dirt not far from us. "'So much depends,'" said Grandpa, smiling at me as he quoted William Carlos Williams's classic poem "The Red Wheelbarrow."*
>
> *Perhaps you know it.*
>
> *My grandpa loved that poem. He knew it by heart, and he taught it to me.*
>
> *From what my uncle Richard tells me, the house at Misty Willow hasn't been lived in since my grandparents died. It doesn't seem to mean much to you, Mr. Sullivan. But for me, everything depends on my children and me living on*

the farm our ancestors carved out of the wilderness over two hundred years ago.

I am pleading with you to reconsider my offer.

Very truly yours,
Shelby Lassiter Kincaid

He touched the blue ink, her neat handwriting, his fingertip tracing the flourish of her *S*. When Richard had given him the note, he'd opened it with idle curiosity. But her words had pressed into his heart until he wanted to know everything about the woman who had written them.

Her note had touched his heart. Perhaps he could thaw her heart with a note of his own.

He wrote what he wanted to say on a sheet of engraved stationery Gran had given him for Christmas a few years ago and folded it into an envelope. He picked up his keys, then put them down again. Shelby wouldn't like it if he showed up and her girls were happy to see him. He'd have to wait till later, when they were asleep, to deliver the note.

Remembering the way Elizabeth and Tabby had run to him in the café made him smile. Tabby's quick laughter and Elizabeth's serious demeanor whetted his yearning for a family of his own. He'd like to have daughters. Just like them.

Snatches of his earlier dream flitted at the edges of his mind. Elizabeth and Tabby playing with another child. A child without a name.

Find Meghan.

AJ started, and his heart raced. *I can't*, he protested. But the admonition, once planted, would not go away.

He battled with himself while he folded laundry, washed dishes, and even mopped the kitchen floor. Finally, he opened his laptop and found the site for the Columbus College of Art and Design. Searching through pages of the archived alumni newsletter, he eventually found a snippet of information. Meghan Jensen Mc-Curry had won an award for a stained-glass project titled *Diamond Morning*.

So she had married. Hope snapped the filament of jealousy that had earlier strangled him. If Meghan were happy, if she had found a man to love and to love her, perhaps she could forgive him. Then maybe he could forgive himself.

Did he dare to dream he'd be free to pursue Shelby's heart?

He did a search, using Meghan's name and the title of her artwork.

Pay dirt!

Her website appeared on the first page of the results. He clicked the link, and Meghan stared back at him. Her pale gray eyes, creased with the tiniest of lines, welcomed visitors to her site.

His head ached as he read her bio. Only one line, short and matter-of-fact, mentioned her attendance at CCAD. He rubbed the sting behind his eyes, acutely aware of why she had abandoned her studies.

The contact information listed an email address. But after all these years, an email seemed too impersonal. Besides, she'd probably delete a message from him without reading it.

Maneuvering around the site, he found a gallery in Brennan Grove, Michigan, that displayed her work. Before he could talk himself out of it, he looked up the address on a navigation program.

Brennan Grove showed up as a tiny dot north of Toledo. AJ leaned back in his chair, rapping out a rhythm on his desk. Only a few hours away.

The thought startled him, followed an instant later by an astonishing assurance that he needed to see Meghan.

But first, he had to see Shelby.

After shutting down the computer, he gathered his keys.

And his courage.

- 18 -

*A*fter kissing her girls good night, Shelby carried a glass of lemonade to the front porch and gazed out over her front lawn. Tiny pinpoints of light glowed in the shadows of evening. Before going to bed, Elizabeth and Tabby had chased the elusive fireflies, catching a few in their jelly jars.

Shelby freed the blinking insects, wishing she could rid herself of her troubles so easily. Embarrassment and guilt pressed into her heart. *Why, God?* she silently prayed. *Why did I even think of letting another man into my life?*

Hard to believe, but she missed her courtship days with Gary. Fun, laughing days when the future beckoned with promising dreams and happily ever after. Tears burned her eyes, and she swiped them away.

All things work together for good.

The Scripture came, unbidden, into her mind, and she grimaced. She'd heard Romans 8:28 repeated so often the verse held little meaning.

All things work together for good to those who are called according to his purpose.

"It's a promise," Dad had often said, encouraging his family to trust in God's providence no matter their circumstances. But it had been a long time since Shelby believed the promise was meant for her.

Certainly no good had come from her grandparents' deaths or from the family losing Misty Willow.

Nothing good?

Her parents would never have gone to the mission field if not for the earlier tragedy.

"The price was too high," she argued, bowing her head.

All things.

Suddenly tired, Shelby settled into the soft cushions of the new porch swing. Up the road, headlights came around the curve. When the vehicle turned into her drive, she recognized AJ's Jeep. Her stomach tightened, and she resisted the impulse to run inside and lock the door.

Better to face him now, when the girls were sleeping, than endure the embarrassment of them climbing all over him if he dropped in tomorrow.

She stayed seated as he parked in front of the porch. As he came toward her, Lila trotted past him and poked Shelby's hand with her nose.

"Hey there, girl." Avoiding AJ's gaze, Shelby rubbed the lab's silky ears. Lila pressed against her legs, then lay down at her feet.

"Hello from me too." He stuck one hand in his jeans pocket and leaned against the porch's wooden column.

"Hi."

"Are the girls asleep?"

"They're supposed to be."

"I thought you'd prefer it if I stopped by after they went to bed."

"Stopped by for what?"

"To give you this."

She took the envelope and examined the bold writing, a legible mix of print and cursive that conveyed confidence.

"What's this?"

"Just read it. After I'm gone."

"Okay."

Chirping crickets and musical frogs, the night's rural orchestra, filled the awkward silence. The swing creaked as her foot pushed against the porch, and the gentle motion eased her tension.

"I'm going out of town tomorrow." He shifted, and the meager light from the house briefly revealed his tired eyes and grim expression. "When I get back, I'll bring over the things from Gran. If that's all right with you."

"I recognized the items in the photos. They were Nanna's."

"Gran left a note saying she bought them at the estate sale. For safekeeping, she said."

"I'm glad of it." At least one of the Sullivans felt remorse for what they'd done to her family, though spending time with AJ was teaching her that he was more like his gran than his grandfather. She met his gaze and gave him a brief smile. "So where are you going? Another camping trip?"

"There's something I need to take care of." He shrugged, obviously ill at ease. "Something I should have taken care of a long time ago."

Dread filled her stomach. "Does this have to do with Misty Willow?"

"My cousins want the farm."

"Why?"

"So they can sell it to some developer."

"Brett thought he could persuade me to give up this place?" Her heart lurched, and she closed her eyes as she remembered Brett's insistence she'd be happier in a newer home. She had foolishly allowed herself to wonder if he'd been thinking of their future together. How utterly stupid she had been.

AJ shifted uncomfortably. "Brett doesn't date moms."

The words hurt, their truth a slender arrow into her heart. "He had to know I wouldn't give up this place."

"I told him that." AJ removed his ball cap, wincing as he ran his fingers through his hair.

"What happened to your hand?"

"I hit something," he said sheepishly.

"Brett?"

"Yeah."

"Did he hit you back?" The concern in her voice surprised her. AJ too, by his expression.

The door flew open, and Elizabeth scurried outside. Clad in a pink gingham nightgown and barefoot, she knelt beside Lila.

"Young lady, what are you doing out of bed?"

"I heard you talking to Mr. AJ, and I came out to play with Lila."

"It's time for sleeping, not playing."

"Can Lila sleep with me?"

"Afraid not, sunshine," AJ said. "She's got to get up early in the morning."

"Are you going camping again?"

"No, just taking a little trip."

"And Lila's going too?"

"Not this time."

Elizabeth's mouth formed a horrified O. "You're going to leave her all alone?"

AJ chuckled. "She won't be alone. I'm taking her to a place that keeps dogs when the owners go away."

"Can't she stay with me?" Elizabeth turned from AJ to Shelby as tears welled up in her eyes. "Please, Mommy. Don't make Lila go to the keeping place."

"Honey, I'm sure Mr. AJ knows what's best for Lila."

"But she wants to stay with me. I know she does." Elizabeth stood, and Lila scrambled to her feet. Swiping her eyes, Elizabeth laid her hand on the dog's head. "I'll take good care of her, Mr. AJ. I promise I will."

He looked helplessly at Shelby and she lifted her shoulders in resignation. "I don't mind if you don't."

"Are you sure?"

"I'm sure." She'd take care of his dog, get Nanna's furniture

144

from him, and then that would be it. No more contact between them.

And this time she meant it.

Elizabeth squealed with glee. "Come on, Lila. You can sleep with me." She hurried back into the house before the grown-ups could change their minds, Lila trotting right beside her.

Another thing to add to the list. Get Elizabeth her own pet.

"Why do I feel like I just lost my dog?"

Shelby stifled a chuckle. "I promise you can have her back."

"I'll drop off her food and a few toys in the morning. If you're sure this is okay."

"I don't think I can pry her away from Elizabeth now." Shelby stood and joined him at the porch rail. "How long will you be gone?"

"Two or three days. Not long."

"You better give me your phone number." She opened her phone to add his contact info. "In case we need to reach you."

"Sure."

They exchanged numbers, and Shelby walked with him to the Jeep. He started to open the door, then faced her. "Will you pray for me? For this thing I have to do." His voice trailed off into the darkness.

Pray for AJ? After all he'd done?

Her mind reeled, clicking off the things "he'd done." Finding a way around Sully's will so she could live in this house. Sheltering her children from a storm. Letting Elizabeth keep Lila.

Always telling her the truth even when it was hard.

"I'll pray for you," she said, her voice barely above a whisper.

"Thank you." He brushed her arm, his touch feather light against her skin. "Good night."

She watched his taillights, mesmerized and lonely, as he drove away. When the Jeep disappeared around the curve, she went inside and checked on the girls. Elizabeth was already asleep, Lila beside her on the bed.

Curling up in the wing chair by the fireplace, Shelby opened AJ's envelope.

> *Dear Shelby,*
> *I know my family has hurt you. Right now, I'd give just about anything not to be a Sullivan. Or at least not to have Brett for a cousin. Except he is and so is Amy. And the truth is, despite our differences, they're still my family. The only family I have.*
> *I'm sorry for all the pain the Sullivans have caused the Lassiters. But isn't it time we put an end to our grandparents' feud? Their fight doesn't have to be ours.*
> *Please tell me that we can be friends.*
>
> *AJ*

He wanted her prayers and her forgiveness? He had no idea what he was asking.

All things work together for good. The phrase echoed in her thoughts.

Not for her they didn't.

All her heartaches could be traced back to the Sullivans.

It wasn't true, but she had blamed them for so long that it felt true.

But the truth, and she had to admit it, was that AJ Sullivan was a decent guy. Elizabeth and Tabby adored him. And pretty much ignored Brett.

Was it possible her children had more sense than she did?

Before Shelby slipped between her covers, she knelt beside her bed. Struggling to find the right words to express her mixed-up feelings, she finally whispered, "Father, I'm sorry. My heart just hurts so much. Please help me. And be with AJ too, and whatever it is he's doing."

- 19 -

AJ drove north, following the directions given by his GPS. The memories he'd hidden away for the past several years threatened to boil over and scald his heart. Pushing through the searing pain, he prayed for guidance.

At the next rest area, he parked and wandered to a secluded picnic table. He couldn't put off the memories much longer, not if there was a possibility of seeing Meghan anytime soon.

What would she do when she saw him? The insistent question prickled his skin, and he scratched his arm. Why had he even come?

Because of Shelby.

He sat on the edge of the table, his feet planted on the bench, and rested his head on the heels of his hands. How could asking Meghan's forgiveness change things with Shelby? Especially after Brett's stupid little game.

A calm assurance eased his pain. He didn't have the answers, but he served a God who did. A God who forgave even the worst of sins. AJ grasped that truth, wordlessly praying as the memories gushed over him.

He was in his first year of law school at Ohio State University, swamped with reading assignments. But the Indian summer day, the sun blazing on red and gold leaves, enticed him from the law library. He took his books to a park not far from his grandparents' home and stretched out on a gently sloping bank leading to a sun-dappled lake. While he napped, Meghan had photographed him as part of her assignment on the urban landscape. She was a junior in a fine arts program at Columbus College of Art and Design.

When he woke, she asked him to sign a release. Naturally, he'd insisted on seeing the photographs. Which led to him renting a paddleboat, then an impromptu supper date at a taco stand. Neither one finished their assignments that day.

Enchanted by Meghan's soft Southern accent, AJ asked her to dinner the following weekend. Juggling their schedules, they spent as much time together as they could that semester.

As Christmas neared, AJ shopped for a special gift, finally deciding on an engraved locket. He planned to give it to her at the annual holiday reception hosted by his grandparents. It was the first time she had met his family.

The first time Meghan met Brett.

I'd have given her back when I was done with her. I always do.

∼

Her head pounding after a restless night's sleep, Shelby shooed the girls and Lila outside after breakfast. She downed the rest of her coffee, then carried a canvas tote containing a three-ring binder and laptop to the patio. Photos of garden retreats overwhelmed her Pinterest boards, and articles torn from gardening magazines bulged from her notebook.

Time to make a few landscaping decisions.

Outside the kitchen door, she almost stumbled on a bag of dog food next to a box with dishes, a leash, and a few toys. She found a ball and threw it out to the grassy oval where Lila played with the girls. The retriever raced after the ball, Elizabeth and Tabby chasing after her.

Lila snatched up the ball and proudly delivered it to Shelby. "Such a good girl," she said, patting the dog's wiggly body. When

Elizabeth reached the patio's bottom step, Shelby tossed her the ball. "Here you go."

"Thanks, Mommy." Elizabeth grabbed the ball with both hands and threw it into the yard. "C'mon, Lila. Go get it!" Lila took off, and so did Elizabeth.

"Let Tabby have a turn too."

"I will," she called over her shoulder.

Shelby settled in a wicker rocker and sighed with deep contentment as she surveyed this bit of her land. The graveled driveway stretched from the road and past the house till it faded into a hard-packed lane near the pasture. The drive also looped next to the house to enclose a large grassy area long ago dubbed the oval.

Along the fence beyond the drive, Paul Norris's son Seth had prepared a long flower bed. The hydrangeas, daisies, marigolds, and petunias Shelby had planted shortly after the move now thrived. Only one other element was needed to set off the purple, yellow, and white blooms, and she was on the lookout for just the right thing.

In her grandparents' time, a ring of stones had formed a gathering place for campfires on the far side of the grassy oval. Only a few of the rocks remained beneath the shelter of two towering oaks.

Grandpa had transported the rocks from Glade Creek. Surely she could too. Maybe AJ would help.

She frowned.

Forget AJ. She could do this herself.

She opened her binder and sifted through photos of lush flowerbeds, wild roses growing along fencerows, colorful blooms bordered by fragile violets, and an assortment of statuary.

Selecting a few favorites for inspiration, she sketched several layouts for the memorial garden to honor her grandparents. Engrossed in her planning, she barely registered the crunch of tires on gravel and the soft whir of an engine until Lila's sharp bark caught her attention. A silver minivan stopped near the patio, and the side door slid open.

Austin Owens, a miniature Jason with his red hair sticking out from beneath a ball cap, jumped from the side, waved at Shelby, and sped toward Elizabeth. Cassie emerged from the front with a bulging grocery sack. "Hi, neighbor. I brought you something."

Shelby set aside her notebook and walked to the edge of the patio. "I thought you were still out of town. How was the wedding?"

"Perfect." Cassie climbed the steps, straining under the weight of the brown paper bag. Shelby reached to help, but Cassie twisted away. "Just get me to the kitchen. Fast."

Shelby opened the kitchen door and steered Cassie inside. She dropped the bag on the table and flamboyantly plopped into a chair. "My sister was a lovely bride, and now she and her new hubby are honeymooning in the Caribbean."

"Lucky them." Shelby took two glasses from the cupboard. "Iced tea?"

"Sure, thanks. Mom cried forever, but I guess that was to be expected. All her babies grown up. After all the wedding festivities were over, it was nice to spend a couple extra days at the old home place."

"Do you wish you still lived there? Near family?"

Cassie tilted her head in thought. "I love going back for the big family events and holidays. But my home is here with Jason."

"'Whither thou goest' and all that?"

"I suppose." She gave Shelby a quizzical look. "I just know I love our farm. Speaking of which . . ." Reaching into the sack, she dramatically pulled out a giant zucchini. "Ta-da! Fresh off the vine. I picked them this morning from my garden."

Shelby hefted the zucchini. "It's huge."

"You'll take them, won't you?"

"Absolutely, thank you." She moved the bag to the counter and sat across from Cassie. "Next year I'll have my own garden produce to share."

"So what's been going on with you while I've been gone? I see you've got a dog."

"That's Lila. We're dog-sitting."

"Lila?" Cassie's eyes widened with curiosity, and she scooted her chair closer to the table. "AJ Sullivan's dog?"

"I know what you're thinking, but it's not like that."

"Not like what?"

"He was over here last night." Shelby reddened as Cassie's smile brightened. "He said he was going away, and Elizabeth heard, and . . . well, we've got Lila."

"Where did he go?"

"I don't know. He just said he had something to do." Shelby absent-mindedly twirled the ice in her glass. "He asked me to pray for him."

Cassie's amused smile faded. "What's wrong, Shelby?"

"He didn't tell me."

"I mean with you. Something's happened, I can tell."

Shelby hesitated, unsure whether to trust Cassie. She'd been burnt in the past after confiding in someone who pretended to be her friend. Since then, she'd been leery of entering into a close friendship with anyone. But Cassie wasn't just anyone. She was Jason's wife, and that meant something. He wouldn't have fallen in love with anyone who was unkind or judgmental.

The day Cassie had helped Shelby paint, before the move from Chicago, she brought along a couple of other women from church. Though they'd chatted about mutual friends, the conversation never slipped into idle gossip. Cassie, especially, seemed to think the best of everybody.

"I know we haven't known each other very long," Cassie said. "But I'd like us to be friends."

"I'd like that too." Shelby breathed a prayer for courage and took a deep breath. "I've been not-dating this guy. Brett."

"Not-dating?"

"It's stupid, I know."

"No, it's not." Cassie folded her hands and propped up her chin. Her eyes narrowed with sudden insight. "You're not talking about Brett Somers, are you?"

"You know him?"

"Not really. I mean, I know he's AJ's cousin and too gorgeous for his own good, but that's about it." Her eyes grew large, and she smacked the table. "You're *dating* AJ's cousin?"

"No, we're not-dating."

"What does that even mean?"

"We've gone out a couple of times, but not on a real date. That was supposed to be tonight. But yesterday . . . I didn't know he and AJ were cousins until yesterday."

"And that's a problem why?"

"Because Brett wasn't dating me for me." Shelby stood and rinsed her glass. Through the window, squirrels chased each other up, down, and around a red maple while a starling scolded them from its perch on a fence post.

Tears welled up in Shelby's eyes. "He wants to take the farm. AJ found out, and he hit him, and now he's gone, and . . ." The rest of her words drowned in the tears spilling down her cheeks. She grabbed a paper towel from the holder and tried to stem the flow. "I'm sorry."

"There's no need to apologize. You're hurting, and a good cry will ease the pain."

"I'm not sure about that." The words came out in a halting stammer.

"Me either." Cassie tore off another paper towel sheet and handed it to Shelby. "But it's something my grandma used to say, so I figure it must be true whether I believe it or not."

"Grandmas know best."

"They often do." She laid a sympathetic hand on Shelby's arm. "Now tell me again what happened. Start at the beginning. Who hit who?"

Despite the lump clogging her throat, Shelby laughed at Cassie's bossy curiosity. "I'll tell you everything, but I better check on the kids first."

"I'll do that. You go freshen up."

Shelby nodded her appreciation and headed for the bathroom. After splashing water on her aching eyes, she joined Cassie outside.

While the children played freeze tag, she told Cassie about Brett's attentive charm, the incident in the café, and AJ's late-night visit. Comforted by Cassie's intuitive understanding, Shelby tried to untangle her knotted emotions.

"From the first time we met, I wondered why Brett would be interested in a stay-at-home mom. But I liked him. And I thought he liked me."

"How did you meet him?"

"My great-uncle introduced us, so it's hard for me to believe he knew Brett's plan. But when I look back on that evening, I can't help feeling like it was a setup."

"Have you talked to your uncle about it?"

"I thought about calling him last night after AJ left. But this morning, I didn't want to think about it. So I planned Nanna's memorial garden instead." Shelby gestured at the notebook lying on the wicker table between their chairs.

Cassie smiled, then focused on the playing children. After a few moments, she faced Shelby. "The girls can come to my house for a while if you want to go into town."

"To talk to Richard?"

"It might help to know his part in all this."

Shelby picked at a piece of loose wicker in the chair arm. "You really don't mind watching the girls?"

"I'd love to."

"Then I'll call Richard and ask him to meet me this afternoon." Shelby pulled out her phone and scrolled through her contacts. "I need to call Mandy, Paul Norris's daughter too. She was going to babysit tonight."

"So you're not keeping your date with Brett?"

"Absolutely not." Shelby hit the send button and made a pouty face. "Though I spent too much money on a new dress."

"Ooh, I want to see it."

Shelby held up her index finger. "Hello, Uncle Richard. It's me, Shelby."

– 20 –

A bell tinkled as AJ entered the gallery, a corner brick building on a quaint street designed to appeal to tourists with its gift shops, restaurants, and courthouse-turned-museum. He stood awkwardly, hands jammed in pockets, in the stillness of the space. Long shelves held a variety of pottery, vases, bowls, and mugs. Painted canvases decorated the walls. Frames of stained glass hung at varying heights in front of the windows, the sun's rays brightening the rich reds, blues, and greens.

He stepped closer to one, a framed rectangle of a brown tree, its branches extending over a broad stream. Wildflowers, purple and red and yellow, grew along the bank, their vibrant colors made brighter by the morning sun. It reminded him of Glade Creek.

"May I help you?"

The voice startled him, and he quickly turned.

A petite woman with spectacles hanging on a chain around her neck smiled at him. "That's a beautiful piece, isn't it? It was designed and created by one of our local artists."

"Meghan McCurry?"

"How did you know?"

"Lucky guess."

"Professionally, she goes by Meghan Jensen. Are you familiar with her work?"

"Not lately, no. I'd like to purchase this one."

"Without asking the price?"

He reddened slightly as dollar signs practically replaced her pupils, then handed over his credit card. "I'm sure it's worth whatever it costs."

"I wish more of our visitors shared your attitude." She put on her reading glasses and glanced at his card. "Anderson J. Sullivan."

"Please, call me AJ."

"AJ Sullivan." She said his name slowly then peered at him over the rim of her glasses. "Meghan didn't tell me she had contacted you, though I'm glad she did. I was tempted to myself, but she'd have been so very angry if I did anything like that behind her back. None of that matters now. At least you're finally here. But why didn't you go straight to the hospital?"

AJ held out his hands, palms forward, in a vain attempt to slow down the woman's rapid speech. In the jumble of words, he pulled out the most important ones.

"Is Meghan in the hospital?"

"She's been there since the accident. Didn't she tell you?"

"I haven't talked to Meghan in years."

"Then how did you know?"

"Know what?"

"About Jonah."

"Who's Jonah?"

The woman heaved an expansive sigh and leaned against the counter. She seemed to have spent all her words in the roundabout conversation that had left both of them confused.

AJ recovered first. "Where can I find Meghan?"

"If she didn't call you, then perhaps she doesn't want you to find her."

"I'll go to every hospital in the region if I have to. Please don't make me."

"Why did you come here, Mr. Sullivan?"

"You'll probably think I'm crazy."

"Try me."

"God led me here."

"I don't think that's crazy at all." She sighed again. "You'll find Meghan in the trauma unit at Toledo Regional."

"Is she all right? I mean, what's wrong with her?"

"Just go to her. She needs you."

~

Entering the coffee shop, Shelby joined Richard at a corner table. He rose, and she pecked him on his papery cheek before sitting in the chair he held out for her.

"Sorry I'm late," she said. "UPS stopped by as I was getting in the car." The cookie jar for AJ had finally arrived, but there had been no time to open the package. She hoped it was an exact replica of the one Tabby had broken.

"You're not late at all." Richard patted her hand. "Where are your darling daughters?"

"With Cassie Owens. You may remember that her husband Jason and I were childhood friends."

"I know Jason and Cassie. Not well, but I see them around town once in a while."

"They've been very welcoming."

"I'm glad to hear it. I want you to be as happy here as you were when you were a little girl." The corners of his mouth tilted, and he gave her a teasing look.

They engaged in idle chitchat till the waitress delivered their orders of strawberry shortcake and coffee. Shelby stirred extra sweetener in her cup, her attention focused on the dissolving granules.

"It's nice to get together with you like this, Shelby. But I have a feeling this isn't a social visit. Why don't you tell me what's bothering you?"

Richard's smooth voice reminded her of her grandfather. Not

that Grandpa ever spoke with such perfect diction. But the concern for her, the warmth of affection was the same. If only he were here now, sitting across from her in this little place. Try as he might, Richard could never fill Grandpa's boots.

She raised her eyes to his, catching a flicker of irritation before his expression softened. Surely she had imagined it. Why should he be irritated at her? He was the one who had lied. Willing her voice not to quiver, she tapped her spoon against the cup's rim. "Why didn't you tell me?"

"Tell you what?"

"That Brett was related to the Sullivans. That he's AJ's cousin."

She searched his age-creased eyes for the answer and saw them darken, shadowed by fear. His smile dispelled the shadow, but it had been there. She wasn't imagining things. What was Richard afraid of?

"I thought you knew." His placating tone barely concealed an odd quiver. "Brett didn't tell you?"

"No, he didn't." Her voice rose in pitch, and she glanced around the shop to see if anyone had heard her. Fortunately, the guy at the nearest table was engrossed in whatever was happening on his laptop screen. Sipping the too-hot coffee to hide her uneasiness, she scalded her tongue. This wasn't going at all well.

"Brett is quite taken with you. Perhaps, knowing how you felt about his grandfather, he wanted you to get to know him without that prejudice." He took her hand in his, his palm clammy against hers. She resisted the urge to pull away. "Would you have given him a chance otherwise?"

"That wasn't why he didn't tell me."

"Then what was?"

If Richard knew Brett's plan, he hid it well. The fear, if that's what it was, had disappeared. Now his light blue eyes showed a curious concern. As he leaned back in his chair, he released her hand.

"Brett hoped to talk me into selling the farm." She jabbed a strawberry with her fork and dipped it into the whipped cream.

"For some kind of development project he and his sister dreamed up."

"He should have known better." Richard chuckled, a hollow and cheerless sound, and the shadow returned. Shelby dropped her fork, its clatter on the floor barely penetrating her senses.

"You knew it." She barely whispered the accusation.

Richard opened his mouth, then closed it again as his shoulders slumped. Impossibly, he appeared to age before her eyes as his tensed jaw emphasized the hollows in his cheeks. Perspiration dotted his forehead as he rummaged through his jacket pocket and slipped something in his mouth.

Concern overshadowed Shelby's anger. "Are you all right?"

He sipped water, then dabbed at his lips with a napkin. "I'm fine. Nothing wrong with me except old age." His attempt at a smile failed, and he lowered his eyes.

"Tell me the truth, Uncle Richard. Were you in on Brett's plan?"

"No." His eyes glistened with regret and something deeper that Shelby couldn't comprehend. "He only asked me to introduce you. I didn't ask him why."

"I find that hard to believe."

He sighed heavily. "His grandfather and I were friends for many years, Shelby. Now that Sully is gone, I have a responsibility to his grandchildren."

"You were more than friends with my grandfather. Nanna was your sister."

"True." The sadness in his voice pressed against Shelby's heart. His eyes looked beyond her, into a past before her time. "We were great friends, Sully and me. Always were. We knew Thad too, but he didn't socialize much. Too busy working on his parents' farm. But then the three of us—Sully, Thad, and me—we got our draft letters. We went through basic training together, shipped out to Korea together. For a while we were like the Three Musketeers. But it couldn't last. Too many things changed between us because of that war."

"What things?" Shelby whispered the question, fearful of breaking the spell that held Richard in its grasp. He shivered, then gazed at her with clear eyes. Affection softened his expression.

"If we hadn't become soldiers, your grandmother would have married Anderson Sullivan."

Shelby gasped, but Richard continued. "And I would have married Joyanna."

"But how—"

"Thad came home first, severely wounded. He and Aubrey spent a great deal of time together. By the time Sully and I came home"—he shrugged—"they were making wedding plans."

Memories of her grandparents flitted through her mind. The special way they looked at one another, the gentle touches that whispered a deep abiding love. A match made in heaven, Grandpa always said. It's what she had dreamed of for herself. What she expected to have with Gary.

Richard's voice drew her from the quicksand of regret. "Sully never recovered from Aubrey's betrayal."

"Nanna would never betray anyone." Would she?

"Sully believed she did. They fought, he and Thad. But in Aubrey's eyes, Sully's bitterness only confirmed she had chosen the right man."

Another puzzle piece clicked into place, revealing Anderson Sullivan's reason for taking Misty Willow, for leaving the house to deteriorate.

"He waited a long time to exact his revenge," she said, her voice trembling. "And it cost my grandparents, cost me, our heritage."

The shadow flitted once more across Richard's face. "It destroyed Sully too." His expression softened. "And Joyanna."

The photograph of AJ's grandmother she had seen in his cottage appeared in her mind's eye. This lovely woman had comforted Shelby when grief over all she had lost threatened to destroy her.

"They were friends, weren't they? My grandmother and Joyanna."

"The best of friends. Until Joyanna married Sully. She thought she could reconcile them, but Sully was too stubborn."

"I should have guessed it before now. They both loved irises. Cary Grant." A sudden longing overcame her to share this news-flash with AJ. Their grandfathers may have been rivals, but their grandmothers had been friends. No wonder Joyanna cared so much about returning Misty Willow to Shelby.

The wrinkles creasing Richard's face seemed to deepen with remembrance and loss.

"You never stopped loving Joyanna. Did you?"

Crimson spots highlighted his cheeks, and he cleared his throat. "The past no longer matters, Shelby. You have Misty Willow, and Brett can't take it away from you. I promise you, with all that is in me, I will not let him."

~

AJ took a deep breath and knocked on the hospital room door before entering. A sandy-haired boy covered with white linens lay in the bed. His pale face looked almost waxen, while an assortment of wires attached him to various monitors. The woman sitting in the chair next to him stared at AJ as she stood.

Meghan.

Her hair, only a shade lighter than her son's, was pulled back in a quick ponytail, and fine lines creased the edges of her gray eyes.

"I've been praying for a miracle." She crossed her arms in front of her chest as if to shut him out. Her lips pressed into a thin line that tightened her chin into a point. "I didn't expect God to send me you."

"I didn't expect to find you had a child. Is he . . . is he mine?" AJ's heart thumped, loud and hard, as the anger in her eyes faded, revealing naked vulnerability. She was afraid of him, and that knowledge pushed him to reach across the bed to her. She drew back, and he let his arm drop to his side. "Why didn't you tell me? I thought you had an—"

160

"That only shows how little you knew me."

"I was wrong." His voice sounded loud in the quiet room. "Wrong to let you go when you needed help."

"Your grandfather was generous." Her words dropped like heavy stones upon packed dirt, solid thuds against his heart.

Remorse squeezed his chest, and a pent-up anger he had never acknowledged welled within him. His eyes stung as guilt gripped his throat. He tried to speak, swallowed, and tried again, forcing the raw words out of his mouth. "What happened to him?"

She tenderly brushed the boy's bangs from his forehead. His eyes seemed to flicker beneath his thin lids. "A car accident. I haven't prayed in a long time, but I've been on my knees again and again the past couple of days, begging God to help my boy."

Her sharp eyes penetrated AJ's as she challenged him with her words. "Are you the answer to my prayer? Will you help us?"

"I won't abandon you, Meghan. Not this time." He laid his hand on the boy's slender shoulder.

Closing his eyes, he said a silent prayer for Jonah. For his son.

– 21 –

*B*rett rotated his phone, tapping the ends on Amy's kitchen counter. Throughout the day he'd ignored Tracie's frequent calls and texts until she threatened to call the local hospitals and the police. He replied in all caps: GO AWAY!

She didn't respond.

Rotate, tap. Rotate, tap.

He should call his apartment's concierge service and arrange for a new lock. Third time this year. A guy never knew if the scorned lady had made a copy. It happened once to a buddy of his. Since that unfortunate mishap, "change locks" had been immediately added to *The Professional Man's Guide to Breaking Up*, an imaginary checklist often referred to by the Monday night regulars at Gallagher's.

A couple of the guys were going to the benefit for the wounded military tonight. They wanted to meet the widowed mom he'd told them about. Truth be told, he had looked forward to showing off his brown-haired, green-eyed date.

Shelby might not be a Tracie. But then Tracie definitely was no Shelby.

He was confident that by evening's end the other guys would have slipped their Golden Date tokens into his hand—tokens he'd later redeem for beers. He wouldn't have told them Shelby wasn't staying the night at his place, an automatic disqualification in the Golden Date contest.

It was all part of the game.

Rotate, tap. Rotate, tap.

The apartment door opened, and Amy entered the kitchen, lugging groceries. "Why are you still here?"

"Hello to you too."

"Playing hooky, are we?"

"I only had a couple of appointments. Canceled them." He stretched across the counter's upper level for the grocery bag. "Anything good in here?"

"Not for you." Amy moved the bag out of his reach. "Sorry to do this, but you've got to go."

"Expecting company?"

"That state senator I was telling you about is coming over. For a strategy session."

"And to break a few ethics rules? You need to be careful, Amy."

"I know what I'm doing."

"Sure you do."

She turned her back on him and retrieved a bottle of white wine from the fridge. "Aren't you going to that charity thing tonight?"

"Looking like this?" He touched his chin and winced. The bruised scrape jagged along his jawline. "Besides, I no longer have a date."

Amy smirked. "Did the high-and-mighty Shelby Kincaid cancel on you?"

"I haven't heard from her, but I think that's a safe bet."

"You never know. She could be pulling her little black dress out of mothballs right now. Praying it still fits."

"Save the claws for someone who deserves them."

"She doesn't?" She poured wine in a goblet without offering a glass to him. "Her sentimental yearning for that blasted farm is causing all kinds of trouble for me."

"You act as if AJ would have turned over the deed to you."

"He hated the place till she came along."

"What about the other farmers? Misty Willow isn't big enough on its own for what you want."

"They have their weaknesses."

"Oh, do they?"

"Everyone does." She sipped her wine, then slowly traced the rim with her manicured finger. "We only need to discover what they are."

"You're not going to give up, are you?"

"The lawsuit will be filed next week."

"On what grounds?"

"Violating the spirit of Sully's intentions."

"That will never hold up."

"Perhaps not." She arched her eyebrows and shrugged. "But I have more resources than Shelby Kincaid. She won't last long."

Grabbing the wine bottle, he checked the label and swigged a mouthful.

"Don't do that. Gross." Amy wrestled the bottle from him and wiped the opening with a dishcloth. "Go home, would you?"

He stood and pocketed his phone. "Tracie might be there."

"Your problem, not mine."

"How long is the senator staying?"

She gave him a stony look, her clear blue eyes flashing fire. "Bye, Brett."

"I'm going." He gathered his keys and headed for the door. With his hand on the knob, he paused. "You know, Shelby might be stronger than you think."

Amy came out from behind the counter and crossed her arms. The tension in her slender posture screamed defiance, but the quiver in her voice exposed her vulnerability. "Whose side are you on?"

When Mom and Dad had fought, screaming vile names at each other, Amy would huddle close to him with her hands over her ears. After the divorce, he'd refused to let them use her as a pawn, risking his parents' wrath to defend her. His role of protector would never change.

"It's always us, Amy. No matter who gets in the way."

She smiled and hugged his arm. "Call me tomorrow, okay? Just not too early."

"Sure."

He said good night and headed to the parking garage. To avoid taking Tracie to the charity event, he'd led her to believe he was going on a weekend golfing trip with a few buddies. She hadn't minded, probably seeing it as an opportunity to secretly move more of her belongings into his place.

He slid into his Lexus, unsure where to go. He'd had the perfect life until Shelby Kincaid showed up. Maybe Amy was right. Maybe forcing Shelby out of Misty Willow would return his world to normal.

Of course it would.

When the skies rained gold coins.

~

Carrying a cafeteria tray, AJ followed Meghan to a secluded corner table. His appetite had disappeared in the trauma unit when a nurse explained Jonah's numerous injuries, but he sensed Meghan hadn't eaten much in the past couple of days. She'd been reluctant to leave the room despite the nurse encouraging them both to take a supper break.

He sat across from her and unwrapped his Italian sub. "Nice-looking salad you've got there."

"They have a lot of options on their salad bar."

"Benefit of a big hospital, I guess." He silently kicked himself. "I didn't mean—"

"I know." She moved the greens around with her fork. "This place puts everybody on edge."

While they ate, AJ resisted the urge to bombard her with questions. Instead he talked about teaching and his recent camping trip while Meghan did a fairly good impression of being interested.

When she shoved away the remains of her salad, he gathered their plates on the tray. "Would you like dessert?"

"I should get back to Jonah." She started to rise, but he grasped her arm.

"Not yet."

She reluctantly sat. "What is it?"

"I want to know how it happened, what the doctors are saying." The words came out in a rush, and he took a moment to calm down and soften his voice. "I want to know everything."

Silence filled the narrow space between them. Meghan tugged her shirt sleeves to her wrists as if she were cold, then fidgeted with her soda straw.

"Why isn't your husband here?"

"Ex-husband," she said emphatically and gulped. "He's in jail."

"Jail?" he asked in disbelief.

"He was driving. Drunk." She momentarily closed her eyes. "Jonah wasn't supposed to be in that car. Travis took him, and I didn't even know until the police came."

"How could you not know?"

Her gray eyes darted to his, and she pressed her lips into a thin line. When she finally spoke, her voice was raw and hoarse. "I have no idea what brought you here. Coincidence? God?" She shrugged, lifting her shoulders high for emphasis. "But understand this. I'm the only parent Jonah knows. And I won't allow you, or anyone else, to waltz in here and give me the third degree."

"I have the right to know how he ended up in that hospital bed," AJ shot back. "And why I never even knew he existed until today."

"I wanted him." She wrapped her arms across her stomach. "I couldn't risk anyone taking him from me."

His flash of anger subsided, replaced by regret. "If I'd known, I would have married you."

"Your grandfather would never have permitted that. He'd have disowned you."

"He did that anyway."

Her eyes widened. "Why?"

"I finally decided to stand up to him, but it was too late. You were already gone." He crumpled his napkin into a tight ball. "I dropped out of law school. He never forgave me."

She glanced at his left hand. "You're not married?"

"No." He grinned, remembering Elizabeth's comical goof. "There's no Mrs. Fourth."

"What?"

"Just a silly joke."

Meghan sipped her soda, then placed the cup on the cafeteria tray. "I've been gone too long."

"Don't shut me out, Meghan. Not anymore."

She sighed heavily. "There's something you should know."

"Tell me."

She wavered, biting her lip as her forehead creased in thought. "Jonah's recovery is going to take a long time. Maybe you should go home and just leave us be."

He sensed that wasn't what she intended to say. But after what happened between them in the past, he understood her lack of trust.

"We'll see this through together." He squeezed her fingers. "I promise."

~

Shelby accepted Cassie's invitation to supper when she stopped by the Owenses' farm to pick up her girls. She put the finishing touches on a green bean casserole while Cassie prepared a salad and Jason removed chicken from the grill. Afterwards, they sat outside in lawn chairs while the children and dogs, Lila and the Owenses' English shepherd Penny, chased each other around the yard.

"Where did you say AJ took off to?" Jason asked.

"I didn't say," Shelby said. "He didn't tell me."

"Strange for him to leave like that. Will he be back in time for next week's game?"

"What game?"

"The Faith Community Church softball game. Against Grace Chapel." Jason's tone grew agitated. "He's our second best batter, so he better get back here before Tuesday."

"Second best?"

"AJ's good, but I'm better." Jason sat forward in his chair and went through the motions of swinging a bat.

"It's their personal rivalry," Cassie said. "Every summer we go through this."

"My batting average put me number one last year. Can't argue with the stats."

"I wouldn't dream of it." Cassie swatted his leg and gripped the chair arms as if to rise. "The kids and I made brownies this afternoon. Anybody interested?"

"I'll go get them." Jason stood and stretched, then swung his imaginary bat again. "You gals just relax."

"Thanks, hon," Cassie said before he disappeared into the house.

"Does AJ attend Faith Community? I haven't seen him there." Shelby shrugged. "Though we've only been a couple of times."

"We don't often see him either. He usually attends the first service, and we go to second service because Austin attends children's church then."

"I wish I'd known."

"Why?"

Shelby shrugged again, shifting uncomfortably in her chair. *Because I would have taken the girls to a different church. Because I'm trying to avoid AJ Sullivan as much as possible.*

She hadn't told Cassie about the bitter history between the Lassiters and Sullivans when they talked earlier in the day. How could she possibly explain the animosity she harbored toward AJ when he was so . . . likeable? Would Cassie even believe she despised him?

Shelby hardly believed it herself.

The proof of her change of heart chose that moment to race toward her for a sniff and a pat. Shelby pressed her cheek against Lila's creamy muzzle as she rubbed both her ears. A few weeks ago, she'd have scorned the idea of dog-sitting for her worst enemy.

But her attitude toward AJ was no longer so black and white. The events of the past twenty-four hours proved she had placed her trust in the wrong grandson.

"How could I have been so stupid?" she murmured into Lila's ear.

"You're not stupid," Cassie said softly. "Don't be so hard on yourself."

Shelby leaned back in the chair, and Lila plopped at her feet. "You weren't supposed to hear that."

"I can't imagine AJ treating anyone like Brett treated you. He's a good man."

"Who's a good man?" Jason appeared behind them with the brownies.

"You are." Cassie took the container from him and called for the children.

Grateful for the distraction, Shelby pulled Tabby onto her lap. Elizabeth and Austin sat close together as they ate their brownies, seemingly best friends. Perhaps another prayer answered for her lonely little girl.

When it was time to go, Shelby herded the reluctant children to the car. Lila slowly stood and limped after them.

Shelby knelt beside the dog and gently touched her front paw. "It's her injured leg. I thought it was all better."

"She's been running a lot today," Cassie said. "Maybe she just overdid it."

"What should I do?"

Jason examined the leg. "Make sure she rests tonight. If she's still limping in the morning, let me know. I can take her in to Doc Buck."

"He's still around? He must be at least a hundred."

"Old Doc Buck retired a couple of years ago, but his son and granddaughter took over the practice. Young Doc Buck and Lady Doc Buck."

"That's what people call them? You're kidding me, right?"

"I promise I'm not." Jason chuckled as he rubbed Lila's ears. "She'll probably be fine in the morning. I'll help you get her in the car."

The drive home took about five minutes, but it seemed a hundred times that before the girls were bathed and tucked in for the night. Lila whimpered and paced, favoring one leg, until Shelby awkwardly lifted her onto Elizabeth's bed.

"She needs a bandage, doesn't she?" Elizabeth rested her arm across Lila's neck.

"Maybe." Shelby ran her hand along the dog's side, wishing she hadn't taken her to Cassie's house. But she had been too caught up in her own concerns to think about Lila's leg.

"Mr. AJ will be sad, won't he, Mommy?"

Shelby smiled and kissed Elizabeth's forehead. "He might be."

"Are you going to tell him?"

"Do you think I should?"

"It hurts to feel sad." Elizabeth's forehead furrowed in thought. "But he might be sadder if he didn't know."

"I think you're right."

"I can call him." Her little voice sounded too grown up. "If you don't want to."

"I'll call him, Bitsy. In just a few minutes, okay?"

"Okay." She nestled closer to Lila, and her eyes flickered shut. "Maybe he'll come home. Lila and I want him to come home."

So do I.

Shelby gasped at the revelation, then shoved it away and kissed

Elizabeth again. The unexpected thought haunted her as she wandered into the kitchen. The unopened UPS package sat on the table.

She'd been curious before about "this thing" AJ had to do. But as she opened the package, pleased to find an exact replica of the broken calico-cat-in-a-basket cookie jar, her curiosity grew. He didn't have to tell her why he went out of town, but he should have told her where he was going. Especially after leaving Lila in her care.

As she made the rounds, turning out lights and checking that all the doors were locked, Lila joined her.

"What's the matter, girl?" Shelby scratched behind her ear. "You're a little restless tonight too, aren't you?"

After checking on the girls one more time, Shelby settled in the wingback chair with her phone. Lila lay on the floor, her head resting on Shelby's foot.

Elizabeth was right. AJ needed to know about Lila's injury.

That was the only reason she was calling. To tell him about Lila.

– 22 –

*A*J leaned against the beige corridor wall, his chin tucked against his chest as he focused on taking slow, deep breaths. The inexpressible wonder of having a son warred with his anger at being shut out of his child's life. He didn't know whether to hug Meghan or shake her. If only she'd come back to him, he'd have done the right thing.

They could have married.

Been a family.

His phone buzzed, and he glanced at the screen, then straightened as his pulse quickened. He cleared his throat and tried to sound upbeat. Or at least normal.

"Hi, Shelby. Everything all right?"

"Everything's fine." Her voice seemed hesitant. No wonder after yesterday's scene at the café and his late-night visit. But yesterday's roller coaster had been a kiddie ride compared to what he'd gone through today.

He rubbed his eyes. "Is Lila behaving herself?"

"I think she misses you."

"Why's that?"

"Because she's trying to eat my phone." Shelby's voice became muffled, but he could still hear her. "It's okay, girl. I'm sure he misses you too."

"You bet I do." *I miss all of you.*

"I called to tell you that something has come up."

"And you can't take care of Lila anymore? It's all right. She'll be fine at the kennel."

"It's not that."

Please, God, no more bad news. Not today.

"Lila is limping. I think she played too hard with the children today. And Penny."

He hadn't realized he'd been holding his breath till he exhaled with relief. "Jason Owens's Penny?"

"Cassie watched the girls for me this afternoon. Lila went too, and then we stayed for supper. I wish I had left her at home, but I didn't think . . ." Her voice faded, sounding as tired as he felt. He massaged his aching neck muscles.

"Does she seem to be in pain?"

"Only when she walks."

He chuckled. For a brief moment, he was tempted to climb in his Jeep and drive home. To pretend he had never found Meghan, that he didn't know anything about Jonah. But that was impossible now.

God had led him to this hospital so he could undo the damage caused by his past cowardice. He couldn't leave until he had a plan for providing the care both Meghan and Jonah needed.

Perhaps not even then. If only he'd found them closer to home.

The ache in his neck crept up the back of his head.

"Jason suggested taking her to the vet. Do you see Young Doc Buck or Lady Doc Buck?"

The heaviness in his chest momentarily eased at the playfulness of her tone. "Either one. Sorry to put you to so much trouble."

"It's no trouble. I'm so sorry I didn't take better care of her. She's such a sweet dog."

"I think we both have had a rough couple of days. In the scheme of things, this isn't the worst thing in the world." He paused, pushing out air. "Lila will be fine, I'm sure of it."

"Are you all right? You sound kind of sad."

"Just tired. If you want, I can make other arrangements for Lila."

"No, please. The girls would be devastated. So would I."

"You're going to give her back to me when I get home, aren't you?"

"Only because we won't have a choice," she teased. "I don't suppose you know where we can find another one just like her?"

"I'll help you look if you want."

"When will you be home?"

He must be more tired than he thought. Her voice sounded almost wistful. Had to be his imagination.

"I'm not sure. Things here are a little complicated."

"Where's 'here'? Or don't you want to tell me?"

"Toledo. I'm in Toledo."

"That's not so far."

In miles, only about a three, three-and-a-half-hour drive. But as far as his heart was concerned, he might as well be on another planet. A future with Shelby had always been a long shot. Yet he'd had a wild idea that God only required a quick reconciliation with Meghan before blessing AJ's far-fetched dreams. But life never was that easy.

He hadn't replied, and Shelby ended the silence with an animated rush. "Jason wants you home by Tuesday. Something about a church softball game. I didn't realize you attended Faith Community. That's where the girls and I have been going."

"Bet you go to the second service because of the children's programs."

"Cassie said you go to the first."

"Most of the time. Gran liked to go to the first service so we could go out to eat before the Sunday crowds hit the restaurants. When she couldn't attend anymore, I still went to the first so I could pick up to-go orders without too much hassle."

"Then spend the afternoon watching Cary Grant movies," Shelby said with a teasing lilt.

"On rainy days."

"What about that softball game? Jason said you're the second best batter."

"Did he now?"

"That's what he said."

"Only because I sprained my wrist and had to sit out a couple of games. We'll see by the end of this season who's the best."

"So you'll be there?"

She sounded hopeful.

His imagination playing tricks on him again.

"Probably not. I'm not sure what's going to happen in the next few days."

"What's wrong, AJ?"

"Nothing I can talk about."

He should say good-bye, but he didn't want to let her go. Not yet.

Again she broke the silence, but this time her words thunked like heavy stones.

"I saw Uncle Richard today."

"What did he have to say for himself?"

"He denied knowing anything about Brett's plan, but I'm not sure he was telling the truth."

"I've never known Richard to lie, but I felt the same way when I talked to him."

"He did tell me something interesting. Our grandmothers were best friends once. Before they married. I bet they used to watch all those Cary Grant movies together."

"They probably did. It's hard to imagine them as young women, isn't it?"

"But they were once. Then Aubrey married Thad instead of Sully, and Joyanna married Sully instead of Richard. Nothing was the same for any of them ever again."

"Sounds like a soap opera."

175

"Except it's real life. And it's sad."

"Would you have preferred it if Aubrey had married Sully?"

"No."

She said it short and sharp, leaving no doubt of her opinion about that scenario.

"I didn't think so."

"But I wish he and Joyanna had been happier together."

"I wish that too. You were the lucky one."

"Why do you say that?"

"Thad and Aubrey loved each other. My grandparents didn't have that magic."

"It wasn't luck or magic, AJ. It was a profound love that radiated all around them. The stuff of fairy tales."

"Sounds like magic to me."

"They believed God brought them together. He blessed them, their life together, and their family."

"Until Sully took Misty Willow."

"You're not to blame for what your grandfather did."

"No." He paused, then lowered his voice. "I'm to blame for what I did."

"You never deserved my anger. I hope you'll forgive me."

"There's nothing to forgive, Shelby." Sliding his back down the wall, he sank to the tiled floor. "I let Sully . . . you have no idea what I let him do."

"I wish you'd tell me what's wrong." Concern heightened the pitch of her voice.

"Just pray for me, okay? For everything."

"I have been. I am."

"I need to go. I'll call the vet's office in the morning—"

"Let me do that."

"You really don't mind?"

"Not at all."

"Call me after, okay? If I don't answer, just leave a message. I'll call you when I can."

"I will. Good night."

"Night, Shelby."

"AJ?"

"Yeah?"

"Take care of yourself."

The connection ended, and he hunched over his knees with his head on his arms. A couple of days ago, he wouldn't have let anyone else take Lila to the vet. But as much as he loved his dog, her injury paled beside Jonah's. Strange how quickly priorities could shift.

Because of one long-ago night he had a son.

A night he didn't even remember.

– 23 –

Unable to sleep, AJ threw back the covers and turned on the table lamp. The light cast a warm glow into the unfamiliar hotel room. A half-formed idea niggled beneath the ache that pounded his head. He turned on his iPad and searched for the Central Ohio Children's Hospital.

As he read through the website, the idea shaped into a plan. If only he could persuade Meghan to go along with it. But first he had a phone call to make.

The green digits on the radio clock displayed the time as 5:33. He placed the iPad on the table and turned out the light. Flinging his arm behind his head, he stared at the dark ceiling.

After checking into his room, AJ had gone online to find news reports of Jonah's accident. The wreckage had made the local news, and AJ replayed the video clip several times, sick to his stomach whenever the mangled car appeared on the screen.

Jonah wasn't wearing a seat belt when Meghan's drunken ex slammed his vehicle into the rear end of a delivery truck. The airbag didn't work, so Jonah had been thrown between the dashboard and the seat. A witness found him crumpled on the floor, unconscious and bleeding. The surgeons set his broken leg and wrapped his cracked ribs. But he hadn't regained consciousness.

The trauma unit had stabilized Jonah, but one of the best pediatric neurocritical care units in the Midwest was only a few hours south of here. That was where the boy needed to be.

Punching his pillow in a vain effort to get comfortable, AJ resolved to do everything in his power to get him there. Even if it meant begging Brett for a favor.

~

Shelby struggled to push the heavy tiller, upturning pieces of sod to reveal rich dark earth. She reached the string marking the boundary of her plot and turned the machine, grunting as she maneuvered it into place. The first awkward row stretched for several yards in front of the house, a black jagged gash cut through lush green grass.

To think she had believed the salesman when he'd said this would be easy. A tiller so light a child could handle it.

Sure. If that child's name was Clark Kent.

She aimed the blade and pushed, gripping the handles as the machine tilted. While trying to get it upright, she stumbled and lost her grip. The engine sputtered as the machine hit the ground. Frowning, she tamped down her frustration.

By the time she'd cut two more rows, her back and shoulders screamed for relief. The tiller had fallen at least half a dozen more times, and the black earth was dotted with grassy islands due to her crooked maneuverings. Despite wearing work gloves, her palms ached.

Maybe she should hire Seth Norris to do this job. But he'd gone to a youth camp and wouldn't be back for several days. Determined to finish the job, she took a couple of deep breaths.

She could do this.

About a third of the way along the next row, she halted as Brett's black Lexus turned into the drive. Anger filled her chest, and she gave the tiller a hard push. It wobbled, and once again she lost her balance trying to prevent it from hitting the ground. Somehow she managed to get it upright and turn off the power. When she let go of the handle, the temperamental thing fell over.

Great! She placed her hands on her hips and pretended not to look at the Lexus.

A wonderfully klutzy performance. Behind his tinted windows, Brett must be highly amused.

Irritated that she cared even a smidgen what Brett thought, she wiped sweat from her forehead and headed for the bottle of water she'd left on the porch. Sitting on the top step, she pulled off her gloves and took a long drink.

The Lexus stopped in the lane instead of proceeding to the parking area beside the house, and Brett emerged with the studied poise of a male model. He wore a royal blue shirt and tan shorts with loafers. A scruff of beard barely camouflaged the bruise on his jaw.

Despite her longing to squash him like a gnat, Shelby's cheeks flushed. And not from the summer heat. Why did the beast have to look so good?

She glanced down at her stained T-shirt and dirt-covered jeans and vainly wished things were reversed. Why couldn't she be the model and Brett the slob? Too late for that. At least her appearance would scare him away. Whatever he was doing here, she need never fear he'd come around again.

Trying to appear relaxed, she leaned against the porch railing and took another drink of water. Lila trotted toward Brett, her injured leg freshly wrapped in an Ace bandage courtesy of Young Doc Buck squeezing them into an early morning appointment. Brett bent to pat her, and she barked a hello. He walked toward the porch, and she followed, furiously wagging her otter-like tail.

The traitor.

"Hi." Brett smiled awkwardly and glanced around. "Where's AJ?"

"Out of town."

"Without Lila?" He scratched behind the dog's ear as she leaned into him.

"He couldn't take her with him."

"Where'd he go?"

"Is that why you're here? To spy on AJ?"

"No, of course not." He looked taken aback. "I was just surprised to see Lila, that's all."

"Then why are you here?"

He sat beside her on the step and clasped his hands. Lila pushed her way between them and sprawled on the porch, her head resting against Shelby's leg.

"I thought about bringing flowers, but I didn't want you throwing them at me."

"I don't want your flowers. I don't want anything from you."

"Not even an apology?"

"You expect me to believe you're sorry?"

"It'd be asking a lot, I know." He leaned his back against the opposite rail so they were practically facing each other. "How about if it comes with a friendly warning?"

"What does that mean?"

"I don't want your farm, Shelby. Not anymore. But Amy still does."

"Why?"

"She has her reasons." He brushed imaginary lint from his shorts. "I tried to talk her out of it, but she won't give up."

Dread burrowed into Shelby's stomach. "What is she going to do?"

"File a lawsuit. Sully meant AJ to profit from this land. He actually leased it to you for less than its value."

"How do you know that?"

"Property values are my business. I only had to do a little research to find out."

"He never said . . . I didn't know."

"It could be argued, and probably will be, that your uncle Richard influenced the financial considerations in your favor."

Shelby massaged the loose skin between Lila's ears as the dread grew, clawing its way into her throat. Wild thoughts raced through her brain, and she grabbed hold of one.

"Joyanna encouraged AJ to find a loophole. Not Uncle Richard."

A cloud passed over Brett's face at the mention of his grandmother, but he blinked it away. "The fact remains there were other options."

"How could there be? AJ's not supposed to sell the land to anyone."

"And yet here you are. Amy is looking for a loophole too, and this deal she's putting together could make AJ twenty times what you're paying him. Probably more."

"Money." She spat the word. "It's all you care about, isn't it?"

"Not all." He patted Lila's side, and she exposed her belly for him to rub. "Though maybe that was true for Sully."

Shelby pressed her lips together and shook her head. "I don't understand how a grandfather could be so mean. AJ didn't want to be a lawyer. So what? Sully had to punish him?"

Brett's eyes slightly narrowed. "There's more to the story than AJ dropping out of law school."

For the first time since he'd arrived, she held her gaze steady against his. "Tell me."

He seemed to consider, then barely shook his head. "If you had asked me a few days ago, I probably would have. And made AJ twice the villain he was. Anything to divert your attention from him to me."

"My 'attention' was never on AJ."

"Oh, really?" He flashed a dimpled smile. "I know it even if you don't."

"Know what?"

"You're attracted to my cousin." He gazed out over the long front yard. "More than you ever were to me."

"That's not true." Realizing her denial implied an attraction to Brett, she flushed. "You know what I mean."

"I know." Regret momentarily crossed his features. As if needing to change the subject, he lifted Lila's paw and examined her injured leg. "AJ told me the bandage had been taken off."

"This is a new one. She played too hard with the children yesterday."

"Where are the Misses Kincaid?"

"A neighbor took her son and Elizabeth to the pool in town, and Tabby got sent to her room after throwing a tantrum because she didn't get to go. Now she's asleep."

"Leaving you to wrestle with that?" He pointed at the downed tiller.

She gave an exaggerated sigh. "It's not my friend."

He abruptly stood. "I'll give it a try."

She rose beside him. "You can't."

"Why not?" He headed for the tiller, and Shelby went after him.

"Brett, stop. You can't till my flower bed."

Facing her, he started to touch her arm but let his hand drop. His soft voice almost pleaded. "Give me a chance to show you I'm not a total jerk."

Hesitating, she searched his face. For all she knew, he was putting on a show, but he certainly looked sincere. "You're not dressed for yard work."

"I'll manage." Gripping the handles, he lifted the tiller. "This thing sure is light."

She threw up her hands in annoyance as he powered up the engine. "Go for it, Clark Kent," she mumbled, turning on her heel and heading for the house.

- 24 -

*A*J stepped off the elevator carrying two Starbucks travel mugs. When he walked into Jonah's room, Meghan gave him a brief smile.

"I hope you still drink caramel lattes."

"You remembered?"

"Hey, I spent a fortune on these things back in the day." When her face clouded over, he quickly added, "Not that I ever minded."

"I like the mug."

"Easier to handle than those disposable cups."

"Thank you."

He stood by Jonah's bed and gingerly caressed the back of the boy's hand between his bandaged fingers and the intravenous needle. His skin was cool beneath AJ's fingers.

"Did he have a good night?"

"Nothing's changed, if that's what you mean."

"What about you? How did you sleep?"

"About the same as usual."

"In other words, not well." Whoever did in a hospital? At least the room had bench seating along the wall that folded out into a bed.

"Why don't we trade places tonight? Let me stay here, and you go to the hotel. Get a good night's sleep."

"I can't leave Jonah."

"I promise I'll call you if anything happens."

"What if he wakes up and I'm not here?" She shook her head. "I won't leave him."

"I just want you to take care of yourself too, Meghan. To let me take care of you."

"I know you mean well. But don't push the father stuff, okay?"

"No pushing." At least not yet.

Praying she wouldn't oppose his plan to move Jonah to the children's hospital, he sipped his coffee. "Has the doctor been here yet?"

"Only the hospitalist."

"'Hospitalist'? That's a new one."

"He oversees everybody else. Kind of like making sure the right hand knows what the left hand is doing."

"Sorry I missed him."

"He'll be back." She fidgeted with the lid on her mug. "Would you mind doing something for me?"

"Anything."

"I have a couple of phone calls to make, and the service seems to be spotty in here. I won't be gone long."

"Take as long as you need. I'll be here."

"You won't leave him?"

"Cross my heart."

She smiled her thanks and swung a large tote onto her shoulder. "There's a seating area at the end of this corridor. If anyone stops in, come get me."

He grinned. "That'd be breaking my promise not to leave Jonah."

"Only exception."

"Got it."

After she left, he pulled a chair close to the bed and clasped

Jonah's small hand in his. "Hey there, sport," he whispered. "We haven't been officially introduced yet, and I imagine your mom doesn't want me saying too much. But I want you to know I'm here. And I'm going to do everything I can to help you get better."

His voice cracked, and his eyes misted. "I'm here for you, Jonah. For you and your mom. And I won't leave you ever again."

~

When Brett finished tilling the staked-out area, he helped Shelby plant yellow and orange marigolds, blue ageratums, and a variety of colorful petunias.

"You're going to a lot of trouble for annuals, aren't you?"

"Perhaps." She dug a hole with her trowel and inserted a marigold plant. "But I didn't want to go all summer without any flowers in front of the house."

"Oh no," he drawled with a teasing grin. "Couldn't have that."

Her shoulders tensed as she averted her face. "I hoped to plant iris bulbs in the fall."

"My grandmother raised irises."

"So did mine. Right here."

"There's no reason you can't."

"Guess that depends on how this lawsuit turns out."

Squatting on his haunches, he shifted his weight and reached for a sunny marigold. Maybe he shouldn't have told her about Amy's plan.

They planted the last of the annuals in silence, then Shelby brought glasses of iced tea to the porch.

"You worked hard today," she said. "Thanks."

"Don't sound so surprised." Brett clinked his glass against hers. "There's more to me than being a brilliant businessman."

"I'd say you were also an unscrupulous cad if you hadn't helped me out."

To hide the sting of her words, he shrugged and plopped in a chair. "You'd be right."

She tucked one foot beneath her on the porch swing and pushed against the floorboards with the other.

The chain creaked as she slowly swung in the seat. "It took a lot of nerve for you to come here after what you did."

"Or stupidity."

"Which was it?"

"Good question." He sipped the tea, savoring the icy cold beverage as it cooled his parched throat. Pushing the tiller had given his upper body and calves a better workout than he ever got in the gym. He rotated his aching shoulders.

"Well?"

He wouldn't tell her that he hadn't been home since Thursday because a woman he despised had taken up residence in his apartment. Shelby didn't need to know those details. But not even a night in an upscale hotel had soothed the restlessness that had haunted him since he'd walked out of the Italian café. He should have turned back then, tried to explain.

But he'd been blinded by the rivalry that Sully had nurtured between AJ and him since they were boys. When Elizabeth and Tabby glommed on to AJ, a sharp pang of jealousy had cut into Brett's heart. Wounding AJ by kissing Shelby was his revenge. But instead of feeling relief, he'd only felt cold.

"It started out as a game. But the more we talked, the better I got to know you, it wasn't a game I wanted to play anymore." He took another sip of his tea. "But I had to keep going."

"Why?"

"I didn't want Amy to do something she'll regret." He gave a sheepish shrug. "And because I wanted to spend time with you."

Shelby stared at her glass, seemingly intent on examining the ice cubes. "Can't you make her stop?"

"You don't know my sister."

"I'm not sure I want to." She raised her eyes to his, and her adorable lips widened in a teasing smile. "No offense."

"None taken." He took a deep breath and stroked his jaw. Time

187

to put the final nail in his own coffin. "You know, AJ cares about you. I've got the proof right here." He winced as he touched a tender spot.

"He shouldn't have done that."

"He was provoked."

She sighed and stared across the yard. "I wish I knew what was bothering him."

Brett stiffened, suddenly curious. "What do you mean? Where is he?"

"Toledo."

"Why?"

"He said it was complicated."

"Let's find out how much." He pulled out his cell phone, found AJ's number, and hit the send button. Just as he thought the call was going to voicemail, AJ answered. His voice sounded ragged and tired.

"Everything okay with you?" Brett asked.

"Fine, why do you ask?"

"I heard you'd gone out of town."

"I'm glad you called. I need a favor."

"Name it."

AJ snorted. "Just like that?"

"Figure I owe you."

"For what?"

"I'm tired of fighting with you, AJ."

"Then leave Shelby alone."

"What's the favor?"

"Don't you know someone at the children's hospital in Columbus?"

"Yeah, I've got a buddy there. Dr. Marc Nesmith."

"I need to know how to get a patient transferred to their pediatric neurocritical care unit."

"Pediatric neuro . . . What patient?"

"A little boy who was in a car accident. He's seriously banged up, and I think he'd do better in a specialty hospital."

188

"Who is he?"

"I'll explain all that later. Could you give Nesmith a call? Ask him to call me?"

"Sure."

"The sooner the better, okay?"

"I'll call him now."

"Thanks, Brett. I owe you."

"When are you coming home?"

"I don't know yet. Listen, I gotta go. Call Nesmith, okay?"

"I will."

The connection broke, and Brett tapped his phone against the chair arm.

"Did you hear any of that?"

"Most of it, yes." Shelby stopped the swing. Concern dulled her expression. "Any idea who this little boy is?"

"None. But AJ's always been a sucker for a good sob story. Probably the kid of one of his former students." He scrolled through his contacts list again, then stood. "I'm going to call Marc."

Tapping the send button, he walked down the steps and into the yard. Typical AJ, getting wrapped up in someone else's problems, taking them as his own. But it still seemed odd he had left town so soon after the blowup with Shelby. In AJ's shoes, Brett wouldn't have left her side.

Maybe it wasn't too late for him after all.

He massaged his neck as Marc answered the phone.

"Hey, pal. Met any leggy blondes lately? I need a new receptionist."

– 25 –

Relief surged through AJ as he ended the call with Dr. Nesmith. For once, Brett had come through, and the pediatric specialist had agreed to review Jonah's records. Now he had to convince Meghan to go along with his plan.

When he returned to the room, she was curled up on the bench seat staring out the window. He paused at Jonah's side and gave silent thanks for the comforting rhythm of the monitors. He gently squeezed Jonah's fingers, the ones not swathed in bandages, then sat beside Meghan.

He stretched his arm across the back of the bench, and she surprised him by resting her head against his shoulder. Her eyes closed as she seemed to draw strength from his presence. If only they'd had a moment like this before she disappeared. How different everything might have been.

Demanding clients instead of awkward adolescents. A home in the suburbs instead of Gran's cottage. Maybe a walking dust mop, like a Maltese or a shih tzu, instead of Lila.

And no Shelby to run into at the 'gagement tree. No running through the rain to get a car seat. No hugs from Elizabeth and Tabby.

Suddenly feeling cramped, he squirmed in the seat. As much

as he hated to disturb Meghan, he couldn't relax when Jonah's medical care was at stake. Only God knew how much any delay in treatment affected the boy's recovery.

"I just talked to a pediatrician at the Central Ohio Children's Hospital in Columbus," he said, his voice low. "They have brain injury specialists there who could help Jonah."

"They have brain injury specialists here," she murmured sleepily.

"The children's hospital has something called a pediatric neurocritical care unit. They do research especially for children. Jonah needs to be transferred there. I know it's the best thing for him."

"You know what's best for Jonah?" She pushed away from him, her voice hardening. "You don't know anything about him."

"That's not really my fault, is it?"

They glared at each other a moment, then AJ lowered his eyes. Sweeping his fingers through his hair, he took a deep breath and met her gaze again. "The pediatrician I talked to is willing to review Jonah's records. If there's even the smallest chance the pediatric team can do something for him that's not being done here, shouldn't we take it?" He immediately realized his mistake. "Okay, you. Shouldn't you take it?"

She wrapped her arms around her legs and drew them to her chest. "I want him to have the best. I just don't know how . . . we have no insurance. I can't concentrate on work." She rested her forehead on her knees. "I'm so tired I can hardly think."

"Thinking seems to be the only thing I can do."

"You've already worked out all the details, haven't you?" Turning toward him, she slightly smirked. "You haven't changed much."

He shrugged one shoulder. "Guess not." But it wasn't true. When Meghan disappeared, practically every aspect of his life had changed. He'd alienated his grandfather and traded the halls of government for the halls of a high school. A profession he would have detested for one he loved.

But the estrangement from Sully? That had been excruciatingly painful. As a teen, AJ had admired and respected his grandfather as a shrewd businessman. Only later did he realize how much Sully's acumen was rooted in vengeful ruthlessness.

They'd never reconciled. And it still hurt.

Meghan nudged his arm. "Tell me your plan."

"We do whatever it takes to get Jonah transferred. You won't have to worry about anything but him."

She averted her gaze. "I'm not sure that's quite true."

"I promise it is." He gently hooked her chin with his finger so she looked at him. "You'll have whatever you need as long as you need it. A place to live. Anything."

"What's the catch?"

"No catch."

"There's always a catch."

"Not this time." He scratched his arm, then propped his elbows on his knees. "I want to make up for the years I missed with him, Meghan. Please let me."

As she leaned back against the seat, her hair fell forward and hid her face. AJ bit his lip to stop even the smallest word from slipping out of his mouth. She needed time to think, and he owed her a few moments of silence. But he wished he could follow her thoughts as she considered his proposal. Her eyes focused on Jonah's bed, though she couldn't see him from her angle. He silently prayed he was doing the right thing, that she would say yes.

"I heard you bought one of my stained glass pieces."

"It reminded me of home. I knew it was yours as soon as I saw it."

"I heard that too." Her gray eyes glistened. "It's not a good time to be an artist, the economy like it is. But things have been getting better. I've been asked to teach a class this fall at the art museum, and my designs are being considered for an aeronautics memorial. I worked so hard researching and sketching plans for my proposal." Her voice cracked, and she took a deep breath. "I'm a finalist." She snatched a tissue and dabbed at her eyes. "Me."

"That's great. Congratulations."

"Don't you see?" She quickly stood and gripped the bed rail. "This was supposed to be my big break. But how can I concentrate on work when my son, my baby, is suffering?"

AJ stepped beside her. "You're a talented artist. There will be other opportunities."

"Not like this one."

"All the more reason to let me help. Just give me a chance."

She sniffed and looked up at him. "I'm afraid, AJ."

"I know. But I'm not going to let you down. Not this time."

Her eyes bore into his. "I believe you."

"Then you don't mind if I talk to the hospitalist about transferring those records?"

"I'm beginning to think God really did bring you to us. It'd been so long since I prayed, I hardly knew the words to say."

"He knows your heart. Sometimes words aren't necessary."

She nodded slightly, then braced her shoulders. "Send the records."

"You're doing the right thing, Meghan."

Her mouth quirked upward. "Time will tell."

Before he could respond, a knock sounded on the door. The woman from the art gallery entered.

"Dawn." Meghan hurried to embrace her. "I'm so glad to see you."

"I'm sorry I couldn't come earlier." She turned to AJ. "I don't think I introduced myself when you stopped in yesterday. Dawn Lahm."

AJ shook the hand she offered him. "Thanks for telling me where to find Meghan."

"She doesn't seem too mad at me, so I guess I did the right thing."

"I think so." He looked pointedly at Meghan.

"I think so too," she admitted.

"How's Jonah?" Dawn asked.

"No change."

While Meghan gave Dawn an update, AJ left to speak to the hospitalist. Shortly after gaining access to Jonah's records, Dr. Nesmith started the paperwork to facilitate the transfer.

"All done," AJ said as he entered the room. Meghan stood by Jonah, and Dawn sat in a nearby chair. "Now we wait."

"How long will it take?" Meghan's voice sounded almost robotic.

Something must have happened while he was out of the room. He glanced at Dawn, but she wouldn't meet his gaze.

"Is everything okay?"

"Fine." Her hand played with Jonah's blond strands, brushing them from his forehead then down again. "What's the plan?"

"They'll transport Jonah in the morning. You can go with him in the helicopter."

"Not an ambulance?" She looked up in surprise.

"Too risky. They don't want to take a chance on him being jarred or anything happening on the drive."

"What about you?"

"I'll drive home this evening if that's okay with you, and meet you at the hospital tomorrow."

"Sure. That'd be fine."

The tone of her voice told him otherwise.

"What's wrong?"

She forced a smile. "I'm just tired."

"You need to sleep." He gripped the bed rail and leaned toward her. "Why don't you go to the hotel for a while?"

"I can't."

Dawn stood and placed her arm around Meghan's shoulder. "You should go, Meg. I can stay with Jonah. All night if you want me to."

"No, that'd be too much. You didn't come prepared to spend the night."

"I'll manage. It's more important that you're well rested for that helicopter trip." Dawn handed Meghan her large tote. "I promise I'll call if you're needed."

Meghan reluctantly agreed, and AJ mouthed a thank-you to Dawn.

After they arrived at the hotel, he encouraged Meghan to order room service while he packed his bag.

Ready to leave, he turned to say good-bye, but she was already asleep. He removed the menu from her relaxed fingers and covered her with an extra blanket.

"Sleep tight, Meghan," he whispered. "See you tomorrow."

– 26 –

$\mathscr{S}$helby entered the brightly lit sanctuary and slid into the pew next to Cassie and Jason. The stained glass windows lining both sides of the wide space dated the building of the church to the early 1900s. But the furnishings had been replaced since she attended here with her grandparents. The cushioned seats, upholstered in a tasteful navy blue, were much more comfortable than the hard narrow pews of her childhood.

She stood to sing the opening song when someone tapped her shoulder. AJ, wearing khaki dress pants and a sage green Oxford shirt, stood beside her.

"Mind if I sit with you?" he whispered.

She scooted over to make room for him. "When did you get back?"

"Last night."

"Is everything okay?"

A shadow crossed his face but was quickly dispelled by a smile. "We'll see."

She returned his smile, and they both joined in the singing. Throughout the remainder of the service, she struggled to concentrate her thoughts on worship. But her mind strayed too often to the man beside her.

After Lila's veterinarian appointment yesterday morning, she'd left a message on AJ's cell phone, but he hadn't returned her call. She'd been annoyed when he answered Brett's phone call but regretted her sour feelings as soon as she heard about the hospitalized child.

But she couldn't figure out why it had been such a big secret—or why he'd asked her to pray for him instead of the boy.

At least he was home now. Perhaps he'd know what to do about Amy's obsession to take Misty Willow. She glanced at his hand. The skin was still broken in places, and she suddenly longed to entwine her fingers with his.

Could Brett possibly be right? Was she attracted to AJ? And did he have feelings for her? As they took their seats, her shoulder brushed his. She folded her hands primly on top of her Bible, but the tingling sensation lingered.

Brett had overwhelmed her with his too-good-to-be-true handsome charm. But it was AJ, with his casual good looks and direct demeanor, who haunted her dreams and tugged at her heart.

She impulsively scribbled *Lunch?* on her bulletin and poked him with her elbow. He took it, wrote something, and handed it back.

Rain check?

Swallowing her disappointment, she smiled and nodded. He squeezed her hand but too quickly let go.

Maybe Brett didn't know as much as he thought he did.

The minister gave the Scripture passage, and she opened her Bible to Psalm 18.

"He reached down from on high and took hold of me," he read. "He drew me out of deep waters."

Shelby closed her Bible as the next two verses were read. She didn't need to see the words to know what came next. Blue ink underlined verse 19, perhaps the first verse she had hidden in her heart, not because of a Sunday school assignment or for a Vacation Bible School contest but by her own choice.

A verse that meant something personal. She closed her eyes and inwardly recited the words with the minister.

"He brought me out into a spacious place; he rescued me because he delighted in me."

AJ stirred beside her. "That was one of Gran's favorites," he whispered.

I know.

Flashing a smile at him, she hugged the memory close to her heart. Fourteen years ago, beneath the willow, her angel—AJ's grandmother—had given her Psalm 18:19 as a special promise. After quoting the verse, she'd said, "God delights in you, darling girl. He will take away your heartache and bring you into a spacious place where all will be well."

Shelby had believed her. At first, she thought to find her spacious place on the mission field with her parents. But if God had tried to give his gift to her there, she'd been too angry to accept it. What she wanted—all she ever wanted—was the farm. Her legacy.

With maturity had come the realization that the verse probably didn't mean a literal place, but she couldn't give up her deep-rooted belief that God meant for her to return to Misty Willow. The spacious place of the verse and the fields of the farm intermingled in her dreams until it was impossible to separate them.

And yet . . .

She tried to squeeze her mind shut, not wanting to acknowledge any smudges on the dreams she'd nurtured for so long. But a speck slipped through.

The dream was no longer enough. Not without someone to share it.

Perhaps God meant much more by "a spacious place" than she ever wanted to accept.

AJ and Cassie stood, and after a moment's confusion Shelby stood too. Lost in thought, she hadn't realized the sermon had ended. AJ gave her a quizzical look, and she ached to lose herself in the depth of his eyes.

The first notes of the familiar invitation song resounded through the sanctuary. Shelby sang with the others, but her thoughts returned to Psalm 18:19.

Heaven, the ultimate spacious place, lay in her future.

But what about now? If Misty Willow wasn't her spacious place, where was it? Was she never to know the peace of fully living within God's promise?

She bowed her head for the closing prayer and wordlessly gave her questions to God. Only he knew the answers.

When the prayer ended, she whispered *amen* and slowly opened her eyes.

AJ brushed her arm with his fingers. "You okay?"

"Yeah."

He leaned on the back of the pew in front of them. "How's Lila?"

"Fine. The bandage seems to keep her from playing too hard."

"That's good. I'm sorry for all the trouble."

"She's a delight. The girls love her."

"What about you?"

"I'll miss her when she goes home. If you'd like, we can keep her a few more days."

"I'm afraid if I don't take her now, I may never get her back."

She tilted her head and gave him a teasing smile. "Possession is 99 percent and all that."

He lowered his voice to an evil growl. "I know where you live."

"But not all my hiding places. The farm used to be part of the Underground Railroad, you know."

"I knew your ancestors were part of it, but you never said anything about hiding places."

"There had to be hiding places. How else could they help the runaways escape detection?"

"Did it matter this far north?"

"Apparently."

"And there are still hiding places on the farm?"

"There's a secret room in the house."

"I want to see it."

She laughed at his eager boyishness. "I'll show it to you some-time when the girls aren't around. I'd rather they not know about it till they're older. It could be dangerous."

"It's a deal." He checked his watch and retrieved his Bible from the pew. "About Lila. Today may be a little crazy. I have to drive up to Columbus, and I'm not sure when I'll get back."

"Is the little boy going to be all right?"

"I'm praying he will be." Wrinkles creased his forehead. "How did you know about Jonah?"

"Brett was at my house when he called you. I heard most of the conversation."

His face darkened. "What was he doing there?"

"I think he came to apologize. He never quite did that, but he tilled the plot for Nanna's memorial garden."

"You're kidding, right?"

"No, he really did. Of course, he saw Lila, and then he asked where you were. I told him I was worried about you, so he called."

"That explains it."

"Explains what?"

"Why he didn't give me a hard time about the favor I asked him." He started to move into the side aisle, then stopped and faced her. "You were worried about me?"

"A little." She stepped past him in the narrow space. "I need to pick up Tabby from her class. The teachers get annoyed when parents dawdle too much."

"Do you mind if I pick up Lila later this evening?"

"As long as it's not too late, sure."

"Maybe we could talk then."

Her heart quickened. "I'd like that."

"Great. I'll see you later." He weaved through the crowd, stop-ping frequently to shake a hand or give a pat on the shoulder. When a group of teens surrounded him, his heartwarming laugh echoed back to her.

The scene reminded her of Grandpa after a church service. He was so well-liked and respected, it seemed everyone had something to tell him before he could leave the building. His car was often one of the last ones in the parking lot. Nanna never minded how much time he took discussing the mission budget or a crop yield. "Find you a man like that," she had advised. "A man you don't mind waiting for. Just make sure he doesn't mind waiting for you either."

Advice she should have heeded.

When AJ reached the sanctuary door, he turned and caught her watching him. A surprised smile brightened his features, and he lifted his hand in farewell. She returned the wave before he disappeared into the foyer.

Heading toward Tabby's classroom, she took a couple calming breaths. A long afternoon stretched ahead of her.

An afternoon waiting for a man worth waiting for.

~

Shortly after noon, AJ caught up with Meghan outside Jonah's room at the Central Ohio Children's Hospital.

"How was the ride?" AJ asked.

"Jonah would have loved it if he'd been awake," Meghan said. "But it made my stomach queasy."

"If there's a next time, I'll go with him."

"Agreed." Her smile faded, and she wrapped her arms around her chest. "I hope there won't be a next time, though."

"I don't think there will be," Dr. Nesmith said as he approached them. "My plan is to keep Jonah here until he can walk out the front door."

"That sounds great, Doctor." AJ offered his hand. "This is Meghan Jensen, Jonah's mom." He waited for her to correct him, to say she was Meghan McCurry now. But she didn't. Perhaps she thought it would be easier to keep things straight since Jonah's last name was Jensen.

"Thank you so much for all you've done," she said.

"Glad to do a favor for a friend. I don't see much of Brett now that I'm an old married man." Dr. Nesmith grinned at his own joke.

"Brett?" Meghan shot a glare at AJ.

"My cousin. You met him at my grandparents' house." Dated him a couple of times too. The old jealousy reared but quickly subsided. This ancient history wasn't interesting enough to dig up. Let it stay buried in the past where it belonged. "He connected me with Dr. Nesmith."

"I remember him." She sounded troubled. "I just didn't know he knew about all this."

"He doesn't. I didn't give him any names. Just asked for a favor."

She nodded, looked away, and rubbed her arms again.

"Why don't we go inside?" Dr. Nesmith gestured toward the open door of Jonah's room.

AJ followed Meghan, and they gathered around Jonah's bed. He lay silently beneath the blanket, his head pressed against the pillow. The monitors hummed softly.

"I'll be Jonah's pediatrician for the time he's here," the doctor explained. "We've already assembled a team, and they're meeting this afternoon to go over everything and form a preliminary plan." He picked up Jonah's hand and felt for his pulse. "The trip may have been a little stressful for him, so we'll prioritize what's needed today."

"Is he going to be all right?" Meghan asked hesitantly.

"I wish I could give you a definite answer," Dr. Nesmith said. "But it's too soon to say. We're going to do our best, though. I can promise you that."

"Hopefully your best and our prayers will bring him out of this," AJ said.

"Prayer can work wonders. I've seen it happen often enough." The doctor tapped on his iPad for a few moments. "Any questions I can answer?"

AJ glanced at Meghan, and she shook her head.

"If you think of anything, just let me know. I'll be back later."

After he left, AJ clasped his hands behind his neck and worked out the kinks between his shoulders.

"What do we do now?" Meghan asked.

"Did you have lunch?"

"A sandwich. I'm not very hungry."

"He's going to be all right."

"How can you be so sure?"

He shrugged one shoulder. "Because I haven't taken him to an OSU game yet."

She raised an eyebrow. "What?"

"Buckeyes. College football. The tuba player dotting the *i* in Ohio."

"You want to take him to a game?"

"Sure I do. He's my son."

She turned away from him and walked toward the window. "I'm glad you showed up when you did, AJ. But you're going a little fast for me."

"I'm not trying to rush anything. But we'll have to work something out. Eventually."

Still facing the window, she shrugged. "I suppose."

"No supposing, Meghan. You can't take him away from me again."

"Just don't push me, okay?"

"All I want is for you to let me be his dad. I don't think that's asking too much."

She faced him, arms wrapped across her chest. "You're going to be a great dad, AJ. Someday. But I can't focus on the future right now. The present is all I can handle."

He dug his hands into his pockets and rocked on the balls of his feet. "I didn't mean to upset you."

"I know." She settled into the foldout chair. "It's been a tiring morning. I'm going to close my eyes for a little bit. You don't mind, do you?"

"Go ahead." He handed her a blanket. "I'll go find some coffee. Do you want anything?"

"No, I'm fine. Thanks."

He gently squeezed Jonah's unbandaged fingers and left the room. Beyond the nurses' station, he paused at a large window overlooking a courtyard. Colorful flower gardens lined paved walkways leading to a central fountain. A man pulled a wagon along one of the paths, the child inside surrounded by pillows.

Maybe he could get a wagon for Jonah. One like Shelby had for her girls.

Pressing his temple against the glass, he shut his eyes. Only a little over a week ago, he had crashed Shelby's picnic at the creek. Eaten hot dogs at her house. Had begun to hope that she'd forgive him for being a Sullivan. Had dared to believe she might care for him at least a little.

When he saw her at church, he headed straight for her pew. After all, he needed to talk to her about Lila. But that was just an excuse to sit next to her.

Sticking his hands in his pockets, he strolled toward the elevators. Snatches of the morning's sermon pressed against his mind. Gran had often quoted Psalm 18:19, especially near the end of her life. The concept of a spacious place seemed to bring her comfort in difficult times. Considering she was married to Sully, most of her life must have been difficult. Until Shelby told him, he hadn't known Gran had dated Richard when they were young.

So why had she married Sully instead? Had she followed her heart, or had there been another reason? Richard was probably the only one still alive who knew the answers to those questions.

He wished he could get the answers from Gran. Maybe she could have helped him sort out his own jumbled feelings. He'd once loved Meghan—or thought he had. But before he had even met Shelby, she had awakened something deep within him with a simple note. Every moment they spent together, even the difficult ones, increased her hold on his heart.

But he couldn't indulge those feelings, not when his son needed him.

Why did life have to be so hard?

Where was his spacious place?

– 27 –

Shelby fastened her sandals, then studied her reflection in the cheval mirror. The floral sundress was one of her favorites but perhaps a little too obvious. Searching through her wardrobe, she selected royal blue capris and a pale blue cap-sleeved pullover.

She quickly changed and scrutinized her appearance. Casual chic. Perfect.

Now what to do with her hair?

Gathering the loose strands together, she held them to one side and then the other before deciding on a French braid. She fastened the strands with a clasp, then struck a model's pose before the mirror. The hairstyle accentuated her cheekbones, and her eyes sparkled with anticipation. Pleased with her appearance, she smiled and took a deep breath to calm her jittery nerves.

AJ should be here in about five or ten minutes. She checked on the girls, sound asleep in their twin beds, and quietly encouraged Lila to join her in the family room. Lilac-scented candles flickered on the mantel, and table lamps cast soft circles of light into the room.

The only thing missing was music.

Again, too obvious.

After all, she wasn't trying to seduce the guy. She only wanted him to know she had changed her mind about them being friends. And if friendship led to something more, well, that might be okay too.

Sinking into the wingback chair, Shelby turned on her Kindle and flipped past the cover for Dickens's *Bleak House*. A BBC adaptation she'd recently seen on Netflix triggered an interest in the book, and she was nearing the end. But the story of a disputed will lingering in the court system through generations was less appealing in light of Amy's pending lawsuit.

The very thought of going to court tightened her stomach. After all the effort she'd made to reclaim the house, all the work she'd done and still needed to do, it didn't seem fair that a spoiled Barbie doll with more money than sense could waltz in and take it all away on a whim.

Her conscience murmured, and she huffed in frustration. Maybe it wasn't nice to call Amy a Barbie doll, but Amy didn't deserve nice.

I know, God, I know. Shelby closed her eyes. *She deserves grace. But why would you give me Misty Willow only to take it away again? We'd have been better off staying in Chicago.*

Except that wasn't true.

In Chicago, she had withdrawn into a tight ball after Gary's death, unable or unwilling to do more than the bare minimum when it came to church or community. The long, cold days were to be endured, not enjoyed, as grief enveloped their tiny home.

Everything was different here. The days flowed into one another in a gentle rhythm of hard work and joyous play. Neighbors stopped by with gifts of produce. Her daughters ran around the yard at dusk to catch fireflies. She'd volunteered to help with the crafts for Vacation Bible School.

Her spirit thrived in the peace and quiet of country living. And so did her daughters'. The weariness in Elizabeth's eyes had practically disappeared, unable to compete with her frequent smiles. Tabby's exhausting outbursts were no longer a daily occurrence.

She expended her exuberance in tricycle races against Lila and exploring the fencerows instead of in fits of temper.

No matter what happened or how devastating it would be to lose the farm, this place had done more to heal their grief-stricken hearts in a couple of weeks than a year spent in the city.

She could never wish these days away.

Besides, Amy might not even file the suit. Or perhaps AJ could persuade her to drop it. When it happened, *if* it happened, they could talk about their options then.

But not tonight.

This evening, she hoped to rekindle the magnetism that drew them together the night of the big storm. AJ would have kissed her if Brett hadn't called.

No chance of him interrupting them, but a phone call from Cassie might. Grinning to herself, she retrieved her phone from the side table and muted the ringer volume.

Headlights swept past the front window as a vehicle pulled into the drive. On the floor beside the chair, Lila perked up her ears.

Going into the hall with the lab at her heels, Shelby turned on the porch light and opened one of the heavy double doors. AJ parked the Jeep Cherokee and cut the motor. As he slid out from behind the wheel, Lila bounded across the porch to greet him. He knelt to pat her wiggling body, laughing and averting his face as she covered his chin with doggy kisses.

"Did ya miss me? Huh? Did ya?"

Lila said yes with a cheerful bark.

After another vigorous pat, AJ climbed the steps to join Shelby on the porch. He smiled as his eyes swept over her. "You look lovely."

"Thank you." Trying not to simper like a silly schoolgirl, she gestured toward the house. "Would you like to come in for a little while?"

"I probably better take Lila and go. We've been enough of a nuisance, haven't we, girl?" He scratched between Lila's ears.

"No, not at all. Please come in." Hearing the desperation in her voice, she tugged at the hem of her shirt. "I thought we could visit for a little while."

"Are you sure it's not too late?"

"Not at all. Besides, I baked cookies."

"Okay. Sounds great." He removed his ball cap and followed her into the house.

After sending him into the family room to wrestle with Lila, she retrieved a pitcher of lemonade and a couple of glasses from the kitchen. When she returned, AJ was sprawled on the floor, his back against the couch. Lila stretched beside him, her paws waving as he scratched her exposed belly.

Shelby set the tray on a table and poured the lemonade.

"You promised me cookies." His teasing tone, so typical AJ, didn't hide the fatigue in his voice. Exhaustion dimmed the brown depths of his eyes, and stubble blurred his jawline. Another few minutes, and he might fall asleep on the floor.

She handed him a gift bag she'd previously hidden beside the couch. "This is for you."

"You gift wrapped cookies?"

"Open it." She knelt beside him, her elbow propped on the seat cushion.

"It's heavy."

"And breakable. Be careful."

"You're giving me heavy, breakable cookies? Not sure I want that recipe."

She playfully swatted his arm. "Just open it."

He pulled silver tissue paper from the scarlet bag. "I like the colors. Scarlet and gray all the way."

"Go Bucks."

"I knew I'd make a fan out of you."

"If I ever cheer for a college football team, I promise you that will be the one."

"A man can't ask for more than that." He gingerly lifted the tissue-wrapped gift from the bag and pulled away the rest of the paper to reveal the calico-cat-in-a-basket cookie jar. "I don't believe this."

"Do you like it?"

"Shelby, you didn't have to replace that jar. It was an accident."

"I know. But it belonged to your mom. And I know this isn't the same, but it's almost as good. At least, I hope it is."

He appeared to retreat into his own world for a moment. In the quiet pause, only Lila's snuffling as she twisted to nose her bandage interrupted the silence.

"It's better." He lifted the lid. "Cookies!"

"Peanut butter with Hershey Kisses. The girls helped, so some of them are shaped a little funny."

"Those will be the ones that taste the best." He bit into one. "Um, that's good. Want one?"

"Nope, those are all for you."

"You're something special, you know that?"

"I try."

"I mean it. Finding this jar. Filling it with cookies. That means a lot to me. Thank you."

"You're very welcome."

Angling toward her, he slipped his hand into hers. The diamonds in her wedding set flickered pure reds and greens with the movement. He shifted his grasp, his strong fingers turning her hand over to hide the rings.

"I suppose it's pride," she said in a low voice.

"What is?"

"The reason I haven't taken them off." Elbow still propped on the couch, she rested her chin against her hand and contemplated his profile. "When I'm with the girls, I want people to know I'm married. Or at least I was."

"That's understandable."

"When I'm not with the girls, they help keep away unwanted attention."

210

"Also understandable." He shook Lila's nose with his free hand. Dark lashes fringed his downcast eyes, and the corner of his mouth drew Shelby closer. She longed to brush the scruff of his day-old beard against her fingers, to inhale the alluring notes of his woodsy aftershave.

"Not that you're unwanted atten . . ." Heat inflamed her cheeks as his head snapped toward her. She drew back, her mind scurrying for something to say, then she leaned forward. Touching the cleft in his chin, she smiled. "How do you shave in there?"

Releasing her fingers, he reached for her, cupping her head in his hand as his thumb caressed the sensitive spot near her ear. She responded without thinking, encircling his bare forearm with her fingers and stroking the taut muscles beneath his tanned skin. He shifted closer, his other hand moving along her arm, then settling at her waist. His mouth hovered above hers, tantalizingly close.

"I'm not unwanted?" He asked the question lightly, but the expression in his eyes was serious.

"No. Yes." Momentarily confused by the double negative, she shook her head. "I'm not sure."

"I'm pushing, aren't I?" Releasing her, he pressed his head against the sofa and flung his arm across his eyes. "I seem to be doing a lot of that lately."

Startled by his sudden change, she folded her hands in her lap. Why couldn't she admit her feelings to him? Why hadn't she kissed him when she had the chance?

He sighed heavily, and exhaustion seemed to drag him to the floor.

"You've had a tough day, haven't you?"

"Yeah."

"His name is Jonah, right? How is he?"

"No change. But he's got a good team of specialists now."

"And he's got you. Your students are so lucky."

"My students?" He gave her a quizzical look.

"Isn't Jonah the son of one of your former students?"

"Where did you get that idea?"

"From Brett." She thought back to the conversation. "Though come to think of it, he was only guessing."

"He guessed wrong." Sitting forward, AJ rotated his shoulders. He put the cookie jar into the gift bag and stuffed the tissue paper around it. "Thanks again for this."

"Let me know when you need more cookies."

"Deal." Pushing Lila off his legs, he stood, then offered his hand to pull Shelby to her feet.

"You're leaving so soon?" They'd barely talked about anything.

"It's been a long day. Besides, Lila needs her beauty sleep."

"Would you like to come over for dinner tomorrow?" She walked with him to the front door. "I bought a grill. We could try it out."

"Afraid I can't. I'll probably be at the hospital."

"Ice cream after the church softball game on Tuesday?"

He made a face and shook his head. "I forgot about the game. I doubt I'll be there."

"Because of Jonah?"

"Yeah."

Did he think she was going to beg him to go out with her? If he did, he apparently was right because that's exactly what she was doing. She didn't know whether she was more irritated with him or herself.

They stepped outside to the porch. The long yard shimmered in the pale light of a crescent moon, and wild honeysuckle scented the warm breezes. Fireflies still flickered in the darkness.

"My schedule is usually flexible. Why don't you let me know when you're available?"

"I'd like to." He reached out to touch her arm, then stuck his hand in his pocket. "More than you know. But right now, I need to be with Jonah as much as possible."

"How do you know him?"

His jaw worked, and his eyes misted. Cradling the gift bag in one arm, he suddenly pulled her to him with the other, holding her close to his chest and resting his chin against her temple.

She lifted her arms to his neck, her fingers cradling his cheek. "Tell me, AJ. What's wrong?"

Instead of answering, he bent his head toward hers. His mouth, eager and warm, demanded she respond with equal fervor. Lost in the shared intensity of their passion, she pressed her lips against his as desire pulsed through her.

Suddenly pulling away, he stepped back and stared at her. "I'm sorry. I shouldn't have done that."

"AJ, I . . ."

Shaking his head, he dug his keys from his pocket and bounded down the porch steps. Interior lights appeared in the Jeep as he opened the door and set the gift bag inside.

"Come on, Lila." He patted his leg.

Lila ran to him, then scampered back to Shelby.

"Lila." Impatience edged AJ's voice. "Get over here now."

When she reached him, he grabbed her collar before she could take off again and shut her in the vehicle.

"You'll need her things," Shelby said. "They're in the hallway. I'll get them."

AJ strode to the porch to take the box from her and stowed it in the back of his Jeep. She followed him, touching his arm when he shut the hatch.

"What's going on with you? With us?"

"Us?" A sad smile momentarily crossed his face. "When was there ever an 'us'?"

"About one minute ago, I'd say."

His jaw jutted forward, and he adjusted his ball cap before meeting her gaze. "You're right. One memorable moment. But it shouldn't have happened. As much as I want to be with you—how much I've wanted to be with you since the first time I saw you—now isn't the time."

"Because of Brett?" Her voice cracked, and tears dampened her lashes. "I don't care about him."

"Because of me. Because of what's going on right now."

"You mean with Jonah." She punctuated her words with wild gestures. "I know you're concerned about him, but what does that have to do with you and me?"

"Everything." As if unable to help himself, he drew her into an embrace. She froze, afraid her slightest movement would cause him to pull away again.

"Jonah is my son." The whispered words, feather soft, floated between them. They seemed no more real than a will-o'-the-wisp caught on a summer breeze.

"Your . . . son?"

"I'm sorry, Shelby." He tightened the embrace, then let her go.

She staggered backward, instinctively seeking the shelter of the porch. Mesmerized by the departing taillights, she clutched the rail.

AJ has a son?

Why hadn't he mentioned the boy before? It would have been the natural thing to do on any number of occasions when he was with her and the girls. Her mind raced back to when she was at his cottage. The only photograph she'd seen was his grandmother's. There were no others, she was certain of it.

As the lights disappeared, she sank onto the cushioned swing and curled into a tight ball. Where there was a child, there was also a mom. A woman who must have some claim, even if a reluctant one, on AJ's heart. She must be at the hospital too, watching over her injured boy and desperate for his recovery.

Shelby pressed her fists against her chest. Her heart ached for Jonah's mother even as she fought against the ugly green monster growing inside her. She couldn't be jealous of this woman, not when her own two daughters slept peacefully in their beds.

But the monster refused to be tamed. And nothing could stop the tears pouring down her cheeks.

~

AJ slammed the cottage door and flung his keys on the desk. Plopping in a nearby chair, he dug his elbows into his knees and knocked his forehead against his clasped fists. How could he have been so stupid?

Lila stuck her nose between his arms and whimpered. Sliding to the floor, he gripped her behind the ears. "Why didn't you stop me?" he murmured. He hadn't meant to kiss Shelby, but in the summer moonlight, the tight control he normally had on his desires had slipped.

He wouldn't let it happen again.

The guilt that gnawed at his heart ever since Meghan disappeared had prevented any meaningful relationship with another woman. Though he despised the way Brett treated the women he dated, what AJ had done to Meghan was worse. How could he get close to someone else after abandoning her when she needed him most?

God was giving him another chance to do the right thing. To support Meghan through this nightmare. To be her hero.

Perhaps God meant for them to be the family they would have been if not for Sully's interference and AJ's cowardice.

He sighed heavily, and Lila licked his chin.

"I'm okay, girl." Except he wasn't. He might not love Meghan in the same way anymore, but that didn't change the facts.

God had brought them together again, and AJ needed to give a relationship with her a chance. If she'd allow him. Didn't they both owe it to Jonah to at least try?

Like an old-time movie, the evening with Shelby replayed in his mind beginning with the moment she touched his chin until he saw her stricken expression in his rearview mirror.

It'd taken every ounce of his willpower not to stop the Jeep and race back to her. But this movie couldn't have a happy ending.

– 28 –

The phone's ring jarred AJ from a dreamless sleep. He grabbed the annoying offender and glared at the display. Shelby.

Clad in pajama pants and a T-shirt, he swung his legs to the side of the bed and braced his heart to hear her voice.

"Hey, there," he said with forced cheerfulness as he inwardly groaned at the clock radio. The display read 9:17. He should have been on his way to the hospital by now.

"Hello, Mr. AJ? This is Elizabeth Kincaid."

Amusement at her formal tone conflicted with concern that she was calling him. "Hi, Elizabeth. Is everything okay?"

"Tabby is here too."

"Hi, Mr. AJ." Tabby's chipper voice blasted against his eardrum, and he momentarily pulled away from the phone.

"Gimme that," Elizabeth said.

He grinned, picturing the girls fighting over the phone. Apparently Elizabeth won because she spoke to him next.

"We just wanted to know something. Does Lila miss us?"

"I'm sure she does." He scratched the retriever's head, and she pawed at his arm.

"We miss her too."

"A lot," Tabby added loudly.

"You both took good care of her, I can tell."

"If you have to go away again, can she come and stay with us?"

"I'm sorry, sunshine, but I don't think I'll be going anywhere for a while." Not until Jonah was fully recovered. Maybe then he could take his son camping.

"What if you have to go to the store?" Tabby asked. "I don't think Lila wants to be home by herself." She sounded disapproving.

He chuckled. "She's kind of used to it."

"Couldn't she come over sometime?" Elizabeth pleaded. "You can come too, and maybe we can have a picnic and go fishing by the 'gagement tree. That'd be fun, wouldn't it?"

"I wanna fish." Tabby again.

"Mommy says no, but you could ask her. Then she'd say yes, I know she would."

"Mommy likes you."

Tabby had more confidence in Shelby's feelings for him than he did. "Where is your mom?"

"Planting flowers for Nanna." She was obviously repeating what Shelby had told them. "My favorites are the purple ones."

"I like purple too." He'd transplanted several plants from Gran's Columbus home when she moved to the house up the road. Lilacs. Lilies. Irises. A memory tickled—something about an old friend giving her heirloom iris cuttings. Even though she hadn't told him a name, somehow he knew as surely as if he had seen it happen that the old friend was Aubrey Lassiter.

If so, Shelby should have them for her garden.

But after last night, would she accept them?

"Mr. AJ? Are you still there?"

"I'm here, Elizabeth. Just thinking about the flowers."

"Will you come for a picnic?"

"I'd love to, but—"

"He said yes."

In the background, Tabby cheered.

"Elizabeth, honey, I didn't . . ."

Before he could say any more, Shelby's voice came faintly through the phone. "What are you doing with that?" Alarm heightened her pitch. "Who are you talking to?"

"Mr. AJ," Elizabeth said. "He said yes."

"Yes to what?"

"Picnic. Picnic," Tabby chanted.

"And fishing. With Lila."

"Give me that phone. Go outside, both of you."

"Bye," Elizabeth said quickly.

AJ waited for the tone indicating Shelby had disconnected the call. It didn't come.

"Good morning." She sounded tentative. And tired.

"I heard you've been gardening."

"Guess I should have taken my phone with me. I'm sorry they bothered you."

"They're never a bother." Walking barefoot to the long room, he pulled up the wooden blinds covering each window. The mid-morning sun warmed his skin as he peered through the glass. Over the hill and beyond the fields, only a few miles away as the crow flies, stood Shelby's house. "I think they miss Lila."

"I thought it would be easier on them for you to pick Lila up while they were sleeping. But they're disappointed they didn't get to tell you how much fun they had with her."

"I'd like to see them too."

"But you're busy." She said it as if she were finishing his sentence. He imagined her standing in her kitchen, perhaps looking out the window above the sink. Toward his cottage.

Toward him.

The few miles between them telescoped into a distance neither seemed capable of crossing.

Except through memory. As long as he lived, he'd never forget the soft warmth of her lips, the alluring fragrance of her perfume, the bittersweet thrill of holding her in his arms.

"When's this picnic-slash-fishing trip supposed to take place?"

He blew out air. "I didn't mean to say yes. Elizabeth misunderstood."

"Don't worry about it. I'll make some excuse."

"You can't do that."

"I think I can," she said firmly.

"How about later this week?"

"You need to be at the hospital. With your son."

"I need to keep my promise to Elizabeth and Tabby."

"You didn't make a promise."

"But they think I did. Don't they?"

"Looks that way," she said, sounding both irritated and amused. "They've already packed the paper plates and napkins."

"That settles it then."

"Does it?"

"I don't want to disappoint them. Or you."

"I'm used to being disappointed."

He opened his mouth, then closed it. How could he ease her pain when his expertise was in disappointing the ones he cared about?

"I'm sorry, AJ. I shouldn't have said that." She sighed, and he pictured her tucking a stray lock of hair behind her ear. "But after last night, it just feels awkward to plan something like this."

"We survived the awkwardness last time we were out there. We'll survive it this time too."

"How about if I invite Cassie and Jason to go along?"

"Sure, if we can make it for Thursday."

"That's right. Tomorrow's the softball game you're not playing in."

"But Jason is. And he teaches a class at church on Wednesdays."

"Thursday then. But only if you're sure."

"I'm sure." He turned from the window and wandered into the kitchen. The cookie jar sat in the center of the table. Shelby's attitude toward him had changed while he was out of town. If he'd never looked for Meghan, perhaps he'd have had a chance with Shelby after all.

Except then he wouldn't know about Jonah.

The same thoughts chased each other round and round, providing no answers and getting him nowhere. All he had to hold on to was the unmistakable prompting to find Meghan. God had whispered that message into his heart, and he had to trust in the perfection of God's plan for each of them.

If only he knew the details of that plan.

– 29 –

When Shelby pulled into her driveway later that afternoon, her stomach tightened as she stared in disbelief. AJ's Jeep Cherokee was parked up by the weathered barn. He had no right rummaging around in there. No one did.

She parked in her usual spot near the kitchen patio, thankful that the girls hadn't noticed the Jeep. The last thing she needed was for them to run up to the barn. Though they'd been warned to stay out of it, AJ's presence would undoubtedly kick that rule right out of their heads.

"Into the house, everybody," she said with more enthusiasm than she felt. They scampered from the car with their bags of library books.

"Mommy, look. Flowers." Elizabeth pointed to a bucket sitting near the kitchen door. Sunny yellow and velvety brown irises overflowed from the container. "They're so pretty."

"They're late-blooming lodestar irises. See how the yellow petals stand up? They're called standards." She gently touched a velvety brown petal. "These brown ones are called falls."

She unlocked the kitchen door, puzzling over the plants and glancing toward the barn. The old brick meat-smoking room jutting from the back porch hid it from view. But it was there, a dark shadow from the past that chilled her bones. And AJ was up there too. Why?

"Change into play clothes before you go back outside," she instructed the girls as she systematically placed her groceries in the pantry. "And put the library books in the basket where they belong."

The girls headed toward their room, and she folded the recyclable bags. She should go see what AJ was up to, but the thought of entering the barn made her weak in the knees. She hadn't stepped foot in it since they moved to the farm. Whenever she walked by, she averted her eyes, pretending it didn't exist. A well-known toddler's game—if she couldn't see it, it couldn't see her.

She hadn't even been able to summon the courage to plant the sunflower house along the side wall but paid Seth Norris to plant the seeds. The sunflowers had to be there, just like they had been when she was younger. But when the stalks reached their full height, she didn't know how she could permit Elizabeth and Tabby to play house among them.

The easiest, the most obvious solution, was to tear down the barn. But destroying it somehow seemed sacrilegious, even though its very existence caused her such pain.

A knock sounded on the door, and she jumped.

"Didn't mean to scare you," AJ said through the screen. "Mind if I come in?"

"Only if you promise never to do that again." She waved him inside. "What were you doing up there?"

"Looking for a spade. Or a shovel." He opened the door and stepped aside for Lila to enter. The girls raced up the hall, eager to greet AJ and his dog. After a boisterous reunion, Shelby managed to shoo them outside.

"Why do you need a shovel?"

"When Elizabeth called me, she said you were 'planting flowers for Nanna.' It got me thinking about Gran's flowers. She told me once a friend had given them to her. Maybe that friend was your Nanna."

"Do you really think so?"

"We'll never know for sure, but somehow it seems right. So I brought you a few plants from Gran's house. I can plant them for you if you'd like."

"You know, September is the best time for transplanting irises."

"Uh-oh."

"Apparently your thumb hasn't gotten any greener."

He held up his thumb and examined it. "Guess not."

"Let's just get them in the ground." She gripped the back of a kitchen chair and smiled. "You're a very thoughtful man. Thank you."

"You're welcome. For the flowers and the compliment."

"The tools are in the back room. I'll get a spade."

"Never mind, I found one."

She jerked upright, her heart pounding. "In the barn?"

"Um, yeah, that's where I was."

"You can't use it. Put it back." Her voice edged toward hysteria, but she couldn't control its pitch. Her heart throbbed against her chest, and her knees weakened. She grabbed for a chair, and AJ grabbed her. After helping her to sit down, he knelt beside her and clasped her hand.

"What's wrong, Shelby? Tell me."

"There's nothing to tell."

"You're white as a ghost, and your hands are clammy."

"I just need to sit a minute, that's all. I'll be fine."

He filled a glass with water from the faucet. "Drink this," he said, wrapping her hands around it. He pulled up another chair and sat beside her. His voice comforted as much as his arm across her shoulders. "Tell me about the barn."

She stared into the glass. Tiny ripples marred the surface of the water. "It's where he died."

"Who?"

"Grandpa." Tears welled in her eyes. "He just . . . he was lying there. In the blood." The image wavered before her eyes, and the kitchen spun around her.

AJ took the glass and guided her head to her knees. "Deep breaths now," he urged, gently rubbing her back. "Everything's okay. Just concentrate on breathing."

She inhaled then exhaled. Inhale. Exhale. The black dots receded from sight, and her dizziness lessened.

"Maybe you should lie down."

"I'm fine now." Fine except for the embarrassment of falling apart in his presence and the confusion of him being so close. "Really, I am."

"I don't think so. Come on." With his arm around her waist, he led her down the hall to the family room and settled her on the leather couch. "Lie still for a little while. You'll feel better."

"I'm okay, honest, I am," she protested. But in the depths of her heart she wanted nothing more than to be wrapped in his arms, to share her secret with him, and have his reassurance that he'd never leave her. But it was too late for that. She'd have to settle for his hand closed around hers as he adjusted a cushion beneath her head and covered her legs with a lightweight afghan.

She shoved away the memories, filling her mind with all the things she should be doing instead of having a nervous breakdown because of a spade.

He perched next to her on the couch. "Can I get you anything?"

"A clone."

"Why's that?"

"There's so much around this place I still need to do, but I don't have time. It's partly my fault. I signed up the girls for swimming lessons, and I registered for a master gardeners class, and I volunteered for the church landscaping committee, and Cassie asked me to contribute something to some bake sale. And crafts for Vacation Bible School. I'm in charge of that too, and there's still so much to do around here."

"Whoa, there, Martha Stewart. What is all this?"

She rubbed her forehead. "I want to belong. To the church, the community. To be a part of a . . . a place."

"You can belong without doing everything by yourself."

"My grandparents were pillars in this community. All kinds of events took place in this house. Wedding showers and potluck suppers. Wienie roasts and cookouts. I want my girls to know what that was like. To be part of people's lives. Their celebrations."

"Years and years went into those memories, Shelby. You haven't even lived here a month."

"I know." Raising herself to a sitting position, she leaned against the arm of the couch. AJ shifted to sit back with her feet across his lap. "The Fourth of July is next week. It'd be nice to have some people over. But there's so much landscaping still to do, and the dining room is half full of stuff I don't know what to do with and partially finished craft projects."

"People won't be coming to admire your landscaping. And if you close the dining room doors, no one will ever know what's inside."

Her ploy to distract him from asking more questions about the barn had worked. But she hadn't meant to take him down this road, either. Her expectations had been so great, her impulse to re-create the past so strong, that she was drowning in to-do lists, landscape diagrams, and an overscheduled calendar.

"It's too much."

The attentive sympathy of his deep brown eyes and the casual pressure of his arms resting on her shins lulled her into admitting a truth she didn't want to face. She was falling for him. Hard.

But what if Jonah's mom was the reason there wasn't a Mrs. Fourth? If AJ still loved her, and if she still loved him . . .

"Maybe you just need a little help."

"From you?" She twisted then separated the strands on the afghan's fringe. "Shouldn't you be at the hospital?"

"I was until a couple of hours ago."

"How is Jonah?"

His eyes dimmed. "Still the same."

"What do the doctors say?"

"They believe he'll come out of it. Given enough time."

225

"Is there anything I can do?"

"Pray."

She impulsively squeezed his hand. "Always."

~

AJ's conscience screamed at him to release Shelby's hand, but he couldn't do it. He might not have the thousand obligations she seemed to have gotten herself into, but circumstances were ripping his heart in two as his responsibility to Meghan warred with his desire to be with Shelby.

For these few moments, the tension that had been dogging him since he first learned of Jonah eased, and he slouched further into the cushions. Behind him, a fragrant breeze slipped through the open bay window. Little girl squeals, punctuated by the occasional bark, interrupted the trills of birdsong.

He had often dreamed of a future similar to this, relaxing with the woman he loved as their children played nearby. Holding Shelby's hand in peaceful silence might be as close as he ever got to that dream.

"Tell me about her."

"About who?"

"Jonah's mother." She pulled back slightly, and he released her hand. The dream ended, and tendrils of guilt squeezed his heart.

"Her name is Meghan." He exhaled heavily. "I was in my first year of law school when we met. She was an art student. A very talented art student."

"What happened?"

"Sully happened."

Her brow furrowed as she gave him a quizzical look.

"He, um, sent her away. And I didn't find her again until last week."

"You didn't know about Jonah."

"Nope." He could almost see the puzzle pieces clicking together in her mind.

"That's why you dropped out of law school. Why Sully punished you."

"Yep." Moving her legs, he rose and walked toward the fireplace. With one hand on the mantel, he stared at the empty hearth. Only a couple of months ago, it'd been cluttered with empty beer bottles and charred newspapers. Since then, the stone had been scrubbed and burnished. If only his past could be as thoroughly cleaned.

But to wish a different past meant wishing away Jonah. That he could never do. The boy already held a claim on AJ's heart.

Ducking beneath his outstretched arm, Shelby rested her hand on the small of his back. His arm slid across her shoulders.

"If Sully hadn't sent Meghan away, would you have married her?"

"If she'd have had me."

"What about now?"

"I want to take care of them. To do whatever I can for Jonah." She gave him a quick sideways hug. "I was wrong about you."

"How's that?"

"You're a fine man, AJ Sullivan." Her engaging smile warmed the lonely ache in his heart. "Meghan should never have given up on you."

"Sully convinced her she didn't have a choice. And it took me too long to realize we did."

"What are you going to do now?"

"Good question." He drew her into a casual embrace and rested his chin on top of her head. Her arms lightly encircled his waist.

"I'm going to call Jillian Ross."

Shelby looked up at him in surprise as he pulled his phone from his pocket. "The girl from the Dixie Diner?"

"You need the help, and she needs the cash. This way, it won't look like charity."

"Help me do what?"

"Plan your Fourth of July party. Help with VBS crafts. Bake Cassie's cookies. Whatever you need." He scrolled through his contacts list. "She's a hard worker, and I know you'll like each other." He held up the phone showing Jillian's number. "What do you say?"

"Okay, but I pay her. Not you." She put her hands on her hips and gave him a stern look. "This is your gravel money."

"How about we go halves?"

"No," she said firmly. "I don't want your charity, either."

"But you'll take Gran's irises," he teased as he hit the send button.

"As long as you plant them."

"Deal." He held out his free hand. After a moment's deliberate hesitation, she shook it.

"Deal," she mouthed as Jillian answered the phone. "Meet you outdoors."

- 30 -

*A*J wiped sweat from his forehead and poured water around the base of the newly planted irises. Shelby had chosen a spot for the yellow and brown flowers in front of the bay window where they contrasted nicely against the brick foundation.

He stretched, working the kinks from his back muscles as he appraised the job. "What do you think?"

"They're beautiful." Shelby leaned on a spade she had retrieved from the back room. The one he'd brought down from the barn was propped against the kitchen door.

"I think Gran would be pleased."

"I'm glad."

"Speaking of Gran, I talked to Jason earlier. We can bring over your furniture on Thursday after the picnic."

"That'd be great. I know exactly where I'm going to put each piece."

"So do I." He took the spade from her and balanced it across his shoulders.

"Where, smarty-pants?"

"Exactly where they were when you were growing up."

She made a face. "You're right."

"You know, Shelby, it's your house now. It's okay to change things around a little."

"I know." She pushed loose strands of hair from her forehead. "But where Nanna had them is where they belong."

He smiled indulgently. "Then that's where we'll put them."

"Thank you." She headed toward the house, and he followed. "Would you like a glass of tea?"

"Sure."

They climbed the patio steps, and AJ gestured at the spade by the door. "Do you want that back in the barn?"

"Would you think I'm crazy if I said yes?"

"Not at all."

"But it is crazy. Is there a lot of stuff in there?"

"You haven't looked? Not even a peek?"

"No. Not since . . . No." She shivered and rubbed her arm.

He supported her elbow. "You're not going to faint on me, are you?"

She shook her head.

"You want to talk about it?"

"I'd rather not." She took a deep breath and forced a smile. "You've been a big help today. Finding me an assistant. Providing special plants for my landscaping."

"Always glad to serve," he said with an exaggerated bow.

Her lips curled slightly upward as she opened the screen door. "Come in and get some tea."

"What about the spade?"

She hesitated a moment then straightened her shoulders with resolve. "Put it in the back room with the other one."

"You're sure?" he asked, searching her face for any sign of misgiving.

"It's only a spade, right?" Her voice slightly wavered, but she smiled gamely.

"That's right."

The barn, and everything associated with it, intensely troubled her. Understandable enough, knowing how much she loved her grandfather. But he sensed her anxiety was rooted in something deeper.

He carried both spades and the bucket into the back room behind the kitchen. A washer and dryer sat against one wall, and tools were organized along another.

Thad Lassiter had died around fifteen years ago, but no one had ever mentioned where or how. What had happened in that barn?

Since Shelby was reluctant to talk about it, perhaps he could persuade Richard to give him the details. The realization that they hadn't talked since the fight with Brett panged AJ's conscience. An apology to the elderly banker was way overdue.

After returning to the kitchen, he washed and dried his hands.

"I'm glad Jillian said yes." Shelby handed him a glass of iced tea. "Though I'd rather just give her your gravel money. Somehow it doesn't seem fair she has to work for it."

"If it makes you feel better, you're paying her more per hour than she'd get anywhere else."

"She's staying on at the Dixie Diner, though, isn't she?"

"Yeah, you'll have to work around her schedule there."

"Glad to." She cut an apple, separating the slices into two colorful bowls for Elizabeth and Tabby. "Thanks for everything, AJ. I didn't mean to fall apart like that earlier."

"Any time you need a shoulder, I'm here."

"The same goes for you." Her eyes dazzled, drawing him into their bewitching depths. "If there's anything I can do for you, for Jonah, please tell me."

He picked up an apple core and twisted the stem. "Could you do something for Meghan?"

Her hand slipped, and the knife crooked through the apple to smack the cutting board. She recovered and sliced into the apple again. "Like what?"

"She doesn't know anyone here, and she won't leave Jonah.

Do you think you could stop by the hospital sometime? Just to say hello."

"Are you sure she'd want me to?"

"She's all alone." He shrugged, slightly embarrassed. "Except for me."

"I can't even imagine how hard it must be to see your child like that."

"He looks so small lying in that bed."

"She should have told you about him before now."

"I wish she had. But this isn't the time for recriminations."

"No, of course not." She retrieved juice boxes from the refrigerator and placed them on a small tray with the apple slices. "I'll go see her Wednesday. Is that okay?"

He resisted the impulse to hug her. Any more physical contact between them, and he'd be kissing her again. For both their sakes, he needed to keep his distance.

"Thanks, Shelby. This means a lot to me."

"Who says I'm doing it for you?" Her teasing smile quickened his pulse. She scooped up the tray and backed toward the screen door. "Coming?"

He glanced at the clock on the stove. "Give me a rain check for snack time, okay? I need to go home and shower."

"Going back to the hospital?"

"I promised Meghan I would." He held the door open and followed Shelby to the patio. "I'll tell her about you."

"Nice things, I hope."

"The nicest."

"Does she need anything? I'm running errands tomorrow so I could pick up anything she wants."

"I don't know. Whenever I ask, she says no."

"It can't be easy staying night after night in a hospital. I'll fix up a little goodie bag for her."

"That's very thoughtful. Thank you."

"You're surprised?" She poked him with her elbow. "I'm a missionary's kid. Thoughtful is in my DNA."

Along with beauty, poise, and smarts. "Call me when you get to the hospital, and I'll meet you in the lobby."

"Sounds like a plan." She stepped to the edge of the patio and called the girls. Lila bounded after Elizabeth and Tabby as they scampered toward the house.

AJ jumped to the ground to meet them, kneeling to their level and listening intently as they interrupted each other to tell him a disjointed story about a secret tower and floating lanterns.

"*Tangled*," Shelby said. "The movie."

"Haven't seen it." He spread his hands in apology.

"You can watch it with us sometime." Elizabeth's eyes, more blue than green today, looked into his with pleading hopefulness.

He playfully tugged her braid. "I'd love to." He met Shelby's gaze and slightly shrugged. Was he ever going to learn to ask her before he made promises to her kids? But instead of being irritated, her lips curved in a soft smile. She held up her little finger and made a winding motion.

The message was clear. He nodded agreement. The Kincaid girls had him wrapped around their little fingers.

And so did their mom.

～

The summons arrived the next day while Shelby was chopping vegetables for a salad. Even though she'd been expecting it, the sight of her name as a defendant on the court document horrified her. With her stomach twisting into a coiled noose, she sat at the kitchen table and read the cold details.

Names. Dates.

Consult an attorney.

But the legal specifics didn't tell her how to sort out her teeming emotions. Anger, resentment, fear. Even unsettling embarrassment.

A couple of pieces of paper, and her most cherished dream teetered on the edge of a nightmare.

AJ's name joined hers as a defendant in the suit. He must have gotten a summons too. She wanted to hear his voice, to have him reassure her that everything would be all right.

But he probably hadn't been home to receive the document. She couldn't call him when he was with Jonah.

With Meghan.

An arrow tipped with jealousy pricked her heart, and she swatted it away. In a moment like this, she wished AJ had been the monster she expected instead of the kindhearted knight he never failed to be.

He would have married Meghan if his grandfather hadn't sent her away. Maybe this was their second chance at the happiness that had eluded them before. To take care of Jonah together and be a family.

Meghan was a fool if she let AJ slip through her fingers again. And Shelby needed to keep her distance, a reluctant advocate of their reconciliation.

Not easy when her daughters insisted on planning things to do with AJ. Nor when he wanted her to become Meghan's friend.

Elizabeth wandered into the kitchen, and Shelby quickly masked her anxiety with a forced smile. "Supper's almost ready. You want to set the table?"

She shrugged and opened the drawer where the place mats were stored.

"Something bothering you, sweetheart?"

"It's always lonely without Lila."

Worse than lonely for her precious daughter. Maybe it was only a coincidence, but Elizabeth didn't sleep well without Lila in her room. She wasn't having the grief-induced nightmares that terrorized her in the months following Gary's death, but she'd woken up crying the last couple of nights.

Shelby idly wondered what the penalty was for dognapping. The only other way she could think of to get Lila was to marry AJ.

The girls would probably love that.

To tell the truth, so would she. But with Meghan back in AJ's life, that dream was unlikely to come true.

- 31 -

*S*helby slid her Camry into a slot in the parking garage and cut the motor. Closing her eyes, she pressed her forehead against the steering wheel. *What am I doing here, Father? I know he won't help me.*

She had called Richard the night before to talk about the summons, but he only offered confusing platitudes. She wasn't sure, but it sounded like he called her Aubrey when he said good-bye.

That left her only one other option.

Brett.

Inside the office building's lobby, she found Somers, Inc., listed on the directory and took the elevator to the eleventh floor.

Outside the double glass doors, she breathed a prayer. Somehow she had to persuade Brett to talk Amy out of the lawsuit.

No one was in the reception area, but raised voices could be heard from the inner office.

Uncertain what to do, Shelby perched awkwardly on the edge of a chair. One of the voices was unmistakably Brett's. This probably wasn't a good time to ask him to stand up to his sister.

Especially if that's who he was arguing with.

Curiosity overcame her embarrassment. She edged toward the closed door, then stepped back as it flew open and a willowy blonde stormed out. Her tight skirt and ultra-high heels hampered her stride, ruining the dramatic exit she was undoubtedly trying to achieve.

She paused when she saw Shelby. "We have no appointments scheduled this morning. Who are you?"

"Shelby Kincaid." She forced warmth into her smile. "I just stopped in to see Brett for a moment. I mean Mr. Somers."

"Shelby Kincaid." The woman crossed her arms and gave her the once-over. "Did you like the flowers?"

"Flowers?" Shelby frowned, momentarily puzzled, before remembering the bouquet delivered to the bed and breakfast several weeks ago. The same day she and AJ ate supper at the Dixie Diner. "You mean the roses? Yes, they were lovely."

"I ordered them. At his request." She jerked her head toward the inner door. "And then he stayed the night with me."

Heat crept up Shelby's face.

"That's enough, Tracie." Brett's tone was eerily soft as he joined them. "Shelby hasn't done anything to you."

"Hasn't she? I haven't seen you since Friday, and you expect me to believe she had nothing to do with it." Fuming, she glared at Shelby. "Where did he take you?"

Stunned by the accusation, Shelby scrambled to respond. "We weren't together at all," she sputtered. "Except Saturday. He tilled my garden."

Tracie's eyes hardened in disbelief. "Mr. Never-Gets-His-Hands-Dirty Brett Somers tilled your garden?"

"It's true, Tracie." Brett flashed both dimples. "And then I planted flowers. It was one of the best days I've had in a long time."

"I don't believe you."

He gave an eloquent shrug. "Doesn't matter what you believe. I want you out of my office and out of my apartment."

"You're not getting rid of me that easily."

"I think I am." He glanced sheepishly at Shelby, then focused again on Tracie. "You're not the first to leave this way. Time will tell if you're the last."

Tracie pursed her lips and averted her eyes as she blinked.

Guilt pinged Shelby's conscience, though she wasn't sure why. This awkward situation was Brett's fault, not hers. Her only mistake was not suspecting he was involved with someone else while romancing her.

She was a fool, but Tracie appeared heartbroken.

"I didn't come here to cause any trouble," Shelby said. "I'm sorry, Tracie."

"Save your pity for someone who needs it." Tracie sneered and pulled her bag from beneath the desk. She sidled up to Brett and slid his tie between her perfectly manicured fingers. "You haven't seen the last of me, handsome. It's about time someone taught you a lesson." Her lips neared his. "Believe me, if anyone can do that, it's me."

To Shelby's surprise, Brett remained relaxed and unconcerned. "Take my advice, sweetheart. Next time you want to seduce your boss, be a little harder to get."

Her face splotched with fury, Tracie pushed his chest, forcing him to step back to keep his balance. She sashayed to the office door, then smirked as she looked Shelby up and down. "You're not his type, you know," she said, her voice saccharine sweet. "He won't keep you long."

"Only as long as I want him to," Shelby said smoothly, her gaze steady.

Tracie slammed the door behind her, and Shelby collapsed in a chair. "I can't believe I said that."

Brett smiled. "Me, either. But she deserved it."

"Did she?" Shelby bit her lip as guilt replaced her pompous smugness. "Not from me."

"Tracie's name is synonymous with trouble." He sat in a chair beside her. "Don't worry about it."

"You shouldn't have been dating us at the same time, you know."

"Excuse me, Ms. Kincaid. At your own request, we were not dating."

"True, but apparently you were more than dating Tracie. Seems to me that's breaking the rules."

"I make my own rules." He playfully tapped her arm. "So how long do I get to keep you?"

"That depends."

"On what?"

"Can you do anything about this?" She pulled the summons from her bag and handed it to him.

He glanced at the top page. "I told you before, this is Amy's idea."

"You're named as a plaintiff."

"Can't help that."

"Please, Brett. There has to be something you can say to Amy to make her change her mind."

"If I could have, I would have. She's got a lot at stake in this deal she's planning, and she's not going to give it up easily."

"I don't want to lose my home."

"I don't think you will. But it's going to cost you something to keep it." He handed her the summons. "I can recommend a couple of attorneys if you want."

"You know I don't have that kind of money."

"AJ does."

"I can't let AJ fight my fight."

"He's a defendant. It's his fight too."

"With everything else he's going through, I can't believe Amy is doing this to him."

"What's he going through?"

"He's worried sick about Jonah." She stuffed the summons in her bag and pulled out her car key. "Only God knows when he'll come out of that coma."

"Jonah? Is that his student's son?"

"His student's . . ." Shifting in the chair to look into crystal blue eyes, she tilted her head. "You don't know, do you?"

"Know what?"

She stood, staring at her key. "It's not my place to tell you."

"Tell me what?"

"I need to go. I promised AJ I'd stop by the hospital."

Brett stood between her and the door. "If something's going on with AJ, I want to know about it."

"As if you care."

"Of course I care. He's family."

"Is this another one of your rules? You care so much about AJ you want to know his private business, but you're also suing him. Yeah, Brett, that makes a lot of sense."

"You don't have any siblings, do you?"

"AJ isn't your sibling."

"He's as good as." His eyes softened, as if pleading with her to understand. "When our parents died, Sully and Gran took us in. All three of us. We lived together under the same roof until AJ went to OSU. No more than fifteen minutes away. We saw him all the time."

"So what happened?"

"Life happened." He paced in front of the receptionist's desk. "Don't you see, Shelby? We can squabble all we want between us. But when push comes to shove, we're all we have."

"If he wanted you to know, he would have told you." She moved toward the door. "I have to go."

Brett pulled his phone from his pocket. "I can call my doctor buddy."

"Call whoever you want." She pulled on the door handle, but he pushed the door shut.

"You're going to the hospital now?"

"Yes."

"Tell AJ I asked about him, okay?" Sincerity softened his eyes to a sapphire blue. But she was no longer susceptible to his handsome charm. Frustration roiled within her chest, bubbling into shaking anger.

"I've got a better idea."

"I'm listening."

"Instead of calling your doctor buddy, call AJ. Give him a chance to tell you what's going on." She yanked on the handle. This time he didn't prevent the door from opening. "And while you're at it, explain this weird family dynamic that gives you the right to sue him."

She sensed him watching as she walked along the hall and waited for the elevator. But she refused to give him the satisfaction of turning around to be sure.

When she reached her car, she slid inside and pounded the steering wheel with her fist. The arrogant lout and his "I make my own rules" attitude. It was past time he learned the world didn't work that way.

Her sympathies slid from Brett to Tracie. "I hope you get him," she said. "Get him good."

~

AJ glanced at the display on his phone. "It's Shelby," he said to Meghan. "She's probably in the lobby."

"I'm still not sure why you asked her to come."

They'd been through all that earlier, and he wasn't rehashing the argument again. "You'll like her," he hissed before answering the call. "Hi, Shelby."

"I'm here," she said, her voice wavering slightly.

"You okay?"

"Of course."

Her tone betrayed her. Hopefully nothing more than nerves. Though he couldn't fathom why she and Meghan were so hesitant to meet each other. They were about the same age. Both moms. Give it a few weeks, and they should be the best of friends.

"This place is a labyrinth," he said. "I'll come down and get you."

"I'd like that. Thanks."

The line disconnected, and he pocketed his phone. "I'll be back in a few minutes."

"No rush." Meghan concentrated on the yarn in her lap. One of the nurses had started her on a crochet project. AJ wasn't sure what she was making, but it seemed to calm her to have something creative to do with her hands.

He reached the ground floor lobby and found Shelby coming out of the gift shop with a stuffed dog attached to a balloon.

"Hey, there," he said. "Thanks for coming."

"I keep my promises too." Her smile didn't reach her eyes.

"There's nothing to be nervous about. Meghan's really looking forward to meeting you." *God, please forgive my little white lie.*

"How's Jonah today?"

"The same." He gestured toward the elevators. "This way."

They started to cross the foyer when Brett came through the automatic doors. "Good. I found you," he said as he approached. "What's going on, AJ?"

AJ shifted his gaze from Brett to Shelby. She looked away, and he shifted back to Brett. "What are you doing here?"

"Shelby said you were in trouble."

"I did not," she said vehemently.

"You said he was going through something."

"That's not the same thing."

AJ drew in air, then slowly exhaled as he faced Brett. "I guess I might as well tell you."

Brett shot Shelby a triumphant look, and she rolled her eyes.

"What's going on with you two?" AJ asked.

"Shelby doesn't understand about family, that's all. She's mad about the lawsuit."

"Lawsuit?"

"I got this summons." Shelby pulled the document from her bag and handed it to him. "We're listed as defendants. You and me."

AJ glanced through the pages. "I didn't think you'd really do it, Brett."

"Blame Amy, not me."

"Your name is on here too."

242

"We can talk about this later, okay? I'll call Amy, and we'll have a family powwow. Right now, you need to tell me about this injured boy that's got you hanging your hat in the city. Most summers you disappear into the wilderness."

AJ handed the summons to Shelby and took another long breath. He might as well get it over with, but it wasn't going to be easy.

"You remember Meghan Jensen." It wasn't a question.

"Art student Meghan?"

"The one and only."

Brett shifted uncomfortably. "I remember her."

"Her son was in a car accident. A bad one. Thanks to your doctor friend, now he's a patient here."

"Must be serious."

"It is. A few broken bones. A concussion. He's in a coma."

"His name's Jonah?"

AJ nodded.

"How old is he?"

"Seven." He tried to smile, but couldn't. "Congratulations. You're an uncle."

"Meaning you're his father."

"Meghan didn't have an abortion." AJ stared at his feet, then peered through the hospital's tinted windows to the parking lot. The cars were an indistinct blur. "She defied Sully."

Something he wished he had done.

"Where has she been all this time?"

"Most recently, a small town in Michigan. Just north of Toledo."

Brett took a couple of steps away from them, then returned. "This is unbelievable."

"There's a little boy upstairs who needs the best medical care we can give him. That's believable."

"That's not what I meant." Brett paced again, seemingly unable to stand still for more than two seconds. "You didn't know about him? Before this accident?"

"Didn't have a clue."

"So she contacted you when she needed help."

AJ tensed, and he shoved his fists into his pockets to keep them from connecting with Brett's jaw. No matter what his cousin said, he wasn't going to hit him again. "It wasn't like that. I went looking for her."

"Why?"

His gaze darted to Shelby before he could stop himself. He was aware of Brett looking at her too. Compassion sparkled in her lovely eyes, and she rested her hand on his arm in a reassuring touch.

"It's complicated," he said. How could he explain a prompting from God to Brett? He'd only scoff. "I had to find her, and I did."

"You're sure you're the father?"

"Meghan's too proud to take help from me if I wasn't."

Brett nodded slowly. "You're probably right."

"I need to get back up there. Don't suppose you want to see your nephew?"

"Another time."

"You don't want to say hello to Meghan?"

Brett gave a short laugh. "I think not."

"No surprise there. Come on, Shelby." AJ held her elbow and headed toward the elevators.

"AJ?" Brett called after them.

He turned back.

"If you need anything, if Jonah needs anything, let me know."

AJ waited for the gotcha, but it didn't come. Brett snapped a casual two-finger salute and strode out the front door. AJ stared after him until Shelby poked his ribs.

"I think someone's impersonating my cousin," he said.

"He's had a rough morning. Do you know Tracie?"

"His receptionist? I met her once."

"She quit this morning. Or he fired her. I'm not sure which."

"Let me guess. They were having a fling."

"Bingo."

The doors opened, and AJ followed Shelby into the elevator. He punched the button for Jonah's floor.

"I take it Brett and Meghan don't get along."

"There's a bit of history."

"And you don't want to talk about it."

He pressed his lips in a tight smile and shook his head. The history wasn't pretty, and he didn't like the part he'd played in it. As much as he hated to admit it even to himself, it still hurt that she'd rejected him for Brett.

Until Brett tired of her.

– 32 –

Brett leaned against his Lexus and called Dr. Marc Nesmith's number. The pediatrician answered on the third ring.

"I'm outside the hospital. Any chance you've got time for a cup of coffee?"

"Cafeteria in twenty minutes?"

"Great. See you there."

Brett found the cafeteria and chose a table by the window. Pressing his forehead on the heels of his hands, he relived the memories revived by Meghan's return.

"Brett?"

He jerked, pasted on a smile, and stood. "Hi, Marc," he said, extending a hand. "Thanks for seeing me."

"Glad to." The pediatrician took the opposite chair. "Have you seen Jonah yet?"

"Um, no. No, I haven't."

"Isn't that why you're here?"

"No, I stopped in to see my cousin. AJ Sullivan." He couldn't seem to stop rambling. "I knew he'd be here, and I needed to talk to him about something."

"I met AJ after Jonah was admitted. Nice guy."

"He told me he's Jonah's father."

"I'm not surprised." Marc swirled his coffee. "I wondered about the relationship."

"You wondered? So AJ's not named in your records?"

"Sorry, Brett. You know I can't answer a question like that."

Maverick Marc playing by the rules? Who knew? "I wouldn't tell."

"Nice try." He leaned forward, hands clasped around his cup. "What's this all about?"

"Meghan left town years ago. Now here she is with a child."

"You don't believe he's AJ's?"

"I just think we should make sure."

"I've seen AJ with Jonah. I don't think he shares your doubts."

"The breakup was a bad one." Brett glanced away with a heavy sigh. Somehow he had to convince Marc to help him find out the truth. "She shows up with a sob story, and AJ feels obligated to help her out. He's always wanted a family, and now he's got one. Ready made. He's not going to ask too many questions."

"But you will."

"Someone's got to keep an eye on the family money." An accurate statement, though this had nothing to do with finances. "Is there any way to check? Without involving AJ?"

"Ms. Jensen doesn't strike me as the gold digger type."

"With all due respect, you don't know her as well as I do."

"I'm sorry, Brett, but I'm not doing a paternity test without AJ's knowledge."

"There's no other way? What about blood type?"

"Old school, huh?" Marc leaned back in his chair. "Typing alone won't give you a definitive answer."

"Explain why not."

"Let's say you and AJ have the same blood type. As long as it's compatible with Jonah's and Ms. Jensen's, either of you could be the dad."

"What if the blood type isn't compatible?"

"Then AJ, you, whoever, can't be the father."

"Do you have Jonah's blood type?"

"Of course."

"Meghan's?"

"Probably." He held up a hand. "But I doubt I have AJ's. And I'm not risking my license to satisfy your curiosity."

"What's the charity *du jour*?"

"Brett . . ."

"How much?" He leaned across the table. "Five thousand? Ten?"

"And I'm supposed to believe this is about protecting the family fortune?"

Brett ignored him. "Let's do it this way. Tell me what AJ's blood type needs to be. That's all I want to know, and you won't be breaking any confidentiality rules."

"If their blood types are compatible, it doesn't tell you anything more than you know now."

"But what if they're not?"

"Then AJ shouldn't expect a tie for Father's Day."

"You'll get me the info?"

"Am I right in suspecting you and Ms. Jensen were more than just friends around the time of her son's conception?"

"My business."

Marc guffawed and eyed him steadily. "Children's Brain Injury Research Project. Ten thousand dollars."

"Agreed."

"But this is it. If knowing the blood type doesn't tell you anything, you're on your own."

"Thanks, Marc." Standing, they shook hands.

"I'll be in touch."

"Soon."

"You've got it."

They parted outside the cafeteria. Brett walked to his Lexus, his spirits less agitated than when he'd walked into the hospital. An action plan always helped him sort things out, though he was

99 percent certain the blood types would confirm what he already suspected.

AJ couldn't be Jonah's father.

~

Shelby followed Meghan out of the elevator when it stopped at the ground floor. AJ had practically pushed them from Jonah's room, insisting Meghan needed a break. She'd finally relented, but for all her reluctance, Shelby sensed she was relieved to get away.

"The cafeteria is this way," Meghan said, gesturing to her right.

"How's the food?"

"Not bad. I usually get a salad."

They turned a corner, and Meghan stopped abruptly. "Dr. Nesmith, hello."

"Ms. Jensen." The doctor's engaging smile warmed his dark eyes. "It's nice to see you out of your room."

"AJ's with Jonah."

"Is he? Perhaps I'll stop in and say hello." He switched his gaze to Shelby. "And you are?"

"A friend. Shelby Kincaid."

"Marc Nesmith."

"You're the pediatrician Brett called."

"You know Brett?"

"A little." Shelby looked past him. "In fact, I thought I just saw him. Walking toward the lobby."

Dr. Nesmith glanced behind him. "You might have. He's planning to make a donation to a research project I'm involved in."

"How generous of him."

"Yes, it is." His posture shifted, and his smile no longer seemed as genuine. "If you ladies will excuse me, I need to get upstairs."

He skirted past them and turned into the hall leading to the elevators.

"He seems nice. Do you like him?" Shelby glanced from the

doctor to Meghan. Crimson splotched her pale cheeks, and dread settled in her gray eyes. "What's wrong?"

"Nothing." Her tight smile revealed a shallow dimple, and she rubbed her arms. "So, you know Brett?"

"Yes. Do you?"

"I met him a few times. Years ago."

Shelby didn't know why she was surprised. After what Brett had said that morning, he definitely would have known who AJ dated. "What was he like?"

"Charming. Self-confident." Meghan affected a careless shrug. "I didn't know him very well."

"I don't think he's changed much."

"Is he married?"

"Are you kidding? I think he's too much in love with himself to ever fall in love with anyone else."

"He doesn't seem to have impressed you."

"At first he did. But that was before I knew he was related to AJ." Meghan's forehead crinkled. "Why would that matter?"

"It's a long story. And complicated."

"Life always is."

Shelby stole a glance at Meghan as they walked toward the cafeteria. Her complexion had regained its natural coloring, but her shoulders remained stiff. She'd been understandably tense since Shelby's arrival. But her agitation had increased after Shelby had mentioned seeing Brett in the hospital.

Apparently, Meghan had her own complicated story where AJ's cousin was concerned.

Throughout lunch, she seemed distracted, pushing her salad greens around with her fork. Shelby did most of the talking, sharing details about the girls and their move to Misty Willow. She had barely finished her chicken wrap when Meghan draped her napkin over her plate.

"I've been away too long," she said.

"I didn't mean to keep you."

"No, this has been nice." This time, both of Meghan's dimples appeared when she smiled. "I mean it. Thank you."

"Is there anything I can do for you? For Jonah?"

"Pray for us."

"Absolutely."

"Home seems so far away." Meghan crossed her arms on the table. "I'm not sure I should have agreed to this transfer."

"Why did you?"

"Because Jonah has a better chance of recovery here. At least that's what AJ said."

"AJ can be quite persuasive."

"I know."

Shelby squashed the temptation to ask Meghan about her relationship with AJ. When she had been in Jonah's room, she'd observed them as closely as she dared without raising their suspicion.

Both seemed more concerned with Jonah than each other. But with her heart on the line, Shelby wasn't sure she could trust her own judgment.

However, one thing was certain. Meghan was hours away from home and going through a horrendous ordeal. She needed a friend.

"I know you don't like to leave Jonah, but I'm having a cookout on the Fourth. Only a few people. I'd love it if you'd come."

"I don't know . . ."

"Don't answer now. Just think about it, okay?"

Meghan hesitated a moment then nodded. "I will. Thanks for asking me."

"You're welcome." Shelby pushed back her chair. "I better get home."

"Isn't AJ expecting you upstairs?"

"I'll see him tomorrow. My girls talked him into a picnic." She smiled broadly. "And fishing."

"They must like him."

"They do. Very much."

"Forgive me for saying this." Meghan dimpled as her eyes shone with humor. "Your girls may be young, but they have excellent taste in men."

"You're right. They do." If only she had been more receptive to AJ's attentions when they first met. Though it wouldn't have mattered. Meghan's claim on him, and Jonah's, came first.

- 33 -

Leaving Jason Owens and Seth Norris to oversee the kids' fishing efforts, AJ stood over the blanket where Shelby chatted with Cassie and Jillian.

"Sorry to interrupt, ladies."

"Catch anything?" Cassie munched on a chocolate-covered pretzel rod.

"No, but they're having fun trying." He stretched his hand to Shelby. "Walk with me?"

She tilted her head as if considering his request. Cassie playfully tapped her knee. "Go on," she whispered.

"If you insist," Shelby said teasingly. He pulled her to her feet, and they walked along the creek bank away from the others.

"Way to go, Coach." Jillian giggled.

He flashed a stern look at her over his shoulder. "Who invited her to this shindig?"

"I did," Shelby said, laughing at his pretend annoyance. "She didn't have to work at the diner this evening, and I got the feeling she didn't want to go home. The girls already love her."

"And Seth?"

"I invited him too."

He gave her a skeptical look.

"If you must know, I suggested she ask him. They'd been texting off and on all afternoon."

"It's about time they got together. I think Seth has had a crush on her forever."

"Jillian didn't feel the same?"

"She's an unusual teen. More interested in school than boys."

"Good for her."

"Yeah, but I feel sorry for Seth. He's going to lose her before he gets her."

"Why do you say that?"

"She's headed to Dartmouth; he's going to Ohio State."

"It can still work. If they really want it to."

He paused to pick up a couple of flat stones and skipped one across the broad creek. "Life won't change much for Seth. He'll be close to home, to his roots. But Jillian is about to enter a whole new world."

"Funny, I've never thought of you as the cynical type."

"I've taught long enough to see it happen. Four years in the Ivy League, and Jillian will never be content in Glade County, Ohio, again."

"Perhaps not." She took the other stone from him, her fingers grazing the palm of his hand. With a snap of her wrist, she sent the stone skimming across the creek's surface. He counted the hops.

"One. Two. Three. Four." He lifted his closed hand, and he and Shelby fist-bumped. "Who taught you to skip rocks like that?"

"Who do you think?"

"The same man who memorized poems about white chickens and red wheelbarrows."

"The very same."

"I memorized that poem too. Memorized your whole letter."

Her cheeks pinked, turning his heart to mush. She flung another stone into the water. It plunked, spreading ripples from where it disappeared.

"Did you get your summons?" she asked, staring across the creek.

He shook his head. "Guess they're having a hard time tracking me down."

Her jaw tensed as she wrapped her arms around her body. "I dread this fight. I'm not sure I can do it."

"You're not fighting it alone." He picked a purple thistle growing wild along the bank and handed it to her. "I'll give Amy a call tomorrow."

"She won't listen to Brett. Why should she listen to you?"

"She may not. But it's worth a try."

"What happens if we ignore it?"

"It's a lawsuit, Shelby. Ignoring it isn't an option."

"But if they win, what happens? They undo our deal, right?" She faced him, the words rushing over one another. "They can't force you into their deal, can they?"

"I wouldn't think so."

"So then we make another deal. Forget the lease option. I'll rent the house."

"There's more to it than our contract. Richard has been accused of fraud."

"As if he'd ever do anything that wasn't aboveboard. It's such nonsense."

"He still needs to be cleared."

"Poor Uncle Richard." Her shoulders sagged. "Having his name besmirched like that."

"He's always been there for us. For Brett and Amy and me. He has to feel betrayed."

"It's a cruel thing for her to do."

"Amy's ambitions don't leave much room for loyalty." Ambition borne of the pain each of them had endured as their parents' marriages fell apart. That unsettling pain had sharpened into unbearable agony when the four of them were killed.

Both he and Brett had coddled Amy, barely thirteen at the time.

Consoling her had somehow made it easier for him to cope with his own grief. Even now, as much as he hated what she was doing to Shelby, he had a hard time blaming her. The stone surrounding Amy's heart was meant to protect her from any more hurt. She couldn't seem to understand how much damage she caused by guarding her own vulnerability.

As he walked in silence along the creek bank, Shelby absent-mindedly twirled the thistle's stem between her finger and thumb.

"If Amy won't listen to reason," AJ said, "I'll call my attorney. She'll know what to do."

"I guess I should call someone, but I don't know who. Any suggestions?"

"Let me talk to Patricia first, okay? We'll see what she has to say."

"What about the fee?"

"I'll take care of it."

"I can't let you do that. They're suing me too."

He didn't want to talk about lawsuits and money anymore. Nor to have his thoughts consumed with Amy's troubles. Not when he was where he most wanted to be—with Shelby.

Squinting beyond the creek toward the western horizon, he adjusted his ball cap. The sun wouldn't set for a couple more hours, but orange and gold streaked the sky.

"Take a look at that. God's handiwork."

"It's beautiful."

So are you.

Their shoulders barely touched as they gazed at the horizon. A flock of geese cast shadows against the painted sky.

"We should probably get back," AJ said. "Jason and I still need to bring over your furniture."

Smiling, she nodded agreement then twisted and focused on a nearby hickory. Its low branches extended from a thick trunk that soared upward in a broad green crown.

"Do you know where we are?" Her face lit up in a bright smile.

"Yeah. Glade Creek."

"No." She drew out the syllable. "I mean yes." Grabbing his hand, she pulled him toward the tree. "Remember the story I told you about my Rebel ancestor?"

"The one who married your I-forget-how-many-greats grand-mother?"

"That's the one. Look up into those branches. What do you see?"

AJ bent beneath a low limb and peered into the tree's spreading canopy. "Boards." He circled the trunk. "Is that a tree house?"

"The remains of one, yes. It was the lookout."

"For what?"

"And you call yourself a history teacher," she teased, then pointed to the tree house. "They waited up there, watching for the boat."

"The Underground Railroad." He stared into the hickory. Shelby had mentioned her family's involvement before, but standing on the same ground where courageous conductors had stood made it all the more real. "Right here."

"Which means the hunting cabin was . . ." She scanned the area to gain her bearings, then scampered away from the tree to a broad rise. Standing at the top, she faced him and spread her arms. "Here! Grandma Eliza nursed her beloved Rebel soldier back to health in secret here."

AJ joined her on the grassy rise, then jumped up and down.

"What are you doing?"

"What kind of floor was in the cabin?"

"Couldn't tell you. I wasn't alive then."

"If it's wooden, we might find pieces of it." Bending, he opened his switchblade and dug into the ground.

"Maybe we could find the tunnel too." She knelt beside him and tugged at the grass.

"There's a tunnel?"

"It ran from beneath this cabin to somewhere near the house."

"Long tunnel." He peered that direction. Was it really possible?

"That's the family story." She shrugged. "Wouldn't it be fun to find out?"

"Maybe we can." He'd walked this section of the creek bank countless times since he moved into the cottage. He was familiar with its bends, the wildflowers that grew along its banks, the rise and fall of the surrounding pastures and fields.

But now, long-hidden secrets tinted the land with mystery. He imagined hiding in the tree house on a moonlit night while a boat slipped silently onto the creek bank. What had it been like to welcome runaways to freedom, to offer them a safe haven and a new home?

"You want a penny?" Shelby asked.

He chuckled. "My thoughts are worth at least a quarter."

"I'll give you a dime."

"Just imagining how it must have been."

"After the girls go to bed, I'll show you the secret room in the house. If you want."

"I'd like that." He stuck his knife in another spot. "I should bring my American History class out here."

"There's not much for them to see."

True, but that could change. One of his professors at OSU, Dr. Wayne Kessler, might be interested in knowing about this place. "You're sure this is where the cabin was located?"

"Positive." Her eyes softened, and her lips curled upward in a tender smile. "This is where Eliza and Jeb fell in love."

- 34 -

*B*rett put his new key into his new lock and entered the apartment. After leaving the hospital, he'd returned to the office and called the apartment's concierge office. His instructions had been explicit.

Nothing the staff hadn't done before.

First stop, the master bedroom closet. He scanned the roomy interior. His Brooks Brothers suits hung on wooden hangers along the side wall. His casual shirts were neatly arranged above a broad built-in of drawers and open shelving.

Tracie's dresses, shoes, scarves, and belts were gone.

Next stop, the master bath. No toothbrush in the holder, no floral-scented moisturizer on the vanity, no Midol in the medicine cabinet.

He owed someone a good-sized tip.

Exhaling in relief, he unknotted his tie and slid it from around his neck, then sat near the foot of the king-sized bed and removed his shoes.

What a day.

At least Tracie was out of his office, out of his home, and out of his life. She had held on tighter than most of her predecessors.

He smirked. Well, perhaps not, but it certainly seemed that way.

He padded to the kitchen in his stocking feet and uncharacteristically splashed Glenlivet Scotch into a heavy glass. He checked the refrigerator for something to eat, but there wasn't much to choose from.

His phone played its jazz melody, and he shut the fridge door to answer it.

"Hi, Marc. It's about time."

"You know my workaholic ways. Seeing my patients took priority over snooping."

"But you did find time to snoop?"

"Before I tell you what I found, I want to remind you that this may not give you any answers."

"I understand."

"You also understand you didn't hear this from me."

"Goes without saying."

Marc didn't respond, and Brett bit the inside of his lip. Give the doc a moment, and he'd talk.

"Meghan is Type B. Jonah is Type A."

"Meaning what?"

"His father is either Type A or Type AB."

Brett's pulse quickened. "You're sure about that?"

"Do you know AJ's blood type?"

"Three or four years ago, Gran had a blood transfusion. AJ and I did our familial duty."

"You gave blood."

"Turns out AJ's a universal blood donor, and I'm a universal plasma donor. It became a sort of family joke." For a while, he and AJ had donated plasma and blood every two or three months. They'd find a Red Cross truck, bare their arms, then grab lunch. Eventually Brett canceled a few times, thinking he had better things to do, and they'd stopped.

He massaged the back of his neck.

"Meaning AJ is O," Marc said, "and you're AB."

"Meaning AJ isn't the kid's father."

"And you could be."

"Sounds possible."

"Are you going to tell AJ?"

"I haven't decided yet."

"Do me a favor?"

"Sure."

"Be good to Meghan. She's already going through a tough time."

"Sure, Marc. Your check's in the mail."

He ended the call and tapped the phone against the counter. Having the right blood type didn't mean Jonah was his son. Who knew what Meghan had done after she disappeared?

Except she'd left because she was pregnant. Because Sully forced her to go.

He wandered into the living room and opened the drapes on the French doors leading to his balcony. The sun, low on the horizon, backlit the downtown skyline.

He'd met her at his grandparents' annual Christmas party. An attractive, small-town girl nervous about which fork to use and any conversational land mines she might encounter.

The first time he saw her standing alone by the sweeping staircase, an anxious smile pasted on her girl-next-door face, he'd known she was AJ's date. The college co-ed his cousin had been shielding from the family for at least half the semester.

Brett should have left her alone. But the temptation to provoke AJ had been too strong. Besides, AJ deserved it.

Brett had learned later what he suspected, that AJ had brought Meghan to a formal uptown affair with platitudes about how everything would be fine instead of schooling her in the finer arts of formal etiquette and small talk. No wonder Meghan had been on edge.

He opened one of the doors, stepped out of the A/C into a wall of heat, and leaned against the balcony's wrought-iron railing.

Only a few miles away, the son he'd never seen was lying in a hospital bed because a traffic accident had broken his bones and put him in a coma.

Strange, AJ hadn't mentioned anything about Meghan's injuries. Given Jonah's condition, the wreck must have been serious. So why wasn't she in a hospital bed too?

He returned to the apartment and grabbed his iPad from his briefcase. Settling on the couch, he put Meghan's and Jonah's names in the search engine and found links to media reports of the accident.

Clicking on one for a Toledo news station, he studied the leading photo. The vehicle's crumpled steel churned his stomach. Scrolling past it, he skimmed the article then returned to the beginning and read it again.

Anger knotted the sickness in his stomach into a tight mass.

Who was this Travis McCurry? And why was Jonah in his car?

After tossing the iPad onto the couch, he interlocked his hands behind his head and paced the room. His breathing slowed as he walked, but his jaw remained tense.

What kind of mom was Meghan to let her son ride with a drunk?

He halted as he caught sight of his reflection in the balcony doors. What kind of dad was he?

~

Shelby spread an embroidered scarf across the top of the oak washstand. AJ and Jason had placed the lowboy in the dining room and the washstand against the wall between the study's double doors and the door leading to the patio.

Just like she remembered it.

If only she still had Nanna's ceramic pitcher and bowl. Then it would have been perfect.

AJ walked in from the hallway carrying two large totes. "Here are the contents from the drawers in the lowboy. Where do you want them?"

"On the floor, I guess," she said. "Is Jason gone?"

"Yep. It's just you and me, kid." After lowering the totes to the floor, he sat on the edge of the couch and removed the top lid.

262

"Veering from Cary Grant to Humphrey Bogart, are we?"

"Gran liked *Casablanca* too."

"Who doesn't?" She knelt on the floor beside the totes, her back against the sofa. AJ slipped down beside her and looked around the room.

"Where's Lila?"

"Three guesses."

"Only need one."

"The girls wouldn't go to bed without her." She combed her hair with her fingers, twisting it into a loose bun, then allowing the strands to slip through her hands. "I'd get them a dog of their own if I knew we'd be staying here awhile."

He shifted to face her. "Why wouldn't you be?"

"The lawsuit."

"I thought we weren't going to talk about that anymore today."

"You asked. Besides, not talking about it doesn't make it go away."

"You can't leave."

"If they win, I'll have no choice."

"Where would you go?" The tone of his pitch tightened. "Not back to Chicago?"

"I don't want to go anywhere." But since receiving the summons, an unexpected idea had niggled its way into her heart. As reluctant as she was to accept it, she couldn't ignore it either.

"Maybe God has a different plan for me."

"Such as?" His voice slightly cracked, and he cleared his throat.

"I moved here to re-create memories." She looked past him to the washstand. "But I'm not a kid anymore. I'm a mom."

"I don't follow."

"I love this place. But I've realized what I love most are the memories I have of my grandparents. All the things we did together, the special connection I had with them."

"It's an important legacy. Not everybody has that."

"I have a responsibility to give that kind of legacy to my children."

"But your parents are in Africa."

"I know."

He stared at her, his eyes widening. "You're taking them to Africa?"

Her eyes burned, and she bit her lip. The mere thought of returning to the mission field filled her with dread. But what if that's where God wanted her to be?

"Maybe that's where we belong." She rubbed her thumb against the solid gold of her wedding band. If she'd stayed at the mission instead of coming back to the States, she would never have met Gary. Never have been in a marriage that didn't work. Never have known the grief of being a twenty-eight-year-old widow.

Never have had Elizabeth and Tabby.

"Wow." AJ turned the exclamation into a two-syllable word. He laced his fingers behind his head and held his elbows tight against his cheekbones.

"Maybe Mozambique is my spacious place."

"Your spacious place?"

She nodded. "It's what your gran told me. That day I ran away, and she found me by the 'gagement tree."

"'He brought me out into a spacious place,'" AJ quoted.

"'He rescued me because he delighted in me.'"

"It was one of Gran's favorite themes. There's another Scripture too, she used to say. 'I will be glad and rejoice in your love, for you saw my affliction and knew the anguish of my soul. You have not given me into the hands of the enemy but have set my feet in a spacious place.' Psalm 31:7 and 8."

"She said that to me too." Shelby closed her eyes and took a deep breath. "I didn't want to leave here. I loved my parents, but I never wanted to go with them."

"But you want to go now?"

Looking down at her hands, she barely shook her head. "It was their dream, their calling. Not mine."

"I'm not a theologian." AJ sighed heavily. "God knows I have my

264

own questions about his will for my life. But Shelby, if God wanted you overseas, don't you think he'd put that dream in your heart?"

"My girls are growing up without knowing my parents." That heartache had been with her since Elizabeth was born. Now, to pursue her own obsessive dream, she'd moved them away from Gary's parents. Guilt pressed against her spirit. Sometimes it seemed nothing she did was right.

"Is there any chance your parents will move back here?"

"They came home when I got married and after the girls were born. But they always seemed restless to get back."

She had tried to understand the calling they felt so strongly, the eternal perspective they brought to every decision they made. But if they wanted to be near their granddaughters, they could come home. As far as she knew, they'd never even considered the possibility.

"Sometimes I think . . ." She hesitated, unsure about sharing her secret fear with him.

"You think what?"

"I think they might love their mission more than us. More than me."

"That can't be true, Shelby." He slipped his arm across her shoulders and drew her close. She nestled her head against his shoulder, breathing in the familiar notes of his aftershave.

"I want to believe I'd do anything for God that he wanted me to do," she said softly. "But I don't have their commitment." Though that was her own fault. Somehow she'd become a Sunday morning Christian, sliding into a meaningless routine of worship, service, and prayer.

Several months ago, convicted of her negligence, she'd lain on the floor beside her bed in tearful remorse. Holding on to the multiple Scriptures promising God's steadfast love, she'd sought his guidance.

"With all my heart, I believed God brought me home to Misty Willow. But what if it was all wishful thinking?"

"He did bring you here, Shelby." AJ rested his chin against her forehead. "He knew I needed you."

"I need you too." A lone tear dampened her cheek. "But Meghan and Jonah need you most."

~

While eating a bowl of stale Cheerios at the kitchen counter, Brett read everything he could find online about Jonah's accident. Next, he internet-stalked Travis McCurry, even paying a public records site to gain information about his employment history. And his arrest record.

This wasn't the first time the creep had been charged with a DUI. What was a girl like Meghan doing with a guy like that?

Brett scanned the next document, then reopened a news site about the accident. It had occurred on Meghan's second wedding anniversary. At least, what would have been their anniversary if not for the divorce that had been finalized two months ago.

But those details didn't answer the question that was eating Brett up inside. Why was Jonah in the car with McCurry?

He ran Meghan through the same public records search firm but didn't find much. After leaving college, she'd somehow managed to stay under Big Brother's radar until her current residential address in Brennan Grove, Michigan, popped up. She'd moved there shortly before marrying McCurry. A few months ago, he had moved out.

Brett set aside the iPad, then rinsed out the cereal bowl and stuck it in the dishwasher. He picked up a glass dessert bowl near the sink and started to rinse it too when he realized it held a ring. Sparkling diamonds surrounded a finely cut amethyst set in a white gold band.

Tracie's birthstone. The only thing about her that wasn't artificial.

The ring clinked as he dropped it back into the bowl, then he placed the bowl in a cupboard. No need to risk losing the ring down the drain before he decided what to do with it. Tracie had probably left it on purpose as a ploy to force another face-to-face between them. But that wasn't happening.

After wandering to his bedroom, he opened the top drawer of a mahogany highboy and removed an ebony box. Inside were a few odds and ends—his father's cufflinks, an old-fashioned diamond tie clip, a few foreign coins. And a jeweler's box he'd found hidden in Sully's office safe after his death.

He lifted the lid, and the solitaire diamond, elegantly set in a white gold band, sparkled brightly as if all its fire were suddenly freed from the box's confines.

When he'd asked Richard about the ring, the old man's cryptic explanation was that Sully bought the ring for the woman he loved, but she'd died to him. Those had been Richard's exact words. "She died to him." But he wouldn't say any more.

So Sully had loved someone before he loved Gran. If he'd ever loved Gran at all.

Brett rotated the ring beneath the soft light of a table lamp, entranced by the crisp lines of color sparkling from the finely cut diamond. Was it a symbol of deep, eternal love? Or of love spurned?

Unless Richard divulged the secret, he'd probably never know.

For too many years, Brett had discarded one luscious blonde for another, knowing from the first kiss she wouldn't claim his heart. A long line of Tracie clones.

After all, that was the point. To be the heartbreaker, not the heartbroken.

He put the ring in the box and snapped the lid, dousing the brilliant fire of a love longed for and never found.

The story of his life.

– 35 –

Shelby opened the closet door beneath the hallway stairs and snapped on the light. "It's through here. In the back."

She removed about a third of the clothes hanging from the rod, opened the opposite door, and laid them across her bed.

"Let me help." AJ removed the remaining hangers.

"One nice thing about moving upstairs is that I'll have more closet space." If she moved upstairs. That stage of her renovation project might never happen.

"I know what you're thinking."

"It's hard not to think about it. I had such plans."

"Don't give up before we've even started the fight."

He was trying so hard to reassure her, and she loved him for it. But some dreams weren't meant to come true.

She smiled gamely and squeezed past him into the closet. With both the doors opened, it formed a passageway from the study, currently being used as her bedroom, and the main hallway.

Kneeling, she crawled toward the back where the ceiling sloped from the stairs. Examining the floorboards with her fingers, she found the notch and lifted the trapdoor. Behind her, AJ held it up while she hooked a latch attached to the sloping ceiling to a metal eye imbedded in the door.

"Will that hold it?"

"Should. Grandpa got stuck down there once when he was a kid, so his dad added the latch."

"Wonder what they did before then."

"They were careful."

"Guess they had to be."

"Are you ready?"

In the dim light, his dark eyes shone with adventure. "Shouldn't I go first?"

"I know where the light is. Just pray it still works." Shelby lowered herself through the opening, her feet seeking a toehold in the ladder built into the wall of the underground room. About halfway down, she reached to the side for the light switch and twisted the old-fashioned fixture. A solitary ceiling bulb flickered then glowed, lighting the dank interior.

She dropped to the floor and scanned the space while waiting for AJ to descend the ladder. The room, its walls lined with brick, hid below the closet and the study. Spiderwebs draped across wooden bunks forming an *L* against two walls, and a rickety table stood beneath the bare lightbulb. Plywood covered most of the dirt floor.

"This is how it was? Before emancipation?"

"It might have been a little more comfortable," she said, amused by the awe in his voice. "You know, mattresses covered with ticking. Quilts. Food and water."

"Do you have any idea how many runaways stayed here?"

"Dozens. Perhaps hundreds." She rubbed her arms, slightly chilled. "I don't know if they kept records."

"Probably too dangerous."

"According to Grandpa's stories, not everyone around here was sympathetic to the cause, at least not until the war started. Then folks jumped on the bandwagon, at least for a while. As the war dragged on, though, resentment seemed to build. That's why Eliza hid Jeb in the cabin."

"A Confederate in Union territory," AJ mused aloud. "They

probably had kin fighting those upstart Johnny Rebs." He said it pompously, as if imitating a staunch Unionist.

Shelby chuckled at him, then grew serious. "They did. But so did Eliza. Her brother almost died in Andersonville."

"But that didn't stop her from loving her enemy."

His eyes revealed the deeper meaning behind his words. But he wasn't her enemy anymore. In the past few days, he'd become something so much more.

Which was only making it harder to listen for God's still, small voice.

~

Pausing outside Jonah's door, Brett took a deep breath to compose himself. Coming to the hospital this late was insane. But at least AJ wouldn't be there, basking in his new role of wannabe dad.

He'd usurped Brett's place at the boy's side long enough. Just as Brett had done with Meghan all those years ago.

She should have told him the truth then.

Stepping away from the door, he stuck his hands in his pockets and leaned against the opposite wall. He couldn't barge in there slinging accusations, not if he was going to get any answers.

Maybe he should forget the whole thing, go home, and get some sleep. Or better yet, get drunk.

Great idea, 'cause he really wanted to be another Travis McCurry.

"God, help me," he murmured, staring at the ceiling as he admitted it was more of a prayer than he'd intended.

He didn't think it likely, but perhaps Meghan believed AJ was the boy's father. And even if she didn't, any woman given the choice between AJ and Brett in such dire circumstances would choose a sympathetic shoulder over arrogance.

As much as he wanted to, he couldn't blame her for naming AJ as the father of her unborn child. Or her naiveté in believing his cousin could solve all her problems. She hadn't reckoned on Sully's ferocious response when the future he'd planned for his favorite grandson was threatened by a nobody from nowhere.

Did she even know what it had cost AJ when he later stood up to Sully? By then it'd been too late for AJ to help Meghan—he couldn't even find her—but Sully refused to forgive him for trying. The grudge benefited Brett, but he'd paid a price too.

He'd fooled himself into believing he could have any woman he wanted, but if that were true, he'd have a woman worth keeping.

His life was in a downward spiral, and Amy's was too. If something didn't change, they'd both be lost.

The door to Jonah's room opened, and Meghan stepped into the hallway. Loose strands of her blonde hair, tied in an awkward ponytail, feathered her temples. Her gray eyes widened, and her complexion paled. "Brett." She stepped back against the closed door.

He straightened but gave her space. "Hi, Meghan."

The cute college co-ed had matured into a beautiful woman, but the weary slump of her shoulders and the dark circles around her large eyes reminded him of Cossette on the classic *Les Misérables* posters.

Her vulnerability tugged at his heart, ripping the scab from a wound he'd denied for years.

"What are you doing here?" Her voice quivered.

Fear or anger, he couldn't tell which.

"I came to see you." He gestured toward the room. "To see . . ." He cleared his throat. "To see him."

"Him?" She huffed and shook her head in disgust. "He has a name."

"Jonah. I came to see Jonah."

"I don't think that's a good idea."

"You can't keep him from me forever."

"Can't I?"

Searching her eyes, he tried to find the truth in their gray depths. But her hardened expression told him nothing.

He nodded at the wallet she carried. "Going somewhere?"

"Vending machines."

"How about we go down to the cafeteria?"

"I can't."

"Okay. The vending machines it is."

"I don't recall inviting you along."

"Then I'll stay here." With two long strides, he was beside her, his hand pressed against the door. "Wait for you to get back."

She stared at him, as if weighing his unspoken threat.

"This way."

At the end of the hall, a few vending machines occupied an alcove in a small waiting area. Brett pulled cash out of his billfold. "Allow me."

"Money's always the solution, isn't it?"

"Just being a gentleman."

"Is that what you call it?"

He bit his lip and slid a couple of ones in a machine containing beverages and a couple more in one with chips and candy. "Take your pick."

She punched buttons for bottled water and pretzels. Brett gathered his change and bought another water and M&M's.

Meghan led the way to a table next to a window. City lights competed with the few stars pinpointing the night sky. Brett sat across from her and opened the water bottles.

"How are you, Meghan?"

"How do you think?"

"You look tired."

"That's probably because I don't sleep much."

"Do you have to stay here?"

She gave him a disbelieving look. "Where else would I stay?"

He squirmed. "I don't know. A hotel?"

"Right." She pressed her lips together and rotated the bottle cap between her fingers.

"If it's a question of money . . ." He held out his hands, palms up, before the retort spitting from her eyes came out of her mouth. "I'm just trying to help you out here."

"AJ offered his grandmother's house."

If she'd meant to wound him by the comparison, she'd succeeded. "Did he tell you she died a few weeks ago?"

Her eyes flickered with regret, but she said nothing.

"Why didn't you take him up on it?"

She stared at the table, her body tense and withdrawn. "I can't leave Jonah here alone."

"How is he?"

"About the same."

"I don't know what that means."

"It means he just lies there. He doesn't move. He doesn't blink. He doesn't do anything."

"What do the doctors say?"

"To give him time."

"That sounds hopeful."

"Yeah." She took another sip of water then suddenly stood. "I'm full of hope." Grabbing her pretzels, she left the room.

"Where are you going?" Catching up to her, he grabbed her elbow and forced her to face him. "I know the truth."

She twisted, but he didn't let go.

"What truth?"

"You know what truth." He released her arm, and she rubbed her elbow. "You may want AJ to be Jonah's dad, but you and I both know he's not."

Tears darkened Meghan's eyes and moistened her cheeks. "I knew this would happen. It's what I've been dreading ever since AJ showed up in Toledo."

Tenderness melted his irritation. "Why didn't you call me?"

"And say what?"

"You could have just told me."

"Could I, Brett?"

He opened his mouth, but no words came. How could he expect

her to notify him about his son's accident when he didn't even know the boy existed? A lump lodged in his throat.

"Let me see him. Please."

Her expression crumpled, and she swiped at her cheeks with both hands. "It's too late."

"Too late tonight, or too late ever?"

"Both."

He sighed deeply and passed his hand over his eyes. Maybe it was time to take another tack. "When are you going to tell AJ?"

She narrowed her eyes. "You haven't?"

"Not yet."

Wrapping her arms around herself as if in defeat, she leaned against the wall. "I should have told him when he showed up." Biting her lip, she shook her head then gazed steadily into Brett's eyes. "I rarely talked about Jonah's father. Only to Travis and my friend Dawn. But I told them the same lie I told AJ. So when he showed up at Dawn's gallery, she believed . . ." Her voice caught, and she took a deep breath. "He just assumed, and I didn't correct him. Then he arranged all this, and it was too late."

"I'll explain," Brett offered. "He'll understand." *I hope.*

"He never knew we . . . that you and I . . ." Her cheeks flushed, and she buried her face in her hands. "I've told so many lies."

"Then it's time to tell the truth. AJ deserves that." Hating himself for it, he played the trump card. "So does Jonah. He should know his real dad."

– 36 –

AJ poured root beer into two tall glasses of vanilla ice cream while Shelby gathered straws, napkins, and long-handled soda spoons. After their excursion to the secret room, she'd invited him to stay for a snack. No way could he say no to that.

"Ready to tackle those totes?" she asked.

"Are you sure you don't mind my nosiness?" He picked up the glasses and followed her into the family room.

"Not at all." She sat cross-legged by the stacked totes. "I still can't believe your grandmother meant for me to have all this."

"Her list for you specifically said the antiques and their contents." AJ sat on the other side of the totes then handed her a glass.

She took a bite of ice cream, then lifted a rectangular photo album from the top tote. The photographs were mounted on black paper with white adhesive corners.

"We probably should get these into some kind of archival album," she said. "Do you recognize any of these people?"

"That's Sully." AJ pointed to a photograph of his grandfather as a young man. "Isn't that Richard with him?"

Shelby peered at the photo. "Yes, I think it is." She turned the page and pointed at a young man wearing rolled-up dungarees and a flannel shirt over a white T-shirt. "There's Grandpa. Look how young they are."

Page after page contained photos of their grandparents, Richard, and other teens.

"You look like Sully."

"I was just thinking the same thing about you and your grandmother."

"Look at this photo." She pointed to one of Sully and Aubrey standing arm-in-arm outside the old high school. "Change the clothes and hairstyle, and they could be us."

"I'm not sure I want us to be Sully and Aubrey." *Please, God, let our future be different.*

"No, I guess not." She turned the page. "Graduation."

The class picture took up the left-hand side of the page. On the right side, a few snapshots showed Richard and Sully in their caps and gowns. Gran and Aubrey stood proudly beside them wearing pastel dresses and white low-heeled shoes.

"They were all such good friends once," AJ said.

"Until Nanna fell in love with Grandpa."

"'Two souls, one heart.'"

She gave him a quizzical look, her green eyes shining. "What's that from?"

"Not sure. Just something I heard somewhere."

"It's true of them." She removed the second album and opened the cover. "This belonged to Nanna."

"How do you know?"

"I've seen it before. I wonder how your grandmother got it."

"No clue. I'm guessing she preserved these things for Aubrey's sake. She probably always meant to give them back to your family someday."

"I'm glad she did."

"Me too."

Most of the photographs were of Shelby's grandparents as a young couple, but AJ found Gran and Sully in several of the earlier ones.

He opened another album. "My grandparents' wedding." He turned the pages as Shelby oohed and ahhed over Gran's dress and the floral arrangements.

"She must not have realized this album was with the rest. You need to keep it."

"I'd like to. Thanks." He turned another page and pointed to a photo of two infants. "My dad and aunt."

"Twins? You never said." She tilted her head and gave him a smile. "Come to think of it, you don't talk much about your parents at all."

"Neither do you."

"Why do you suppose it is that we both seem more, I don't know, somehow affected by our grandparents' lives than by our parents'?"

"My parents traveled a lot." He closed the album and set it aside. "I sometimes think I spent more time with my grandparents than with them. They died when I was sixteen."

"You must miss them."

"I do." Planting his feet, he laced his fingers and rested his forearms on his knees. "Parents shouldn't die until they're really old."

"I'm not sure we handle it well even then."

"Probably not." He ran his fingers through his hair, resting his head on his palm. "Sometimes, what I think I miss most is the idea of them. I guess that doesn't make any sense."

"I understand." Shelby stirred her ice-cream float. "You want to remember them as being more than what they were."

"Feet of steel instead of feet of clay."

"Something like that."

"But I don't want to follow in their footsteps. Not Sully's. Not Dad's."

"You won't. You're not." She touched his arm, her eyes intent and tender. "You care more about people than about money."

Drawing back, she stared into her soda glass. "You care about doing the right thing."

Even though he couldn't see her expression, he knew what she was thinking. In her quiet way, she was telling him she understood his responsibility to Meghan and Jonah.

They were his priority for now, but his heart belonged to Shelby. He'd do everything in his power to keep her at Misty Willow.

"One more," Shelby said, pulling a thick manila envelope from the tote. She upended it, and a handful of newspaper clippings slid out.

"What are those?" AJ asked.

"I don't know." She unfolded the top one, then dropped it to the floor. Covering her mouth, she gagged, swallowed, and gagged again.

"Shelby." Shoving the totes out of his way, AJ sat next to her and put his arm around her. "What is it?"

She drew her knees to her chest, hid her face, and rocked back and forth.

AJ picked up the newspaper article and read the headline. "Local Farmer Found Dead." The accompanying photo showed the barn's grainy interior. The lighting appeared ghostly and dim as if the photographer had planned the photo to look mysterious.

"Why would she keep these?" Shelby gasped.

"I don't know." He squeezed her shoulder. "She probably didn't remember she had them."

A second clipping included a studio portrait of Thad Lassiter. Shelby glanced at it. "That's from their sapphire anniversary picture."

"Sapphire?"

"Forty-five years." Her voice cracked. "I was with them that day. When the portrait was taken. We went to lunch, just the three of us." Sobbing, she buried her head again.

He pulled her closer, resting his jaw against her hair. The floral fragrance of her shampoo mingled with the faint notes of her perfume. "It's okay, sweetheart," he murmured. "Cry it out."

After a few moments, her sobbing subsided. She grabbed a napkin and wiped her eyes.

"Are you all right?"

She nodded, then broke again.

AJ rubbed her back and lifted her chin. "What is it, Shelby?"

Struggling to regain her composure, she met his gaze and blinked. "I found him," she whispered. "Richard . . . Richard told them . . . he did." She gulped. "But it was me."

A chill went up AJ's spine as she buried her face in his shoulder. "I'm sorry, Shelby. I'm so sorry." He wrapped his arms around her, holding her close as the sobs wracked her body. Tears burned his eyes and dampened his cheeks.

Her heart was breaking. And so was his.

~

AJ had been reluctant to leave Shelby, but she'd finally convinced him to go home. He placed Gran's wedding album and the manila envelope on his desk, then hung his OSU ball cap on its hook. The cottage was lonely without Lila, but leaving her at Shelby's gave him an excuse to return tomorrow. He dug out his phone and sent her a text.

"Home. You okay?"

A couple moments later, she replied. *"I'm fine. Thank you."*

He repeated what he'd said before he left her. *"No more tears. Promise?"*

"Promise. Good night." The smiley face icon ended her message.

"Night."

He carried the envelope into the bedroom and propped his pillows against the headboard. Relaxing on the bed, his legs stretched before him, he dumped the envelope's contents on the comforter.

Most of the news articles were from the local Glade County paper, but a couple of them came from the *Columbus Dispatch*. After sorting them by date, AJ read every word and studied every photograph.

Thad Lassiter's body had been found by his brother-in-law, prominent banker Richard Grayson, in the Lassiters' barn. The recent loss of Misty Willow due to financial difficulties had been a cruel blow to the prominent farmer, and rumors had swirled that he had taken his own life. But authorities determined Thad died after tripping on a pig trough.

Thad's loss of the farm was a win for Sully, a bitter old man who couldn't get over the rejection of his first love. But surely even he regretted his one-time friend's tragic death. At least, AJ hoped he did.

The final two clippings were obituaries, one for Thad and the other, dated less than two weeks later, for Aubrey. The list of survivors was almost identical in each. But one name stood out. He lightly caressed it with his finger.

One granddaughter, Shelby Eliza Lassiter.

Haunted by the warmth of her hair against his skin, the dampness of her tear-moistened cheeks against his fingers, he closed his eyes and relived the anguish of her sob-choked confession.

"Richard told them he did. But it was me."

She'd only been fourteen. Just a kid.

No wonder she'd spent years despising his family.

He stuffed the newspaper clippings into the envelope and stuck it in his nightstand drawer. Before going to the hospital tomorrow, he'd stop by the newspaper office and check their archives for any other photographs. Figure out how to get a copy of the sheriff's report. And contact Professor Kessler to tell him about the tunnel beneath the hunting cabin.

He slid beneath the comforter and turned out the light. Maybe Shelby would let him take her and the girls to the Dixie Diner for supper. Or perhaps he could pick up a pizza. They still needed to watch *Tangled*.

A movie night with his favorite gals. If only Gran could be with them too.

~

As Shelby closed the dishwasher, her phone signaled AJ's incoming text. *"No more tears. Promise?"* The same thing he'd said before leaving.

She tapped out her reply. *"Promise. Good night."* Smiley face. *"Night."*

Slipping the phone in her pocket, she returned to the family room. The totes, still in the middle of the room, taunted her. It'd been fun at first, looking through the albums at their grandparents' photos. But now she wished Joyanna had given them to someone else.

She scooted the totes against a wall and collapsed on the couch.

"Mommy?" Elizabeth stood in the doorway, Lila by her side.

"What are you doing out of bed?"

"I have to ask you something."

Shelby patted the couch. "Come here then."

Elizabeth scurried across the room and snuggled close while Lila lay at Shelby's feet. "Did Mr. AJ go home?"

"Um-hm." She absentmindedly stroked Elizabeth's hair.

"But Lila is still here."

"He said she could stay the night with you and Tabby."

"I'm glad."

"What did you want to ask me?"

"Are we moving again?"

Shelby's heart fell to her stomach. "Why do you ask that?"

"I heard you and Mr. AJ talking." Elizabeth shifted and pulled her nightgown over her feet. "I like it here. Don't you?"

"Yeah. I do."

"Then why are we leaving?"

Instead of answering, Shelby wrapped her arms around Elizabeth's slender body and kissed the top of her head.

"Africa is too far away."

A world map had hung on the kitchen wall in their previous house. A blue pin marked Chicago, and a red pin marked the Mozambique mission. How many times had she offhandedly said her parents lived "too far away"?

"If we move," Elizabeth's small voice cracked, "I won't see Austin anymore, will I?"

"You like Austin?"

"He's my best friend."

Her oh-so-serious tone made Shelby smile. She had been about Elizabeth's age when she claimed Jason as her best friend. It looked like history was repeating itself with a younger generation.

The friendship of two six-year-olds wouldn't persuade Amy to drop the lawsuit. But was it enough reason to keep Shelby from leaving Glade County?

− 37 −

Shelby hung up the phone and rubbed her temples.

"Another no?" Jillian asked sympathetically as she rolled out pie dough on the kitchen table. The teen had spent the last few days with them, and Shelby had enjoyed every minute with her.

"Everybody I've asked already has plans for the Fourth." She slunk in her chair. "I should have known."

Jillian lifted the dough and arranged it in the pie dish. "I'm sorry it didn't work out."

"Me too. Lemonade?"

"Sure."

Shelby pulled the pitcher from the refrigerator. "My grandparents had such great Fourth of July celebrations. We'd go to town for the parade, then race back here to get everything ready." Ice from the dispenser clinked into two glasses. "I had my heart set on reviving the Lassiter Fourth of July cookout tradition."

"You still can. Just pick another day."

"To celebrate the Fourth?"

"To have a cookout." Jillian spooned fresh blackberries into the pie dish, then added the top crust. "Start your own tradition."

"Maybe you're right."

"Of course I am."

"Tomorrow's Saturday. Too soon?"

"There's only one way to find out. Get back on the phone."

"What about you and Seth?"

"We don't mind giving up the movies for the First Annual Kincaid Cookout."

"You may not, but Seth might."

"I promise you, he won't."

Shelby grinned as a shy smile lifted Jillian's flushed cheeks. This teenage romance might turn out to be more than a summer fling. Score: Shelby, one. AJ, zero.

"Bet I can guess who you're thinking about." Jillian finished crimping the edges of the pie crust.

"I was thinking about the cookout."

"Are you inviting Coach Sullivan?"

"Maybe."

"Why don't you call him?" Jillian's blue eyes glinted with mischief.

"He's coming by later to get Lila. I'll ask him then."

"You know he'll say yes."

"I don't know that."

"Yes, you do." She put the pie in the oven and set the timer. "Just like I know Seth will say yes."

"You and Seth are dating. You're a couple."

"Aren't you and Coach dating?"

"No, we're not."

"Well, you should be."

"Jillian!"

"Just sayin'."

Shelby pretended to give the teen an icy glare as she picked up her phone. "I'm going to call Cassie again. Wish me luck."

"Luck."

Taking a deep breath, she called Cassie, got a yes, then called Paul Norris's wife Renee. Another yes.

"We're having a cookout." She rummaged through a drawer

for a notepad. "Do you mind getting the girls ready while I make a shopping list? We'll go to town as soon as the pie's done."

"Sure."

"I almost forgot. Would you like to invite your parents?"

Dread narrowed Jillian's eyes, and her cheeks turned crimson. "Thanks, but no."

"Is everything okay at home?"

Jillian responded with a grim smile. "It is what it is. I better get Elizabeth and Tabby inside."

"If you ever want to talk—"

"I know. Thanks." She went outside, letting the screen door close with a thwack.

Shelby walked to the window and moved the curtain. Elizabeth and Tabby surrounded Jillian as she grasped both of them by the hand. Their little girl voices, though indistinct, were cheerful. Jillian swung their arms as they returned to the house, a broad smile lighting her attractive features.

Let my home be a refuge for her, Father. A safe and spacious place.

~

AJ emailed Dr. Kessler before leaving the cottage, then waited at the sheriff's office for about twenty minutes to receive the requested report. After paying the copying costs, he drove to the newspaper office.

An administrative assistant listened to his request with interest, but she wasn't sure whether unused photographs from that time period were stored in the newspaper archives. She promised to do some research and give him a call.

Next stop, the hospital.

He bounded off the elevator and greeted the nurses working at the central station.

"Mr. Sullivan," one of them called after him as he headed toward Jonah's room. "Excuse me. Sir?"

Turning back, AJ removed his ball cap and approached the counter. "Is something wrong?"

"I'm sorry, but only approved visitors are permitted in the Jensen room."

Every muscle in his body tensed. "Did something happen? Is Jonah all right?"

"I'm not allowed to answer questions about Jonah's medical condition."

"I've been here every day. Something must have happened."

"Ms. Jensen made the request. No visitors without her approval."

"That doesn't make sense."

"Again, I'm sorry. But Ms. Jensen was adamant, and we must respect her wishes."

"It's okay. I'll call her." He dialed Meghan's number, but the call went to voicemail. "It's AJ. I'm here, but they won't let me past the nurses' station. Call me." Hanging up, he faced the nurse. "I don't understand. When did Meghan decide this?"

Another nurse spoke up. "It was late last night. After that other man left. She was very upset."

"What man?" Surely her ex-husband wasn't bailed out of jail.

"I don't know his name."

"What did he look like?"

"Blond hair. Incredibly blue eyes." She practically swooned, and AJ clenched his jaw. "Very good looking."

"Brett."

The first nurse picked up a clipboard. "Here it is. Brett Somers. Ms. Jensen specifically stated that you and Mr. Somers were no longer allowed to visit."

"Do you know him?" the second nurse asked.

"Yeah. I know him." He strode to the elevator and punched the down button.

~

Shelby walked with Jillian and the girls to the library door. "While you're in there, I'm going to walk over to the bank and invite Uncle Richard to our cookout. Mind Jillian, okay?"

"We will," Elizabeth said.

"We will," Tabby echoed.

"Good. See you soon."

Inside the bank, she had to wait only a few moments before Chandra Coleman, Richard's assistant, escorted her into his office. He stood as she entered.

"Shelby. It's so good of you to stop by."

"Hi, Uncle Richard." She smiled brightly to hide her shock at his frail appearance. His cheeks seemed more deeply wrinkled, his shoulders even more stooped than when she'd seen him the week before. "Thanks for seeing me."

"I always have time for you." He gestured at the chair across from his desk.

"How have you been?"

"Fine, fine. And you?"

"I'm good." She folded her hands in her lap. "I know it's short notice, but we're having a cookout tomorrow afternoon. I'd love for you to come."

Blinking, he passed his hand across his eyes. "I thought you were angry with me."

"No." Her knuckles whitened as she gripped her fingers. "Disappointed, but not angry."

"I'm sorry about that."

"Me too." She smiled again. "But you're family. The only family I have within a few thousand miles. Will you come to the cookout? About four o'clock?"

"I will. Thank you."

"Great." She rose, adjusting the strap of her bag on her shoulder.

"Would you like me to bring anything?"

"Just you."

He stepped from behind the desk and touched her arm. "Did you receive the notice? About the lawsuit?"

"Yes."

"I talked to Amy. She believes you will give up rather than endure a trial."

"She may be right."

"You'd give up the farm?"

"I may not have a choice. But what about you? Brett said you could be in trouble."

"Don't worry about me."

"I can't help it."

His pale eyes searched hers. "You favor your grandmother more every day. I miss her."

"So do I." She kissed his soft cheek. "I've got to go. See you tomorrow?"

"Tomorrow."

~

AJ yanked the door to Brett's office, but it didn't open. He yanked again, but to no avail. So Brett was playing hooky after his late-night hospital visit. He brought up his cousin's name on his cell, then hesitated.

Confronting Brett over the phone wasn't a good idea. Too easy for him to hang up.

He hurried back to the parking garage and drove to Brett's apartment. Outside the door, he took a deep breath, then firmly knocked.

A few seconds later, Brett opened the door and grimaced. "I've been expecting you."

"Have you?"

Brett turned back into the apartment and AJ followed. "Coffee?" Brett asked over his shoulder.

"This isn't exactly a social call."

"Oh, I know that." Brett retrieved a mug from a side table and carried it to the kitchen sink. "You made your daily trek to the hospital this morning, talked to the lovely Meghan, who finally told you the truth about her son, and now you're here to break my jaw."

AJ took off his ball cap and laid it on the counter that separated them.

"The truth about her son?"

"So she didn't tell you." He set a carousel of assorted coffees in front of AJ. "Choose one."

"She banned me from visiting." He carelessly spun the carousel. "Banned you too."

Brett grunted.

"Why did you go see her?"

Leaning against the stove, Brett folded his arms and scowled. "You can't have them both, you know."

"Have both what?"

"Not what. Who." He held AJ's gaze. "Meghan *and* Shelby."

"What are you talking about?"

"This is the moment of truth for you, cuz. Who do you want most?"

AJ chewed the inside of his mouth. His heart trumpeted the answer, but he couldn't trust Brett with it.

"You may not believe this," Brett said, "but I'm doing you a favor."

He shook his head in disbelief. "How's that? *Cuz.*"

Brett placed his palms on the counter and leaned forward. "Do you know Meghan's blood type?"

AJ furrowed his brows. "No."

"She's a B. Her son, on the other hand, is an A."

A knot strangled AJ's gut as he braced for the rest.

"From what I understand, Jonah's dad can only be Type A or AB."

AJ swallowed the lump choking his throat. They'd been typed, he and Brett, when Gran got ill that time. Given blood and plasma regularly for a while. Joked about how they were nothing alike, not even their blood.

"I'm not Jonah's dad."

"No. You're not."

Disbelief fought with accusation in AJ's voice. "You didn't."

Brett's lips tightened, then he exhaled. "I'm not proud of it, okay?"

AJ clenched his fist, then turned away and massaged his neck. The infatuation with Brett hadn't lasted long. Then Meghan had shown up at AJ's apartment, begging him to give their relationship another chance.

"How could you, Brett?"

"If it's any consolation, I felt guilty enough to break it off."

"She said she broke up with you. That it had been a mistake."

"Meghan doesn't always tell the truth."

"She should have told me the truth about Jonah."

"Why would she, AJ? You came sweeping in like you always do, the hero slaying the dragon."

AJ paced the room, then plopped on the couch. Elbows propped on his knees, he pressed his forehead against his interlaced fingers. "I didn't know you'd slept with her." Bitterness soured his mouth.

Brett sat in a nearby chair and crossed his ankles on the coffee table. "Meghan doesn't care about either of us, AJ. Her only concern is that boy."

The words echoed through AJ's brain as the truth he thought he knew turned inside out. The apartment was silent except for the hum of the A/C and the beating of his own heart.

"You don't have to worry about Meghan anymore. Or Jonah."

"I can't turn my back on them."

"I'm not telling you to. After all, you're still his uncle." He paused, and AJ raised his eyes. "But I am asking you to give me a chance to, I don't know, make amends somehow."

"You? What about the blonde-of-the-week?"

"Maybe it's time for me to hire a brunette."

"Right."

Brett's eyes bored through him. "Go to Shelby, AJ. Win her heart and be a dad to those two little hooligans who are so crazy about you."

The perfect plan. If only she stayed at Misty Willow. "Shelby may be moving."

"Why?"

"That little thing called a lawsuit. Have you talked to Amy?"

"I'll call her this afternoon."

"It won't do any good. When did she ever give up anything?"

"Never." Brett planted his feet on the floor and leaned forward. "I'm starving. How about I buy you lunch?"

AJ blew out air. He needed time to figure things out, to decide what to do about Meghan and Jonah.

"What do you say?" Brett asked.

AJ shrugged. "Why not?" He stood and grabbed his ball cap from the counter. "One condition. I don't want to talk about Meghan."

"Okay. I don't want to talk about Shelby."

"Or your hunt for a new Tracie."

"What does that leave us?"

"Sports?"

"Sports."

As he waited for Brett to put on his shoes, AJ rotated his shoulders and consciously relaxed his tense muscles. He hated to admit it, but Brett was right about doing him a favor. If what he said was true—and Brett would never admit to fathering a child that wasn't his—then AJ's heart no longer needed to be torn in two.

He'd still do whatever he could to help Meghan. But now he was free to give his whole heart to Shelby and her girls.

If she'd let him.

- 38 -

With hands on her hips, Shelby surveyed the kitchen table. American flags of assorted sizes, patriotic bunting, and miniature tin pails were scattered between packages of red, white, and blue napkins, plastic plates, and tableware. A bouquet of red-tinted white carnations lay across a pile of candles, stencils, paints, and brushes.

"Let's get these things sorted out," she said, "and we can start painting."

"Can I paint this one?" Tabby grabbed the nearest pail.

"In just a minute, okay?" Shelby moved the bouquet to the sink and split open the plastic wrapping.

"These are going to be so adorable." Jillian rummaged through the pile for the stencils. "What a fun idea."

A knock shook the screen door, and Shelby turned from the sink.

"Mr. AJ!" Elizabeth scampered to the door and pushed it open. "We're having a party tomorrow. Look!"

"Tomorrow? That's sudden." He rubbed Lila's head as she pressed against his leg.

"Everyone I asked to come for the Fourth already had plans," Shelby said as she trimmed the flower stems and stuck them in a pitcher. Later she would arrange them in smaller containers. "So we decided to have our celebration cookout tomorrow. Will you be able to come?"

"Wouldn't miss it."

"Lila can come too, can't she, Mommy?" Elizabeth said.

"If Mr. AJ wants her to, she can." She focused on the flowers and prayed her voice didn't quiver. "Which reminds me, I invited Meghan for the Fourth, so I need to let her know about the change. But I don't have her number."

"Who's Meghan?" Jillian asked, and Shelby shushed her with a look.

"An old friend," AJ said, fidgeting with the paints. "Her son's in the children's hospital in Columbus. I doubt she'll leave him even for a party as grand as this."

Relief eased the jealous bile upsetting Shelby's stomach but didn't comfort her. Meghan needed a friend, not a rival. And Shelby should be that friend.

After sauntering to her side, AJ sniffed the carnations. "Anything I can do to help?"

He stood too close, his minty breath and woodsy aftershave tormenting her senses. She cut the last stem and slipped the carnation into the pitcher. "There are boxes of mason jars in the trunk of my car. Could you bring them in?"

"You're canning something?"

"They're for flowers and candles." She washed and dried her hands. "The extra car key is on that hook."

"I remember." He grinned and disappeared out the door with Lila following after him.

Shelby and Jillian cleared one end of the table and covered it with a craft cloth. By the time AJ brought in the last box and stacked it against the wall with the others, the girls were using the stencils to paint stars and "Happy 4th of July" on the silver pails while Jillian supervised and Shelby sorted the flags.

"That's the last box." He waved one of the larger flags. "What are you going to do with all these?"

"I haven't decided yet," Shelby said as she opened the cloth bunting. "These go on the front porch railing."

"I can do that." He gathered the other packages. "Got a staple gun?"

"I'll get it." Retrieving the toolbox from the back room gave her a few moments to calm her breathing. All the emotion from the previous evening welled up within her. He'd been the rock she needed, his arms holding her safely together when grief melted her skin. But after a sleepless night, she had resolved not to allow such intimacy again.

A resolution made and broken before.

She returned to the kitchen and handed him the toolbox. Their fingers brushed, shooting warm tingles into her heart. "Here you go."

"Thanks." As he entered the hall, she pulled a chair from the table and reached for a pail. "Aren't you coming?"

She looked up in surprise. "Do you need me to?"

"Yeah." His brown eyes drew her into their depths. He obviously needed to talk, and she couldn't resist his silent plea.

She turned to Jillian. "Do you mind?"

"Go ahead. We'll be fine, won't we, ladies?"

Elizabeth and Tabby, engrossed in their stencils and paints, cheerfully agreed.

When they reached the porch, AJ dropped the bunting packages onto the swing and dug the staple gun out of the toolbox. Shelby unfolded the patriotic cloth along the rail. "It's festive, isn't it? I think we can fit three of these along here and one on the side."

"Who all's coming to your cookout?"

"Cassie and Jason, Jillian and Seth, Seth's family. I stopped in to see Uncle Richard when we were in town and invited him."

"How is he?"

"I'm not sure. He seemed fine, but he doesn't look very well." She held the edge of the bunting against the underside of the rail while AJ knelt to staple it in place. "He needs to retire. Take things easy."

"He'll never leave that bank."

"Probably not."

AJ finished stapling the center bunting, then opened another package while Shelby arranged the red, white, and blue cloth.

"You'll never guess who I had lunch with today." AJ unfolded the fabric, then gave it a shake.

"Not Amy?"

"No, but you're close. Brett."

"They're not going to drop the lawsuit, are they?" Knees wobbling, she pushed aside the unopened packages and dropped onto the swing. She hadn't expected Amy to stop her fight, but deep inside she'd been hoping for a miracle.

AJ moved the packages to the floor and sat beside her. "I don't think so, but that's not what I need to talk to you about."

Dread tightened her stomach, and she shifted away from him. "Sounds serious."

"I made a mistake."

"About what?"

"Turns out I'm not Jonah's father."

"What?"

"Brett is."

Her mouth dropped open. "But why," she stammered, "why would Meghan say you were?"

"She didn't." He shrugged and spread his hands. "But neither did she tell me I wasn't."

Shelby bit her inner lip. She hated admitting that in her heart of hearts she wanted this—for AJ to be free of Meghan and Jonah. So why did she feel sick to her stomach?

"I'm sorry," she said, bowing her head. AJ reached for her hand, and she laced her fingers with his. Though soothed by the warmth of his skin against hers, indignation kindled into resentment. "Meghan was dating both you and Brett at the same time?"

"*We* were dating. Apparently she and Brett were doing more than that."

"You weren't . . ."

"No, we weren't."

"Then why did you think you could be Jonah's father?"

"I woke up one morning with a horrific hangover, and she was lying there beside me. I didn't remember anything, but a few weeks later when she said she was pregnant," he said with a shrug, "I believed the baby was mine."

"Even after all these years, finding out that he isn't has to hurt."

"It does." He nodded grimly as he propelled the swing. "I wanted Jonah to be my son. And I hoped to be a dad he could look up to."

"He'd have been lucky to have you."

"He'll be lucky to have Brett too. If Meghan gives him a chance." Shelby huffed. "I'm not so sure about that."

"Before today, I wouldn't have been either. But spending time with you changed something in him."

"Me?"

"You." AJ let go of her hand and slipped his arm comfortably across her shoulders. Her earlier resolve forgotten, she scooted next to him, resting her head in the curve of his neck right where she belonged. Sitting beside him in the swing, rocking gently back and forth, she listened as he told her about Meghan's no-visiting policy and Brett's news flash about the blood types.

"We went to lunch at this little wings place downtown, and the whole time we were there, we didn't talk about Meghan." He grinned and stroked her arm. "Or you."

"What did you talk about?"

"Nothing really. College football. The Bucks."

"Naturally. What else?"

"We reminisced a little about when we were kids. Before things started going wrong with our parents. Then I told him about my students, and he told me about his development projects. You know, it takes vision to run a company like that, and Brett's a smart guy. He's good at what he does. Really good."

"You aren't angry with him?"

"I was." He shifted to face her. "I still want to help Jonah any way I can. But I can't change what happened in the past. Or let it ruin my life now."

He cradled her face, and her breath caught as his enticing lips drew her closer. "I'm more interested in the future."

She touched his jaw, her fingers brushing against the stubble, and tilted toward him. His mouth barely skimmed her lips, and her hand slipped behind his neck.

"Mommy, see what I made."

Shelby jerked as Tabby ran onto the porch, swinging her decorated pail, Elizabeth and Jillian right behind her.

"Oops," Jillian said, flashing a grin. "Guess we interrupted something."

Tabby climbed onto Shelby's lap. "Isn't it pretty?"

"Beautiful, honey. Did you paint these stars?"

"All by myself. See?"

"You did a great job." Shelby smiled at AJ. "Can you stick around for a while? We have a lot to do to get ready for tomorrow."

"I'll stick around as long as you let me."

She hid her impulsive smile behind Tabby's hair then let it fade. AJ's heart might be free, but a romance only complicated things for her. She loved this farm and the happy memories it evoked. She loved the new memories she and her girls had made in the short time they'd lived here.

But what if they couldn't stay?

If it was God's will to leave it all behind, then that's what she had to do. No matter how difficult it was or how much it hurt.

~

AJ had dreamed of moments like this one. A hot summer day scented by gusting breezes. The pleasant contentment of believing, for just a little while, all was right with the world. He wouldn't trade this moment for anything—not even Buckeye national championship tickets.

His arm rested across the back of the gently moving swing. Beside him, her shoulder against his chest, Shelby held Tabby on her lap. Elizabeth, sitting cross-legged, relaxed on the floor with her arm across Lila's neck. Even Jillian, propped against the rail and furiously texting, added her own youthful glow to the day's radiance.

This was the life he wanted, the life he prayed God would give him.

Jillian looked up from her phone. "Seth can bring over a couple of picnic tables from his house if you'd like."

"That'd be wonderful," Shelby said, "if it's not too much trouble. I was trying to figure out how to make mine longer before tomorrow."

"You can do that?" Tabby asked, her voice full of wonder.

"No, I can't." Shelby gave her a squeeze. "That's why Seth is bringing his."

"He said they're already loaded on the truck," Jillian said. "He'll be here in five minutes. I told him Coach was here to help unload."

With that announcement, the peace of this particular moment ended, but not its contentment.

AJ stopped the swing and retrieved the staple gun and bunting from the floor. "Guess I better get this finished before Seth gets here."

"Can I help?" Elizabeth asked.

"Sure. Hold the fabric tight against the wood like this, okay?" He placed her delicate fingers on the material and stapled it. "Perfect. Now here."

Shelby moved Tabby from her lap to the swing and headed down the steps. "I'm going to the oval to decide where to put the tables."

"I'll go with you." Jillian pocketed her phone, and Tabby clasped her hand.

"Me too."

"Race ya." Jillian chased Tabby around the corner of the house while Shelby meandered after them. Before rounding the edge of the porch, she glanced at AJ, and her captivating lips curved into a sweet but slightly embarrassed smile.

"Wait a minute." AJ stapled another section of the cloth, then strode to that part of the rail.

She stepped to the edge of the flower bed. "What is it?"

"You're beautiful," he whispered so Elizabeth wouldn't hear.

Shelby's smile broadened, and her cheeks flushed. "You're sweet."

He started to turn away, then paused. "I forgot to tell you I talked to Dr. Kessler on my way here. You remember, the history professor I told you about. He's intrigued by your secret room. Would you mind if he came out to see it sometime?"

"What secret room?" Elizabeth's chameleon eyes grew round with curiosity as she joined him at the rail.

"The secret room that's a secret," Shelby said, pretending to be stern.

"Sorry," he mouthed over Elizabeth's head.

Annoyance twisted her features, but her eyes sparkled.

"Where is it?" Elizabeth asked.

"Never you mind, Bitsy." Her gaze came back to him. "Tell your professor I'd love to give him a tour."

"Thanks."

She disappeared around the corner of the house, calling to Jillian and Tabby.

"Do you know where the secret room is, Mr. AJ?" Elizabeth held another section of the bunting.

"I do." He added another staple.

"Will you tell me? I can keep a secret."

"I'm sure you can. But you don't want to get me in trouble with your mom, do you?"

"No." Her forehead furrowed as she helped him arrange the bunting over the rail. "Have you been inside the secret room?"

"Once."

"What was it like?"

"Secret." He tapped her nose, and she grinned. A black pickup kicked up gravel as it pulled into the drive. Saved by Seth. "Let's hurry and get this last one finished, okay?"

"Okay," Elizabeth agreed, but from the concentration in her eyes, he could tell she was imagining the delightful horrors of the mysterious secret room.

- 39 -

After the picnic tables were unloaded and placed in just the right spots, Shelby surveyed the oval area. Across the drive, colorful moss rose cascaded from an old wheelbarrow angled in a corner surrounded by irises and daisies. Next year, she planned to add more flowers, perhaps a small bench. At least that had been her original plan.

"The wheelbarrow is a nice touch," AJ said as he approached. "Now you need a couple white chickens."

She grinned. "Only if they're painted statuary."

"What have you got against live ones?"

"I got chased by a rooster once. They scare me."

AJ chuckled. "So the farm girl has her limits."

"I had a few piglets once." Her eyes involuntarily darted to the barn, then to her feet.

"Something wrong?"

"Nope." She walked over to the remains of the fire ring beneath the giant oak. Only a few stones remained from the original circle.

"Why the frown?"

Evading what she didn't want to talk about, she gestured to the burnt area. "Just remembering the fire ring. We used to roast hot dogs and marshmallows here. Make s'mores." She basked in the comfort of the past. "Sometimes Nanna wrapped potatoes in aluminum foil and buried them in the embers. So many good memories."

"Do you want to roast hot dogs and make s'mores tomorrow?"

Shelby poked at a nearby rock with her foot. "I'm not sure it would be safe."

"What if we rebuilt the circle? We could bring stones from the creek bed. It wouldn't be that hard."

"It wouldn't be that easy."

"A section of the creek runs behind Gran's house before it crosses beneath the road. We can get to it without too much trouble."

Shelby bit the inside of her lip as she considered his suggestion. One of the items on her master projects list was enclosing the fire ring with stones from the creek.

"Are you sure there's nothing else you need to be doing today?" she asked.

"You aren't trying to get rid of me, are you?" His brown eyes gleamed with amusement.

"No, but I don't want to take advantage of you, either." She sauntered toward the picnic table where Jillian and Seth sat across from each other, deep in conversation.

AJ clasped her elbow, and she turned toward him, squinting against the sun as she met his gaze. "You need to know," he said, "that there's no place I'd rather be than right here."

She shaded her eyes. "You didn't always feel that way about this place."

Grinning, he removed his ball cap and placed it on her head. "The place means something different now than it did then."

"Your grandfather punished you for something that wasn't your fault."

"He was unfair. But the way things have turned out, I can't say I'm sorry. I'd have hated practicing law. If Sully and I hadn't fought over Meghan, I'm sure we'd eventually have fought over something else."

"I still don't like thinking of Misty Willow as your punishment."

"All things work together for good . . ."

"I've heard that before." She stuck her hands in her pockets, then poked him in the ribs with her elbow. "Romans 8:28. One of my dad's favorites. But some things seem too hard to work out."

"It doesn't have to be hard, Shelby. We just can't give up too soon."

Except that the longer she stayed, the harder it would be to leave. If they were meant to go, whether to Mozambique or to somewhere she hadn't thought of yet, she begged God to reveal it to her soon.

AJ slightly raised the cap's bill, and she gazed into his eyes.

"Stay," he said. "Give us a chance."

The longing to do exactly that pulsated through her veins with each beat of her heart. It's what she'd asked him to do only a few days before.

"You like me, don't you?" he teased.

"Too much for my own good," she retorted. Time to change the subject. "Do you really think you can get enough stones for the circle?"

"I can. On one condition."

"What's that?"

"Tell me what you're doing for the Fourth now that your cookout has been rescheduled."

"I'm not sure. Cassie invited us to join them at some big family get-together. It was nice of her, but I'd feel like a gate-crasher."

"How about spending the day with me?"

"Doing what?"

"I don't know." He grinned sheepishly. "We can go into town for the parade. Then plan something special for Elizabeth and Tabby. Something they'll remember."

She should say no, but her heart was beyond listening to reason. If her future included moving halfway across the globe, then she wanted as many memories with AJ as she could get to take with her.

"A treasured memory." She nodded approval. "There's no greater gift."

~

Shelby picked up a sheaf of official-looking papers lying on the Jeep's passenger seat before climbing inside. She didn't mean to look, but her grandfather's name caught her eye. She glanced back at AJ, who was focused on buckling Tabby into her car seat. She scanned the front page, her hand shaking.

AJ slid into the driver's seat and started the engine. His hand covered hers. "I'm sorry. I forgot that was there."

"What are you doing with it?"

"I picked it up this morning. After reading through the news clippings last night, I guess I got curious. Maybe too curious."

"What does it say?"

"To be honest, I haven't had a chance to read it."

"There's no mystery about it. He fell and hit his head."

"I am sorry."

"It doesn't matter." She stuffed the pages into her bag. He meant well, but she wished he'd leave this part of the past alone.

"Ready to go find some rocks?" His voice sounded tentatively cheerful.

"Yes! Yes!" came the chorus from the backseat.

"Let's go." Shelby forced a smile.

AJ drove to his grandmother's house with Seth and Jillian following behind in the pickup. The girls, excited about riding in AJ's Jeep, chattered away. Shelby focused on the passing scenery.

"There's Austin's house," Elizabeth announced as they passed the Owenses' farm. "Can we ask him to get rocks?"

"Not today, sweetheart."

"But Austin likes rocks. He could help."

"I can give Jason a call," AJ said softly. "Another pair of hands couldn't hurt."

Shelby nodded agreement, then turned back to the window.

She barely listened to AJ's side of the conversation or Elizabeth's gleeful squeal when he announced Austin was coming with his dad.

"He can come, Mommy. Isn't that great?"

"It's wonderful." Shelby put as much enthusiasm in her voice as she could.

"Thank you for asking him, Mr. AJ."

"You're welcome, Elizabeth."

Shelby glanced at the backseat. She couldn't see Elizabeth, who was sitting behind her, but she could imagine her little girl's delighted expression. The fun of this impromptu outing didn't need to be dampened by Shelby's sour mood.

She touched AJ's arm. "Thanks from me too."

He glanced at her in surprise as he turned onto his road. "For what? Calling Jason?"

"For making Elizabeth's day. And mine."

"I thought I'd ruined yours."

"You just shook it up a little. But you've had it tough too."

"Kinda started out that way, but I've got no complaints."

"None?"

"Well," he drawled. "Tabby's timing could have been better." He glanced at her and winked.

Heat warmed her cheeks at the memory of their interrupted kiss.

"What's my timing?" Tabby asked. "Where is it? I want it."

Shelby's laugh mingled with AJ's. She also wished Tabby had waited a minute or two before running onto the porch, but AJ didn't need to know that.

"Here we are." AJ turned into an asphalt drive lined on one side by a row of elegant dogwoods. The one-story bungalow, surrounded by colorful landscaping, nestled in a stand of mature red and silver maples.

Shelby gasped. "It's beautiful."

"You really like it?"

"I do."

"I knew you would." AJ drove slowly past the house. "The house is bigger inside than it looks. The nurse had her own little suite."

"Look at the rose garden. It's breathtaking."

"Her pride and joy. She selected each rose, but Brett and I did the planting."

"That's what I would love to do."

"Plant roses?"

"Design gardens."

"You mean professionally?" Leaving the drive, AJ maneuvered the Jeep across open pastureland to a gated fence.

"It's silly, isn't it?"

"What's silly about it?"

"I don't know." She shifted restlessly. "I'd have to go back to school."

"Is that all that's stopping you?"

"AJ, I'm a mom. A single mom. I can't do whatever I want to."

"I think you should consider it." He stopped the Jeep in front of the gate and shifted to park. "And not just because it would keep you in the United States."

He opened his door and slid from his seat, then turned to her. "God gives you talents for a reason, you know."

Before she could reply, he jogged to the gate, unlatched it, and swung it open. Wearing jeans and a Glade High School T-shirt, he moved with an athlete's confident agility. She couldn't take her eyes from him as he waved to Seth, whose truck idled behind the Jeep, and returned to the driver's seat.

They bumped across the rough ground to the creek, then AJ drove parallel to the bank till they reached a bend.

"Safer for the kids here," he said. "The water is shallow by the sandbar." He parked, and as they got out of the vehicle, a horn blared. Jason's pickup bounced toward them.

Shelby and Cassie sat on a rock slab near the sandbar as the children threw rocks into the water and waded along the shore.

Jillian and Seth hunted for rocks downstream while AJ and Jason went upstream.

"AJ's hat looks good on you," Cassie said.

"I forgot I was wearing it." Shelby flushed and put her hand on her head. "How did you know it was AJ's?"

"Are you kidding?"

"Maybe I've become an OSU fan."

"You better. Come football season, we'll all be wearing the scarlet and gray."

On the sandbar, Tabby splashed water with her palm and giggled as it sprayed her face. Elizabeth and Austin, heads bent together, examined the pebbles in the creek bed. Beside the bank, Lila and the Owenses' English shepherd Penny played their own game.

Shelby tucked the moment into her heart, then faced Cassie.

"AJ's cousins filed a lawsuit to overturn our contract."

"Can they do that?"

"Amy—do you know her?"

"I think I've met her a couple of times."

"She knows I don't have the money for a long court fight."

"But AJ has money . . ."

"No." Shelby tensed her jaw. "I may have to let the farm go."

"But it's your home. You just got here."

"I know. But I don't really have a choice."

"I can't believe this." Cassie's eyes narrowed, and her mouth formed a grim line. "You have to fight."

"It could cost me everything I have."

"Then we'll find you a new place." Cassie rubbed Shelby's back as her words tumbled together. "It won't be Misty Willow, but there has to be something nearby. And we'll paint all the rooms, and AJ will move all your plants for you. You know he would."

"I don't want to dwell on it, not right now. But I wanted to tell you, to ask you to pray."

"You know I will. I waited too long for a close neighbor like you. I'm not letting you go without talking to God about it."

Shelby smiled, then breathed in the sun-scented air. For the next few days, till at least after Independence Day, she planned on pretending all was right with her world.

No lawsuit. No grieving over the past. No worrying about the future.

Instead, she'd enjoy an afternoon at the creek with her family and friends. Tomorrow's cookout would be so much fun. And then she'd look forward to spending the Fourth with AJ. A special memory for the girls.

"AJ probably would do that, wouldn't he? Move the flowers?"

"He'd do anything for you." Cassie snorted. "Do you know how long I've been trying to get Jason to build me a fire ring?"

Shelby chuckled. "Now's your chance."

"Oh, you better believe we're getting rocks for me too."

"Then I guess we'll be here a while. Seth's mom said the same thing."

"Don't you see how much us old married women need you, Shelby? You can't leave us. Besides, I was hoping to see your initials linked to AJ's at the 'gagement tree instead of my husband's," she teased.

"There should be a way to change my initials to yours."

"Except neither of us are Lassiters. Our initials don't belong on the willow."

"I wouldn't mind." She pulled at a tuft of grass near her shoe. "You're a good friend, Cassie. Jason is blessed to have you."

"You bet he is." Her mouth curved upward into a contented smile. "But I'm blessed too."

Only a few yards upstream, AJ picked a large stone from the creek bed and heaved it to the bank. Standing upright with one hand on his hip, he wiped sweat from his forehead with the back of his arm. As if he knew Shelby was watching him, he turned toward her, smiled a gorgeous smile, and waved.

She responded by tipping the bill of his hat. Cassie wasn't the only one who was blessed.

308

~

Shelby yawned as she peeked into the girls' bedroom. Both slept peacefully while Lila sprawled on the floor between them. Lately, the Labrador spent more nights with them than with AJ. If they stayed in the United States, she'd have to find them their own dog.

She padded through the family room to her bedroom and turned on the light. Her bag, the sheriff's report sticking out of the top, lay on the bed where she'd tossed it earlier. After pulling out the papers, she scanned the first page.

Only a few hours earlier she'd promised not to think about Grandpa's death, but her curiosity squashed her resolve. She carried the report to the family room, curled up in the wing chair, then flipped through the pages to the investigation's final account.

She read it through, her stomach tying itself in knots, then read it again more slowly. The report didn't make sense.

Closing her eyes, she leaned against the soft upholstery and forced herself to remember that horrible day. The memories came easily, reinforced by all the times she had relived them in the months following Grandpa's death.

She had found him on the concrete floor, a pool of blood around his head. Praying he was okay, she'd pushed him over and pressed her ear against his silent heart. *Open your eyes, Grandpa,* she had pleaded. *Please. Open your eyes.*

Uncle Richard appeared and pulled her away. Bits of straw clung to her knees, and the four baby pigs in the corner pen squealed for her attention. But she had barely heard them above her own uncontrollable sobs.

She read the nonsensical words again. Whoever wrote the report must have made a mistake. Flipping back to the initial report, she found the same error there.

Suddenly fidgety, she walked to the kitchen for a drink of water. The mistaken detail was minor, but the investigators should have known better. Were they just sloppy? Didn't they care about the truth?

The clock on the stove displayed 10:33.

Leaning against the sink, she sent AJ a text. *"Are you still up?"*

A few seconds later, her phone beeped. *"Sure am."*

She called him on her way back to the wing chair.

"Hi, Shelby. Long time no see."

"I read the sheriff's report." She bit her lip, picturing him massaging the back of his neck as she waited for him to respond.

"You want to talk about it?"

"It's wrong. They messed up."

"Who did?"

"The deputies who investigated. They're so stupid." She pressed the heel of her hand against her forehead. Behaving so childishly was out of character, but irritation at their carelessness boiled her knotted stomach.

"Tell me how they messed up."

She breathed a prayer of thanks that AJ's tone neither belittled nor downplayed her exasperation.

"It says Grandpa hit his head when he tripped on the pig trough. But that's not possible. The trough was in the pen. With the pigs."

"I don't understand."

"Grandpa gave me four pigs to raise for 4-H." She took a deep breath. "The trough was in the pen. He couldn't have tripped over it."

"Are you sure? Maybe he moved it."

"I'm positive. Nanna had gone to Columbus that day. I fed the pigs. I gave them water. That trough was inside the pen."

"Was your grandpa in the barn?"

"He had been working on a tractor outside the barn. After I fed the pigs, I went for a walk back to the woods. On the way home, I stopped at the barn and that's when . . . that's when I found him."

"Could he have tripped on something else?"

"Both the initial report and the final report say the same thing. A pig trough. But I know they're wrong."

"Yeah, it looks that way."

"The report references photographs, but they aren't here. I want to see them."

"I don't know, Shelby. That might not be a good idea."

"I just want to see if there are any photographs of the trough. Or whatever it is they're saying he tripped on. Do you think you could get that for me?"

"Of course I can. I'll stop by the sheriff's office first thing in the morning."

"Thank you."

"Are you sure you're okay? I can be over there in ten minutes."

"I think I'm more mad than anything else. Is that weird?"

"No. Not at all."

"I just needed to talk to somebody. To explain about the report."

"I'm glad you chose me."

The huskiness in his voice awakened a dormant yearning. Her breath caught in her throat.

"Me too."

She said good night and hung up, then crawled into bed.

Grandpa hadn't taken the trough out of the pigs' pen, she was sure of it. But then what had he tripped on? And how did the deputies make such a stupid mistake?

– 40 –

*A*J breathed in the familiar mouth-watering aromas of cinnamon rolls and brewed coffee as he entered the bakery. He'd arrived late enough to miss the early Saturday morning crowd, so it wasn't difficult to find an empty table.

Slurping an iced coffee, he spread out the photocopies and studied each one. A deputy at the sheriff's office, a dad whose three teens he'd taught in the past five years, had done him a favor by making black-and-white copies of the photographs he wanted.

Though the copies were slightly grainy, the details were clear enough. The outline of a body drawn on the barn floor was shown from different angles. The dark stain near the head in one close-up could only be blood. At least three of the photos showed a pig trough lying on its side near the outline's feet.

For reasons they'd never know, Thad Lassiter must have taken the trough out of the pen. That innocuous decision had apparently cost him his life.

And forced Shelby out of a protective cocoon where bad things didn't happen. He'd been devastated by his parents' deaths, but he'd learned before then that life was a series of challenges, and there were no heroes.

But Shelby's golden childhood had shielded her from the harsher realities of life outside the doting family world of Misty Willow. She didn't know the pain of feuding parents who viewed their ping-pong betrayals as a blood sport. Or the loneliness of feeling less important than his dad's latest sports car or his mom's newest diamond.

Only Gran had been there for him. Every time his little boy's heart was broken by another quarrel or an unkept promise. Every single time.

He wished she were here now to soothe the whiplash from the past couple of days. Maybe she could have helped him work out his contradictory feelings toward Meghan and Jonah. Despite the surprise of Jonah's existence, he'd been eager to fulfill his responsibilities to the boy. And he still wanted to do anything he could to ensure Jonah received the best possible care.

Though initially angered at Brett's revelation, AJ also had been relieved.

And disappointed.

The little boy, pale and still beneath institutional bedding, had wormed his way into AJ's heart without a word or a glance. He loved the kid. Brett's newsflash hadn't changed that.

"Hello, AJ. Such a nice surprise." Richard hovered near the table, his eyes intent on the papers. Barely touching the nearest sheet with his index finger, he gave it a slight twist so it faced him. "What is this?" He attempted to sound merely curious, but bitter indignation edged his voice.

"Morning, Richard." AJ gathered the papers into a single pile. "Have a seat?"

Richard glanced at the bakery goods on display at the counter, then pulled out the opposite chair. His back as straight as his stooped shoulders allowed, he lowered himself to the seat and held out his palm. "May I?"

AJ handed him the papers, and Richard, with a pained grimace, shuffled through them.

"Why do you have these?" He laid them on the table, then adjusted the stack so it was parallel to the table's edge.

313

"You've seen them before?"

Richard slowly shook his head. "I was in the barn when the photographs were taken. An experience like that is not easily forgotten."

"I imagine not." AJ felt a rush of pity for the old man. After all, Thad was his sister's husband. It couldn't have been easy to see him lifeless on the barn floor. He had probably been the one to break the sad news to Aubrey.

"I remember every detail of that day." Richard involuntarily shivered. "The smell. The overbearing stuffiness. When I saw him lying there, I tried to revive him. But it was too late. He was gone. Then Shelby came in." His voice trailed away, and his watery eyes stared again at the bakery display.

"You found Thad?"

Obviously replaying that long-ago day, Richard barely nodded.

Hands clasped around his iced coffee, AJ leaned forward. "Shelby told me she found her grandfather."

Richard slowly turned his head. His pale eyes appeared unfocused before fixating on AJ. "I shouldn't have let her go into the barn." His quiet, dreamlike voice held little emotion. "Night after night, I hear her scream."

AJ narrowed his eyes. "You *let* her go into the barn?"

"Such a dear child." Richard sighed heavily, and his eyes blurred. "Thad's death, and then Aubrey's only a couple of weeks later. The shock was so great, she barely spoke for months. Her parents were right to take her so far away from such heartache."

"I'm not sure Shelby thought so."

As if deliberately removing himself from his memories, Richard's eyes cleared. "But she's come back to us, hasn't she?"

AJ shrugged in puzzlement. *Come back to us? What does that mean?* "I suppose so."

With a slight smile, Richard stiffly leaned forward and gestured at the photocopies. "You aren't going to show these to her, are you? I doubt she could handle seeing them."

"No." AJ swept them away from Richard's side of the table

and folded them in half. "Unless she insists. Then I'll give her the close-up of the trough. She doesn't believe Thad tripped on it."

"Why not?" Richard asked sharply.

"She said the trough was in the pen with the pigs."

"She's wrong." His mouth snapped shut, and his eyes flashed with sudden anger.

"I think *mistaken* might be a better word." Though it wasn't a surprise that the photocopies seemed to be stirring up painful memories, the old man's behavior appeared odd. Maybe he should give Richard's daughter a call.

"You care about her, don't you?" Richard smiled indulgently, his demeanor swinging like a pendulum to the opposite extreme. "I'm not surprised. She's very much like her grandmother. And you are very much like Sully."

"I think you have me confused with Brett."

"I assure you I do not."

"Since Aubrey dumped Sully, I'm not sure I want any relationship I might have with Shelby compared to theirs."

"Aubrey belonged with Sully." The faraway look returned to Richard's pale eyes. "Thad never should have interfered."

"Two souls, one heart."

"What?" The pendulum swung back to anger.

"Aubrey loved Thad. Not Sully. They had a good life together until this happened." AJ tapped at the folded papers.

"Yes. They were happy." Another pendulum swing as his eyes bored into AJ's. "Don't show Aubrey the photographs. Her heart can't take it."

"You mean Shelby." AJ spoke quietly. "Aubrey's dead."

Richard gripped AJ's arm, his fingers surprisingly strong as he dug into flesh. "We shouldn't have done it, Sully. I told you we shouldn't."

A shiver raced through AJ's spine as he pulled his arm away. "Done what?"

"Thad won't listen. I tried to explain I wasn't to blame. But he's so angry."

"Why was he angry, Richard?"

"If Thad tells Aubrey, she'll never speak to me again." His fist slammed the table. "This is your fault, Sully."

"Richard, it's me. AJ." He definitely needed to call Richard's daughter. "What did Sully do to Thad?"

Richard pushed back his chair and closed his eyes.

"Tell me what Sully did."

Richard took a couple of deep breaths, then opened his eyes. "AJ?"

"Yes, Richard. It's me."

"Are you going to Shelby's cookout this afternoon?"

"Of course."

"Please make my excuses." Richard passed a hand over his forehead. "I don't seem to be feeling very well."

"Would you like me to drive you home?"

"No, that won't be necessary. I'm walking to the bank. Only please, do tell Shelby I'm sorry."

"She'll understand."

"Thank you."

"Any time."

As Richard walked toward the door, AJ pulled out his cell phone and searched his contacts list. Finding the right number, he hit the send button. When the call went to voicemail, he left a message asking Richard's daughter to contact him.

He unfolded the photocopies, then sifted through them again. They confirmed the investigator's report that Thad had tripped on the pig trough and hit his head in a fatal accident. But the conversation with Richard raised unsettling questions.

What had Sully done to anger Thad? Most likely something to do with the ownership of Misty Willow. But what did that have to do with Thad's death? Even more troubling, though, was Richard's admission he'd found Thad. Just like the newspaper accounts said.

But if that were true, then where was he when Shelby walked into the barn? And why did she believe she found Thad first?

- 41 -

*S*helby placed a platter of deviled eggs in the refrigerator then lingered at the kitchen window facing the oval. The stones from the creek made an almost perfect circle beneath the outstretched limbs of the oak. Within the circle, AJ knelt and struck a match while Paul Norris squatted nearby. Jillian, Seth, his sister Mandy, and the girls gathered near one of the picnic tables, snacking on grapes and apple slices.

After the match's tiny spark flared on the dry kindling beneath the logs, AJ coaxed it into a sizzling flame. Paul must have said something humorous because he laughed as he added more kindling.

"They got the fire going." Shelby gathered a few tomatoes and faced the table where Renee Norris stirred a homemade vinaigrette dressing. "My first."

Perhaps my last.

She dismissed the thought, resolving once again to focus on the present. Neither the unknown future nor the difficult past would intrude on today's festive mood. That's why she hadn't asked AJ if he'd contacted the sheriff's office about the photographs, though she suspected he had. Ever since he arrived, he had avoided being alone with her. Though that wasn't difficult considering how much Elizabeth and Tabby monopolized him.

She retrieved a knife from the counter and sat at the table to cut the tomatoes into juicy red slices for the hamburgers.

"I remember coming here for church cookouts when I was a teen." Renee's easygoing smile and twinkling brown eyes brightened her attractive features. The mother of two teenagers and a jewelry designer, she participated in frequent 5Ks to maintain her trim figure. "You've done so much with the place in such a short time. Your grandparents would be pleased."

"I had a lot of help. Including your husband. I can't thank Paul and Seth enough for cleaning out that horrid attic." She almost gagged at the memory of the carcasses. "Though now, that floor may be cleaner than this one."

"I heard stories." Renee wrinkled her nose and chuckled. "I wasn't surprised Paul took on something like that, but I was thrilled when they'd finished. He had to burn their clothes."

"Why did he do it?"

"That's the kind of man he is. A good neighbor."

"There's more to it than that." Shelby dipped a baby carrot in the vinaigrette and took a bite. "Um, this is good."

"Thanks." Renee funneled the vinaigrette into a tall cruet. "It's an old Norris family recipe. His grandmother won a blue ribbon at the county fair with it."

"I can see why." Shelby absentmindedly rotated another carrot between her fingers. "Paul told me once he owed my dad a favor, but he wouldn't say what it was. Do you know?"

Renee's eyes became solemn, but her smile didn't fade. If anything, a serene glow lit her expression. "I do." Her tranquil sigh seemed to momentarily transport her into the past, then she gazed at the window.

Shelby followed her gaze. From their vantage point seated at the table, Shelby could see the oak stretched across a perfectly blue sky. Because the house stood several feet above ground level, they couldn't see anyone, but Shelby could tell Renee's thoughts were preoccupied with her husband and children.

"I didn't mean to pry," she said apologetically.

"You're not." Renee put the topper on the cruet and set it aside. "We are the family we are because of your dad."

Shelby mentally repeated the words. "I don't understand."

"It's an old story. Paul and I dated in high school. I became pregnant." She shrugged. "We both had college scholarships. Dreams for the future. And parents who wanted the best for us."

"What did my dad do?"

"He asked Paul to imagine ten years had passed. To think about his profession, his home, even what kind of vehicle he would be driving. To dream his perfect life."

Intrigued, Shelby leaned on the table, her chin resting in her palm. "How did that help?"

"To my great joy," Renee said as she unconsciously patted her heart, "Paul realized that his only perfect life included me. Ten years, twenty years, forty years. It didn't matter how far into his future he tried to see. I was his constant."

"His constant." Shelby's heart flipped with longing and mild envy. "I love that."

"I've loved it for twenty-two years."

"Twenty-two? But Seth is only . . ."

"He's eighteen." Renee leaned against the table. "I miscarried a week before we were going to be married. So, because our parents wanted it, we waited one more year."

"Then lived happily ever after?"

"Mostly, yes. Not that we haven't had our share of problems and heartaches. But we've faced them together."

"You're very lucky."

"Not lucky. Blessed. And all thanks to Adam Lassiter."

"He gave you good advice."

"The best. We use it whenever we have a big decision to make. Usually we only go a few years into the future. Seldom more than ten." Her smile flashed. "But it does seem to give us needed perspective."

"And it got my attic cleaned," Shelby joked. Perhaps her dad's advice would work for her too. Where did she want to be in ten years if she couldn't be at Misty Willow? Elizabeth would be almost seventeen, Tabby thirteen.

Teenagers!

She got up from the table and peered out the window. Tabby clung to Seth's back as he jogged around the yard. Elizabeth sat with Jillian and Mandy, her slender arm slung across Lila's creamy neck. AJ and Paul, apparently deep in conversation, lounged in lawn chairs near the circle.

Shelby gasped as her restless thoughts and the yearnings in her heart slid together in perfect precision. With blinding clarity, she realized her grandparents' legacy wasn't bound by a place.

Though she had struggled to re-create Misty Willow into the golden home of her childhood, she'd neglected Grandpa and Nanna's most treasured gift—their deep abiding love for each other.

Two souls. One heart.

AJ leaned forward and poked at the fire with a long stick. The inevitable OSU ball cap shaded his features, but beneath the brim were warm brown eyes, an engaging smile, and an adorable Cary Grant cleft. All belonging to a man she'd have been proud to introduce to Grandpa.

As if he sensed her thoughts, AJ gazed toward the house. Seeing her, his smile broadened, and he waved.

Abiding love was the legacy she most desired, and he was the constant she yearned to hold in her heart.

No matter where she lived, at Misty Willow or an African hut or in whatever spacious place God set her feet, she prayed for AJ to be there too.

~

As AJ poked at the fire, an undeniable impulse drew his eyes toward the house. Shelby gazed at him from the kitchen window. She wore her chestnut hair in a French braid tied with a red ribbon, and loose wisps framed her lovely features. Though too far away to see the color of her eyes, he sensed the gleam of their emerald depths. She returned his casual wave then disappeared.

He had given her Richard's message when he first arrived without going into details. Preoccupied with preparations for the cookout, she hadn't asked for any, so his offhanded "I bumped into Richard in town" had been enough of an explanation. After that, AJ busied himself with the stones for the circle and building the fire. That is, when he wasn't throwing a tennis ball for Lila or a Frisbee to Elizabeth and Tabby.

Anything to prevent Shelby from asking about the photographs.

"Sittin' by this circle sure does take me back." Paul's relaxed voice broke into AJ's thoughts. He gestured toward Elizabeth. "That little miss is Shelby's spitting image at her age."

"You knew Shelby? When she was a child?"

"She practically lived here. Each spring I sold her three or four pigs for 4-H." He propped his boot-clad foot on one of the rocks and crossed his ankles. "It was a sad time when Thad died."

"Do you know anything about that? About how he died?"

"My parents still lived at the farm back then." Beneath the bill of his John Deere ball cap, his forehead furrowed. "I remember my dad saying something once about it all being a bit strange how they said it happened."

"Shelby thinks so too." AJ explained about the trough and the photocopies.

"That does sound odd. Mr. Lassiter wasn't one to leave things lying about. And even though at the time I thought he was ancient, he wasn't feeble. I think that's what bothered Dad. He couldn't picture anything as senseless as Thad dying the way they said."

"The report doesn't leave much room for doubt."

A silver minivan pulled into the drive. "Here come Jason and Cassie."

As he stood, AJ turned back to Paul. "Don't mention any of this to Shelby, okay?"

"What is it the kids say these days?" He rose beside AJ. "Duh!"

With a chagrined smile, AJ nodded his gratitude.

"Renee and I have been speculating that you're sweet on our nearest neighbor. Or is it none of my business?"

"Is it that obvious?"

"We see your Jeep here often enough as we're driving by."

"Her daughters are crazy about my dog."

"Is that what it is?" Paul chortled. "Sully's grandson and Thad's granddaughter. I bet your granddaddy is just a-spinnin' in his grave."

- 42 -

The arrival of the Owens family sparked a flurry of excitement. AJ unloaded a portable grill from the rear of their minivan.

"Where's Penny?" he asked.

"Stuck at home." Jason hoisted an ice chest. "She's in heat."

"Are you going to breed her?"

"Maybe next time. Are you wanting a puppy?"

"Not really. Though I seem to be losing Lila to Elizabeth."

"Maybe if you're real nice," Jason teased, "Shelby will adopt you too."

"Ha-ha. Come look at the stone ring."

While he showed off the fire circle to Jason, Shelby and Renee came out of the house then disappeared inside again with Cassie and a large picnic basket. Elizabeth and Austin retreated into the old brick meat-smoking structure jutting from the side of the house with Lila following close behind.

The women soon reappeared with veggies, chips, and iced tea before joining the others around the circle. AJ scooted his chair to make room for Shelby's. She looked around with a satisfied smile, then lowered herself into the canvas chair.

"I love today," she said softly.

"I hope you have a lot more like it." He bit his lip, mentally kicking himself for such a stupid response. But if he'd reminded her of the lawsuit, she hid it well. No flicker of worry dimmed the green sparkle in her eyes. Instead she smiled as if safekeeping a secret.

"Me too," she whispered.

When the charcoal briquettes turned to hot embers, the men gathered around the grills. As the burgers and brats sizzled, the women retrieved food from the house. Soon the picnic tables, festively decorated with the flower-filled pails and flags, were laden with casseroles, salads, condiments, and desserts.

Jason retrieved long sharpened sticks from the floor of his minivan. "Who wants a hot dog?" he shouted. "Let's put this fire to use."

"I do, I do." Tabby singsonged as she danced around Jason. AJ took one of the sticks and helped Tabby pierce a hot dog onto its end.

"Where's Austin?" Jason asked, scanning the area.

"I think Elizabeth wanted to show him a book she got from the library," Shelby said as she put serving spoons in the potato salad and coleslaw. "I'll go get them."

AJ pulled his chair closer to the circle, then helped Tabby balance the long stick. "Like this, honey."

"Let me do it."

"Just not too close, okay?"

A few moments later, Shelby's voice, edging on panic, sounded from the front of the house. "Elizabeth! Austin!"

AJ's throat constricted, and he scoured the area. The children were nowhere in sight. "Jillian, come help Tabby, will you?"

"Sure, Coach." Jillian gave her stick to Seth and took AJ's place. "Is everything okay?"

"I'm sure it is." He glanced at Jason's and Cassie's anxious expressions and jogged toward Shelby. Jason followed close behind.

They met up with Shelby near the bay window.

"Are they out here?" Her eyes restlessly searched the huge yard, the nearby fields, the curving road.

"Aren't they in the house?" Jason asked.

"I looked everywhere. Even upstairs." She shook her head. "They weren't there."

"How about the attic?" Paul asked as he approached them.

"The door was locked so I didn't go up there."

"I'll check it out." He headed into the house.

"Elizabeth was curious about the secret room." AJ put his arm around Shelby's shoulder. "Maybe they're down there."

"She doesn't even know where it is."

"Still worth a look," Jason said. "Remember how much we liked sneaking down there when we were kids?"

"You and Jason check it out," AJ suggested. "I'll go around the house."

"And the . . . the barn?" Tears swam in Shelby's worried eyes.

AJ gave her a sideways hug. "There too."

Walking the perimeter of the house, he scanned the adjacent pasture and beneath the brush lining sections of the fence. The cellar door remained padlocked and the low windows were still intact. In the barn, he quickly checked the stalls and climbed into the straw-scented loft.

Nothing.

As he descended the ladder, he couldn't resist taking another look at the corner pen where Shelby must have kept her small litter. The trough was gone. Would it have been taken in as evidence?

He deeply exhaled. It didn't matter. Whatever had happened in this barn fourteen years ago wasn't nearly as important as finding Elizabeth and Austin.

Jogging down the drive, he met the others near the picnic table. The children hadn't been found inside the house. He glanced around the oval. "Where's Lila?"

Jason perked up. "Haven't seen her. Which means—"

"She must be with the kids." AJ whistled, then listened for an answering bark. Nothing. "They have to be around here some-place."

"Could they have gone to our place?" Cassie asked. "Austin wasn't too happy about leaving Penny at home."

"They're at the engagement tree." The fear in Shelby's eyes subsided as she gripped AJ's arm. "Elizabeth told me she didn't want to move away and leave Austin. He's her best friend. I know that's where they went."

"Just like we did." Jason huffed out air and glanced at his watch.

"They wouldn't know how to get there," Cassie protested. "I think we should check our house first."

"Let's go." Jason dug his keys from his pocket.

"You go ahead. Shelby and I will head to the creek." AJ glanced up the drive toward the pasture. "We'll take my Jeep as far as it will go. Everyone has a cell phone, right?"

Seth held out a key. "Take my truck, Coach. You'll get farther."

"Thanks, Seth."

"How did they get past us to go up the lane?" Renee asked as they all faced her. "Think about it. We know they went into the house, and we've been out here the whole time. At least somebody has. They couldn't have gone up Shelby's lane without being seen by somebody."

"They could have gone out the front door," Paul said, "and up the pasture on that side. Seth and I will go that way. The rest of you stay here in case they come back."

AJ and Shelby climbed into Seth's truck. Sticking the key in the ignition, he glanced her direction. Though wearing a seat belt, she leaned slightly forward as if propelling the vehicle with the force of her energy. "We'll find them," AJ said. "Everything's going to be okay."

She bit her lip and nodded. "I'm positive they headed for the willow. I'm less confident they could find their way there."

"If they aren't there, we'll call the sheriff's office. Get a search party out here."

"At least Lila is with them. I'm glad of that."

"Me too. She won't let anything happen to them. Besides, even if she comes back, she can lead us to wherever they are."

He maneuvered the truck along the lane as it disintegrated into a barely visible track and disappeared as they entered an empty pasture then passed a stand of hardwoods and pines.

"If they came this way, Elizabeth might recognize the woods."

"Would she go in there?"

"I don't think so, but"—she shrugged—"I don't know."

AJ drove several hundred feet before the ground became too rough to go any farther. "We'll have to walk from here." He opened the door, then balanced on the edge of the floorboard. "Lila! Come here, girl."

Shelby slid out of the truck and joined him. "I'm ready to lock one little girl in her room until she's eighteen."

"Don't be too hard on her. If I thought it would keep you here, I'd camp out at the 'gagement tree myself." His phone buzzed as he got out of the truck. "Hey, Jason. Did you find them?"

"They aren't here. We're headed back to your place."

"We're on foot now, but we'll be at the creek before long."

As they walked, AJ whistled and called for Lila. When the willow's crown appeared beyond a slight rise, her gleeful bark resounded through the still air.

Shelby gasped in relief, and AJ clasped her hand. Together they sprinted toward the creek.

Elizabeth and Austin stood next to Lila beside the willow's delicate branch. A knapsack lay on the ground beside them. Lila jumped in place, raced to AJ, then wheeled and returned to the children.

Shelby released AJ's hand and fell to her knees in front of her daughter. "Oh, Bitsy. I was so worried about you. What were you thinking taking off like that?"

Elizabeth glanced at Austin. "We had something to do."

"If you ever do anything like this again . . ." Shelby pressed her lips together and pulled Elizabeth into an embrace.

AJ grasped Austin's shoulder. "How about you, buddy? You okay?"

"Yeah. We just took a walk." Frowning, Austin fiddled with something in his hand.

"A long one, I'd say. What you got there?"

"Dad gave it to me." He held out his hand, palm up, to reveal a penknife. "I'm puttin' our initials on the tree. Mine and Elizabeth's."

"On the engagement tree?" AJ stifled a laugh and glanced at Shelby's stunned expression.

"You didn't." Her eyes darted from Elizabeth to Austin and back again.

In rare defiance, Elizabeth raised her chin. "I don't want to move again."

"I know you don't, sweetheart."

"But now Austin and me will always be together." She gestured toward the willow. "It's tradition."

Shelby kissed the top of Elizabeth's head and took her hand. "Why don't you show me? You can come too, Austin."

AJ pulled out his phone. "I'll pass on the news." Tapping the keys, he sent texts to Jason and Paul, then ducked beneath the willow's overhanging branches.

Elizabeth traced the rough carving with her finger. E. K. + A. O. in an incomplete heart.

"I need to finish it," Austin said. "It's kind of hard, though."

"I can do it for you," AJ offered, ignoring Shelby's glare.

Austin held out the knife, then took it back. "Will it still count?"

"Well, buddy, that's up to you and Elizabeth. And whatever God has planned for the two of you." He winked at Shelby. "You're not eloping any time soon, are you?"

"Not until I have a job." Austin's serious tone matched the earnest expression in his hazel eyes as he gave AJ the knife.

"That's a good plan, buddy." AJ snapped open the blade and turned to Shelby. "You don't mind, do you?"

Shelby gazed at the heart-surrounded initials of her ancestors, then touched the ragged *E*. "Not much I can do about it now, is there?" She placed her hand on AJ's shoulder, the slight touch of her fingers burning through his shirt. "But if they get married before she's thirty, I'm holding you responsible."

"Thirty?"

"Okay, twenty-five." Taking Elizabeth by the hand, she led her away from the willow. "You and I are going to have a little talk, young lady."

AJ grinned at Austin, whose squatting posture matched his own. "You sure about this?"

"Elizabeth is my best friend," he said solemnly. "I heard tell you should marry your best friend."

"I've heard that too."

"I figured I better speak up before she moves away."

"Maybe something will happen, and they won't move."

"That's what I've been praying about."

"Me too, buddy." He cut the bark to finish the heart. "Me too."

– 43 –

After church the next day, AJ joined Shelby and the girls for lunch at the Dixie Diner. When they'd finished their meal, the waitress laid the check on the table.

AJ picked it up and pulled out his wallet. "My turn."

"I don't think so," Shelby said as she wiped ketchup from Tabby's face. "You picked up the check last time. At the café."

"That one doesn't count." He glanced at his knuckles and flexed his hand. The skin was still slightly discolored from where it had connected with Brett's jaw.

Shelby's lips slightly curved upward, but fine lines accented her eyes. He longed to kiss away her doubts and worries, to tell her everything would be all right. To beg her to fight Amy's lawsuit.

"Are you sure you still want me to come over this afternoon?" *Please say yes*.

Her eyes widened with uncertainty. "Don't you want to?"

"Of course I do."

"You promised," Tabby asserted. "So we can watch *Tangled*."

"I know, honey." He leaned across the table to hold her gaze. "But your mommy looks tired. She may not want company."

"Mommy can take a nap if she wants to." Tabby's no-nonsense tone added to her gold-flecked eyes boring into his made it difficult for him to keep a straight face. "Always keep promises."

"Guess she told you," Shelby whispered with a chuckle, then rested her hand on his. "With this rain, it's a perfect Sunday afternoon for watching movies. Please come."

He turned his hand so her fingers slipped into his grasp, and he got lost in the depths of her eyes. Something had changed within her, and he couldn't wait to find out what it was. "Let's go."

Genuine delight warmed her smile as she helped Elizabeth and Tabby put on their jackets. As he put cash in the check folder, his phone rang. "It's Richard." Probably mad about the call to his daughter. "Do you mind?"

"We'll see you at the house." She herded the girls to the exit, turning back to wave before disappearing around a corner.

He nodded, then answered the call. "Hello, Richard."

"AJ?"

"Yes."

"Are you with Shelby?"

"I was, but she just left."

"Where are you?"

"At the Dixie."

"I've been thinking that we should talk. About your grandfather and Misty Willow."

"What about them?" Was Richard finally going to tell him how Sully had gained ownership of the farm?

"Not on the phone. I'm almost to the cottage now."

"I'm still in town. How soon will you be there?"

"In a few minutes."

"Okay, just wait for me. I won't be long."

"You won't say anything about this to Shelby, will you? At least not till after we've talked."

"Sure, Richard. Whatever you say." He hung up then headed for the Jeep. Shelby already expected him to run home first to change clothes. Hopefully this strange meeting with Richard wouldn't take too long. And the old man would stay lucid.

~

Shelby bent her head against the downpour and hurried the girls inside the house. This was one of those days when she really missed an attached garage. Or any garage.

"Change your clothes," she said, shooing them down the hall. "And hang up your dresses."

In the back room, she shook out their wet jackets and hung them on hooks. As she returned to the kitchen, a knock sounded at the door. She glanced through the window, then opened the door.

"Uncle Richard, come in. What a surprise."

"Thank you, dear." He fussily swiped at the dampness on his shoulders. "I didn't expect you to take so long getting home from church."

"We went out to eat first." She frowned. "Have you been waiting for us? I didn't see your car."

"I parked behind the barn."

Anxiety niggled at the edge of Shelby's mind, but she dismissed the odd sensation. "Why there?"

"It's the safest place."

"Safe from what?"

"I saw you with AJ at church."

"Yes," she said hesitatingly. "We were both there." Sitting together with Cassie and Jason. Almost like a couple.

"You don't dislike him anymore?"

"Why don't you sit down, Richard?" After pulling out a chair for him, she reached for the glass coffeepot and carried it to the sink. "Would you like coffee? Or hot tea?"

He waved his hand to decline and stayed standing.

"It would be a mistake to leave him."

"Leave who?"

"After all this time." His voice rose in anger. "How can you let your heart be swayed by someone else?"

Shelby returned the pot to its burner. "Are you talking about Brett? I'm not interested in him."

"I'm talking about Thad."

Elizabeth appeared in the kitchen door, her eyes furrowed in concern. With a knot in her stomach, Shelby hurried to her daughter and gently clasped her shoulders. "Why don't you and Tabby watch a video?"

"But we're supposed to watch *Tangled* with—"

"And we will. Soon." She turned Elizabeth around and gave her a slight push. "Go on now."

Elizabeth reluctantly slunk down the hall, turning back periodically to see if Shelby still watched her. Shelby gave her a reassuring smile. "Stay with your sister, okay?" With a brief nod, Elizabeth turned past the stairs.

Leaning against the doorframe, Shelby faced Richard. He hadn't moved, but his pale blue eyes stared past her.

"You have a daughter? Does Sully know?"

"Sully's dead. He's been dead for about six years."

"Did Thad kill him?"

Shelby gasped. "No, of course not." Taking a deep breath, she allowed compassion to push away her indignation. Richard obviously was stuck in the past, but he was still her great-uncle. A kind and caring old man.

"You killed Sully."

Too stunned to speak, she shook her head.

Richard's eyes narrowed into thin slits, and the furrows in his forehead pleated together. "I remember now. Sully destroyed Thad. But Thad blamed me. I tried to tell him it wasn't my fault. I tried to tell him."

The knot returned, expanding against her chest. Somehow she had to bring him back to the present. Forcing a smile, she walked to the cupboard and pulled down two cups. "Wouldn't you like a

333

cup of coffee, Uncle Richard? Just have a seat and tell me all the news from the bank."

"The bank?"

"We missed you at the cookout yesterday. Cassie and Jason Owens were here. And Paul and Renee Norris and their kids, Seth and Mandy. Do you know them?" When he didn't answer, she continued. "Oh, and Jillian Ross. She's one of AJ's students. Of course, they all are. Or were. The kids, I mean. Jillian and Seth graduated this year. Mandy's a sophomore."

She folded her arms tightly across her chest and bit her lip to stop the babbling. Where was AJ? "Are you sure you wouldn't like to sit down?"

"It wasn't my fault, Aubrey. It was yours."

"Uncle Richard, please. I'm Shelby."

"Why didn't you stay with Sully? He loved you." He stepped closer, his eyes menacing. "You're to blame for everything that has happened. But you wouldn't listen. Thad wouldn't listen."

Her phone, tucked inside her bag, rang, and she instinctively reached for it. *Please let it be AJ.*

Quicker than she would have thought possible, Richard gripped her arm. "No."

"I need to answer it."

"I said no." His long fingers tightened, and he yanked her toward the door. "Come with me, Aubrey."

"Leave Mommy alone." Elizabeth grabbed Richard's other arm, and he flung her to the floor. Tabby stood wide-eyed in the hallway door.

"Stop it," Shelby shouted, sidling past him to clutch Elizabeth. Tabby joined them, and Shelby wrapped her arms around both girls. "Please, just leave us alone."

"Thad's in the barn, Aubrey. I didn't mean it, but he blamed me." He passed his hand across his face, and his eyes hardened. "But you have to listen to me. This time, you'll listen."

Shelby's limbs turned to rubber as the hammering of her heart pounded against her ears. She momentarily closed her eyes. Somehow she had to get Richard out of the kitchen. Away from the girls. "I'm listening."

"In the barn. I have to show you how it happened. That it wasn't my fault."

Her thoughts in a whirl, Shelby tried to resist the horrific suspicion triggered by Richard's ramblings. What he was insinuating wasn't possible. He had entered the barn *after* she found Grandpa.

But where had he been?

A long-forgotten detail, sharp and vivid, emerged from the murkiness of memory.

Her fourteen-year-old self walked down the lane from the back pastures toward the house. Approaching the barn, she saw Richard's car, a late-model Cadillac, parked beside it. A strange place to park, almost as if he was hiding it from anyone who might be in the house. But that was silly. What did Uncle Richard have to hide? Dismissing the thought, she entered the barn. And had her world turned upside down.

Richard had come in behind her. Except he hadn't. Not through the door. He'd just been there, hidden in the shadows.

Taking a deep breath, she scooched the girls behind her as she slowly rose to her feet. Controlled anger steadied her voice. "I'll go to the barn with you, Richard. But you mustn't scare the children."

A slow smile added another crease to his wrinkled face. "You'll see, Aubrey. This changes everything. You loved Sully once. Now you can love him again. And Joyanna and I can be together. Just like we were supposed to be. Remember, Aubrey, how we said it would be?"

"I remember, Richard. You can tell me how it happened. And then everything will be all right." She knelt by the girls as they huddled together in the hall doorway. "We'll be back in a few minutes. Then I'll make cocoa, and we'll pop popcorn. Okay?"

"Don't go, Mommy." Tears streaked Elizabeth's cheeks.

"Stay in the house and take care of your sister." She glanced at her watch. AJ should have arrived by now. Maybe that's why he called, to say he couldn't come. If only Richard had let her answer the phone. "Be good now. I won't be long."

Elizabeth nodded and tightened her hold around Tabby's small shoulders.

Pushing past her abhorrence, Shelby pasted on a smile and hooked her arm in Richard's. "I'm ready."

He patted her hand. "You'll see, Aubrey. I didn't mean to hurt him."

Together they walked out into the rain.

~

After changing from dress shirt and pants to long-sleeved pull-over and jeans, AJ stared out the cottage's rain-spattered window. Where was Richard?

He had waited for the old man long enough. He shrugged into a lightweight jacket, pulled on a ball cap, and raced Lila to the Jeep. Once on the road, he called Richard for the third time. And for the third time, the call went straight to voicemail. He tossed the phone on the passenger seat.

Strange Richard wasn't answering his phone.

Strange too that Shelby hadn't answered when he called her.

A disturbing shiver raced up his spine, and his muscles tensed. Gripping the steering wheel with one hand as he accelerated, he reached for his phone with the other. As his fingers closed on the case, the phone rang. Glancing at the screen, he sighed with relief.

"Shelby, hi."

"Mr. AJ?" A sob choked the small voice. "This is Elizabeth Kincaid."

The tension returned, gripping his stomach with an iron fist. "What's wrong, sunshine?"

"Tabby's scared." Another sob. "Me too."

"Where's your mom?"

"She went to the barn with Uncle Richard. But Mommy doesn't like the barn."

The fist twisted, and AJ forced himself to breathe as he slowed to cross the bridge, then accelerated even faster. "Why did she go with him?"

"Because it wasn't his fault."

"What wasn't?"

"I don't know." The intermittent sobbing was replaced by a tearful sniff. "He called her Aubrey, and he said she could love silly again."

"Love silly?"

"That's what he said."

No, not silly. *Sully*. Richard wanted Aubrey to love Sully. But why?

"Where are you and Tabby?"

"In the kitchen."

"Stay there, okay? I'm almost at your house."

"Is Lila coming too?"

Despite the grim circumstances, AJ grinned. "Yes, Bitsy. Lila's coming too."

"Thank you, Mr. AJ."

Before he could reply, the line went dead.

Decelerating as he approached the stop sign, he prayed the poor visibility wasn't hiding any traffic. He braked only enough to make the left turn and sped toward Misty Willow.

As he passed a rambling farmhouse, he punched a button on his smartphone. "Call Jason Owens."

– 44 –

Despite her revulsion, Shelby was forced to rely on Richard's support as they trudged through the heavy downpour. Why hadn't she changed her high heels into something more practical before leaving the house? Or put a jacket on over her dress?

One simple reason. To get Richard away from her girls as quickly as possible.

Head bent to protect her face from the pelting drops, she allowed him to lead her on the slow trek. As they neared the barn, her stomach roiled. Cold beads of sweat mingled with the rain on her bare arms and legs. Her aversion to entering the vile place where Grandpa had died devoured her desire to hear Richard's explanation.

The weathered structure loomed before them, and she dug into Richard's arm. "I can't," she said, swallowing the acrid bile that rose to her throat. "I can't go in there."

"But you must." Determination seemed to give him strength as he pulled her forward toward the narrow gap created by the slightly opened sliding door. She retched, emptying the contents of her stomach into a standing puddle as the relentless rain beat her back and shoulders.

As she wiped her mouth with the back of her hand, tires spun on gravel, and AJ's Jeep broke through the downpour's veil. Tears of relief eased her anguish. She started toward the vehicle, but Richard pushed her into the gap. Stumbling as the heel came off one of her shoes, she smacked the concrete floor with her knees and hands. The sour smell of old straw and blighted feed pressed into her nostrils.

"Stand up, Aubrey." Richard clasped her elbow. "I have to show you."

The sliding door groaned as it opened wider, and AJ stepped inside. "Leave her alone, Richard."

Shelby scrambled to her feet and staggered into his arms. He held her close, protectively shifting his body to shelter her from Richard's demented gaze.

"Sully, you're here."

"I'm not Sully."

"Aubrey loves you again. I knew she would if Thad went away."

Shelby raised her head from AJ's chest and forced herself to look into Richard's clouded eyes. "You killed him, didn't you?"

"No." He shook his head, then nodded. "Yes." He took a step toward them, and she shrank against AJ. "I didn't mean to, Aubrey. But he wouldn't listen. He was going to tell everyone I cheated him out of the farm. I pushed him, and he fell."

His eyes looked wildly around the barn. "I moved the pig trough. Moved it here." He pointed at the floor. "It was an accident, Aubrey. A tragic accident. I'd have been ruined." Tears filled his eyes, and his voice shook. "You're my sister. You have to protect me."

Shelby gasped and clutched at the sob caught in her throat.

"Did you cheat him?" AJ asked, his voice hard and cold.

"Sully, you know I did." Richard's tone was placating, subservient.

"Why? After so many years had passed, why?"

Richard bristled. "You dare ask me why? Haven't I always done what you told me to do? Cleaned up your messes? Covered up your tracks? And how do you repay me? You marry Joyanna." Tears coursed across his wrinkled cheeks. "It should have been you instead of Thad. You!"

His eyes darted around the barn's dim interior, then he picked up an abandoned beer bottle and flung it at them.

AJ turned and raised his arm. The bottle barely scraped his shoulder and crashed to the floor. He gently pushed Shelby away, then faced Richard.

"There's no need for this, Richard. Let me take you home."

Outraged, Richard emitted a loud bellow and bent his body forward as if to rush AJ. But he lost his balance and staggered, clutching his left arm as he fell.

AJ patted his pockets, then spoke over his shoulder to Shelby as he knelt by Richard and felt for a pulse. "My phone's in the Jeep. Call 911."

Shelby hurried to the door as Jason entered. He gave her a quick hug, then tugged AJ from Richard.

"I'll make the call," he said. "Cassie's with the girls. You take care of Shelby."

AJ enclosed her in a warm embrace. "Are you all right?"

She nodded, gripping her aching stomach as the dam of tears broke loose.

"It's over," he whispered. "It's all over."

"He's . . . dead?"

"Yeah."

"He killed Grandpa."

"I'm sorry, sweetheart. So very sorry."

"I'll never forgive him."

AJ pressed his chin against her temple. "I think Sully's the real villain here."

Despite her horror, she glanced at the still body sprawled on the concrete floor. If she hadn't returned, hadn't reopened old wounds, he'd still be alive with his secrets and his regrets. A pathetic old man haunted by the past.

Tilting her head, she gazed into AJ's soft brown eyes. "He did one good thing."

"Richard?"

She nodded.

"What did he do?"

"He brought us together." She swiped away a fresh onslaught of tears, then lightly kissed his upper jaw. "At least I can be thankful to him for that."

"The sheriff and an ambulance are on their way," Jason said. "Go back to the house. I'll stay here."

Shelby glanced at the lifeless body, then closed her eyes. *Help me to forgive him, Father. Someday, help me to forgive him.*

Wrapping her arm around AJ's waist, she hobbled in her broken shoe to the door. The rain had decreased to a light drizzle, and a shaft of sunshine pierced a cloud. Perhaps it was only a coincidence. Or perhaps it was a heavenly sign that her prayers for peace had been answered.

~

AJ pushed shut the barn's sliding door. Richard's body had finally been removed, and the deputies had taken statements from AJ, Shelby, and Jason. Rain no longer fell from the sky, but thick clouds darkened the horizon. Another storm was headed their way as AJ and Jason sauntered from the barn to the house.

"Thanks again for coming over."

"That's what neighbors are for," Jason said. "If Shelby wants the barn removed, you should have her call Nate Jeffers, the contractor. He's involved with a nonprofit architectural salvage group that might be interested in the boards."

"I'll talk to her about it."

"She's not really planning to move overseas, is she?"

"I don't think she's made a decision yet."

"Think you can convince her to stay?"

"I hope so."

341

"I hope so too. Though you know, I'm the nearest thing she has to a brother," Jason said dryly. "So if you do anything to hurt her, you'll answer to me."

"Guess I better be real careful then." They reached the patio, and AJ opened the screen door.

Inside the kitchen, Shelby sat at the table, nursing a cup of cocoa. She'd changed into jeans and a dark green V-neck sweater that enhanced her lovely green eyes. Her chestnut hair, still damp from her shower, hung straight down her back. At the stove, Cassie stirred the homemade cocoa.

"Want a cup?" she asked as they entered.

"Love one." Jason stood behind his wife and kissed her neck.

"Me too, please," AJ said as he pulled a chair close to Shelby and curled a damp strand of hair around his finger. "How're you doing?"

"Fine," she said with a weary smile. "Thanks for being here. All of you. I've never had such good friends before." Her smile brightened. "Except for Jason, of course, when we were kids."

Jason wagged his thumbs at his chest. "Like her brother," he bragged in a singsong voice.

"So you say," AJ retorted.

"Did I miss something?" Shelby asked.

Before anyone could respond, Tabby rushed in from the hall, hands behind her back, and ran to AJ's side. "Ta-da," she said, holding out a *Tangled* DVD. "You promised."

"So I did." He set her on his knee and grinned at Shelby.

"You did promise," she said.

"Tell you what, Tabby. How about if I run home and change into dry clothes. I'll be back in less than an hour, and we can watch your movie."

"That's a good plan," she said, then pointed her finger at him. "But don't dawdle."

"I won't." He matched her tone and gave her a tickle. She giggled, then ran out of the kitchen.

"Cassie, you'll all stay, won't you?" Shelby asked. "I'd really like you to."

Cassie and Jason exchanged looks and agreed. "I could go pick up a couple of King Karl pizzas," Jason volunteered as he pulled out his phone. "Figure out toppings."

"I'll let you figure it out." AJ dug keys from his pocket as he rose. "I guess it's okay to leave my dog here."

"She's in the other room with Elizabeth," Shelby said.

"Where else would she be? See you soon."

"Wait a sec." Shelby spontaneously clasped his hand. "Would you, um, come out to the front porch with me? Just for a minute."

"Sure." He shot Jason a puzzled look. Jason shrugged and looked at Cassie, who also shrugged.

Shelby took a deep breath. "Come on."

He followed her to the front porch. "What's this all about?"

"This is where we first met. Remember?"

"How could I forget?"

"I was so angry with you. For no good reason."

"After what we heard from Richard, I think you had a very good reason."

"To be angry with Sully. Not you."

"Shelby—"

She placed her fingers on his lips. "Please. Just let me do this."

"Do what?"

"Meet you again. Like that first time."

"You want to reenact when we met?"

She nodded enthusiastically and scurried down the steps. "I was standing about here when you came out the door. You walked toward me. I held out my hand. And you said . . ."

AJ approached her and took her hand. "I'm—"

"My hero." She beamed, waiting expectantly.

"Is this where I'm supposed to tell you I'm not your contractor?"

She stepped closer and held his gaze. "*You* are my hero. And my knight in shining armor and the man of my dreams." Her eyes filled with tears, and AJ's heart ignited a fire in his chest. "I don't want to go anywhere without you beside me."

He cradled her face in his palm, his pulse racing as he inhaled the floral fragrance of her shampoo, the delicate notes of her perfume.

"You mean it?" He blinked, annoyed he couldn't think of something more profound to say in this memorable moment. His eyes flickered to her alluring lips. Maybe words weren't necessary.

He wrapped his arm around her slim waist, drawing her close as his mouth hovered over hers. Her eyes closed as their lips touched, the pressure increasing as passion enveloped them. His hand moved down the silky dampness of her hair as she slipped her arms around his neck, her fingers burning his nape. The intensity of the kiss lingered as their mouths barely separated.

"I love you, Shelby. Since that first day, I've loved you."

"I love you too. With all my heart, I love you."

He kissed her again, enchanted by the sweet taste of her lips against his.

Pulling away, she smiled impishly and stuck her finger in his cleft. "How do you shave in there?"

～

After the Owens family left and the girls were tucked in bed, Shelby wandered into the kitchen with her hands behind her back. AJ turned from loading the dishwasher to greet her.

"Ta-da," she said, holding out a handful of Cary Grant DVDs. "Unless you need to get home."

"I don't have a curfew."

"Choose one."

He tilted his head as if in deep thought. "After everything that's happened today, definitely a comedy."

"Agreed. We've got *Bringing Up Baby*, *I Was a Male War Bride*, and *His Girl Friday*." She shuffled through the DVD cases. "Also *My Favorite Wife* and *That Touch of Mink*."

"*I Was a Male War Bride*."

"You were?" she teased.

"Ha-ha."

"It's the perfect choice."

"Before we watch the movie, can I ask you something?"

"Sure."

He reached for her hand. "Where's your wedding ring?"

Warmth crept up her cheeks. "In my jewelry box. I thought it was time."

"I agree." He drew her close and clasped his hands behind her waist. "Does this mean you'll stay? Let me help you fight the lawsuit?"

"I love this place." She rested her hands on his muscular biceps. "But it's not what I love most. Nor was it the most important legacy my grandparents left me."

"What was?"

"How much they loved each other. And how much they trusted their lives to God's plan for them."

"What Sully didn't do. Or my dad."

"You have their name, Mr. Fourth." Standing on tiptoe, she kissed the corner of his mouth. "But you're not them."

"I don't want to lose you, Shelby. Please don't go overseas."

"I won't. I can't." She smiled warmly. "My constant is right here."

"Your constant?"

"You." She stepped away and hooked her arm in his. "Let me tell you about the favor my dad did for Paul Norris."

∼

AJ plopped onto the blanket beside Shelby as the girls waded in the creek with Lila. "Has it been a good Fourth of July so far?"

"A picnic at one of my favorite places. The promise of fireworks this evening." An adorable smile lit her face as she nodded slowly. "I'd say it's perfect."

"Great." He tugged at a blade of grass and chewed on the end. "I need your permission to do something."

"Name it."

"I know your initials are already on the 'gagement tree with Jason's. What about joining them to mine?"

Her eyes grew round. "Are you . . . ?"

He stood, then reached down and pulled her to her feet. Digging in his pocket, he pulled out a jeweler's box, then knelt on one knee. Shelby covered her mouth as he took her hand.

"I love you, Shelby, more than I can put into words. And I love your girls as if they were my own. I promise to follow in your grandparents' footsteps, to honor their legacy of devotion." Swallowing the lump in his throat, he smiled. "Will you marry me?"

"Yes," she breathed. "A million times yes."

He slipped the diamond on her finger and stood.

"It's beautiful," she said, tears welling in her eyes as he kissed her. "I love you. So much I love you."

"Two souls. One heart."

"My hero."

- 45 -

*S*helby stood between AJ and Dr. Wayne Kessler next to the chain-link fence surrounding the excavation area. While clearing out the barn, Nate Jeffers had found an old tack room with a solid wood floor. After removing the walls, Nate pried up the floor and found another floor underneath.

One with a trap door.

"What do you think, Kess?" AJ asked.

The professor tugged at his graying moustache. "It's an amazing find. Thank you for allowing me to be part of it."

After investigating the secret room beneath the study and the hunting cabin by the creek, the professor had put together a special archaeological team. A couple of weeks ago, they had found a tunnel entrance beneath the cabin's foundation.

Today, they were systematically sifting through the earth and debris beneath the barn's trapdoor.

"Consider it payback for teaching me how much fun history can be."

Kess chuckled. "You were a good student, AJ. And still one of my favorites."

AJ beamed as he bumped Shelby with his elbow. "Hear that? One of his favorites."

Shelby returned the bump. "My very favorite," she whispered.

In the weeks since his proposal, AJ had been the constant she'd dreamed of, the shining knight she knew him to be. He'd stood beside her, a strong and comforting presence, during Uncle Richard's funeral. On the day Nate pulled down the first wall on the barn, AJ planned a trip to the zoo to get them away from the farm.

And he let Lila spend every night with Elizabeth.

"Perhaps this is a second tunnel," Kess mused. "Is it even possible it could connect with the cabin?"

"Grandpa said it did, but I don't really know."

"Given time, we should uncover the answer. Where was the next stop on the Station?"

"My family provided clean clothes. Hot food." Shelby shrugged. "When it was safe, I think the travelers went back to the creek and headed farther north."

"Another mystery for us to solve." He pulled an old-fashioned silver watch from his pocket. "But for now I need to be going. You'll let me know about the sign?"

"I still can't believe this is happening."

"Believe it, Shelby," he said as she and AJ walked him to his Buick. "If all goes as planned, Misty Willow will be a premier research center and museum in another year or two."

"You're not worried about the lawsuit?"

"Once the property is listed on the state's historical registry, it will be protected." He opened his car door and gave her a reassuring smile. "Now don't forget to let me know what you decide."

"Later today, okay? I want to show AJ the designs."

"Just give my office a call." He slid into his Buick, waved, and drove down the lane.

"What designs?" AJ asked as they sauntered toward the house.

"Before you got here, Kess gave me a folder of mock-ups for a sign to put in front of the house." She clasped his hand. "The Lassiter Family Underground Railroad and Civil War Research Center."

He gave a low whistle. "Pretty impressive."

"They're on the kitchen table. You need to help me choose one."

"Glad to help."

"Your darling professor also told me something rather remarkable."

"What was that?"

"An anonymous donor gave a million dollars to the project." Shelby stopped in her tracks and tugged on AJ's hand so he faced her. "It was you, wasn't it?"

"A million dollars?" His teasing grin tugged at her heart. "Nope, I didn't give a million."

"How much *did* you give?"

"Five hundred thousand. In memory of Gran."

"Who gave the other half?"

"Brett. In memory of Gran."

"You're kidding me."

"He really did. His way of apologizing."

"Neither of you should have done it." She reached up and gave him a lingering kiss. "But I'm glad you did."

"It's a worthy project." Hand in hand, they followed the loop around the oval to the patio. "Besides, my students can come here for a field trip into the past. Maybe help with the museum."

"I'm still flabbergasted about that tunnel beneath the barn. I got a note from Dad, and he didn't know about it either. Which makes me wonder if Grandpa even knew."

"We'll never know which Lassiter forgot to pass that secret along to future generations," AJ said. "But look at the legacy you're giving to your children. To the entire state."

"Kess said the donation will fund a nonprofit foundation that will take over the restoration of the house. I get to be on the board. And he thinks we should make the secret room more accessible and rebuild the hunting cabin."

"Does that *we* mean you and me?"

"Technically, the farm still belongs to you. Besides, even though it's my grandparents' name on the sign, this will be our legacy. Yours and mine. If you agree."

"What about the 'gagement tree?"

"He wants it too, but I think we can negotiate picnic and fishing rights to Lassiters and Sullivans in perpetuity."

AJ chuckled and drew her into a casual embrace at the top of the patio steps. "We'll have lots more picnics there, but I doubt any will be as memorable as that first one."

"You mean the one you crashed?"

"I mean the one where I rescued you from the storm."

"Someday I'll pay you back by rescuing you from something," she teased.

"You already have." He lifted her chin, his eyes dark and intense beneath the brim of his ball cap. "You rescued me from my past. And gave me a future I can't wait to explore. With you."

Despite the August sun beating down on them with its fiery rays, Shelby relished the warmth of AJ's body against hers, the saltiness of his sweat-moistened lips that demanded her willing response.

The honeymoon couldn't come too soon.

As Elizabeth and Tabby crashed through the screen door, followed closely by Jillian and Lila, Shelby broke from the embrace.

"Guess I better get used to this," AJ whispered before grabbing Tabby and swinging her around.

"More. More," Tabby squealed.

"Me too," shouted Elizabeth.

Shelby and Jillian stood on the patio while AJ chased the girls into the oval and around the oak trees. Lila scampered after them, her gleeful barks echoing through the summer air.

"This has been the best summer." A wistful expression flitted across Jillian's face. "I'll never forget these days."

"We're going to miss you." Shelby gave her a quick sideways hug. "I wish you weren't going so far away to college."

"Sometimes I wish that too. But it's too good of an opportunity to pass up."

"At least you'll be back for the wedding. My prettiest brides-maid."

"Your only bridesmaid," Jillian said pointedly. "Cassie is matron of honor. She doesn't count."

Shelby chuckled then focused on her fiancé as he gently rough-housed with her daughters. Soon to be his daughters too.

Her gaze wandered to the variety of flowers waving their color-ful blooms against the fence, the old flower-laden wheelbarrow, the newly formed stone circle. She had moved here searching for the place she belonged only to learn that she didn't belong to a place at all.

She belonged to people. To her close friends, Cassie and Jason. To her near neighbors, Paul and Renee. To Jillian.

And most of all, to AJ.

The man she came here wanting to hate had reopened her heart to the most intense, head-over-heels, amazing love.

A future with AJ Sullivan wasn't at all what Shelby had expected when she moved her girls here from Chicago. But after a few short weeks, she couldn't envision a future without him.

Two souls. One heart.

God had most definitely set her feet in an exceptionally spa-cious place.

COMING FALL 2016

BOOK #2 IN THE

Misty Willow Series

READ AN EXCERPT

LATE AUGUST

Blue light, the muted shade of a twilight sky, shone through the rectangular panes of the brick building's ninth story window. Last night, the light had been yellow. The day before, red.

Brett Somers pressed his hand against his heart. But he couldn't ease the unbearable pain that threatened to break him in two.

I'd give everything I own if he would only open his eyes.

Not even the scars of his own childhood had engulfed him like this. He hadn't known such pain was possible.

As the skies darkened with the promise of rain, the random colors became more vivid, more numerous. Beneath the gathering clouds, the lighted panes created a brilliant kaleidoscope of hope.

The children on the other side of the windows controlled the color of their ambient night-lights.

Unless, like the boy in room 927, they were in a coma.

Brett leaned against his Lexus and forced a smile as footsteps ambled toward him. Finally.

"How is he?"

"No change, man." A mass of curly red hair framed Aaron Wiley's round Santa Claus cheeks. Come Christmas, he'd don a white wig and beard for the young patients whose vital signs he monitored.

"He just lies there, sound asleep."

Brett swallowed the sigh building up in his throat. "The accident was weeks ago."

"Head traumas take time to heal."

"What about Meghan?"

"She seems to be doing better now that she's not spending

twenty-four hours in this place. More rested. I overheard her talking about a church giving her an apartment, no charge." Humor twinkled in Aaron's gentle eyes. "Don't suppose you had anything to do with that?"

"She was going to end up in a bed next to him if she didn't . . ."

"Take care of herself?"

Brett shifted uncomfortably. He wouldn't have to resort to these cloak-and-dagger tactics if Meghan wasn't so stubborn. So unforgiving.

Not that he hadn't given her a good reason to despise him.

He pushed away from the car and retrieved a colorful gift bag illustrated with zoo animals and balloons from the backseat. "Tomorrow's his eighth birthday. I want you to give him this."

Despite the blue and yellow tissue paper sprouting from the top, Aaron peered inside. "What did you get him?"

"It's not from me."

"'Course it isn't."

"Come up with something, okay? There's got to be a group or some kind of foundation that donates toys to these children."

"Several." Like the big kid he was, Aaron slightly shook the bag as if trying to get a hint of what was inside. "They donate books. Hand-carved wooden toys. Stuffed animals."

"That works. It's a stuffed monkey. With an MP3 player inside."

"Good choice."

"Wearing an Ohio State football jersey."

Aaron grinned. "Even better." He held out his closed fist, and Brett obliged him with a friendly bump.

Brett's smile quickly faded. A rain-tinged breeze swept along the quiet street, and he shoved his hands into the pockets of his khakis. "She can't know it came from me. I'm depending on you, Aaron."

"I'm always here for you, man. You know that." A rare frown pulled at his mouth. "But I can't do this anymore."

Brett closed his eyes and bowed his head. The words he'd been dreading settled like a boulder in his gut.

With anyone else, he'd pile on the charm. Or the pressure.

But Aaron wouldn't succumb to either. The certified nursing assistant risked his job every time he gave Brett an update. Even if the update never changed.

Brett stared toward the ninth floor window. "I understand."

"You should just talk to her, man."

"I've tried." He shook his head. "She hates me."

"Not used to that, are you?"

"No, Aaron. I'm not."

"Tell you what." The Santa Claus twinkle returned to Aaron's eyes, and his voice lowered to a conspiratorial whisper. "When he wakes up, I'll make sure you know it."

A sliver of hope slipped past the boulder. "I'd appreciate it."

"I better go, man. My shift's about to start." Aaron's characteristic smile beamed as he cradled the gift bag. "Don't worry, she'll never know this came from you."

Brett nodded his thanks, and Aaron sauntered toward the hospital.

Suddenly light-headed, Brett bent over the hood of the Lexus, his hands pushing against the black frame.

If only he'd known . . .

He sucked in air, then exhaled.

If he'd known, he wouldn't have cared.

Not back then. Not when it mattered.

~

The camera shutter clicked multiple times in quick succession, then Dani Prescott slouched against the medical building across the street from the hospital. By the sun's fading light, made dimmer by the rain-heavy clouds, she checked the Canon Rebel's digital display. The images of two men, a handsome blond and an unruly carrot top, appeared in the square screen. In the final image, the Adonis stood alone, his chin lowered.

As Dani looked up from the display, he interlaced his hands

behind his head. She caught a momentary glimpse of his pained expression as he lifted his eyes to the heavens.

Compassion stirred her heart, but it lasted only a single beat. Taking a few steps forward, she lifted the camera and took another quick succession of shots, though she wasn't sure why. She didn't need more photos of the guy.

Waiting for him to emerge from his office building then tailing him seemed like a good idea a few hours ago. The thrill of playing detective and all that.

But the reality had been mostly boring. And puzzling.

He'd stayed later at his office than she expected considering it was a Friday night. When he had finally emerged from the parking garage's elevator, she'd expected him to drive to a restaurant or to pick up a date. By then it was past six-thirty, and she couldn't wait to snap furtive photos of him out on the town with some Barbie bimbo as shallow as she knew him to be.

But hanging around a children's hospital? Why?

A blaring siren broke the brooding peace of the lonely street. Dani pivoted, and her stomach clenched as an ambulance sped her way. She blinked, and her breathing accelerated as if racing the siren's crescendo.

Gripping her stomach with her free hand, she concentrated on deep inhales and exhales. This emergency had nothing to do with her. Nothing.

The ambulance came nearer, then turned and followed the curving drive around to the ER.

"Are you okay?"

Dani spun toward the voice and gazed into the most attractive blue eyes she'd ever seen. A faint smile creased the man's gorgeous face, revealing deep dimples.

Busted.

Her surveillance plan for learning more about Brett Somers's personal life hadn't included actually speaking to the guy. Heat crept up her neck and warmed her cheeks.

"I didn't mean to scare you." The smile disappeared. "You look a little pale."

Her voice stuck in her throat. Good-looking and self-assured, he was just the kind of man who made her stammer and trip over her own feet. The kind of man who looked right through her or only noticed her because she'd done something clumsy or stupid.

Like secretly taking pictures of him.

"Are you going to be sick?"

"Fine," she blurted, flushing again at the squeak in her voice. She cleared her throat. "I'm fine. I just don't like ambulances."

"Who does?"

She followed his glance toward the hospital. An assortment of bright colors shone through the windows.

"Taking photos of the lights?"

"Um, yes." She nodded in support of the lie and forced a smile.

"Can I see?"

"No!"

He appeared taken aback by the force of her objection but only for an instant. Holding out his hand, he smiled. "Please."

Her knees turned to jelly when his dimples reappeared. He obviously expected her to succumb to his charms. Most women probably did.

But no way could she show him the images she'd taken. He'd think she was a stalker.

Who was she kidding? She *was* a stalker.

Though for a very good reason.

"I'd really like to see them."

She couldn't let him know how much he intimidated her. If only she could be as poised and self-confident as her favorite classic movie actress. No matter the circumstances, Audrey Hepburn always said and did the right thing.

Of course, Audrey had a scriptwriter.

Dani wished she had one too. With a quiet sigh, she straightened her shoulders and carefully placed the camera in its bag. "The pictures are personal."

He dropped his hand. "Which window?"

"Excuse me?"

"Which window is yours?"

She crinkled her eyes in confusion. "None of them."

"You don't have someone here? A sick child you're worried about?"

"No."

"So you take hospital photos for the fun of it?" His gaze bored into hers, and a hint of suspicion weighted his words. "Strange hobby."

Dani silently agreed. If that were the truth, it would be. She needed to distract him. Maybe a conversation wasn't such a bad thing after all.

"Which window is yours?" She tried to sound nonchalant but didn't think she'd quite succeeded. Small talk with handsome men never had been her forte.

The brilliancy of his light blue eyes faded, and he carelessly shrugged. "Just looking at the lights."

So he could lie too.

From her research, she knew he'd never been married. Since the death of his grandmother a few months ago, his only family members were a sister and a cousin, both single as far as Dani knew.

So there should be no children in Brett's life.

Or maybe he was telling the truth, and the present he had given the other man wasn't for a patient but for someone on the hospital staff. Perhaps he was playing secret admirer.

The image of his earlier pained expression appeared before her as clearly as if she were staring at a printed photograph. His secret didn't have anything to do with romance. She gazed at the colored lights. Behind one of those windows was a child he cared about.

A mystery.

What would Audrey do?

Feeling his eyes upon her, she met his gaze and awkwardly smiled.

"I'm Brett Somers."

I know.

"And you are?"

Dani's eyes shifted, and she stared at the tan toes of her canvas shoes. He wasn't supposed to know her name. At least not yet. Her mind flashed to the classic movie she'd watched last night.

"Regina Lampert." The lie surprised and emboldened her. Suddenly tickled by her audacity, she grinned.

He arched an eyebrow. "Regina Lampert?"

She nodded.

"As in *Charade*? Audrey Hepburn's character?"

Busted again.

"You know that movie?"

"Why wouldn't I?"

She mimicked his earlier casual shrug. "You just don't seem the type."

"What type?"

"The type to know about old movies."

His eyes crinkled in amusement. "What type am I, 'Regina Lampert'?"

"I don't know." *Careful, Dani. He can't suspect you already know anything about him.* "The never-alone-on-a-Friday-night type. The let's-fly-to-New-York-in-five-minutes type."

"I never fly, and New York doesn't interest me." The amusement eased into a broad grin, and he spread his hands. "And I'm all alone here."

She nervously twisted the camera bag's strap. "So how do you know so much about Audrey Hepburn?"

"My grandmother was a huge Cary Grant fan. I watched *Charade* with her several times. You?"

She lifted one shoulder and bit her lip. "Too many Friday nights alone, I guess."

"Pretty girl like you?"

Immediate heat burned her face, and a strange deprecating sound escaped her lips.

"How many stars would you give *Notorious?*"

"Cary Grant and Ingrid Bergman's *Notorious*? I love it."

"It's playing at the Ohio Theater. Part of their summer classic series." He checked his watch. "We've got about fifteen minutes."

"Fifteen minutes?"

"Before the movie starts." He flashed that knee-weakening smile again. "I know we've just met, but I promise I'm a respectable businessman. Successful too. I own a thriving property development company. And my cousin is engaged to the daughter of missionaries. We used to not-date, so she can tell you what a gentleman I am."

Dani's head spun as she tried to keep up with his chatter.

He pulled out his cell and flicked the display. "Should I call her?"

As if it had a mind of its own, her hand shot out and covered the phone's screen to stop him. "You don't need to do that." Her fingers lingered against the warmth of his skin. She drew away and took a step backward. This could not be happening.

"Then you'll come? My treat."

"To the movie? It's probably sold out."

"I know the manager."

Of course he did.

"Come on, 'Reggie.'" He shoved his cell into his pocket and bumped her elbow with his. "Historical theater. *Notorious* on the big screen."

Twisting the camera bag's strap, she tried to think of another objection.

Just say no. N. O. One easy syllable.

But her voice didn't cooperate.

"A giant bucket of buttered popcorn."

She grinned. Couldn't help it, he sounded so pitiful.

"We'll drive separately. Where's your car?"

362

"Around the corner." She tilted her head to the side street next to the medical building. "Where's the theater?"

"Just a few blocks over. So how about it?"

Perhaps this wasn't such a bad idea. A movie meant little time for small talk, which meant she might find out something useful without giving anything away. Seeing one of her favorite movies on the big screen was a bonus.

"Okay," she said.

His dimples deepened. "Okay."

As they walked to her car, he gave her directions in case they got separated. She tried to pay attention, but her stomach tightened at what he must be thinking about her eleven-year-old Honda Civic. The rusted spots seemed to take on a noticeable and vibrant hue beneath the street lamps.

Shoving her not-good-enough feelings aside, she unlocked the driver's door. So what if she didn't drive something new and shiny. At least she worked for what she had.

That is until she'd quit her job to follow her dream to nowhere.

Brett grabbed the door as she slid into the seat. "Remember, follow me to the light and take a left."

"I've got it."

"Good." He shut the door and waited.

The engine coughed then smoothed into a solid hum. She lowered her window. "Something wrong?"

"Just wanted to be sure you got it started."

"It usually does." Her voice held that defensive snap she hated.

"Usually?"

"We're going to be late."

"You're right." He tapped the window frame then jogged to his car.

A few minutes later, she pulled into the street behind his polished Lexus and gripped her steering wheel.

She was on this lonely street to spy on Brett Somers. How in the world did she end up on a date with him?

Johnnie Alexander is the award-winning author of *Where Treasure Hides*. Johnnie is an accomplished essayist and poet whose work has appeared in the *Guideposts* anthology *A Cup of Christmas Cheer*. In addition to writing, she enjoys reading, spending time with her grandchildren, and taking road trips. She lives near Memphis, Tennessee.

MEET
Johnnie Alexander

AT JOHNNIE-ALEXANDER.COM